PARADISE ISLAND

MIAMI BEACH

Nelson Hamel & Charles Sibley

Paradise Island. Miami Beach

© 2017 Charles Sibley & Nelson Hamel

ISBN: 978-0-9998300-3-1

Library of Congress application number: 1-6600529371

Publisher: Erasmus Press

Cover photo: Cristina Fernandez

Editor: Elisa Arraiz Lucca

Proofreading: Janet Bratos

Printed in USA, 2018

Paradise Island glitters with wealth and power, but behind the sparkling façade lies a darker reality, of adult transgressions, "peccadillos" and lack of morals. All of these are inevitably imitated by their offspring – which includes the gang rape of a childhood friend.

PREFACE

The three teens had planned this moment for a long time. They knew her weekend routine like clockwork. After quietly docking their water ski boat, a $100 tip was all that it had taken for the unaware waitress, about to finish her shift, to allow them to slip the date rape drug in the virgin piña colada that was being delivered to cabaña #1.

Sixteen-year-old Hillary Zathlyn is in a haze. One moment everything is foggy and out of focus and the next moment the room starts to spin. She gets dizzy and feels as if she is falling into a void. She is vaguely aware that despite her best efforts to remain in control, she is losing it. As she passes out, she is hit with a wave of cold fear as she sees the blurry images of the people that she knows, but did not invite there…

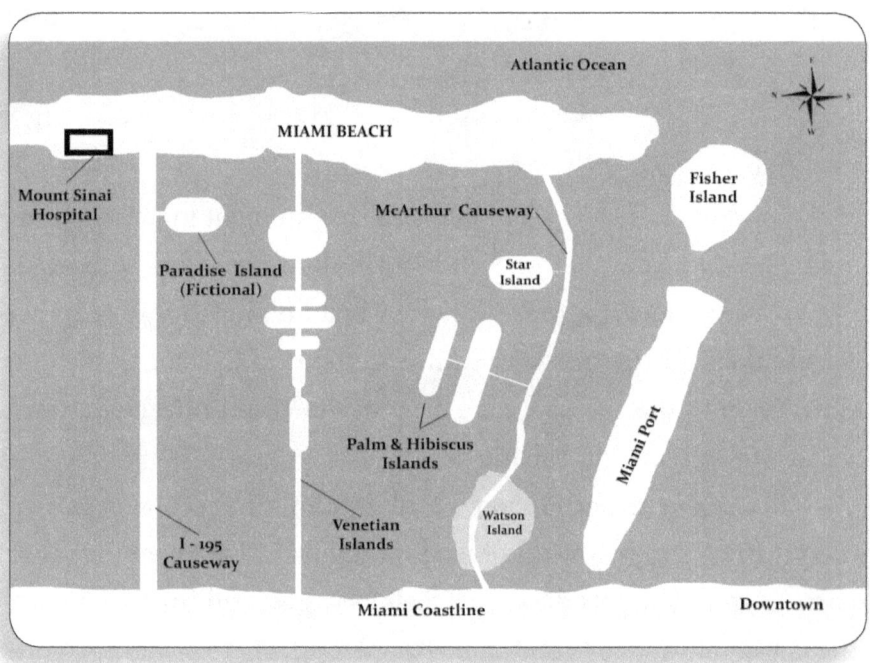

Atlantic Ocean

MIAMI BEACH

Mount Sinai
Hospital

Paradise Island
(Fictional)

McArthur Causeway

Fisher
Island

Star
Island

Palm & Hibiscus
Islands

Miami Port

I - 195
Causeway

Venetian
Islands

Watson
Island

Miami Coastline

Downtown

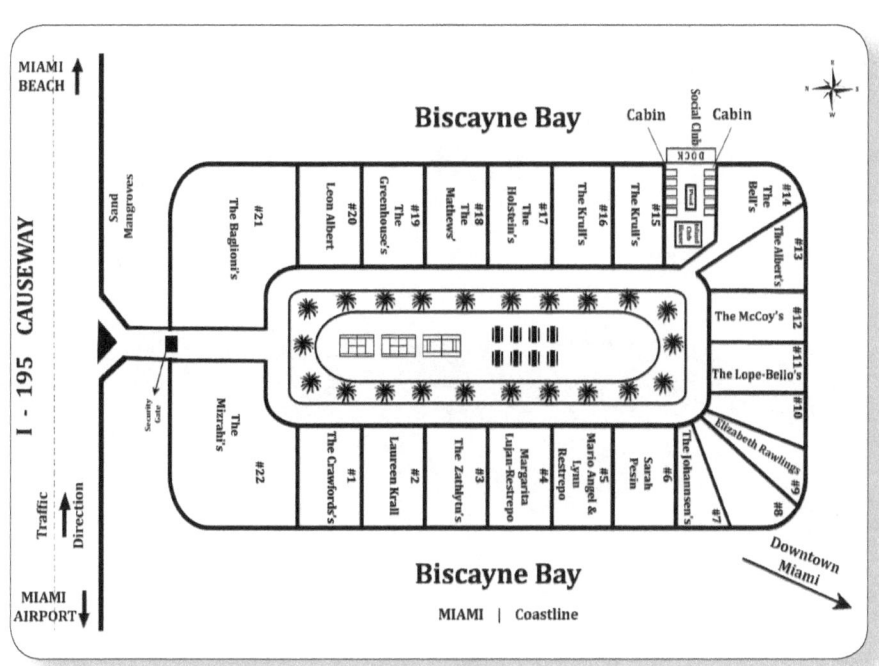

MIAMI
BEACH

I - 195 CAUSEWAY

Sand
Mangroves

Traffic

Direction

MIAMI
AIRPORT

Security
Gate

Biscayne Bay

Cabin   Cabin

Social Club

DOCK

The Baglioni's #21

Leon Albert #20

The Greenhouse's #19

The Mathews' #18

The Holstein's #17

The Krull's #16

The Krull's #15

The Bell's #14

The Albert's #13

The McCoy's #12

The Lope-Bello's #11

Elizabeth Rawlings #10

#9

#8

#7

The Johannsen's

Sarah Pesin #6

Mario Angel & Lynn Restrepo #5

Margarita Lujan-Restrepo #4

The Zath&yn's #3

Laureen Krall #2

The Crawford's #1

The Mizrahi's #22

Downtown
Miami

Biscayne Bay

MIAMI | Coastline

INTRODUCTION

Miami's I-195 causeway stands out from all others, as it is an 8-lane highway that connects the beach to the mainland in a 3 to 5 minute drive, and downtown or the airport in 10 minutes. What sets it apart is that there aren't any residences built along the side of the road, just sand, beaches and mangroves with just one island connected to it, known as Paradise Island.

At mile marker #2 off the south side of I-195 going towards Miami Beach there is a perfectly paved road that ends at a small bridge. After traversing over the bridge, a small security hut appears on the right at the island's entrance. High-definition video cameras record everything and everyone coming onto the island. The world beyond the 70-year-old bridge appears perfect, or so it seems. The island is an elongated oval with one road that starts at and circles back to the entrance. The 1930s man-made island faces south directly towards Biscayne Bay and downtown Miami.

After stopping at the gate, the residents can gain access by placing their thumbs on an infrared scanner. Within a fraction of a second, the security bar raises and voilà, they are literally in paradise. But, if you could read minds, the frequency of curses, smirks or twisted faces would divulge that the briefest of waits for entry would seem like an unbearable waste of time to most of the highfalutin residents. For them, Paradise Island's security is never enough. Nothing is ever up to the expectations of the opulent Paradise Island residents. There are 20 waterfront homes on Paradise Island sitting on lots ranging from 2 to 5 acres. Only 2 lots remain empty and their asking price is $25 million per acre. This is the most expensive piece of real estate in the United States.

All of this leads us to the obvious. The residents of Paradise Island are individuals with seemingly very deep pockets who can afford to pay $50 million+ for their homes and $500K a year in real estate taxes. They have gone way beyond the American dream, through extraordinary success, careers, ideas and enterprises. Some residents of Paradise Island though, have done none of the above, but instead, have gotten theirs through inheritance, thievery, unlawful means or monetization of power.

The most desirable homes on Paradise Island face south towards the Port of Miami and downtown Miami. When the giant cruise ships leave the Port of Miami, they can be seen in the distance from these palatial homes. The center of Paradise Island is lined with giant Royal Palm trees that were planted when the Island was rebuilt after the hurricane of 1926. A 1-mile running track weaves around and through the Royal Palm trees. There is a group of tennis courts, a beach volley-ball court and an Olympic-size swimming pool available to the residents. However, nothing on the island is what it seems. Under the glitter and wealth lie all kinds of secrets, mostly about the price paid to be and stay in Paradise.

As some of the Island's teens enjoy themselves by the pool, they are totally unaware of what is taking place in Hillary Zathlyn's poolside cabaña.

CHAPTER 1
THE PARADISE ISLAND SOCIAL CLUB AND THE ZATHLYN POOLSIDE CABAÑA

A group of teens are hanging out at the Paradise Island pool. The sun is setting after a lazy Saturday afternoon. Not a cloud in the sky. A gentle breeze tousles the hair of the teenage girls. The temperature is in the 90s. Another idyllic day ends in south Florida… or so it appears!

"I don't believe you!"

"But, I took the picture," says Johnny Baglioni.

"How do I know that, actually, how do we know that?"

"Hey, this is my phone. I was there. Just a few feet away from him."

"For all I know, anyone could have emailed you that picture. You have a picture, but you're not in it. No selfie, no proof, not true, period!"

They all laugh in unison at him. Although Justin Bieber is a well-known winter visitor in Miami Beach and Paradise Island, nobody would give Johnny the benefit of the doubt that he ran into the "Beib" and took his picture.

"Where's Hillary?"

"She went to take a nap," replies Megan.

"Home or here in the cabaña?"

"Johnny, why do you always ask the same questions over and over again? You know the answer," Megan says annoyed.

Johnny has just come off the water and his kite surfing sail and board are lying on the ground, equally wet in salt water and in need of rinse, wash and grooming as is their owner.

"Chill out Meg, what's wrong with you? A guy has the right to ask about his gf."

"She isn't your girlfriend, baloney head!" snaps back Megan.

"F… off, she may not be yet, but she will be my gf, she will!"

"Not in your wildest dreams. Listen to yourself. You think we are all gf's to you, but I have news for you, you are so full of yourself…if you keep on going the way you are, pretty soon you'll find yourself without any girlfriends to hang out with at all," says Megan, finally getting it off her chest.

Johnny, the youngest son in the Baglioni family, wisely decides on two courses of action: First, to shut-up and second, to take a shower before going to Hillary's cabaña.

Inside the Zathlyn family poolside cabaña, 16-year old Hillary, the only daughter of the surgeon to the stars, Steven Zathlyn, is slumped on the big sofa, her legs bent in an awkward position.

"She certainly doesn't look picture perfect now! The little brat had it coming. Ever since I can remember, she was always teasing and posing," states a fired-up Louis Matthews III.

"When I think about all of my childhood friends on the island, I never think about her. When I think about her, it's only about sex," states Andy Holstein as he removes Hillary Zathlyn's bikini, which leaves her totally naked.

"Geez, this girl is so fuckin' beautiful!" says a wild Thor Krull as he spreads her legs and thrusts hard into her. Hillary lets out a short involuntary, muffled grunt, as young Thor Krull pushes harder. Hillary's face contorts in pain. Andy Holstein abruptly yanks Thor back and jumps right into the action. His movements seem awkward and jerky. Predictably, climax comes within seconds. Louis Matthews III fares no better and instantly climaxes as well. The boys look dejected. All of that planning and risk for a lousy 5 minutes with a lifeless body. When they head out, one of the three mumbles, "This was not a good idea. Let's pray they don't catch us."

Johnny is rinsing off in a nearby cabaña. Instead of whistling and singing as he normally does in the shower, he thinks about the many ways he could kill Megan Greenhouse. Clenching his fists and teeth, Johnny lets out a guttural and prolonged grunt of a spoiled teen brat not having his way. Hurtful as Megan's words were, they had been dead on! While he vents and lets out steam, his thoughts drift from sweet revenge on Megan to his lust for Hillary.

He's known and grown up with the object of this lust, Hillary Zathlyn, and he's been in love with her ever since he can remember. He knows she loves him as well. If only he could get her to act on it.

Johnny, clean and fresh, wearing basketball shorts showing his colorful boxers around the waistline, walks by Megan and company and tries to ignore them. He's actually grateful to her, but testosterone and adrenaline prevent him from showing it. He heads towards Hillary, glances back and sees Megan staring right at him. It is a fraction of a second glance between confidants, hers of amusement and friendship, his of self-confidence and wickedness. They both smile to themselves after turning away.

Johnny knocks at the cabaña door and he decides to make a move. This time he'll be calm and polite when Hillary rejects him. Thinking to himself, 'maybe I should wait for the right moment and kiss her, a real kiss, tongue and all.' No answer. Maybe Hillary is asleep. He knocks again and it gives in a bit. Strange! The door is ajar. He steps in the room. Everything is pitch black. Johnny decides to tiptoe his way into the cabaña's bedroom and wake Hillary with a kiss - the kiss that he's been dreaming about. His eyes adjust when he enters the bedroom and he sees a shadowy figure slumped on the sofa, legs spread. The bed is empty. He recognizes Hillary as he approaches the shadowy figure. She is naked and appears to be wasted. But, she doesn't drink or take drugs!

Not sure what to do, Johnny opts for not embarrassing her, covers her with a blanket and lets her sleep. At first, the smell just hits him, then it registers, it's the smell of sex and semen. He bolts for the door. He suddenly freezes and looks back at Hillary's face. He's overwhelmed with pain and anger, and then as he walks back, she opens her eyes.

"Hey."

"Johnny?"

Her eyes feel heavy; every part of her body is hurting. Slowly she comes out of a deep and foggy stupor.

"Where am I?" asks Hillary as she turns on a table lamp.

"In the cabaña."

"Oh yeah. I came to take a nap…how did you get in here… Johnny? I'm naked!" Hillary is now crying and almost yelling.

"You tell me, the door was unlocked. I knocked, but you didn't answer. I almost left, but decided to check on you to make sure you are okay. This is how I found you."

"Johnny Baglioni, you saw me naked?" an almost hysterical Hillary snaps at him.

"Well, I only saw shades of you slumped on the sofa, I covered you with a blanket. You seemed… wasted."

Just then, the blurry images of uninvited guests comes back to her … Hillary starts to shake and becomes inconsolable.

The expression on her face is one of sheer terror as she comes to the realization. "What happened to me Johnny?" she says in disbelief, her voice bordering on the verge of an emotional breakdown. "Everything hurts!" she blurts out in despair. Touching the source of the warm and wet sensation, she lets out a muffled cry, "I think I am bleeding!" She starts to take out her rage on Johnny, but his eyes only speak of love and concern. Her anger morphs into a cry for help.

"You want to call 911?" asks Johnny.

"No, I have to call my father."

"Do you want me to leave?"

"No, please stay…and hug me."

Hillary sees the phone on the floor next to the sofa that she's lying on.

"Johnny, can you hand me my phone please?" says Hillary weakly.

Her phone flashes a new text message. It's a delayed message from Megan.

"Hey girlfriend, Johnny is on his way to you. Hope you are awake by the time he shows up."

Hillary texts back, "Megan please come over now, I need you."

Hillary curls up in Johnny's arms. His heart races with mixed emotions that have him confused between sympathy and sexual desire as he feels the warmth and smoothness of her skin, so close to his for the very first time. Suddenly, some new emotions erupt - a chill of fear and impending danger. They both freeze when they hear a knock at the door.

"Hillary, it's me," Megan calls out.

"Come in!"

Megan storms in quickly and the first image she sees is Johnny's tender embrace. "What's going on, Johnny?"

Before he can answer, Hillary says, "Meg, something happened while I was asleep!"

"What do you mean?" asked Megan.

"I'm pretty certain that I've just been raped!"

"WHAT?" "How do you know?" asks Johnny. His fears are suddenly confirmed and his level of fear and anxiety raises to a crescendo pitch.

"I woke up in pain and naked on this sofa and noticed blood and other foul fluids all over me."

"What's that smell?" asked Megan.

"That, Megan is the smell of sex," answers a disheartened Johnny.

"We have to call the police," says Megan.

"Noooo! I have to call my father first," insists Hillary. She gives a voice command to her iPhone: "Call Dad." At the first ring, the phone is answered.

"Hi, Sweetie, your Dad is busy for the next hour. Is there anything I can do for you?"

"Aida, please get him on the phone. This is an emergency."

"But he just went in 15 minutes ago."

Hillary responds with a cry for help. "Aida, get him now, please."

"All right, I'll get him for you."

A few minutes later, Steven Zathlyn is on the line. "Hillary!"

"Daddy, Daddy." Hillary starts to cry hard and loud.

"Baby, what's going on?"

"Dad, I've just been raped!"

"What? Are you hurt?"

"I'm bleeding, Daddy!"

"Where are you? Are you alone?"

"At the cabaña, Megan and Johnny are with me."

"I'm on my way. I'll be right there."

"It hurts, Daddy, it hurts so much. I don't want anyone to see me," Hillary says as she continues to cry inconsolably.

"I'm walking out the door right now."

"Hurry up Dad, please."

"Who did this to you, baby?"

"I don't know Dad. I came from the pool to get a quick nap and woke up like this."

'Was this a break in? He would have to find out. Whoever it was, was going to pay.'

"Put your friends on the speaker please. Guys, please take care of Hillary until I get there."

"Yes, Mr. Zathlyn," answered Megan.

"Baby, I have to make a couple of calls in reference to this. I'm going to put you on hold while I do that, okay?"

"Okay, Dad, okay."

He puts Hillary on hold and speed dials retired General Robert Pinkus, CEO of Zapco International, one of the largest security firms in the country.

"Steve, what can I do for you today?"

"General, I have a delicate situation and I need your assistance."

"What's the nature of your situation?"

"My daughter has just been raped."

"Where is she now?"

"Paradise Island club house, cabaña #1."

"Are the police there?"

"No. We'll handle this ourselves, General."

"Understood, Steven."

"Has she been evaluated yet? Does she need medical assistance?"

"I don't know, but I'll see to that, General, she's waiting for me."

"Make sure that nothing is touched."

"All right, General."

"Steven, I'll be heading your way immediately."

"OK, I'll leave word at the security gate."

Dr. Zathlyn hangs up with the General and switches back to Hillary.

"Baby, have you cleaned yourself up?"

"No, Dad."

"Then don't do anything, just wait for me."

"OK, Dad."

Now, directing his questions to Megan and Johnny, he firmly states, "Where were you when this happened?"

"By the pool until Hillary texted me to come to her cabaña," replies Megan.

"Sir, I was kite surfing on Biscayne Bay off the east end of Paradise Island. When I finished I took a quick shower and stopped by the pool, argued for a few minutes with Megan, and then decided to pay a visit to Hillary. Megan said, she was in her cabaña. I found the door open, the lights out and Hillary was naked and passed out on the sofa," replies Johnny.

Dr. Zathlyn then asks Johnny, "How long between the time you came into the cabaña and when Hillary texted Megan?"

"Five to ten minutes, Sir."

Steven Zathlyn is boiling inside, gripping his steering wheel as if he could squeeze it and choke it. This is the only way to relieve some of the pressure that he feels, as he does not want to show his rage in the tone of his voice. "I'm just around the corner, baby, I'll be right there."

"Okay, Daddy."

Finally, Steven Zathlyn arrives at the cabaña. He runs to his daughter, takes her in his arms and hugs her a tad too tight. He embraces her and keeps saying, "I'm sorry baby, I'm sorry baby." He turns towards Megan and Johnny and says, "Thanks for your help in being here for my daughter. Don't go far in case we need you." He then walks the two teenagers out.

"Tell me exactly what happened?" Dr. Zathlyn asks his daughter while holding her tight to his chest.

"Daddy, I came in here for a nap like I usually do, fell asleep and woke up like this."

"You must have been drugged," says Dr. Zathlyn, frowning as he now realizes that this was not a random crime of opportunity, but one perpetrated by someone close to his daughter and in all likelihood, premeditated.

"How Daddy? While we were at the pool, I didn't have anything to eat or drink."

"What about before you got to the pool?"

"Let me think. I had breakfast at nine, that's all."

"What about while you were in here?"

"Nothing, wait a minute, I ordered a virgin piña colada." They scan the cabaña, but see no empty glass.

"Hillary, we're going to take care of this matter privately. A private security firm will arrive shortly and they'll help us find out who did this to you."

"What about the police?"

"We're not going to subject you to humiliation, baby, besides it will be much more effective to quietly find out the truth. This will shield you from the media and social networks."

"Who are they?"

"A private security firm that has worked for me for the last 20 years. They're going to interview all your friends at the pool, any people at the Club at that time and the Island's security guards on duty.

"All right."

"They're going to come in here and gather up forensic evidence."

"But, aren't the people they interview going to find out everything that happened to me?"

"No, we'll say this was a breaking and entering while you were sleeping, but with no harm to you." At that moment, Dr. Zathlyn receives a text message. General Pinkus and his assistants have arrived and are about to enter Paradise Island.

And that's how the wheels of justice get into motion on Paradise Island – revenge among the rich and powerful is swift, brutal and done with the utmost discretion.

Paradise Island long-time resident Mario Angel Restrepo's vast fortune cannot provide him the fidelity, much less loyalty, of his much younger wife. But, justice and revenge for Mario Angel Restrepo do not fit within the Island's standards – as ruthless as they may be. His sense of honor and manhood were acquired in the Colombian jungle oil fields where life resembles the old wild west and unbeknownst to them, that's what Lynn Nichols-Restrepo and her trainer, Piero Tomba, are facing – jungle law...

CHAPTER 2
THE RESTREPO FAMILY

The sun is setting, ablaze with intense colors, while in the Restrepo home another type of fire has been flaring up. Thirty-two year-old Lynn Nichols-Restrepo has been face down on her gym massage table for the last 30 minutes. Judging by her combination of giggles, screams and laughter, the mansion's help are supposed to believe that she is having an intense and animated workout with her Italian personal trainer. However, they know not to judge a book by its cover, but for what is underneath, and that is precisely, down deep inside, where Piero Tomba has been working out the lady of the house in more ways than one.

"Mr. Tomba has the sweetest job in the world. He gets to do her three times a week while being paid handsomely for it," says Marta Lopez, the household head of staff.

"And without any fear, as the rotor blades of Señor Restrepo's helicopter always give them plenty of time to get unhinged," replies Guy Robinot, the Haitian house driver, with a smirk on his face.

"I still think it's a mistake that neither you, Marta, nor you, Guy, tell him about what's going on. When he eventually finds out, heads are going to roll, probably ours," warns the cook, Dora Rojas.

"Since he met, courted and married Mrs. Nichols, after he was alone for so many years, this is the happiest I have ever seen him," replies Marta.

"Let me rephrase it, we must tell him! He's been really good to each of us, especially to you two," counters Dora.

Marta feels guilty and deep inside knows Dora is right. Yet, she can't get herself to do it. Ever since 70-year-old oil tycoon, Mario Angel Restrepo Nuñez, decided three years ago to marry the vivacious Texan and former lingerie model, 38 years his junior, Marta knew that the bride was only in it for the money. She also sensed, as was confirmed today, that Lynn Nichols was too hot to handle.

The hired help are all standing around in the kitchen when the door suddenly opens. "How's everybody doing today, the helicopter is in maintenance," says Mario Angel Restrepo. His staff's stone silence reaction is instantly replaced by his wife's sexual concerto a cappella.

Mario Angel Restrepo immediately heads toward the concerto and, once there, simply stands at the door and watches. He's livid. The veins in his neck are ready to explode. Then suddenly, unnoticed, he turns around and walks out of the gym, straight out of the house, to his waiting limo.

Thirty minutes later, the trainer walks out of the gym with a big smirk on his face. He waves goodbye to the house staff and quickly rides away on his brand-new Harley. Minutes later, she walks out of the gym and into the kitchen. Her face is flushed with a woman's expression and aura that only multiple consecutive orgasms can create. However, she's up for a rude awakening. The staff quickly brings her back to the reality of what has just taken place. Again, she lets out a muffled scream, but this time it is one of fear and anxiety.

CHAPTER 3
PARADISE ISLAND HISTORY

The majestic body of water that surrounds Paradise Island, between Miami's coastline and Miami Beach is called Biscayne Bay. After the 1926 Hurricane, causeways and roads were built over the expanse of Biscayne Bay from Miami Beach to the City of Miami. The Army Corps of Engineers were brought in by City of Miami officials to transform the swamp land and mosquito-infested bogs into ocean-blue bays and waterways. The Army Corps of Engineers dredged the existing swamps and bogs in order to build the roads that would allow travel from the City of Miami to Miami Beach. Additionally, dredging was undertaken to improve the waterway system to allow commercial and private boating. The material that was dredged up was used as landfill and deposited at intervals lining the causeway over Biscayne Bay. These landfills became separate small islands, linked by small bridges to the causeway. The most beautiful island that was created by the Army Corps of Engineers was called Paradise Island.

Without the promotional genius of Carl Fisher, Paradise Island would not be in existence. Carl Fisher was an American entrepreneur, *inventor and promoter of auto racing, as well as a real estate developer. He invented and then secured U.S. patents for automotive headlamps and automobile lighting systems. He opened the first automobile dealership in the United States and developed the Indianapolis Motor Speedway.*

In 1913, Fisher conceived and helped develop the Lincoln Highway, the first road for the automobile that stretched across the entire United States of America. A convoy trip a few years later by the U.S. Army along Fisher's Lincoln Highway was a major influence upon then Lt. Col. Dwight D. Eisenhower. Years later, as President, Eisenhower developed the Interstate Highway System. In 1914, after the success of the Lincoln Highway, Carl Fisher developed the north-south Dixie Highway system, which eventually led to the US1/I-95 highway system that ran from Key West, Florida to Maine. During this period of time, Fisher became involved in the successful real estate development of the new resort city of Miami Beach. From an unpopulated barrier island, Fisher developed a causeway system that linked the new Miami Beach to the City of Miami. Fisher is the best known and the most active promoter of the Florida land boom of the 1920s. By 1926, he was worth an estimated $100 million. In today's dollars, Fisher would be worth $10+ billion. One of his last projects in South Florida was the redevelopment of the hurricane-ravaged Paradise Island.

The Island is a glorious embodiment of wealth and grandeur. There are 20 mega-million-dollar mansions on it occupied by mega-rich billionaires, internationally-known sports figures, movie stars and entertainers, most of whom got their mega-millions through exceptional talent, extraordinary success and great timing, but others have made it through inheritance, thievery and Ponzi schemes.

However, the decadence and delight of moneyed Paradise Island had a tumultuous and turbulent past. In 1926, Miami, the city in which Paradise Island is located, was growing rapidly and preparing for a financial and population boom. Suddenly, on September 11, 1926, the U.S. Weather Bureau issued a warning that a hurricane had formed 1,000 miles east of the Lesser Antilles. The system moved quickly westward and intensified into a major hurricane. On September 15, 1926, the hurricane blew past Puerto Rico and continued into the Turks and Caicos Islands. Ninety miles west of Miami there is a group of barrier islands known as the Bahamas. On September 17, 1926, the hurricane decimated the Bahamas with 150 mph winds.

The U.S. Weather Bureau told Miamians that this vicious storm would not hit them. As was typical with hurricanes, the skies over Miami, just west of the hurricane, were clear and the seas were calm. Just hours later, on September 18, 1926, a category 4 hurricane made landfall in Florida with the eye passing directly over the City of Miami. The hurricane, with cyclonic winds, produced the highest sustained winds ever recorded in the United States. A storm surge of over 30 feet was reported on Miami Beach. Paradise Island, a mere ¼ mile west of Miami Beach, between the city of Miami and Miami Beach, was enveloped and decimated by the 30-foot plus storm surge.

The great Hurricane of 1926 ended the economic boom in Miami. Paradise Island was in ruins, flattened of the exotic and hypnotic palm trees and the colorful Royal Poincianas. All residential structures were washed away. After many months, people reluctantly returned to the area and were amazed to see that some of the natural beauty of Paradise Island survived the devastation.

CHAPTER 4
PARADISE ISLAND
SOCIAL CLUB, CARD ROOM

The clubhouse on Paradise Island contains a card room. There is currently a card game in progress, attended by four regal and pompous senior lady residents of the Island. Their twice-weekly card game is just a means to a non-stop gossip rampage about the latest Island rumors and innuendos, followed by their sharp tongues spewing out their opinions and predictions, sprinkled with their uncanny knowledge about the Island's history. Today, the Bayfront card room is buzzing. As the group of Island teens chill by the pool, the old matriarchs start to chitchat.

The first item on the chitchat agenda is gossip about the Greenhouse and Mizrahi families. Richard and Leonor Greenhouse have a mega mansion at # 19 Paradise Island. Dr. Greenhouse, one of the best neurosurgeons in the country, is a kindred spirit that donates most of his free time to the homeless, handicapped children and the citizens of Haiti, where he runs and funds a clinic. Their daughter, Sarah, is the image of her father. She is a talented humanitarian. She is eager to head to college and has been accepted at Harvard University. She is currently engaged to Steven Mizrahi, who lives with his family at # 22 Paradise Island.

Sarah seems to be a catch for Steven, but not in the eyes of the four old Island crows, as almost all of the residents call them.

"She is certainly marrying up; this is a catch for the ages. Leonor Greenhouse's lifelong ambition of marrying her little girl to the richest of all princes is now a reality, chapeau!" sarcastically states 70-year-old Nicole Albert.

"Steve Mizrahi could have spared himself so much trouble by marrying an equal in wealth. I've tried to help the family over the past two years, but Steve has shown no interest in anything whatsoever but that little Greenhouse girl," laments 65-year-old Sarah Pesin.

"Ladies, you all know that the Mizrahi family has wealth that ranks them the richest in Florida. When Steve's grandfather retired, their cruise ship line, Jubilee, had 3 vessels. Today, under Ariel's helm they have acquired five of their largest competitors. They have 32 ships now and are the biggest in the world. Rumor has it that they are worth $20 billion dollars," stated the pensive 64-year-old Margarita Lujan-Restrepo.

"And the Greenhouses live well beyond their means. Richard Greenhouse is a darling with lots of talent and good deeds, but no ambition. If it were up to him, they would be living where they belong, perhaps in Coconut Grove or somewhere similar. My educated guess is that they are worth $20 million tops, and the house is 90% of that," speculated sarcastic 69-year-old Elizabeth Bell.

The four matriarchs now switch subjects, jumping as if in a shark attack frenzy, into the debacle they have all been waiting to share and shred with their tongues. The shocking events they are now going to get into have kept the old bags salivating all the way until this moment.

"Everybody knows he beats her," says Sarah Pesin.

"He has done it for years, but as of late, it has been escalating," counters Nicole Albert.

"Why does she stay? Why doesn't she simply leave him?" adds Maria Lujan-Restrepo.

"Money and power my dear, what else would a former stripper and escort like Ornella do without the status and lifestyle of Alessandro Baglioni?" states an opinionated Elizabeth Bell.

What the old crows are getting into happened the previous night, close to midnight, when scandal erupted out of house #21 as Ornella Baglioni, half naked, screaming her lungs out and seemingly running for her life, put up a show for the whole island to see. Right behind her, driving his brand new convertible blue Bentley, her husband Alessandro gave chase, and in stereotypical Italian fashion, yelled back at her, demanding she go back to the house.

"Well, it appears that he caught up with her and beat the crap out of her right there in the middle of our Island park, conveniently out of range of the security video cameras," adds Sarah Pesin.

"Then he marched her into his car and drove her back to their home, where in all likelihood, once corralled, he beat her some more," interjects Elizabeth Bell.

"Why don't we call the cops on them?" questions Margarita Lujan-Restrepo.

"And acquire Alessandro as an enemy? No thanks, I pass," states Nicole Albert.

Then all four ladies remain quiet and mute, perhaps in realization that their talk and words are simply just that, talk and words.

As if to break the ice, Mrs. Albert starts to relate lighter news. "Leon is finally finishing the house," she says.

"About time Nicole, your poor old son living in an empty mansion, an empty kitchen, and with nothing but a bed to show for it!" snaps back Margarita Lujan-Restrepo.

"Your son has been doing nothing but work and work since his divorce," laments Sarah Pesin.

"His house is one of the nicest on the Island. Living in that empty shell of a mansion is such a waste," adds Elizabeth Bell.

"Tell me about it, haven't we all cooked for him and stuffed his fridge for months? But, nothing has changed," reflects his very own mother, Nicole Albert.

"I bet you anything there is a woman behind it," challenges Elizabeth Bell.

"I was wondering that myself," replies the smiling mom.

Leon Albert is the CEO of one of the largest homebuilders in the country. The company was formed in the 1950s by his father, who passed away a couple years earlier after a long battle with liver cancer, leaving Leon in charge of the company. Leon turned out to be a great manager and the company doubled in size during his tenure. He has three grown children and recently went through a nasty and stressful divorce. His mansion faces Miami Beach to the east and is just down the road from the humbler home occupied by his mom.

In a cloud of smoke and gossip, the four old crows' sharp tongues are a never ending plow into the life of the Island, but they should know better, they do so at their own peril…

CHAPTER 5
THE HOLSTEIN FAMILY HOME
ON PARADISE ISLAND

 You cleaned me out tonight guys."

"Well it's about time, Mr. President, and we will have to do it about 50 more times to pull even with you."

Earlier that evening, a fundraiser had been held at the Paradise Island Holstein mansion, where the charismatic former President had performed his well-rehearsed 'act' to the delight of the super wealthy guests. More than $500K had been raised, right on target and not bad for a quick visit to Miami Beach, Florida.

Once the fund raiser event was over, most of the Holstein family except their son, Andy, left on the family plane and went to their winter home in Telluride, Colorado. Mr. Holstein, an old buddy of the former President, has stayed behind for their customary poker game. Five powerful and rich Miamians have joined the President for the poker game. The President has lost $250K and is promptly covered by the funds Mr. Holstein holds in trust for his buddy. With the game over, the other poker players have gone home. Holstein and the President walk to the back of the property, dockside, and both enter a small bungalow wedged between the pool and the mansion's waterfront. The bungalow is Holstein's retreat. And no one is allowed in, except him and the former President. It is windowless and soundproof. It has a high-ceiling living area, kitchen and a plush inviting bedroom with a state-of-the-art entertainment system. It is stocked with all kinds of goodies. It is restocked, cleaned and swept for electronic eavesdropping devices on a periodic basis.

However, there is something unique about the bungalow. The bedroom closet has a false wall, which once opened, has a hatchet door on the floor where a ladder goes underground one story down. At the end, there is a tunnel that goes straight towards Biscayne Bay and ends at a waterproof door on the mansion's water's edge. That's where Holstein and the former President stand as a small boat arrives and four young girls in tight body suits proceed to disembark and head towards the men. Holstein lends a hand to each of the girls. A few minutes later, they are all upstairs in the bungalow. The four girls are shocked and surprised to learn who is one of the mysterious hosts. Each of the girls has been body searched beforehand. They have left all their personal belongings and electronics at their departure point. They were scanned when they boarded the boat, and again, when they disembarked on Paradise Island.

Up in the bungalow, the former President takes his old buddy aside and says, "how old are these ladies?"

"Mr. President, tonight we have four young ladies between 18 and 20 years old. Tonight, I went not only for quality, but for freshness as well. They have all been thoroughly vetted. They are all college students and their tuition and student loans have been taken care of on a continuing basis as long as they keep their mouths shut. If you like them, they will be available every time you stop by."

"God help us, Bart, but you know once you present me with this kind of opportunity, it is very hard for me to resist, especially since it involves teen girls." The former President and his old pal have been doing the same charade ever since his term at the White House had ended. Bart has been among the few that has stood behind him throughout the ups and downs of his political life. Both Bart and the former President are incorrigible philanderers. They feed on each other's sexual drive. The bungalow has resolved many anxieties and problems since it was put into use a few years earlier.

The two old friends walk back in and are welcomed by giggles and laughter. All the girls have made themselves comfortable and appear to be chitchatting about their soon to be encounters. After a few drinks, the scene changes dramatically. The former President has a girl sitting on each leg and is stroking their hair incessantly, something he loves to do.

"Who wants to be the first to provide a great service to their country?" states Bart, sarcastically.

"What do you two guys have in your dirty little minds?" asks the blonde sitting on the President's right leg.

The former President heaves her off his lap with both hands, sighing and grunting from the exertion. He straightens up and grabs the blonde girl's hand.

"Bart, do you care to join us?" he says with a wicked smile.

"Your orders are my command, Mr. President."

Bart grabs the girl's other hand and the threesome heads into the bungalow's adjoining bedroom. Shortly thereafter, the other three girls are called in as well.

But even in "Paradise" there are boundaries that shall not be crossed or pushed as perilous cliffs may be waiting unannounced on the other side.

CHAPTER 6
THE ZATHLYN FAMILY

"General Pinkus, Dr. Zathlyn, we are done with the testing," says Lynn Albert, an MD on staff at Zapco International.

"What are your findings?" asks Steven Zathlyn.

"Dr. Zathlyn, she has been sexually molested, traumatized and is in need of urgent care."

"Dr. Albert, they are waiting for you both at my clinic."

"Fine, Sir, we'll be on our way in a couple of minutes."

Steven Zathlyn's veins are about to explode. He thanks everyone and asks for privacy. He joins General Pinkus and a few of the investigators to discuss the search for the perpetrators.

General Pinkus is the first to speak: "We found a group of teens sitting by the pool, four old farts playing cards and five club personnel. We were able to eliminate all these people as suspects, except for a waitress that we are locating as we speak. We did discover that there are video security cameras posted around the pool area. However, of the four cameras covering the area, none were directed towards the cabañas."

After the update, General Pinkus heads to Paradise Island's security booth at the entrance. "Good morning, I am General Pinkus and I am conducting an investigation of a possible burglary at Dr. Zathlyn's club house cabaña. We would like to review the security camera images recorded this morning."

"Yes, sir," states the guard. "We have notified the head of our security team and are awaiting instructions."

"We need to see the videos right away. We cannot waste any time here."

"I understand, but I have to wait for clearance. Our standard procedure is to contact the police first, and let them handle any alleged criminal activity."

An irate General Pinkus speed dials his old friend, Richard Oranski. Mr. Oranski immediately picks up… "Oranski, how are ya?"

"General, what a surprise, it's been a while."

"Yeah, that's right."

"Oranski, is your firm still running security at Paradise Island?"

"Yes, sir."

"I thought so, listen, I am here with one of your employees at the front gate. A client of mine had his cabaña burglarized while his daughter was inside taking a nap."

"Did anything happen to her?"

"No, but you need to authorize your man to let us take a look at the security footage."

After a brief pause, Oranski responds, "Of course, General, anything you need. Let me speak to him please."

The security guard picks up the phone and a few seconds later sheepishly hands the phone back to General Pinkus.

"Oranski, we want to conduct this as a private investigation."

"Oh, ok, let me speak to the security guard again please."

After a brief phone conversation, Oranski confirms to General Pinkus that the guards have been instructed not to call the cops. General Pinkus then proceeds to review the video tapes in earnest. An hour later, he is totally frustrated. "Nobody coming or going to the cabaña, how do you explain that?" he barks to the security guard. "No camera view of the cabañas? If someone went to the cabañas from the pool area, wouldn't they be filmed?"

"The only way is from the water. Which means that the interlopers are very familiar with this island and its security cameras."

General Pinkus continues, "Are any cameras in the dock area?"

"No sir," replied the guard, "besides those you are looking at, which are all around the clubhouse, we only have video cameras around the main street and here at the gate."

"What about the homes closest to the clubhouse area?"

"Some have them at their docks to alert them if intruders get near their yachts."

"Is there a way to find out if the two neighboring houses have security cameras at the water level?"

"Yes, let me call each house, give me a second."

Moments later, the security guard confirms that both houses have security cameras at the docks. General Pinkus quickly and forcefully addresses the security guard, "Can you ask if we can take a look at their security video from this morning?"

Minutes later, he secures clearance. General Pinkus, the security guard and two uniformed colleagues of General Pinkus sit down to check the security videos. A while later, a familiar scene repeats itself.

"Nothing! No one coming in or out. Absolutely nothing!"

Suddenly, "What is that?"

"What, Sir?"

"Stop the video! Right there!" The General points to the upper right corner of the video. There was a small blurry image in the distance, a clip that everyone could have easily missed as it lasted less than a second.

"It's a boat, Sir."

"Download it into your laptop, blow it up and clean it up."

Once he has reviewed the information, General Pinkus walks back to cabaña #1. He knocks softly at the door. There is a terse response, "Who is it?"

"General Pinkus."

"Come in please."

As the General walks in, he is shocked to find his old friend disheveled and staring with empty eyes at him. "How is she?"

"She is resting."

"She is obviously very badly injured inside, General. It will take a while for her to heal both physically and mentally."

"We have suspects, Peter."

"What!"

"I think we know who they are. Video footage shows 3 guys coming in and out by boat, let me show you."

As they stare at Pinkus' laptop, they see an image of a small boat. Then, an enhanced photo of the boat comes into view. Steven Zathlyn goes numb. First thing he recognizes is the registration number on the boat. "I know who they are, I know all of them, they have all grown up on the island. General, let's go talk to Johnny Baglioni, he may be a witness."

They don't need to go very far, as Johnny is hanging out just outside of the cabaña. This is as close as Dr. Zathlyn would allow him to be to his daughter. Johnny looks scared and apprehensive. Dr. Zathlyn is blunt and to the point.

"Johnny, I have a couple questions for you. You were kite surfing just before you came to visit Hillary, right?"

"Yes, Sir."

"Did you see any boats near the island?"

"Let me think…of course I saw Thor Krull, Andy Holstein and Louis Matthews. They were water-skiing."

"Did you see them come back to the island?"

"As a matter of fact I did, they docked…" Johnny abruptly stops the conversation and his eyes widen and look like they are about to pop out of his head. He looks straight at Dr. Zathlyn and the General and yells, "Did they do this to Hillary?"

"Johnny keep your mouth shut, not a word to anybody, not a word, do you understand?"

"All right Sir, I'll do that, but I'll make sure that if they did it they will pay for it."

The General quickly responds, "Young man, let us handle this, if they are guilty, they will get what they deserve, rest assured they will." After Johnny leaves, General Pinkus and Dr. Zathlyn discuss what they are going to do.

Revenge is all Dr. Zathlyn has in mind – but he needs proof – unequivocal proof.

CHAPTER 7
THE BAGLIONIS

I t's 11:00 p.m. and Ornella Baglioni, for second time in a week, is running for her life down Paradise Island's only road. The dim streetlights barely touch her. There is a sliver of a moon and she is running through shadows. She is sobbing uncontrollably. Her face is badly bruised and her nose is bleeding. Her blouse is ripped open and her tan torso is exposed. Her sandals are held tightly in her right hand. She is running barefoot and with each step she gasps in pain. As she approaches the Island's exit, two headlights are reflected off her back. Her husband, Alessandro Baglioni, in a blue Bentley, is coming after her. He slows down right by her side.

"What are you doing?!" He yells with eyes filled with rage. She does not respond and continues to run forward. "Get in the car Ornella! Right now! Let's go home."

The night security guard sees the activity and comes out of his gatehouse. "Mrs. Baglioni are you alright?" the guard shouts.

"Shut up and stay out of this," yells Alessandro Baglioni.

The security guard calls the head office to report the incident. As he looks up after punching in the numbers, he stares in disbelief as he watches Ornella Baglioni jump from the bridge coming out of the Island, into the dark, night waters of Biscayne Bay.

Some of the Island residents seek attention – that is all they care about and live for.

World famous Island resident, Lars Johannsen, is too self-absorbed to fulfill his duties as a single father and pay attention to his only son, Jasper, whose antics are not only dangerous but blatantly illegal.

CHAPTER 8
LARS JOHANNSEN'S HOME

The west facing lot, #7 is the Johannsen's beautiful Spanish-style home. A single parent, Lars Johannsen has lost control of his 21-year-old son, Jasper. It began when Jasper was 12 years old and started experimenting with drugs. He had a string of close calls that kept getting more serious in nature. It started with trespassing at 14, silenced; then, rolling the family's SUV at 16, traffic violation quashed, no breathalyzer taken; and then, Jasper overdosed at 20, clinically dead, followed by two weeks in a coma and two months in recovery. It was a chronologized downward spiral.

Jasper's self-destructive lifestyle has not changed the self-absorbed life of his father. His jet setting and socializing has never changed. Lars Johannsen's availability to help his troubled kid is sporadic as his time is spent running one of the largest architectural firms in the United States, called Johannsen's Urban Design. He also teaches conversational Spanish at the University of Miami, Coral Gables, Florida. Luckily, maybe for all, Jasper is a computer genius. His hedonistic father believes that in the end his son's talent will take care of any flaws and lack of maturity. How wrong he is. His son is completely, totally and utterly lost.

Turning the victim's computer camera on while hacking it, is always the safest way to know that no one is using or about to use the defenseless piece of hardware that has been penetrated. Jasper Johannsen's target today is to find out if the user has any software applications on his computer where the computer user may have stored all of his passwords and user IDs to be used across the web. There it is…then he freezes. He hears a loud bang and the door opens. Her face is covered in blood. She stumbles into the room. He watches her through the hacked laptop's camera. Suddenly she disappears from view. He can hear the thump on the floor and the mattress' springs. He guesses that she has slid to hide under the bed. Seconds later, he sees another person walk into the room. He has a stun gun in his right hand and a flashlight in his left. Jasper Johannsen can see that the second intruder has kneeled down and apparently fired the stun gun. This is followed by an intense but brief muffled scream. The second intruder exits, but not alone. He is pulling a big canvas bag with him. The intruder turns off the light as he is leaving and suddenly everything turns dark. Jasper can no longer see anything in the hacked room, except for a flashlight that turns toward his line of sight and blinds him for a second. He briefly squints, then quickly opens his eyes and to his shock the intruder's face now occupies the entire screen of the hacked computer. The intruder appears to be looking straight at the hacker. As he is leaving the room, the intruder must have seen the red light blink indicating the computer was on.

Jasper is about to learn that when you break into other people's lives, property or their privacy, the unforeseen consequences can put your own life and freedom in peril…

CHAPTER 9
Zapco International Headquarters

“ Sir, as you instructed, while we had the three suspects under surveillance, we were able to retrieve three empty soda cups they were drinking from and that they had discarded in a garbage can. We have the DNA results from the semen samples from Miss Megan, as well as from the soda cups,” says Dr. Lynn Albert.

“And?”

“They all match. We also interviewed the waitress who they paid to slip something in the drink. The three teens are not the smartest in town. They came on and off the island almost undetected, but left a witness. They committed the rape, Steven.”

“Thank you, Dr. Albert.”

General Pinkus immediately calls Dr. Zathlyn. “Steven, it’s a match. We are moving to the next phase. I’ll let you know a few days in advance, the exact date and location.

“All right, I’ll be ready.”

The fate is sealed on the three young Island residents. The three culprits are now hunted animals – they just don't know it yet. Being reckless is all they know, so the three young rapists continue to do what they do best, party non-stop.

ULTRAFEST, TWO DAYS LATER

The three suspects, Thor Krull, Andy Holstein and Louis Matthews III, have been dry humping their way through Ultrafest for about three hours now. General Pinkus' field operators have been surreptitiously following the three suspects. The teens have gotten progressively more intoxicated. At last count, each of them has downed at least five big draft beers. Besides the surveillance inside Ultrafest, other field operators are watching the boys' car that they parked before going into Ultrafest. The operatives are lying in wait.

Ultrafest is a worldwide global journey of electronic music that culminates in a 3-day hyper music-sex event held in Miami once a year. Ultrafest takes place at 15 different venues through a calendar year, such as Sao Paulo, Brazil, Seoul, Korea, Tokyo, Japan and Bangkok, Thailand. Lots of young fans follow Ultrafest from country to country and wind up at the crescendo of the Ultrafest journey in Miami, Florida. This is the second year in a row that the three boys have gone together to Ultrafest. They know the ropes. They have sampled the music and the hyperphysical sexual contact that accompanies the bump and grind of the electronic vibe.

Thor Krull has split off from the other two boys and has moved into a crowd in front of the Bayfront Park bandstand where the Black

Eyed Peas have just finished their hit "My Humps" and started their 15-minute version of "I Gotta Feeling." Thor has gotten in the mood during the song "My Humps" and he squeezes and slithers through the crowd to get as close to the lead singer Fergie as he can. When Fergie and the band move into "I Gotta Feeling," Thor rips off his tank top and throws it into the crowd. He then pulls his basketball shorts down a couple more inches to show more of his boxers. Glued to him on his right is what looks like a blond high school cheerleader wearing cut-off jeans and a half-shirt that shows her belly button. When Fergie and the band start singing, the chorus: *"That tonight's gonna be a good good night, tonight's gonna be a good good night, tonight's the night, lets live it up,"* Thor looks to his left and sees an Oriental girl that had obviously followed Ultrafest from the Orient to Miami as she is wearing an Ultrafest, South Korea 2016 T-shirt.

Suddenly, Fergie and will.i.am start screaming: *"Let's do it, let's do it, let's do it and do it and do it and do it, do it, do it... I gotta feeling that tonight's gonna be a good good night... Tonight's the night, let's live it up, let's love it up."*

Thor, the blonde girl and the Oriental girl are sandwiched together. As the crowd ebbs and sways to the sexy and undulating music, Thor inadvertently (but kind of deliberately) moves the back of his hands along both girls' butts. Then, they start to move to the music in unison, touching, caressing and exploring. Thor and the blonde girl pair up.

She whispers in Thor's ear, "Let's go to the back."

They weave their way through the crowd to the beat and crescendo of: *"That tonight's gonna be a good good night, tonight's gonna be a good good night, tonight's the night, lets live it up, let's love it up."* The crush of the crowd, the power of the music and the closeness of the young girl gets Thor intensely aroused.

Then, the girl whispers in Thor's ear, "Walk towards the fence by the exit and I'll follow you there."

Thor thinks of the old Aerosmith song, "Love In An Elevator" and does as he is told. Thor is so turned on he can hardly breathe. He starts to walk towards the fence, but suddenly, he is engulfed by the ebb and sway of the massive crowd. He loses contact with her, then in frustration, pulls his cell phone out of his pocket and sends a text message to Andy and Louis, telling them to meet up with him at the exit gate near the American International Arena.

Together, the three boys exit and stumble and fumble their way to their car. But, the moment Thor clicks the car door open, the three teens are hit with darts. In a few seconds, they are unconscious on the ground and the General's operators quickly load them into a van.

Later, the boys would wake up again, in the same spot, but this time seated in the car. What happened in-between will haunt them for the rest of their lives.

They asked for it. They are about to get it in spades. It will be a devastating blow.

The stage is set, a world class of surgical skills will be used for the purpose of extracting "exacting" revenge.

CHAPTER 10
BIMINI ISLAND, BAHAMAS

The yacht, Happy Ending, is anchored on the east end of the quiet and tranquil Bimini Island Cay. Everything is ready. The main living area has been completely sealed, wrapped and covered in plastic. Around 2:00 a.m., the roar of the jet engines of a speedboat can be heard in the distance. It has taken, with perfect weather, about 90 minutes for the speedboat to cross the Gulf Stream from Miami. The speedboat docks next to the Happy Ending. The three limp bodies are transferred onto the yacht. Their pulse and vital signs are checked. Dr. Lynn Albert carefully preps them. Thirty minutes later, Dr. Zathlyn is ready to start. He works with great care. Anesthesia is the trickiest part and it is the area where he has the least amount of practical experience. He first starts with local anesthesia, then after verifying that all vital signs are in order he makes the first surgical incisions. He conducts several procedures at the same time, always suturing while severing to prevent excessive bleeding. Once the initial task is completed, he makes sure to leave enough skin tissue behind, and then starts the painstaking task of reconstruction. He stretches the skin and creates smooth walls on each side. The most difficult part is to set the outflow tracks. He carefully sews everything back in place. Next, he repeats the same procedure on Andy Holstein and then finally, on Louis Matthews III. When Dr. Zathlyn is finally done, he contemplates with satisfaction the results of his work.

Then, Dr. Albert and Dr. Zathlyn put everything they have extracted in plastic bags to be fed to the sharks. Dr. Zathlyn dresses his three patients and asks Pinkus' crew to take them back to Miami. Dr. Zathlyn quickly leaves the ship for his waiting private seaplane and flies back to Miami.

MIAMI, FLORIDA

Thor opens his eyes to a blinding morning sun and a strong headache. The car is steaming and he is leaning against the car steering wheel drenched in sweat. He tries to move, but his body hurts in every conceivable spot. He feels like a truck has run over him. Andy is slouched next to him on the passenger seat and Louis is lying flat out on the back seat. He shakes both sleeping beauties up.

"Hey, guys! Time to wake up."

"So, what happened last night, someone slip something in our drinks or what?" said Andy.

"Must have been very strong, I feel like shit," says Louis.

"Hey, Louis, you've been acting funny ever since the gang bang we had with Hillary."

"Like what, speak up, dude."

"Yea, Johnny was kitesurfing when we approached the island," replies Louis.

Thor comes out of his stupor and interjects, "You seriously think he paid attention to us?"

"I don't think he consciously did, but if asked, he will remember us," replies Louis. A pregnant pause follows.

"I'm going to take a leak over in the bushes, quite a night last night, might as well pee over there by the security fence," says Louis.

He staggers over towards the outskirts of Ultrafest and looks in both directions to make sure no one is staring at him. He unzips his pants, reaches in his boxers, but finds nothing. All he feels is pain and two lips of flapping skin. His scream of sheer agony and horror can be heard blocks away and the power of it shocks his two buddies in the car. Both Thor and Andy jump out of the car and see Louis running toward them with his face contorted in horror and his fly open.

He looks straight into Thor's face and screams, "We shouldn't have done it, we shouldn't have done what we did to Hillary."

"Chill out, dude, what's the matter with you?" yells Thor.

"I'm not a man anymore," cries Louis hysterically.

Realizing that a crowd was starting to form, Thor yanks Louis into the car, Andy hops in and they speed away.

"I got no dick, all I can feel down there is a vagina," screams Louis from the back of the car.

"Has he gone nuts or what?" Andy asks Thor.

The blurred image of being hit by the darts comes to Andy and suddenly a brutal fear grips the three of them.

"Thor, stop the car, stop the damn car now," yells Andy.

As Thor pulls over, Louis pulls his pants down. All that can be seen on Louis' crotch is a perfectly shaped triangle of pubic hair and a… vagina! Fear and horror rips Thor and Andy as they both zip down their pants and look for their lost treasures. All that can be heard are endless screams, hard and soft cries, followed by total uncertainty and fear about what to do with the rest of their lives. Their worst nightmare has just come true.

"We cannot let anyone know about this," says Thor.

"This must have happened after we left Ultrafest and got knocked out," replies Andy.

"Who did this? How was this done to us?" asks Louis.

Finally, they all go home, not knowing what to do except keep their mouths shut.

"Island law" is swift, brutal, exacting and remorseless.

The Baglionis' glitter hides the depravation, as well as a dangerous psychopath, Alessandro Baglioni.

CHAPTER 11
THE BAGLIONIS

On the north end of Paradise Island sits a 27,761 sq. ft. mansion on 6+ acres of some of the most valuable real estate in the United States. The 10-bedroom, 12-bath home is owned by Canadian born, Alessandro and Ornella Baglioni; both naturalized American citizens of Italian ancestry. The Baglioni's have two children, 18-year-old Johnny, Hillary Zathlyn's platonic rescuer, and 16-year-old Antonella.

The couple proudly brag about their still outstanding 10-year-old record as the youngest couple, when in their 30's, they moved onto Paradise Island. Everything about Al, as everyone calls him, is big, flamboyant and ostentatious. Whether it is cars, planes, yachts, art, jewelry or clothes, it is big and expensive. However, his character, ego and temperament were honed, not on the grandeur of Paradise Island, but on a less than auspicious beginning thirty years earlier.

30 Years Prior

Fifteen-year-old Alessandro Francesco Baglioni Rossi is running for his life. At 6'2", his height and long legs should have been an advantage, but his lack of fitness and his teen gawkiness do not allow him to either outrun or hide from his pursuers. His big leather soled shoes keep sliding and provide no grip on the wet cobblestones. He is out of breath and is running out of energy. The pursuers' footsteps are close. Fear overwhelms him. He tries to run faster. He takes an ill-advised right turn and suddenly finds himself in a dark, narrow dead-end alley. In this confined area, the echoes of his own footsteps are strangling his eardrums. His six pursuers storm into the alley's only way out, locking it. Alessandro can see the shadows of their body frames and the pipes, chains, knives and guns they are carrying. Their jerky movements show their tension and anger. There is no place to run or hide. The tallest member of the pursuers comes to a stop in front of Alessandro. Both pursuer and pursued are out of breath and exhausted. "So you like beating up small girls? You enjoy making them suffer and inflicting pain on defenseless youngsters? Let's see how it feels for you low-level scum to be on the receiving end." Alessandro braces himself for the worst.

He does not die that night, but comes close to it. Two titanium plates, one on his right cheek, the other on the back of his head and screws through his right femur are testimony to it. He learns later that night that right in the middle of the six men beating, an M-16 submachine gun had been fired into the air from the back door of a nightclub. The club bouncer had come out for a smoke and stumbled onto the scene. Alessandro could not recall any of the events after he lost consciousness, but he had learned later that the club bouncer that had saved him drove him to the hospital and contacted his family. His parents, Massimo and Gina Baglioni, had rushed to their son's side and had nursed him back to health over the following six months. They both knew that their son was a psychopath and had no remorse or conscience about his acts. Ever since he was a young child, even though brilliant and a fast learner with a curious mind, he showed signs of cruelty and violence. At first, it showed itself with the family pets and the wild animals he would catch in the woods behind their home. Then, in high school, he became a bully and physically abused his class-mates. They knew their son had a serious problem. Therapy was started, but to no avail. The incidents kept occurring and increased in viciousness.

Fortunately, the bouncer that had saved his life, took a liking to Alessandro and offered him a job as a worker in the nightclub's back room. He became the protégé of the bouncer and the staff of the nightclub. Alessandro also engaged in three years of weightlift-ing and martial arts training. On his 18th birthday, he was officially promoted to bouncer. His cravings for violence remained the same, though. At least now, the bouncer job allowed him to release some of his dark desires for violence. His fixation to hurt the defenseless remained. It was simply that he learned how to be smart about it. A wolf in sheep's clothing.

Reality hits home as one of the young rapists goes home and faces his father.

CHAPTER 12
THE MATTHEWS MANSION

L ouis III drives himself to Paradise Island. He slowly parks his convertible inside the 5-car garage. Having ruined his life, he is determined to put an end to it, right now, right there. He leaves the car running and gets out. He then pulls out a half-dozen beach towels from the trunk of his car and soaks them in water. He places them around the door openings of the garage. He opens the car's convertible top and sits down in the driver's seat to wait for the inevitable.

"So, this is your way out of this, as always, the easy way out." Louis jumps out of his seat. "Get out of the car right now," demands his father, Louis Matthews II.

As soon as Louis gets out of the car, his father gives him an uppercut, which knocks him to the floor and he loses consciousness. A couple of hours later, Louis slowly opens his eyes. The first thing he sees is the contorted face of his father sitting right in front of him.

"I just spent a couple hours with the Zathlyn family attorney, and he presented key evidence that they have and it implicates you and your two moron friends in a very serious crime. Now tell me, did you rape Hillary Zathlyn?"

"Dad…"

"Yes or no?" Louis stays completely still. "Didn't you understand my question?" Louis II is now inches from his son's face. "Did you or didn't you?" Again, silence from his son. "So, is it true?" Louis II starts pacing around the room, cursing to himself. Then, he turns around and faces his son. "We gotta get you a good criminal attorney, pronto. But, first I'm going to call Steven Zathlyn to apologize."

He then dials his childhood friend, not knowing exactly what to do or say, but determined to do whatever is necessary to try to mitigate this horrendous problem. "Steven, I'm here with my son. I and my entire family are so sorry about this." Silence is the only response he gets. "Steven, are you there? Listen, we've been friends since we learned how to walk. I'm sure you want to avoid any scandals, we certainly do." More silence.

Finally, "Louis, I agree with you on that."

Louis II is a little relieved that his old friend is acting with benevolence and is communicating with him.

"I frankly don't know what to do with my son," states Louis II.

"I believe he will need a lot of counseling to adapt to his new life," replies Dr. Zathlyn.

"What life? He isn't going to have any in the foreseeable future. I want him to redeem himself through severe and prolonged punishment," continues Louis II.

"He's been punished enough already, Louis. That's why I am talking to you. After this conversation, I don't want anything to do with you or your family. Never, ever," firmly states Steven Zathlyn.

"Now you lost me. I called you to apologize and work things out. I'm even asking for help for what to do with my son."

His former long-time friend interrupts him, "He hasn't told you anything??"

"Told me what, Steven?"

"Believe me, Louis, you are not going to want to hear from us or see us again, either! You guys have your own hell to live through. Always remember this, he did it to himself. Goodbye."

The line goes dead and Louis II sits in disbelief looking at his son. As he looks into his son's eyes, slowly at first and then coming on strong, a cold shiver starts to creep up his spine. "What did he do to you?" He is met with silence, except that his son crawls into a fetal position and starts to cry like a small child. "What did he do to you?" Louis II jumps on his son and starts tearing his clothes off. His son curls up even more. When he gets his son's shirt off, he can see no scars our wounds on his chest or back. He starts pulling his son's pants down and finally pulls them off and sees no visible injuries or any trauma. Louis is now sobbing uncontrollably with his hands covering his genital area.

Suddenly, Mrs. Matthews walks into the room. "What's all the commotion…?" She sees her husband's face in a gaping grimace, a kind of rictus of startled alarm. "Louis what are you doing?"

"Leave us alone, Eleanor."

"You're hurting our son." She then moves in between her husband and their son, and is face to face with her husband.

"Eleanor, are you sure you want to be a part of this?"

"Of course, I'm sure, what's going on?"

"He raped Hillary Zathlyn."

"Our son would never do that."

"Ask him."

"Louis is this true?"

The teenager remains curled up, sobbing uncontrollably. Eleanor's maternal instincts of protection of her son turn to anger.

"Louis, why are you holding our son's clothes?"

Louis then explains to his wife the contents of the call he just had with their former long-time friend, Steven Zathlyn.

"Do you think he might have done something to our son?" she says in an anguished half crying voice.

They both turn and see Louis, not only curled up, but also covering his genital area with both hands. They looked at each other in horror.

"Louis, what did he do to you?" they both scream uncontrollably in tandem.

In an instant, their castrated son shatters their perfect world. Louis Matthews II meteoric rise as a self-made man has been brought to a sudden halt – after so much work, starting in the oil fields of Venezeula.

25 YEARS PRIOR

Louis Matthews II's father was in the oil business for 40 years. By the time of his death, he owned thousands of wells throughout the state of Texas. But, his lifestyle held him back. It was only fitting that at the age of 76 his chaotic and selfish life had ended in a brothel, totally drunk and surrounded by middle-aged, sagging and sad prostitutes. In total, Louis Matthews was married six times, had

13 children and never had time to speak with any of them or their spouses. He lived, from boom to bust, from nightclub to nightclub and from escort service to escort service. He was a functioning alcoholic for the last 40 years and he loved to pay for sex, especially if the women were from Eastern Europe. Louis Matthews was loud, foul mouthed and accustomed to imposing his will on the unfortunate people and employees in his orbit. He was a self-made man. He came from a mid-west middle-class family. His dad was an IRS employee and his mom was a math teacher at the local high school. They provided the rebellious Louis with stern discipline, a deeply religious upbringing and the best education. Louis was wild and bright since his early years and ended up graduating with top honors from Carnegie Mellon. The very next day after graduation, he left home never to return again. First, he went chasing black gold in California and then back to Texas.

Louis II shared his dad's passion for oil and as a child spent time with his father in the oil fields. Later in life, he accompanied his father on his nightly escapades. When the will was read, Louis II inherited 90% of his father's wealth. His 12 siblings each received an annuity, but nothing else. Only 22 years old and a recent industrial engineer graduate of the University of Texas, Louis II was poised to grow and modernize his father's business. However, there were massive debts and lawsuits that strangled all the oxygen out of Louis II's dreams. Within six months, everything crashed and Louis II ended up worse financially than his siblings…with nothing… or that's what he thought at first.

Louis Matthews II witnessed his father's business evaporate in liquidation. However, as the days went by, he realized that the knowledge and experience he had acquired working close to his father was as valuable as the business itself. And, sure enough, it happened.

A headline and accompanying story in the 'Dallas Morning News' was shocking with regard to the world oil market and supply. The story read: "Venezuela's major oil company goes on strike. The majority of PDVSA's workers, executives, contractors and freelancers walked off the job today, paralyzing the company's operations in protest against the government of Hugo Chavez. This country with the world's largest oil reserves is now paralyzed, as its main source of income has simply stopped."

Louis Matthews II remembered that his father always said the biggest opportunities in business are lying in wait when everyone is running scared. Louis II had a great advantage in Venezuelan matters since he spoke fluent Spanish, having been raised at home by a Mexican nanny until he was a teenager. The next day after the Venezuelan oil news, he was on a plane to Caracas via Miami. He flew into town with no idea about what he was going to do. He was just following his gut instincts. Once in town, he found out that the President had threatened to fire all striking employees. Louis II followed his gut instinct by visiting the main office of PDVSA every day. He first offered his services to supply anything that would be needed in the crisis. The Venezuelan authorities met with him multiple times, but that got him nowhere. However, he did learn what the major problem was, that is, how to keep production running and how to deliver and transport the product. So, he opted to apply for a job as a means to get inside the beast. He was finally hired and dispatched to the northwest main refinery, where he found total chaos. The striking workers had even disabled the IT systems and software that ran the company.

He earned a great deal of respect in the following weeks, as he became a key troubleshooter. His efforts helped PDVSA to partially resume operations. Nevertheless, it became obvious to all that although there was production of oil, there were no oil cargo vessels available to transport the oil to the world markets. It appeared to Louis II that they were rapidly heading to a devastating bottleneck. It was at that moment that Louis II's real inheritance came to him in spades. Thinking ahead, Louis II called his dad's closest friends and talked them into sending two massive oil tankers to Venezuela. In that there were no transportation jobs booked in advance, something never done in the industry; Louis II had to have perfect timing. He was dealing with Chavez's new, inexperienced and indecisive management. These political hacks did not have the requisite knowledge of PDVSA's entire supply chain. As Louis' two oil tankers arrived, they were immediately booked and with the authorization of Chavez himself, Louis II became the virtual monopolist of Venezuelan oil transportation. In a few years, he earned over $100 million.

The massive scandal is quickly approaching the life of Island resident, lobbyist Bart Holstein, he just doesn't know it yet.

CHAPTER 13
THE HOLSTEINS

He is the ultimate enabler. He is the discreet and loyal facilitator. The poker game had run late into the wee hours of the morning. Then, the usual routine had followed wherein his close friend, the former President, had morphed into – as he always did – a sexual acrobat. The previous night, Bart Holstein had entertained his powerful friend and himself with four ladies. But, this time had been different and riskier. Group sex was a reckless act. What good had it done to strip the ladies of their phones and electronics, when now, if all hell broke loose, they could back up each other's stories? Why does he keep pushing the limits? Why does he keep cutting it closer and closer to the edge? One of these days, Bart realizes, he is not going to be able to prevent a catastrophe. His cell phone has been ringing for a while and he finally checks the caller ID on his screen. What he sees sends chills up his spine and he answers reluctantly. "Why are you calling? This is not the protocol."

There was a quick answer, "We've got a serious problem, Sir."

"What is it?"

"One of the girls is a minor."

"Come and see me now. Get off the phone!"

As he hangs up, he thinks of only one thing, damage control.

Crossing the line with a minor was a catastrophic mistake – one that could bring down a former president and his lobbyist pimp.

CLANDESTINE FBI PROBE

The rogue FBI agents are doing something illegal. They are eavesdropping without a warrant and their motives are political. They operate on the fringes of what is permissible and they do it with the tacit consent of their supervisors. Don't ask, don't tell. They are on an open-ended fishing expedition against the former President. But, in a way, he has opened the door for them, the rumors, the off-the-record testimonials. The problem, though, is that he is slick. He has learned from past mistakes. So, time goes by and zilch, nadda and yet…they don't stop, they go on chasing their prey. They know something is going on with the President and the women, they just can't prove it.

But, suddenly, at this very moment, they can't believe their ears as the perennial philanderer is served to them on a silver platter. Years of surveillance and frustration; days, weeks and months away from the family; chasing the elusive target; it has finally paid off. The team of three has heard and copied the conversation on the clone phone, as they had hacked the original days before. Bart had just broken his communication pattern by speaking about the forbidden subject over the phone. Bart was so disciplined. But, by speaking about the forbidden subject over the phone, the cover had been broken. Now the trio will go into action and track the minor by whatever means necessary. But Bart Holstein's world is about to turn upside down, faster and more serious than the fallout from his off-hour trysts. And much closer to home.

Island resident, Oleg Krull, one of the most famous criminal attorneys in the United States, has the Midas touch with an unblemished record in the courts as jurors seem to side with him on every occasion.

CHAPTER 14
THE KRULL PROPERTIES

Property, 16 Paradise Island, consists of 120K square feet of property, about three acres, owned by the Krull family. Currently, a 70K-square-foot home is under construction on the property. The home will have underground parking that surrounds an open lagoon with a waterfall, yacht dockage, a library, chef's kitchen, billiard game room, cabaña bar, wine room, gym, commercial elevator and more. The underground parking will accommodate 32 vehicles. The cost of the mansion is expected to be over $100 million, which should be no problem for Oleg Krull, the most successful criminal attorney in the southeast United States.

Property, 15 Paradise Island, is a historic 1931 mansion designed by the renowned architectural firm of Kiehnel & Elliott. Oleg Krull, having a Bachelor of Arts degree from Stanford University and a JD degree from the University of Miami, decided to move this over-2-million-pound Paradise Island mansion to the front, roadside area of the lot, where it will become an entrance building and guest house. The waterfront area of the property will be developed into a new ultra-mansion to compliment the tropical and aquatic nature of the property. Mr. Krull is developing this property as a spec property to be sold at a profit in the future.

Oleg Krull is the epitome of an American success story – self-made and wealthy beyond imagination. However, his secret source of strength and self-confidence is his wife.

The Krull Family History

For almost two years he had been going through the motions, doing what he was supposed to do and what was expected of him. Neither of his parents had finished college and he couldn't find any ancestors that had attended college either, that is why his scholarship to Stanford had been treated by his family as a defining moment. The festivities surrounding his Stanford scholarship, at least that is how Oleg felt about the meaningless, endless celebrations and congratulatory gestures that had lasted for days, had become a surreal ritual. He felt they were inappropriate because he was at the beginning of a journey and not at the end. The end would be graduation with honors. This was an underserved reward before the effort and the journey, and this double-edged sword created tremendous pressure on him to succeed.

He had left home rebelling at all the expectations placed on him and upon his arrival at Stanford, he fell into a mood of apathy and social isolation. He knew he had a duty and an obligation to perform, but he lacked the passion or enthusiasm he had in high school. Each and every night he went to bed without a clear recollection of what happened throughout the day. He was on time for every class and completed all his assignments. He scored in the top 10 percent in all of his courses. His only extra-curricular activity was playing on the Stanford volleyball team as a setter. On the weekends, he would get stoned. He maintained little or no contact at all with his family back home, except sending them his end of semester academic record. He had become a hermit.

Oleg's lifestyle suddenly changed the first time he saw her. He would never regret having made the decision to go hiking the San Juan Mountains. He was hiking steep terrain at Telluride when the path he was on cleared the tree line and a valley opened up. He was at 10,500 feet, now surrounded by huge mountains and a valley of a sea of flowers opened up ahead of him. As he proceeded along the path, a small waterfall appeared on the right, and there she was all by herself, sitting in yoga position, munching a sandwich. She was muscular, athletic, stunning and Japanese! She was from Nagoya, studying in California and they became inseparable ever since the fortunate encounter. Also, Mrs. Sakito Krull was totally responsible for making Oleg Krull the most successful criminal attorney in the southeastern United States.

Contrary to most women living on Paradise Island, Sakito Krull is a well-grounded and independent woman and responsible for keeping order in her husband's world.

The Courtship Of Sakito And Oleg Krull

The bullet train speeds across the landscape. Mt. Fuji was left behind 30 minutes ago. Oleg Krull and Sakito had hiked it the previous weekend. But, today it has been only a post card image to a panoramic view from the speeding train. He has noticed though, that from a distance, the snowcapped mountain shaped like a narrow volcano seemed to have a lot less snow than when he hiked up its trails. First class on a Japanese train is quiet and peaceful. Japanese riders, whether on a plane, subway, bus or as here, on a bullet train, keep mostly to themselves, reading, sleeping and seemingly meditating. Many, if not most of them, keep their heads down and their attention is totally absorbed by their electronic gadgets. Sakito is totally exhausted and deep in sleep with her head resting on Oleg's shoulder. Her face exudes peace, contentment and beauty. Their last two weeks together have been a whirlwind outdoor adventure combined with a crash course in Japanese culture, tradition and religion, sprinkled with a bit of history and geography. They had snorkeled in Okinawa, skied near Sapporo, prayed and meditated in Kyoto, bargained in Ginza, and contemplated in awe the faith and fervor of worshippers at the Shinto Shrine. Of course, they ate and ate seafood, cooked or raw, in 2,000 different ways, with lots and lots of rice wine sake. Her parents had been warm and open and, thanks to them, all of Nagoya had welcomed him. And their music followed them everywhere. They had travelled with a Sony Walkman and 100 or so cassettes that they listened to non-stop, 24 hours a day.

But it was the conversation with her uncle Akiro that impacted him the most. He was a child survivor of the first atomic bomb blast in Hiroshima. His recollection of the event and his subsequent life as a Japanese immigrant in America, post-World War II, his marriage into a Japanese-American family and his subsequent return to Japan caught Oleg's full attention. It was his story about the atomic bomb that had prompted Oleg to book a ticket to visit Hiroshima and its Peace Memorial.

Her uncle Akiro had said, "I am a Hibakusha (Hiroshima survivor). I was three years old when the bomb fell and I wandered the streets of the outskirts of the city for hours before I was rescued. My parents and siblings all died that day. But, after many, many years, it was in Hiroshima where I reached atonement and found the answer to fundamental and existential questions like: Can a country as a whole really apologize? Can the collective consciousness of a nation express remorse? Can the people of an entire society state unequivocally, we are truly, truly sorry? And if so, can the living soul of such a nation reach atonement in this way, then, begin to heal, make amends and receive forgiveness? The answers came to me through an iconic old war picture, one that I would come across several times throughout my life. I was a young teenager in 1960 when, as I was reading about Hiroshima, I noticed a black-and-white photograph taken a few days after the nuclear attack. The image, taken by an American photographer, showed total desolation and devastation. The city had literally been leveled. Nothing was standing, except a few power lines, a handful of trees and the city's municipal building, which had been close to the bomb's explosion that took place a few hundred feet above ground. Several decades later in 1980, as my family and I were visiting the Hiroshima Peace Memorial and walking through the park, we saw a gigantic watch lying flat on the ground. It showed forever the time of the explosion. There was a walking path that circled the watch. As we walked, we descended underground and entered a room beneath the watch's sphere. The room was totally dark, except for a thick cylindrical ray of light that came down from the sphere's center hole. Slowly, my eyes adjusted to the circular room, which was the exact same size as the watch. Then, my eyes grew larger as they adjusted to the lack of light. There it was, the same photograph! But this time, it was huge and in a 360-degree view. The image was plastered all around the circular wall. Now I could see every critical point in the city. Again, there was nothing standing. Everything had been obliterated. That moment, in front of an image of total destruction, I thought about the hundreds of thousands of people that, within days, died in Hiroshima and Nagasaki and asked myself, over and over again: 'Why don't the Japanese hate and despise Americans? How is it that we are not their enemies forever?' That day, as we spent 12 hours visiting the entire Memorial Park grounds and exhibits, the thought never left me. Then it happened, as we were approaching the exit and walking past the municipal building that had withstood the blast, there was a plaque. I froze. The inscription on the plaque was written by the fallen Emperor, to his people, right after the bomb fell. It reads something like this: "Let's ensure that never again because of our own actions, we bring upon our Nation this type of retaliation. Let's ensure that humanity never does this to itself again. We are responsible for our actions, we are to blame no one else." Hirohito 1945. That is why there is no hatred or resentment between Japan and America. Then, I asked myself, 'Has Germany apologized to the Jews for the Holocaust or Japan to China for Manchuria and what about America to all blacks for slavery?' The answer is NO in each case, just to name a few. Not because it is not possible, but because the collective will to repent has not been there. But eventually it will be, because otherwise, deep wounds and resentment will outlast any desire or pretense that the past be forgotten or ignored. Japan has demonstrated after Hiroshima and Nagasaki that a nation and an entire society can show remorse and apologize, turning pain into strength, hatred into love and a farce into forgiveness."

But Oleg Krull's fairy tale life, as well as his extraordinary achievements mean nothing compared to the new reality he faces. His son, Thor, is about to reveal that he is no longer a man.

PRESENT DAY

As Oleg has been reflecting on this story about life and forgiveness and the impact it has on him, his world is about to be shattered and his true beliefs put to a test.

"Dad," the voice of his first born takes him out of the trance he is in. Then, he sees his son's face.

"What is it, Thor?"

Thor Krull is standing by his dad's home office door. Oleg Krull isn't in the mood to see anyone.

"What do you want Son?" he asks angrily. He hasn't looked at his son yet. Thor does not reply. Oleg quickly glances at him.

"I don't have time now, come back later."

Thor still does not move. This time Oleg stares intensely at his son and his anger evaporates. As he sees his son's face, he stands up sensing something is seriously wrong and places his hands on Thor's shoulder.

"What's wrong, son?"

Thor is crying, but still not talking.

"Has something happened to your Mom or sisters?" He frantically asks Thor as his gut sends a cold shiver through his body. He freezes in fear. Are the police at the house to arrest him for the 'sex with minors' incident? He is in a panic.

"Dad, I am no longer a man," interrupts Thor.

Right then, Oleg and Sakito's life comes crashing down in an instant.

Ten minutes later, Oleg Krull is on the phone in a frantic state with Louis Matthews II.

Maybe, just maybe, Steven Zathlyn has messed with the wrong guy. After all, he is Oleg Krull, the undisputed king of Miami's criminal justice system, with plenty of judges and prosecutors in the palm of his hand...

Revenge on Paradise Island sometimes goes both ways, and that's how wars are started by powerful resident egos clashing and burning everything around them. In this case, Steven Zathlyn vs. Oleg Krull is an ugly game of survival of the fittest.

Lynn Nichols-Restrepo's trainer Piero Tomba is about to get a taste of Colombian "jungle law."

CHAPTER 15
THE RESTREPOS

The Harley-Davidson rider fits the South Beach scene by wearing a tank top over his tan and perfect physique. Piero Tomba is in a good mood. He has just had his favorite client in every way possible. 'She is too hot to handle even for me,' he mumbles with a half-smile, 'And right under the old man's nose.' He knows full well that doing it there with the staff listening is just part of the thrill that she and he get. Banging the life out of each other is more intense when there is danger and risk involved. Sometimes, it even feels like a performance with a live audience.

He parks and dismounts the bike with the same carefree attitude. He is carrying a small bag of organic groceries as he walks into this home.

Piero Tomba lives in a three-story, 70-year old art deco, blue pastel building, three blocks from Ocean Drive in South Beach. He walks into his third-floor condo, after running up the stairs. That is the last thing he remembers. A sharp pain in his back wakes him up. He opens his eyes, but all he can see is darkness. 'It is evening already,' he thinks. He tries to stand up, but stumbles face down. His limbs are not responding. His face is now smashed and compressed against the floor carpet. He realizes that within the darkness there are no shadows or any inkling of light. Then he hears the voice from above.

"If I ever see you near my wife again, the paralysis and blindness you are now experiencing will be permanent. Next time, I will also cut your tongue out. You have 24 hours to move out of Miami Beach. The physical effects you are now experiencing will wear off in a few hours." Mario Angel Restrepo leaves quickly. He isn't quite certain how to handle his promiscuous wife, yet! However, most importantly he has underestimated the intensity of the lust between the trainer and his hot wife.

But Piero Tomba and Lynn Nichols-Restrepo did not learn their lesson...

Four Weeks Later, Orlando, Florida

Mario Angel Restrepo has been lying in wait for hours. He is reading a newspaper and sipping an authentic Cuban coffee. He has an unobstructed view of the non-descript 5-story building. His wife has been coming twice a week to a clinic on the 3rd floor. He sees her metallic light-blue Mercedes convertible at a distance. She drives into the parking lot at high speed. Seconds later she walks toward the building. Restrepo raises the newspaper and hides behind it. She seems nervous and in a hurry. She enters the building and he goes back to his paper. Three hours go by without any further sign of her. He is now enjoying a light salad for lunch while reading Chernow's Hamilton.

Then, suddenly, a petite 32-year-old blond walks out of the building. She is wearing different clothes and brandishing a broad smile. She looks very happy and the walk back to her car appears carefree. This is exactly what the private investigator has reported to him. And, that's where the mystery begins. The clinic, one of the best in the country, is legit and entirely run by women. He decides to wait. He has all day. He has developed patience, even though anger is boiling up inside him.

It is now dusk and the light is fading. He has gone through 150 pages of the 731-page book. He has matched the surveillance photos with all of the clinic's personnel and doctors that have left the premises. 'The treatments last 30-40 minutes,' he keeps reminding himself, at least a dozen or so times. There are hormone clinics in Miami, so why drive all the way to Orlando? And what's the deal with the different clothes when leaving? Restrepo is distracted and deep in thought. Then, he snaps out of it and focuses on one figure leaving the building. Long surfer shirt, baseball cap sideways, checkered Van shoes, shoulder length hair and skateboard under the right arm. But his body movements give him away. So, he was right and the PI was wrong. He sees him skateboarding away from the building. Restrepo quickly pays the check and heads for his helicopter for a 1 hour and 20-minute flight back to Miami. He now has to decide how and when, as Tomba has already erased the "if" from the equation.

Both lovers are going to pay a heavy price and will be the subject of Mario Angel-Restrepo's burning rage.

Island resident, corrupt lobbyist Bart Holstein's reckoning has begun in the form of his son Andy no longer being a man – how can this be happening to him?

CHAPTER 16
The Holsteins

The whole family rushed back from Colorado. The herd is in full crisis mode. The scene is bloody, literally bloody. Junior, as young Andy Holstein is called, is lying face down; his big frame slumped against the living room main entrance door. His face is swollen big as a volleyball and his mouth and ears are bleeding like water fountains. His pants are pulled halfway down. He is drifting in and out of consciousness with each of his father's screams, blows and kicks. Holstein Sr. is out of control. The effect of his bi-polar medicine is blown away by his rage. For trying to interfere, Arsenio, the family driver, has been floored with a full-force "knuckles backhand". His left cheek is inflated like a balloon.

Blood is boiling in Mr. Holstein's veins. His son is no longer a man! But, the worst part for him is the public shame; not being in control; and the fear that he will not be able to handle the problem as quietly as the fathers of the two other boy/girls that live on the Island. The phone keeps ringing incessantly, but Mr. Holstein does not answer it. Louis Mathews II and Oleg Krull keep on calling and he knows why.

"So, what do we do now? We start dressing you like a woman? And we find you a cute boyfriend? Or perhaps we should disown you and throw you out into the street."

"And you, yes, you, piece of useless ass. I blame you. What kind of a mother are you? You live like a queen. You produce nothing. Your only usefulness is opening your legs to me and parading your face and body around," screams Bart Holstein at the top of his lungs.

The doorbell rings, but none of the house employees dare to come out of their hole and eavesdropping station in the kitchen. Mr. Holstein reluctantly walks to the mansion door and looks through the peephole. Oleg Krull and Louis Matthews II are standing outside. "Open up."

The Baglionis' antics of apparent spousal abuse and her suicide attempt
jumping from the Island bridge are exposed and the real truth about
their behavior and motivation is revealed.

CHAPTER 17
THE BAGLIONIS

The Miami Herald headline reads:
"Paradise Island Resident Tries to Commit Suicide by
Jumping Off a Bridge:"

"Allegedly, domestic abuse caused Mrs. Ornella Baglioni to run barefoot through Paradise Island, in an act of fear and despair as she was chased by her husband, who was following her in his Bentley convertible. She jumped 20 feet into Biscayne Bay from the Paradise Island Bridge that connects the Island to the Miami Highway system. She was safely rescued with no apparent injuries by three good Samaritans, one in a passing boat, the other, the Island's security gate guard and the third, her own husband, Alessandro. Alessandro had brought attention to the incident by yelling and blowing his automobile horn. Although she refused medical assistance from the paramedics that were called to the scene, she was taken for observation purposes to Mt. Sinai Hospital, Miami Beach, Florida. The emergency room staff at the hospital initially determined that they were dealing with injuries resulting from a fall. However, further review resulted in a trauma specialist being called in. The trauma specialist determined that Mrs. Baglioni's injuries to her breasts, arms, legs and face were from lashes and burns. The Miami Beach Police were called in to review the situation. Thereupon, they arrested Mr. Baglioni who was in the Mt. Sinai Hospital waiting room. Based on the statements made by Mrs. Baglioni to one of the duty nurses, the police obtained a search warrant for the Baglioni residence."

The Miami Herald article goes on to state: "The Miami Herald has obtained a copy of the search warrant and the court documents in regard to what the search discovered. The Baglioni home at #21 Paradise Island, a Spanish-style mansion, was built in the 1930s. The house has been fully renovated using the best woods and marble. It is furnished with extraordinary masterpieces. The countless balconies, terraces and patios make the big house feel homey and inviting. However, appearances can be deceiving. About 30 minutes into the search of the home, Detective Bustamante leaned a bit too far backwards into a mirror wall in the Master bedroom and the wall gave way. There was a secret door. He opened the door, then one by one, the Detective and other police personnel went into the room. The entire search was recorded on film."

"The Miami Herald has interviewed Chief Detective Bustamante, who was an eyewitness and has reviewed all the evidence and documentation on this matter. Detective Bustamante has stated the following: "Obviously, he left in a hurry and could not clean the place up! It was a room of pain and pleasure. Every conceivable S&M device was in plain sight, either neatly organized, hanging on the walls or on display around the room. The center of the room had a table with leather leg and wrist restraints. There was a "riding crop" on top of the table along with a pair of nipple clips. There was a large butt plug on the floor. The room had a sound system. The room was filled with sounds of pain and pleasure. There were speakers all around the room and the crescendo of sexual sounds was in surround sound. Suddenly, a video screen came down from the ceiling and the image of Ornella Baglioni appeared on the screen. She was strapped to the table face down. Then, an image of her husband, Alessandro Baglioni, lashing the buttocks of his wife with the "riding crop" appeared on the screen. Mrs. Baglioni appeared to be crying and pleading for him to stop. Then suddenly, she appeared to climax and scream with pleasure. The images on the screen were a well-crafted and produced movie."

"The Miami Herald interview of Detective Bustamante concludes with the following: It is directed and ordered that Alessandro Baglioni be released from custody. The Baglionis are into S&M practices and this type of behavior does not violate any State of Florida criminal statutes."

A couple of hours later, the Baglionis sit at their dining room table having breakfast, laughing their asses off. Their unstoppable desire to be noticed has been fulfilled. They have played everyone to perfection. The couple is ecstatic as they watch the video of the Detectives' faces.

"They fell for it, look at their faces," states Alessandro.

Then Alessandro Baglioni, while looking straight into his wife's eyes, presses a key on his hand-held device. Instantly, Ornella Baglioni jerks and jumps, closes her eyes and appears to be in ecstasy. She experiences wild sensations of pleasure as the instrument inside of her starts to move sinuously while gently vibrating. Mrs. Baglioni starts to slowly open her eyes and look at her husband. He then presses a second key on the device and Mrs. Baglioni grabs the table with both hands as the elongated device starts to grow in thickness and length and undulate in a serpent like movement. Mrs. Baglioni closes her eyes again, this time quivering in absolute delight. Mr. Baglioni then pushes a third key and the device in Mrs. Baglioni starts to slowly warm up. He keeps the key pressed as he stares intently at her, raising his brows as if asking when to stop. She then closes her eyes for the third time signaling that it is hot enough. It is like molten lava from a volcano, which is what she becomes seconds later. She starts experiencing a continuous orgasm that lasts as long as he leaves the device on, which is in the end, in excess of 30 minutes. She collapses in exhaustion and plenitude.

They have both played themselves by seeking pleasure and attention through manipulation of the public opinion. But, he has played them all, including his wife, by bringing the police right to the room where he hides all his treasures. He is still reeling from it. This is a whole new world of pleasure for him. His lifetime of crime is simply not enough anymore. He has to have many others come into his S&M world. This kind of pleasure is unbearable for the psychopath. The thrill is irresistible. Alessandro Baglioni then helps his wife walk back to her room and he puts her to bed to sleep, a very deep sleep.

Johnny Baglioni is glad he has not confided in either of his parents with what has happened to Hillary Zathlyn. He is so embarrassed by the Miami Herald headline, that if he had a choice he would move out of his parents' home immediately. He loves his father, but he does not like his ways, specifically with women. His mom is broken and at his father's mercy. She has grown accustomed to the poisonous cocktail of love and pain, reward and punishment. Johnny has been in the "room" and has seen the videos. His father knows that, but has not said anything.

However, in the Baglioni family, the apple has fallen quite far from the tree. Johnny could not be more different from his father and that eventually will be a big problem for Baglioni Sr.

In typical Paradise Island fashion, one of the least deserving set of parents, the Baglionis, have a jewel of a son and they don't even know it.

Different levels of wealth exist on the Island. The Mizrahi family, owners of the largest cruise line in the world, are in the mind-blowing wealth category, meaning they are billionaires. The Greenhouses on the other hand, live on a medical doctor's income – a pretty substantial one indeed, but in the millions, meaning they belong to the common joe's millionaire's club.

CHAPTER 18
THE MIZRAHIS AND THE GREENHOUSES

For the last two weeks, Sarah Greenhouse has been helping her dad in Haiti. Just yesterday she had been in the foothills of Labadee, at an elementary and middle school built by her fiancé's family. This one is located in a remote forest on a mountainside facing the emerald green Caribbean Sea.

Sarah, about to head to Harvard, is the 'sandwich' of the three Greenhouse sisters, Megan being the youngest and Lindsey the oldest.

Her fiancé surprises her upon her return from Labadee. He is waiting for her on the Port-A-Prince airport tarmac. He has flown in unannounced from Miami on his Gulfstream G650 in order to pick her and her dad up. Then, they drop Dr. Greenhouse off in Miami and immediately fly to Nassau, Bahamas, for a well-deserved vacation.

The Mizrahi yacht is three stories high. It has a clinic and on its bottom hull an army of tender boats, jet skis, water toys and even a two-seater 'state-of-the-art' floatable wings seaplane.

The young couple is having breakfast on the upper deck surrounded by the magnificent views of Highbourne Cay. The massive boat is anchored on the northwestern tip of the Island. The half-moon bay in front of them is empty of other mega yachts. In the distance are the 5-star Bahamian hotels and on the hills surrounding the half-moon bay are Key West-style villas. The engaged couple is surrounded by a paradise of powder sand and translucent green water.

Steven Mizrahi loves diving at Highborn Cay. Today the couple will be chauffeured by the Captain of the yacht and guided around the island paradise. Another couple has joined the group. Leopoldo Arrieta is Steven's oldest friend. Leopoldo is chubby and a short 5'7". Nevertheless, if there is a book that cannot be judged by its cover, then such a book would be Leopoldo. He is one of those spear gun fishermen that can stay down without air for 3-4 minutes. He will not kill anything and he will not hunt any fish that is shorter than 5 feet and weighs less than 100 pounds. Leopoldo's date on this day is a Swedish model he met a few weeks earlier. The two friends have an agreement. This morning, they will only dive; no spear gun fishing. Today the dive is for underwater sightseeing. The two couples and the Captain will dive together.

The five of them head north on a tender. Within minutes, they reach the northern tip of the Island. They go around the tip and leave the quiet serene waters of the western side of Highbourne Cay and enter the deeper, rougher waters of the east side. Shortly thereafter, they see a diving buoy. They secure the tender to the buoy and within minutes, they are in the water and begin the descent. At 50 feet, a forest of coral is awaiting them. The colorful coral branches are up to 10 feet tall. The five divers get inside the magnificent coral garden through the corridors and alleys that circle the natural wonder. There are yellows, reds, greens and blues. They snap pictures and videos. Young Mizrahi's tranquil thoughts are interrupted by Leopoldo. He is indicating with hand gestures that his air-pressure gauge is not working and pointing up, to indicate an ascent. The rest of the group stays down. They enter into small coral gardens populated by tropical fish of all colors and sizes, stingrays and giant groupers. Cruising around above them are menacing barracuda and sharks. Morea eels are peeking out of their holes, intimidating and scary-like miniature sea monsters. The one-hour dive is over, seemingly in just a few minutes. The group of four circles back towards the buoy's anchoring point in the seabed. The tender is straight above them. The dive has been over 100 feet. They have to decompress, stopping for specific amounts of time at different depths before they can reach the surface. They use the buoy rope to guide them up and to hold on to it at the interval stops. At their 30-feet decompression stop, they hear the swoosh of a spear being fired. The waters are crystal-clear and there is endless visibility. As they turn toward the direction of the sound, they see him! At the sea bottom, at the edge of the coral jungle is Leopoldo, who is wrestling and trying to pull a spear out of a grouper. The four are startled at the struggle and their eyes seem about to pop out of their masks. Steven Mizrahi is livid. 'He cannot keep a promise. He can't control himself. We agreed no fishing while we dove.'

Leopoldo goes up to the surface in a relaxed motion. Then goes right back down after inhaling some precious air. His round figure and potbelly are moving swiftly towards his prey. After another two minutes of additional struggle, the group of four can see Leopoldo's catch. It's a grouper of easily 120 pounds and 5-feet long. Leopoldo goes up quickly this time with his prey in tow.

Steven Mizrahi looks down and sees the cloud of blood around the coral formations where Leopoldo caught the grouper.

They still need to decompress for several more minutes. The first sharks come cruising slowly toward the coral formations and the accompanying blood cloud. Then, more and more sharks arrive. Their movements become jerky and lightning fast. It is when a couple of smaller sharks, which are more immature and reckless, separate from the herd of twenty or so, that Steven Mizrahi realizes that they have to move up towards the surface although they have not decompressed. Two young sharks start circling the buoy's rope attached to the sea bottom. Steven Mizrahi orders everyone to start ascending. They reach the surface. There is panic to get into the boat. They are frantic. The two women get in first and then the Captain. Steven Mizrahi gets in last and lunges straight at Leopoldo, landing a right-hander straight into his fat gut. "Reckless imbecile! You can't help it, it's all about you, only you."

The divers head back to the yacht. Later that night, under the calming effects of the full moon, Mizrahi and Leopoldo make up.

"I've got something important to tell you. It is really serious. It happened on Paradise Island while you were in Haiti." Then Mizrahi tells his fiancé what happened to her childhood friend, Hillary Zathlyn.

For a Paradise Island resident, there is nothing worse than a situation that he has no control over. Corrupt lobbyist, Bart Holstein, has completely lost it when facing the reality of a castrated son. He is looking for a way to seek revenge on the Zathlyns.

CHAPTER 19
THE HOLSTEINS' FAMILY HOME

B art Holstein looks like he should be in a strait jacket in a sealed room in the nearest nut house. The front door of his house is slightly ajar, but his two neighbors have not been invited in yet. His eyes denote a man lost within himself. He seems defeated while standing with an open bathrobe, his hair disheveled and blood stains all over him. Krull speaks out after several minutes go by, but Bart Holstein does not seem to recognize them.

"Bart, are you going to let us in or not?"

He stares at them for a second, but does nothing. His neighbors, Oleg Krull and Louis Matthews II, decide to march in and do so by simply pushing Bart Holstein to the side. Bart offers no resistance and absentmindedly closes the door and slowly walks back into the mansion's living room. Krull and Matthews are at the bar helping themselves to a couple of drinks. The living room is a mess. Expensive items are laying on the floor. In the meantime, Arsenio, the wounded chauffeur, is gingerly walking Andy Holstein upstairs.

"Bart, come on, man, get over it!!"

Bart remains silent.

"Bart, he did the same surgery to Thor and Louis Jr.!"

Bart's head turns towards his friends, "What?"

"Yeah, that SOB has to pay."

"We came here to ask you to join us in regard to the legal proceedings to put Zathlyn in jail."

Bart moves his head sideways several times.

"Bart! Speak up! Respond!" demands Oleg Krull.

Bart's voice suddenly comes across loud and clear, "We can't just decide that you're going to prosecute one of the wealthiest, most powerful and well connected persons in this town. It will take a small army of the best attorneys money can buy to make even a small dent in Zathlyn's defense shield.

"Bart, I make my living keeping people out of jail," states Oleg Krull.

Louis Matthews II, eager to give his opinion, quickly states, "In other words, Bart, he knows how to put people in jail too."

Bart is now at least partially engaged. "Go on," he says.

"We will share the cost to engage in an expensive, but effective, investigation seeking to produce and provide evidence of wrongdoing. I know this guy, he is one of the best in the security business in the country, and his organization has the resources, know-how and connections to virtually fry anyone under our flawed American judicial system," says Krull.

"Justice of destruction for hire?" asks Bart Holstein.

"Absolutely!" replies Matthews II.

"Let me call him right away and set up a meeting."

Both Matthews and Holstein nod their heads in agreement. Krull puts the speaker phone on and dials the familiar cell phone number of the man he has worked with for years.

"Krull?" A grave voice asks through the speaker.

"Yes, sir."

Silence.

"Sir, I need to meet you about a personal matter, along with two friends of mine."

Silence on the other end.

"Are you there, sir?"

The sudden click signals that the call has been cut.

"What happened, Krull?"

"I don't know, let me dial again."

The phone rings until the voice mail kicks in and a female voice greets the caller. "You have reached the phone of retired General Robert Pinkus, please leave your name, number and the reason for your call."

"General, please call back ASAP."

"Something must have come up and he had to drop our call. I'll try him again later," states Krull.

As far as General Pinkus is concerned, the battle lines have been drawn. It was to be expected. He never liked Krull anyhow, not one bit. He decides to call Steven Zathlyn on the spot. "Steven, they are on to you, the three of them. Krull just called me, as I expected. I did not enter into any conversation with him and hung up."

"General, please don't tip our hand to them. Staying close to them plays to our advantage. For example, now, because of their approach to you, we know they want to handle this matter quietly. So, remember to keep your friends close and your enemies even closer. Call him back and find out exactly what they are up to."

"Will do." As the call ends, General Pinkus wonders how he missed the point just made by Zathlyn. But he still has time to make amends 'and keep the enemies even closer.'

"Krull?" his voice is again coming out of the speaker and the three Paradise Island neighbors are listening.

"General, thank you for calling me back. I would like to meet you ASAP about a very serious personal matter. I'll come along with two of my neighbors, Louis Matthews II and Bart Holstein."

"All right. What about tomorrow 9 a.m. at my office?"

Everyone nods, so Krull confirms it.

This is only the beginning, reasons Pinkus, the fight is yet to come.

Perhaps the parents of the castrated boys should have been more cautious in what they wished for - in this case by unknowingly jumping in bed with the enemy.

Island resident, the largest home builder in the country and the son of one of the old crows, Leon Albert, is a divorcee' that lives in a palace that is not a home but rather a largely empty and unfurnished structure. He is a workaholic and has very little time for his son – but that is about to prove costly and very dangerous.

CHAPTER 20
THE ALBERTS

E xactly as his mom had narrated to the old crows in the card room, the billionaire's home is almost empty. Twenty thousand square feet and there is no furniture, except for the bedroom. He has just snorted several lines of cocaine and the rush has made him extremely hyper. He puts on a pair of running shoes and shorts. He jogs out of Paradise Island and through the emergency lane of the beach causeway. He runs towards Miami Beach. He crosses Alton Road with the Mount Sinai Hospital on his left, then runs past Arthur Godfrey Road and reaches the boardwalk and the long hot sandy beach. He heads south down the boardwalk. The wind is still and the sea is totally calm. The boardwalk seems abandoned. He reaches the intersection where the boardwalk crosses Lincoln Road. He heads west on Lincoln Road and finally reaches his destination, the French bakery, 'Paul'. He has been running for 45 minutes and plops down at the counter to have his breakfast. He orders a croissant, flaky and crispy. The French waiter sets the item down in front of him. He opens it up and spreads it with real butter and organic strawberry marmalade. The accompanying latte's foam has a nice decorative design drawn in it. He stirs a couple of spoonfuls of brown sugar into it. The extra-large orange juice, on ice, has a bright and inviting yellow color. This is his routine when he has breakfast at 'Paul's', though some days he substitutes the flaky croissant with several slices of a warm French baguette spread with honey that he dips in his latte.

"Good morning, Dad," states his oldest child, as he arrives a bit late.

"Hi, son," replies Leon Alberts, flashing a big smile while hugging him.

At 26 years old, Eleazar (Eli) Alberts is sort of a late bloomer. Today is the day Eli has been hoping and waiting for, for so long. Eli has been raised by his mom, so he has not gotten to see much of his dad. The last time he saw him was almost 12 months ago on New Year's Eve. And he has almost never gotten to see his dad in a one-on-one situation. But, in the next 5 minutes, Leon Alberts is in for the shock of his life

"Dad, I've got something to tell you. I've been sneaking into your house for months," mumbles Eli as he bites his croissant. Leon Alberts erupts inside, but refrains from expressing it in the spirit of rebuilding a new relationship with his son.

"Son, you don't need to and you should not break into my house incognito," states Leon in a controlled voice dominated by stern eyes. "Besides, why would you do that in an empty house..." He stops and subconsciously raises his hand to his mouth. "Did you go into the panic room?"

"Yes. Dad, I have known from the beginning that the room was more than that..."

"How? I've always been so discreet about it."

"With your family, yes, but not with the guests you bring there. For example, my girlfriend's mom was there and you showed it to her."

"What's her name?"

"Eleanor Golohing." Leon Albert remembered her vividly. Father and son sit in silence for what appears to be an eternity. The secret room is located in his bedroom, behind a mirrored wall. It contains a large collection of sex toys and porno materials. Also, he almost always has a stash of drugs on hand. However, what makes it one of a kind is that about 80% of the space is covered by his gun collection that is displayed wall to wall. And now his son has seen it all. He remains silent but with an accusatory look.

"That's not all, Dad!" Now alarm bells are going off.

"OK, Eli, spell it out."

"I took some of the guns and all of the cocaine."

"What? They are chained to the racks."

"I picked the locks."

"Where are the guns? Have you returned them?"

"All but one, an AK-47."

"Where is it?"

"I sold it, Dad, and now it is part of a murder investigation."

"Holy shit, are you crazy or what?"

The three Island neighbors, parents of the castrated teenagers, are about to fall under the spell of Dr. Zathlyn and General Pinkus.

CHAPTER 21
THE KRULLS,
THE HOLSTEINS & THE MATTHEWS

Oleg Krull, Bart Holstein and Louis Matthews II sit uneasy in the lobby of Zapco International. None of them is accustomed to waiting. Instead of walking right through security, they have been asked to wait in the lobby. The elevator's electronic ring announces its arrival to the lobby floor. As the doors open, a mountain of a man steps out. Retired General Robert Pinkus comes forward and heads straight towards them. He glances at them without flinching. There is no movement in his face; if anything, his rictus is sober, straight out serious, dead serious.

"That's the way he is guys, still behaves as a General," states Krull, as they all size up the big man walking in.

"My apologies, gentlemen, I got stuck in traffic. Oleg, how are you?"

"Fine, General, let me introduce Bart Holstein and Louis Matthews II." They all shake hands.

"Follow me please." He leads them into a soundproof conference room with a large 20-chair board meeting table. The three agitated parents all sit together facing the General, who is at the head of the table. General Pinkus is staring at each of them, intently sizing them up.

"Oleg, how can I help Mr. Matthews, Mr. Holstein and you?"

"What do you have on Steven Zathlyn?"

"The surgeon?" asks Pinkus, while internally amusing himself.

"Yeah!" eagerly answers Krull.

"Isn't he y'all's neighbor?" Pinkus questions with a puzzled face while enjoying their jerky body language.

"Yes, he is," replies Krull with a stern face. "We want you to dig up all the dirt you can about him."

"Why don't you gentlemen explain to me what's going on. What is the beef?"

The three amigos sit in silence staring back at him. They certainly have not anticipated the obvious, that investigator Pinkus was going to ask – the why question!

"That's none of your concern, General. We just want you to dig, whatever it takes, whatever it costs."

The General abruptly stands up without a word, starts to walk out, and then at the door, he turns his head back and states, "Gentlemen, I'll let you know if I'm interested in the job under the conditions you have outlined." He leaves the door open and poof... is gone.

"What was that all about?" asked Matthews II.

"An arrogant prick, so full of shit, so full of himself," states Holstein.

"Guys, he is the best there is. He is also one of the best connected in town. When you unleash Pinkus' dogs on someone, you can start counting how much time they have left in the free world."

As they drive back to Paradise Island, Krull's phone rings.

"$100K retainer…, are we all on board, Krull?"

"Of course, General, we are. I will send you a check today."

Pinkus had already called Zathlyn. 'Keep your friends close and your enemies even closer.'

The afflicted parents of the "clipped" boys think they have a reason to be hopeful, but in reality, they are locked onto a road to nowhere.

World famous architect and Island resident, Lars Johannsen's son, Jasper's hacking activities have yielded a bounty of cryptocurrencies – along with a boatload of looming troubles.

CHAPTER 22
THE JOHANNSENS

J asper Johannsen's heart is beating as if it wants to jump out of his chest. He canvasses the information he has stolen from the laptop while he replays the video recording of the wounded woman. The driver's license file, once open, stares at him. The same woman he saw in the room, Regina Schlusche. Then he stumbles onto gold, passkeys for a bitcoin digital and an Ethereum wallet! He runs across the room and logs into the internet using an encrypted laptop. He quickly transcribes the numbers and turns off his tablet. He checks the balance and the Ethereum cryptocurrency...$1.7 million. He breathes deeply in awe. He then checks the bitcoin digital wallet balance...$12.3 million. He quickly uploads both account balances into new passkeys. He has just stolen $14 million! But, what about her, the victim? Who is she? What does she do? What is her trade? How did she get all that money? What happened to her? Was she kidnapped or killed?

He turns his tablet back on and quickly finishes canvassing the stolen ID files and erases them. He then logs back into the victim's computer and not only erases all of the contents, but also, places a virus that will render it totally useless. He wipes all of the tablet information out, but not before copying the residential and work addresses of the assaulted woman. He then turns off his tablet for good, before smashing it to smithereens. Within half an hour, Jasper is in South Beach, walking down Alton Road until he runs into the pedestrian-only boulevard of Lincoln Road. He stops in front of a 5-story building. It does not have any active businesses on its ground floor. The directory, however, shows the names of companies on the upper floors. Why does he want to get in trouble? Curiosity perhaps. The Google office where she works is on the 3rd floor. He waits until a couple of people are about to exit. He holds the door for them. He is now in the building. He has bypassed security. The elevator door opens, he gets out and bumps into a woman. She trips and falls. She is down at his feet. As the elevator leaves, she raises her head towards him. His eyes pop out of their sockets. She is the woman in the video! She is alive and healthy. She does not look hurt, but only frustrated by stumbling right in front of her office. He extends his hand and helps her stand up. She thanks him and disappears on the next down elevator.

Young Jasper willingly drops further into a perilous "real life" labyrinth.

Island resident and Colombian oil tycoon Mario Angel Restrepos' wife's trainer, Piero Tomba, is doomed, he just doesn't know it yet. It happened the moment he crossed Restrepo for the second time – now there is no going back.

CHAPTER 23
THE RESTREPOS
(Orlando, a couple of weeks later)

Tomba heads for the beach. Mrs. Restrepo is driving him crazy, sexually speaking. She is insatiable. Each time they meet, it is a marathon that leaves him exhausted. She is a perfect match for him if she would just shut up. What was funny and kinky in the beginning has slowly begun to irk him, and now flat out irritates him. And she won't stop belittling her husband. She ridicules almost every aspect of Mr. Restrepo's character and manhood. Tomba has tried to sway her away from the repetitive conversations, to no avail.

But it is time for another kind of pleasure. He pulls the strings ever so slightly and the kite's sail inflates. He then runs through the sand towards the edge of the water. He hops on his small board with his feet firmly locked on it as he zooms into the water. The harness takes on all the wind pressure. His arms only steer the sail. He brushes up against the water with his left side, then with his right side while leaning into it at impossible angles. He tacks against the wind at considerable speed.

'I wonder whether I should be wearing a helmet and a life vest while doing this.' Finally, the exertion and pleasure of kite surfing starts to make the latest sexual marathon with Mrs. Restrepo fade away. Suddenly, he hits a small wave head on and the bump propels him twenty feet into the air. He gets an intense rush. That seems to be the story of his life, one intense rush after another, until now...

Later in the afternoon, Tomba walks back to his new hide-away. He has an early dinner at a "trattoria" run by a distant cousin. He gets half-drunk and bloated with Italian pasta, cheese, bread, you name it. Except for the stupid disguise he is wearing, he feels relaxed and happy. It has been weeks now since the encounter with Mr. Restrepo, and the fear, which was actually sheer terror, has begun to fade away. There have been no repercussions concerning this matter that Mrs. Restrepo has told him about. If there would have been at least some type of interaction between the Restrepos, he would feel safe. Something is not right, he keeps repeating that to himself. However, as the weeks have gone by, bit by bit, he has let his guard down. He lives hours away from Miami, in the same building where Mrs. Restrepo goes for her treatments. 'Clever and safe,' he repeats to himself one more time. Whistling, he lets himself into his love pad, and for the second and last time in his life, that is the last thing he will remember.

"Jungle law" has been applied by Mario Angel Restrepo. But the deed is not complete unless he sees with his own eyes his young wife's reaction to what he did.

Two Days Later

Mr. Restrepo is again sipping a large macchiato while reading the Wall Street Journal. He has been there for quite a while and has already read through the New York Times and the Washington Post. Then, 'there she is in a hurry, as usual.'

She parks and walks down the street at a brisk pace. 'I got to find a faster way to get here, this drive is way too long,' reflects Mrs. Restrepo. She goes through the motions at the clinic, then runs up two flights of stairs. She is aching to be taken, to be totally possessed by her lover. She fumbles the keys twice. She finally lets herself in. She loves to wake him up and jump all over him. She takes her blouse and skirt off as she walks through the apartment. As she steps into the bedroom, she rips her lingerie off and sits on top of his limp body. She starts to caress him, then slightly ride him with her legs. He is covered with a blanket and he slowly starts to move.

"Wake up soldier, your commanding officer is here," she says in a whisper. She then gets up and turns her back to him. That's her signal she wants to be taken from the rear. His hand starts to caress her and slowly finds its way down. Something does not feel right. His hand goes limp and weak, which is not part of the usual scenario. She quickly turns around and looks at his face. His eyes are swollen and puffy. He opens his mouth, but only a guttural sound comes out. She turns the bedside lamp on and sees his handsome but pale and distressed face.

"What's going on?" Don't scare me!"

Then suddenly, she sees his mouth open and he lets out a muffled scream while gasping for air.

"What have they done to you? my beautiful stallion," she cries in anger.

She feels his arousal and in a perverted way this turns her on as well. Then while on top, she penetrates herself by plummeting into him, thrusting downward with such intensity and speed that she loses complete control of herself and explodes into a continuous climax and shakes and trembles for more than three minutes. She then drops exhausted and falls into a deep sleep.

When she wakes up, the room is lit up like a Christmas tree, but Piero Tomba is nowhere to be found. She calls out his name, but doesn't get a response. She tiptoes naked around the small condo. Fear suddenly grabs her as she recalls what she had just done. 'Was it a fantasy or a dream?' She hopes that it wasn't. As she opens the bathroom door, she sees her lover's reflection in the mirror. She is frozen in horror. His arms are covered in blood, his face and eyes are lifeless.

Mr. Restrepo is finishing his meal as he sees her storming out of the building with her clothes and hair in total disarray. As she speeds away, he finally feels vindicated and with a smile on his face, he pays the bill and heads for the nearby helipad to catch a ride back home.

Behind the shiny and imposing mansions of Paradise Island, unspeakable tales of power, greed, lust and swift but discreet revenge take place – this is just one of them.

The reason why jurors listen and Oleg Krull wins at trial is simple. The Island resident and nationally recognized criminal attorney fixes them – and he has done it for years.

CHAPTER 24
THE KRULLS

A permanent resident of Saint Thomas with a second home in Miami, Emmanuel Oquendo makes a living out of locating people, gaining their trust and persuading them to do something seemingly "trivial" in exchange for a handsome reward. Every time he succeeds, he earns a substantial fee. He has been working for a Panamanian company for 15 years. The company deposits his salary punctually, on the first of every month, along with any expenses he has incurred. His bonuses are paid immediately after every success. But, those are only deposited in his Cayman Islands account. His assignment instructions are never given to him in the United States. So, he has to travel to the Caribbean, to the island of the month, and literally every month the designated Bahamian meeting place changes. Nothing about his job is in writing. There is no paper trail.

He's always known when he has a new job because the trigger for the clandestine meeting is when his monthly salary is short exactly $1.00. When he sees the shortfall this time, he knows that he must immediately fly to Antiqua, the island of the month, to get his instructions that are always couriered to him and picked up in the front lobby of the Ritz Carlton Antigua before check in.

The instructions are always the same, a picture and a name. In Antigua, the payoff spot would be Banco Popular. He would appear there with his passport and inquire about a wire transfer. A bank officer would escort him to a private room and hand him cash sufficient to fulfill the mission. He never returns to the United States on a scheduled airline flight. For the last 15 years he has worked for them, there is always a private boat available to take him from the designated island to the South Florida coast. Under cover of darkness, he easily enters the United States without having to go through Customs or Immigration control. That is the mechanical part. It is well oiled and he has executed it countless times over the years. The difficult part is to gain the trust of the targeted person.

For the last six months, he had been idle. So, he has had time to occupy himself with his other interest, a small Caribbean export business. Over the years, he has developed a solid costumer network of small local businessmen on the same islands that he visits to pick up his orders. His service is to locate and deliver any product, part or service they may need. It is an opportunistic business that is always in emergency mode and always last minute. The key to his success is to deliver fast and collect promptly. It is a close-knit operation of 12 workers. It requires substantial effort, but produces a strong profit. However, the monetary reward of his sideline business is only a fraction of the money that he makes from his other clandestine activity. He also has substantial investments in real estate and he isn't getting any younger. But, greed always makes him postpone and postpone again any plans for retirement. His greed also drowns his voice of conscience, along with any innate prudence or good judgment.

Emmanuel figured out years ago, through press and television accounts, precisely what he does for his employer. At first, he tried to convince himself that the catastrophe shown on television was just a coincidence. But, the third case in a row where he recognized the confirmation he dreaded, sent cold shivers through his core. He has over time learned to cope.

He is browsing the internet and checks his payroll deposit made that day. There it is. $1.00 is missing. He realizes it is 4:00 p.m. Damn it, he forgot to check earlier. He is mad as hell. 'I guess I have become complacent,' he thinks. He rushes to pack, grabs his passport and heads for the airport. He is able to book and hop on board a plane bound for San Juan, Puerto Rico. In Puerto Rico, he rents a private plane, takes off and at approximately 10:00 p.m. lands in Antigua.

This is a change in routine. He is flying by private plane out of Puerto Rico, which is a United States free associated state. This trips alarms in several U.S. government agencies as the DEA and Homeland Security routinely monitor private flights in and around Puerto Rico. The DEA and Homeland Security, in turn, notify the FBI and the Treasury Department. The ID that Emmanuel uses to rent the plane is run through the system and he is put on a "watch" list. Emmanuel Oquendo has awakened the giant and hereafter is going to be a targeted man.

Emmanuel Oquendo, a jury fixer for Oleg Krull has operated flawlessly for years. He does not know who he works for, but greed is going to get him to break protocol and with it, threaten the entire operation.

Next Morning

He has been staring at the picture for a long time. When he goes to the bank and asks for the wire transfer, he is shocked when he opens the package to find $5 million in cash. This is ten times more cash than he has ever previously received. He goes back to his hotel. He is concerned. He keeps staring at the picture and staring at the $5 million in cash. The cash is nice, the main problem is the picture of the target. He knows the target. He knows him up and close, he is already like family to him. His name is Albert Harrington, his sister's fiancé. Alarm bells are ringing; 'don't do it, can't do it, not to my sister, not to my future brother-in-law. Not worth it, time to call it quits, this is what you should have done a long time ago!'

At noon the next day, Emmanuel flies out of the island and later that day flies into Bimini, Bahamas. Then, under the cover of darkness, he travels by speedboat from Bimini to Miami and that evening disembarks at his home on Biscayne Bay. He has not officially entered the United States.

Days later, DEA agents verify his address, and find out he is in the United States. Homeland Security cannot verify his entry into the country, so an investigation is launched concerning him and his activities. It is assumed by the government agencies that Emmanuel Oquendo is either likely involved in drug smuggling or that he may have ties to radical groups and may be linked to terrorist activities.

Emmanuel's greedy nature gets the best of him again. Instead of resigning and quitting, he is in the United States with the $5 million in cash that is now stashed in his home's basement. The instructions are clear. Two days after the pickup, he is to locate and approach the subject. His two days are almost up. He has to approach the subject that evening. When he leaves his home, FBI agents take pictures and note his departure, but do not follow him.

At this stage of the investigation, FBI protocol is to investigate, but not follow the subject. Emmanuel sets up a meeting with Harrington to have a drink and talk about the wedding. Emmanuel could not be happier with his sister's choice. As they sit sipping Blue Moons with a splash of orange juice, Emmanuel states bluntly, "Albert, I have a proposition for you."

Harrington tilts his head slightly and stares back with an intrigued expression without uttering a single word. An uneasy silence follows.

"You can simply say no, keep this conversation confidential, and then nothing happens."

Harrington is now even more puzzled, but says nothing.

"Within the next few days' time you will meet a man wearing a suit with a red tie and red handkerchief. This person will also be wearing alternately a blue or a brown double-breasted suit, but always with the same red tie and red handkerchief."

"You now have totally lost me. Who is this guy?"

"I don't know him. We have never met."

"What is this all about?"

Emmanuel interrupts him, "let me finish."

"All right."

"When I say meet, it does not mean you will shake hands or even talk to each other, but you will be together at a location."

"Where?"

"I don't know, I'm not privy to that."

"Are you pulling my leg or are you serious?"

"Absolutely serious!"

"Okay, go on, what do you mean by all of this," says a visibly shaken and irritated Albert Harrington. "If you do what he wants, you will be handsomely rewarded."

"Are you proposing for me to do something illegal, Emmanuel?"

"I don't know."

"How can't you know?"

"Because I don't know who, where or what. All I know is what I just told you."

Albert Harrington stands up and starts to walk out. Emmanuel raises his voice slightly and states, "they will pay you $5 million in cash. I have the money in hand at my house."

Harrington stops abruptly and turns back towards his future brother-in-law. He looks at him straight in the eye and says, "tell me you are fooling around with me please!"

"No."

"Emmanuel, are you trying to bribe me?"

"No, I am not."

"Do you want me to believe that you don't know what you are doing or talking about?"

"Yes, I don't know."

"Even if you don't know, which I don't believe for a second as you must have some inkling about it, are you really ready to do something illegal and possibly jeopardize your sister and my future together?"

Emmanuel Oquendo feels like a jerk and the scum of the earth. "Of course not, Albert, of course not. Let's just forget about it okay?"

"Tell you what, Emmanuel, I'm not stupid and do understand that this could set your sister and me up for life and I presume you'll benefit as well. I cannot promise that I will follow through completely, but I will go with an open mind and if I am persuaded morally so I will go along and accept your offer. Otherwise, you can simply return the money. What do you think?"

"Excellent, Albert, it's a deal."

"Let's go, show me the money!!!"

Emmanuel Oquendo hesitates, he's never shown the payout to anyone, but he is soon to be family, after all. "All right, I'll take you there."

These are unchartered waters for him as unknowingly his employer chose his brother-in-law. They have no way of knowing the link between Albert and him. That night shortly after midnight, he emails the agreed signal that the target accepted. His email reads, "Gentlemen, I've noticed that my payroll is short, please correct the mistake." The next morning, he receives a reply, which means that his message has been received and accepted. The reply reads, "You are right, we will correct the mistake."

The wheels are now in motion and Emmanuel has to wait in Miami and see whether he is going to be paid for this assignment and whether his brother-in-law and sister will quickly become rich. Otherwise, he will have to unwind the transaction and return the money.

Jasper Johannsen is quickly realizing that real life and the world of adults is far different than the dark cyber world fantasy he inhabits like a hermit.

CHAPTER 25
THE JOHANNSENS

Young Johannsen is freaked out. The woman he has stolen the bitcoins from, is not only not dead, but has just walked right by him. And she looks like nothing has happened to her. 'What the heck is going on? Has she found out about the missing money? She probably hasn't found out yet. If she had, she wouldn't look so good,' he thinks to himself.

'So, what are you a web hacker and a thief pretending to be a gentleman with the ladies? Hot, that's how she looks, hot! You moron. You like her and you steal from her. You are a creep!' he muses to himself.

After the initial shock of seeing her, his algorithmic mind kicks in. He opens his smart phone and accesses his encrypted file cabinet. He has erased all of the personal data he has stolen from her, except her web passwords and account's user names. It is reckless and risky and he knows it, but his compulsive urge to invade her is strong. It is all about control. Already at his young age, in his seriously twisted mind he has an uncontrollable need to be in charge. There it is, her phone user ID and password. Then, in just a few seconds, through a "dark web" app, he connects his phone to hers, opens it up and clones it. He is so obsessed and engaged, that he stumbles as he approaches the end of the walkway. He fights to obtain his equilibrium, but out of balance, momentum takes over and he falls and lands hard in the street. A taxi driver screams at him as he dodges him and zooms by. Then, he hears the brakes screech and watches in horror from ground level as a car approaches him at lightning speed. Fortunately for him, the car stops inches short of a direct impact. Then he hears a voice.

"Are you all right?"

He looks up in total surprise.

"Are you all right?" she repeats, "You want me to call 911?"

'It's her, it's her!' His street shock breaks into panic. "I am fine, thank you."

She helps him stand up and smiles. "Second time we stumble into each other today." He ignores her pleasantry.

'Where is my phone?' He is frantic. He scans the ground.

"Here you go. This must be your phone, right?"

Again, she brings him back to reality. He sees his phone and forcefully grabs it from her hand.

"Hey, mister, careful, I am just trying to help you."

He quickly turns his phone off and by doing so her phone home screen page also disappears. He then turns around and smiles at her in a disarming way, with fake external appreciation and real internal relief.

"Thank you so much. I thought I'd lost it. My phone is every-thing to me."

But, that last part of his sentence falls on empty ears as she has abruptly left the scene, 'what a jerk' she mumbles as she speeds away.

Jasper's life is about to get ugly – he has ignored all of the warning signs he has received.

CHAPTER 26
THE HOLSTEIN,
MATTHEWS & KRULL FAMILIES

A t least, through the intended plan they will keep them together. But there is no joy in that decision. Their families
simply did not know what else to do, except send them
away as far as possible. Hopefully, the final decision is to be made
at the Mayo Clinic. Today, the three boys' family members have had
a hush-hush appointment there, and by noon, the three boys have
been medically evaluated.

The Holsteins, Matthews and Krulls sit motionless staring at
the eminent Dr. Venkataram. They have all flown in together earlier in the morning on the Krull's new G-650. The three couples have
something in common, they are all a little loaded as they drank
their way through the flight. But, this moment is sobering and
adrenaline takes over as their escape from reality through liquor is
about to end.

"The surgery is irreversible. It was a masterful job done by an
outstanding surgeon. Your sons, and pardon the bluntness, have
been thoroughly castrated and almost perfect vaginas have been
created in replacement. The blood vessels and nerves and urinary

tracts are all perfectly reattached and are functioning as if they were part of a female body."

Dr. Venkataram is at a loss about the circumstances surrounding the three kids. He doesn't know if they are transgender and changed their minds after surgery. This seems, at first glance, to be the only explanation. But, he reminds himself that it is not his job to get into the minds and the feelings of his patients. His thoughts are interrupted.

"Doctor, so what are they supposed to do with their lives?" questions Sakito Krull.

"That, Mrs. Krull, is for a therapist to counsel you on and render a professional opinion about it."

On the flight back, the couples hardly speak to one another. As the finality of the tragedy sinks in, they find themselves wishing to be alone and are uncomfortable with each other. They know very well that they are going to be bound forever by their common shame, embarrassment and dark secret.

Berkeley, California, is where the three boys land. A new college, a new life and each of them in therapy. Their biggest problem quickly becomes denial. They engage in furious daily routines of weight lifting and at night continue dating the most gorgeous girls they can find. But, as reality sets in, Louis Matthews III starts to drink heavily and gets hooked on hard drugs. Young Holstein completely loses it and experiments with men, only to learn that he only likes girls. He and young Krull make a serious effort to find a new identity through therapy. Then, through it, a whole new world opens up to them.

CHAPTER 27
THE ISLAND'S SOCIAL CLUB
THE FOUR OLD CROWS

The four old crows have been staring at each other for a long time. Each of them is waiting for the others to talk. They have all been waiting for this day and are dying to spill their guts. They want to know what the others know. The bottom line is that today is a contest about who knows more, who has the scoop and who doesn't. Today, there's not even a card game going on. The tension is palatable, there is incessant tapping of the ladies' fingers and legs, as well as chain smoking and yes, lots of drinking. Then, 74-year-old Nicole Albert loudly clears her throat.

"OK, ladies, who is first?"

No replies. She decides to go ahead, even though she knows she is not addressing   the biggest and juiciest story.

"So, finally Ornella and Alessandro made it to the front pages of the Miami Herald."

Still no takers, just smirks and twisted mouths. Nevertheless, she still pushes forward.

"A 15-feet jump into the Bay off the Island by a former competitive swimmer does not look like a real suicide attempt to me."

More silence.

"C'mon, ladies!" snaps Nicole Albert, and this seems to do the trick.

"Definitely not, but more like an attention-seeking, headline-grabbing deliberate act," states 65-year-old Sarah Pesin.

"I have always seen her as a victim, but now I am not sure anymore," jumps in 69-year- old Elizabeth Bell.

"Why so?" asks Nicole Albert, thinking that there is more to the rhetorical question.

"A couple of the inside sources on the spousal abuse and suicide attempt investigation have told me that an S&M room was found at the house, and as a result, the investigation has been suspended," busts out Elizabeth Bell.

"Then, it isn't abuse, but pleasure?" questions the malicious 64-year-old Margarita Lujan-Restrepo.

"Whatever it is, this was their last hurrah in the public eye," states Sarah Pesin.

"I heard that the Zathlyn's was not a robbery," states Margarita Lujan-Restrepo.

Sarah Pesin cannot control herself, and jumps in and almost cuts Margarita off, "What I heard was that it was a rape."

"By three boys from the Island," matter-of-factly states Nicole.

"And the matter has been taken care of privately by Dr. Zathlyn," adds Sarah.

Elizabeth sits wide-eyed with one hand on her mouth.

"That's why you are out of the loop, Elizabeth, because all of your contacts are from the law enforcement agencies, so you know as much as they do, which is zero, zilch, nothing!" states Nicole, exercising revenge on the usually informed Elizabeth.

"But, what does it mean 'taken care of by Dr. Zathlyn'? Did the parents of the three kids pay off the good old Doctor?" asks Elizabeth.

"No, I hear he took care of the boys himself," states Margarita.

"But how?" asked Elizabeth.

"Something must have happened, but the fact of the matter is the Holstein, Matthew and Krull boys are in hiding and nobody has seen them for several days," states Nicole.

"They can't be hurt or they would be at a hospital," states Elizabeth.

"So, what did Dr. Zathlyn take care of with the boys?" asks an incredulous Elizabeth Bell.

The other three ladies look at each other in complicity, but the grand old dame, Elizabeth Bell misses it.

"Embarrassed, that's what the three families seem to me," states Elizabeth.

Then, suddenly Elizabeth Bell understands the stares of the other three. She blurts out, "nooo, tell me it's not true!"

"Yes, it is, they have gotten what they deserve. It was a long time coming," state the other three in a chorus.

The four old crows are both judge and jury, without the prosecutor or the defense allowed to speak – that's how they operate.

Island resident and world famous architect Lars Johannsen's old philandering ways are about to come to an end - he is about to fall for someone completely foreign to his comfort zone.

CHAPTER 28
MR. JOHANNSEN – OSLO, NORWAY

As his son is getting tangled in his own web in Miami, Johannsen Sr. has arrived in Oslo. He does not need to, but he has booked himself into a 3-star hotel and the only belongings he is carrying with him are two backpacks stuffed with shirts, jeans, running and hiking shorts and shoes, as well as a Spanish lesson curriculum. His only indulgence are two pairs of Sam Hubbard dress shoes with rubber soles. He simply hates leather-soled shoes. He wears his trusted stainless steel and gold Rolex watch with a lapis lazuli blue sphere dial and golden Roman numerals. He bought it 40 years earlier when he was 18-years old. The bedside clock is blinking silently. It is 5:30 a.m., time to go for a run. He steps onto the cobblestone street. The air is a bit breezy and mildly cold, not bad for a summer day, he thinks. Then, as he hits his stride and keeps an 8-minute –per-mile pace, his mind drifts to another place in time.

Why of all places is he in Oslo? Why not Switzerland or, perhaps, St. Barts? He certainly isn't here for business or artistic reasons. He only has one goal in mind and if he fails, he will move next door to Sweden and then to Denmark, until he reaches his goal.

There are few vehicles in the deserted city streets, except for a few food trucks. The streets are lined with magazine stands. He and a handful of runners have it all to themselves. As he zips along the charcoal brick and stone-grey facades, he drifts back to his plan. Soon, the breeze picks up as he approaches the Aker River. He then runs in front of the Parliament building, the old university, the national theatre, the royal palace and, finally, through a beautiful park that leads him back to his hotel.

Later, that morning, at 8:30 a.m., he is at the faculty lounge and 15 minutes later, he is in front of 50 graduate students at the University of Oslo. "Let me begin by debunking the notion that Spanish is a very hard language to learn. It isn't, and in this class you will be learning a method to learn Spanish in about ten lessons."

Lars Johannsen, at 58, is a very wealthy man, among the richest in the world. But, in his academic life, he tries to be incognito. He has been teaching "conversational Spanish" for over 25 years and has taught it all over the world at the best universities. He teaches under a pseudonym. Most universities respect his right to privacy and those that don't, he simply abandons. He is beloved by his students and that's the way he likes it. He teaches the language with a simple purpose in mind: to find young beautiful women. He likes them smart, disciplined, organized, savvy and strong. His method is simple. During his classes he identifies his target, then, proceeds to observe and learn everything about the student from a distance. When classes are over, knowing her routine, he orchestrates a chance encounter at a public place. To him it doesn't matter if the girl is engaged or hooked up with a boyfriend. The thrill for him is for them to like him, not knowing who he really is and then, be agreeable to a non-committal relationship. So, over the years, he has enjoyed romantic and passionate affairs with countless university students. Some of them have fallen hard for him, but, he has never committed to any of them. Eventually they do find out who he is or he tells them himself and then there is a breakup. But, three months ago, Catalina Garcia Suarez, a stunning Chilean student in the Computer Science Department at Cal Tech had committed suicide after breaking up with him. And even though he had been relieved when she took the initiative to break up, he felt deeply guilty this time, even after he found out that she had been having an affair with another woman. So, after the tragedy, he decided to call his philandering lifestyle quits and get married. Anyhow, that is his plan, find a wife, but this time she will know who he is when she falls in love with him.

True love blesses Lars Johannsen while he is attending the Wimbledon tennis tournament in London, England.

LONDON, ENGLAND

At 26, American tennis phenom, Gabrielle Lareau, is at the peak of her career. This is her breakthrough season on tour, with 51 straight matches won and only three losses. She has won the first two majors of the year, the Australian and the French Open, and is now facing the lightning fast grass surfaces of Wimbledon. At 5'11", she is among the tallest players on the WTA tour. She is certainly one of the prettiest professional tennis players in the world. Her blonde hair is cut extremely short, almost like a man, and parted to the right. Her pale skin has a permanent tan in a light brown color. Her deep blue eyes point just a tad upwards, giving her the look of a cat, a precocious and intense feline ready to… well, in tennis terms, attack, and attack she does.

Today, the first round match is not going well for her at all. Her opponent, a fierce 18-year old Italian, has come out swinging bullets right and left. She feels flat footed and slow on the court. Perhaps on clay she could get away with it, but not on grass, not at Wimbledon. Her unforced errors mount. Her first service is not working and, as another service return zooms by, unreachable for another winner, she feels dejected and frustrated. Oddly enough, even at age 26, today she feels old against this teenager. She needs to hang in there. Be patient, she tells herself. There is no way the young Italian can keep that level of play for two straight sets. Besides, without much experience, the teenager will probably choke when she is about to win.

The tall blonde is now facing break point. She is on serve. She tosses the ball high up and the service clock registers 110 mph. The young Italian is already on the move before the ball crosses the net. She has read the direction accurately. The service skids on the grass gaining more speed. The ball has hit the ground at an impossible angle right on the sideline of the service box. The ball runs away from the court at an impossibly low trajectory. The Italian is on her way. She slides through the grass as if she is playing on clay. She stretches as she loads her backhand. She produces a controlled half-swing that connects with the ball, well outside the service line. The stroke is animalistic, devoid of style, but filled with power and timing. The ball comes back at an even faster speed and in an angle that is insanely low. The cat lady takes a step forward towards the net, as her plan is to serve and volley. Suddenly, she sees the ball sailing towards the net, literally grazing the top. The Italian's shot has caught her by surprise. And so, another clean winner goes by without her being able to even put her racket near it. Thereafter, it seems to go further downhill. The Italian hits two service aces and now has a double match point.

He cannot take his eyes off her. The tennis match is irrelevant to him. He is captivated by the tall stunning player. Then, as the Italian prepares to serve one more time at match point, he is fixated and transfixed. It's hard for him not to look at her. She is about to lose and she looks the part. Her body language shows frustration, but also confidence. 'She is just hanging in there, waiting for the other one to blink, just one blink,' he guesses.

The young Italian's first service hits the net. Got it! Got it! That's who she reminds him of, Hope Solo, with curly short blonde hair. That's it! He is in trouble and he knows it. The second service is out, double fault. The young Italian has indeed blinked. He is intoxicated with attraction after such a long time of searching through the world. With just a couple of blinks, the Italian has lost the game as she cannot convert either of the two match points. After weeks of teaching in Oslo, Stockholm and Helsinki, he has flown to London just to watch Wimbledon and voila, of all people he falls for, a professional tennis player. It is all on him now as to the best way to approach her. He also knows that his great attraction is a huge first step, but there are still many other hurdles that await him and most of them are out of his control.

In 30 minutes, the match has turned upside down. The object of his desire has won the second set and is now serving for the match. He knows the match is hers. He stands up and lets his instincts guide him. The cat starts to circle his prey, seemingly another cat like him.

"That was close', she thinks as she quickly leaves the hallowed grounds of the All England Croquet and Lawn Tennis Club. She feels drained, yet restless. It is a very lonely life on the road, up to 40 weeks a year. She has come to hate hotel rooms and airports with a passion. Yet, she is heading to her central London hotel suite to try to get some sleep. She feels the anxiety creeping through her and a sensation of emptiness in her stomach. A massive tennis racket bag is hanging over one shoulder. She sees the limo right at the agreed spot. Then, she hears him for the first time.

"Care for a ride?" he says.

She turns and what she sees makes her smile. There is a guy holding two rental bikes with a bunch of balloons tied to the handlebars. She glances at him and his stare sets a jolt of electricity through her. She continues to walk to her limo and hands her bag to the driver.

"A change of pace, a different routine, may do you a lot of good. I promise to stay quiet while you laugh," he insists.

This time the pull is more intense, and she reacts out of primal instincts.

"Who are you?" she asks in a challenging tone.

"Just a fellow life traveler trying to share a magic moment with you." He exudes intensity and his voice makes her feel tempted.

"What is your plan?" she asks with contempt but with a touch of curiosity.

"The plan is that there is no plan."

"Is it safe?"

"Actually not, bicycles and cars moving together down the wrong side of the road do not mesh at all."

She walks towards him while still challenging the idea. "Then, why should a professional tennis player in her work clothes, displaying a very high skirt, ride on an old fashioned bike with a perfect stranger on city streets filled with crazy drivers?"

"Because you can, because it is different and because it will do you a lot of good after the close call you just had inside," he says confidently.

"Did you…?" She is amused and stops mid-sentence.

"Yes, I enjoyed the whole match a great deal, but, knew all along you would win after you saved the two match points."

She waves the driver off, but instead, the doors of the limo open and her trainer, coach and manager start to come out. She raises her hand and waves them off. The manager tries to talk but she puts a finger to her lips pleading for him to remain silent. Finally, they get it and leave. She is now left alone standing in front of a total stranger that is holding two bikes and a bunch of balloons…

"As you already know mine, why don't you begin by telling me yours?" "Lars… Lars Johannsen."

They have now "walked" the bikes for what seems to be just a few minutes. In fact, she knows they have walked miles through narrow sidewalks, only touching the streets when crossing roads. The coffee shop smells of freshly baked bread and attracts both of them. The city of small stores, with hand-painted signs surrounds them with all of its noise, bumper-to-bumper traffic and humungous cabs. But they are completely oblivious to all of it, as they are in their own world.

"Did you ever intend to ride?"

He smiles, her eyes smile back.

"I don't know what my intentions were. Perhaps, somehow just this, only this. I felt it at the match way before it ended and simply followed this amazing pull." As he speaks, his gaze totally captivates her. Whatever he means, she can feel it as well, and the intensity is all bottled up inside her. Every breathe she takes feels awfully good, as happiness spreads throughout her.

"Bikes with balloons!" Her smile is totally naked, as are her senses.

Her every move and gesture gets magnified to him because of an overwhelming magnetism. "Sometimes an absurdity is the only key to a riddle."

"A riddle?... yeah, at this moment that's what you seem like to me." Though, an overwhelming riddle of desire is what real unspoken thought is about.

And just like that life changes for inveterate womanizer Lars Johannsen – nothing is ever the same again.

CHAPTER 29

The McCoys

William McCoy, "Billy", has grown up in a home where hard work is the norm. He was just 10 years old when Barack Obama was elected President of the United States. Thereafter, he refused to go to church on Sundays. He did not believe a word preached to him about 'you can't do this, you won't be able to do that...' All he knows is that the President is proof that anything is possible in America. Billy has been raised by successful parents that still feel they are intruders in a predominately white world. In time though, his preacher has changed his message, so he returned back. At 18 years old, all Billy knows is that a fellow African-American has led the nation. Billy's friends and his girlfriend are all millennials. They are all of different ethnicities; African-American, Spanish, Asian and White, and they couldn't care less what their parents think. All they care about is themselves. Billy's parents, Denzel and Sherryl McCoy, are both stage actors and stand-up comedians. They are among the most popular and beloved artists in the country. Ten years ago, the McCoy family moved to Miami, and then to #12 Paradise Island. They came looking for a better climate than New York. Billy loves to write, especially plays. His talent has just recently been discovered, after one of his plays won a Young Screenwriters national award. The award consists of a 2-week run on Broadway, where his play will be a pre-show warmup for the main attraction.

Today, three actors are rehearsing Billy's play and are doing it in front of an empty theatre with the curtains drawn behind them. Later that day, they will have the full audience hopefully eager to experience the award-winning play as a short intro into the night's show.

The director kicks off, "Ok, guys, go…"

DRESS REHEARSAL

"Martin Luther King believed that society's three evils were: MILITARISM, RACISM and MATERIALISM. Today, decades later, we could easily argue that all of them remain among the biggest threats we face: 1) With events like Russia & ISIS, we see the danger of militarism; 2) With Ferguson, New York and Orlando, we see the lingering poison of racism; 3) With income inequality, the lack of social mobility and the lack of a fair shot for all, we see evidence of the darker side of materialism. And yet today, Reverend King's dream lives on and, as the name of this play goes, it is…" "No Longer Just a Dream"

"What if Dr. King could take a look, a peek into what happened to his dream? Well, according to prominent physicists, including Einstein and Goddard, time travel, at least mathematically, is possible."

"We are now in 1964, 53 or so years ago."

"Who are you?"

"Reverend, I am a time traveler assigned to you."

"A time traveler?"

"Yes Sir, I have been sent straight from heaven to track the lives of exceptional men like you."

The Reverend looks at the time traveler with total skepticism.

"I have been following you, sir, all the way, but recent events have changed my task."

"I don't have time for this. Now, if you would excuse me!"

Unfazed, the time traveler quickly swipes his hand across and in front of them. Dr. King's key life events flash in front of him in rapid succession. Suddenly, the scrolling of the images slows down and on the floating image, Dr. King can watch himself speak to a large crowd in Selma, Alabama, in March of 1965. Dr. King states emphatically: "We can do this, we must do this, we will take their power through the vote."

Then, the image fast forwards again, and now Reverend King speaks to an enormous crowd at the footsteps of the Lincoln Memorial in Washington, D.C: "I have a dream... that all men are created equal..." Then, the images fast-forward again. In rapid succession, Dr. King is shown receiving the Nobel Peace Prize in Stockholm, Sweden; then standing next to President Johnson in 1964, while he signs the Civil Rights Act; then on August 6, 1965, the Reverend is witnessing the signing of the Voting Rights Act.

"Reverend King, the seeds you've planted will have a profound effect in our country. I have been instructed to take you forward in time for you to observe what happened to your dream." And, before the Reverend can react, the time traveler is standing with the Reverend on a barren island outside of what appears to be an abandoned one-story prison made of stone blocks.

"Where are we?"

"We are at Robben Island, Sir, it is the Alcatraz Island of Capetown, South Africa. As you can see and feel, it is bitterly cold, humid and windy. It is a place damned by immense human suffering, like Devil's Island in South America's French Guyana, and Auschwitz in Poland."

"Why are we here?"

"In here, an extraordinary man, following in your footsteps, spent the majority of a 27-year sentence, imprisoned for opposing the racist system of South African segregation…"

"Apartheid?" states a visibly shaken Dr. King, completing the sentence.

"Reverend, let me introduce you to this remarkable South African." They are now in 1993, in a place familiar to Dr. King. Overcome by emotion, he witnesses the King of Sweden presenting the Nobel Prize to a tall white haired man.

Suddenly, the setting changes and they are now standing inside the South African Congress Building, in the country's capital of Pretoria. "Reverend, it is now May 10, 1994 and this great man is addressing the nation as he has just been elected South Africa's President. Let's listen to what he is saying."

"This is a victory for justice, for peace, for human dignity. At last, we have achieved political emancipation. Never, never and never again shall it be that this beautiful land experiences the oppression of one by another… the sun shall never set on such a glorious human achievement, let the freedom reign, God Bless Africa."

The Reverend is, at first speechless, then he states, "What a remarkable achievement, the end of Apartheid through a democratically elected member of the oppressed." He asks, his voice trembling, "What is his name?"

"Nelson Mandela." Dr. King is in a trance, shaken to the core as he holds back blissful tears of pride. The image changes again and South Africa's Press Secretary is answering questions on behalf of President Mandela.

"The National Rugby Team uniforms should be changed to reflect the colors of the majority in the country," states a reporter.

"Absolutely not. We will respect and participate in the traditions and preferences of one another. This will not be a witch-hunt. This process is about unity and integration, and not about dominance or oppression or imposing the will of one, some or even many others."

"Reverend, in the future you become famous and revered all over the planet. Your ideas and life struggles resonate all over the world. Testimonials of your life and you are all around us. In the United States alone, there are some 650 streets named after you. Also, there are streets, parks and monuments dedicated to you in Australia, Austria, France, Germany, India, Israel, Italy, Senegal, South Africa and Zambia, among others."

In front of his eyes, the floating screen moves from place to place, showing his name across cities, countries and continents. "I wish that I could tell you that I am pleased, but accolades about me are not something I particularly enjoy. I am more interested in what happened with my ideas."

"Well, Dr. King, your ideas and persona have grown significantly over time and Mr. Mandela is a great example of your legacy. But, the definitive crystallization of many of your dreams took place years later when the improbable, the impossible and the unthinkable took place. However, to witness that, we need to move closer to home.

"Reverend, we are now in Chicago at the 2008 Democratic Party National Convention. Here is another remarkable man. An African-American Senator launching his political career nationwide. Let's listen to what he has to say."

"How long will justice be crucified and truth be buried? There is no blue or red, black or white, native or Hispanic, liberal or conservative American, there is the United States of America."

The Reverend is visibly impacted by his words. "Who is he?"

"A Harvard graduate, Sir, specialized in constitutional law, son of a Kenyan man and an American woman from the mid-west who was raised in Hawaii and Indonesia. He is married to another Harvard graduate and they have two daughters.

"What is his name?"

"Barack Obama."

"Reverend, let me take you a bit forward to January 2009, but let me prepare you, sir, it is going to be emotional, very emotional for you."

The Reverend sees a familiar image, the D.C. Mall that runs from the Lincoln Memorial through the Washington obelisk, all the way to Congress. As with Dr. King's very own speech at the same place 45 years earlier, there is a huge crowd gathered. He realizes it is a lot bigger crowd than what his was.

"There has to be half-a-million people out there."

"Actually, the estimates are between three-quarters of a million up to a million, Sir."

"Why are they all here?"

"Let's get closer and find out, Reverend."

They are now standing on the footsteps of the US Congress building. They are now facing the crowd, from the opposite end, which extends all the way to the Lincoln Memorial. The elevated and sizable stage is filled with people. The Reverend does not recognize anyone or the event at first, but picks up what the ceremony is about right away.

He asks, "Why are we here?"

Then, as Senator Obama stands up and places his hand on Lincoln's bible, a bolt of emotion overcomes the Reverend, sending chills down his spine. His lower lip trembles, his stare is intense and teary at the same time. He is rendered speechless with a tight knot in his throat.

"I, Barack Obama, swear to uphold…"

"Yes, we can… oh Lord, we did it, we did it with the power of the vote."

A new image quickly flashes and is familiar to him. With a broad smile and in amazement, the Reverend observes: "So, as Mandela and myself, he also received the Nobel Peace Prize."

Then before he can react, they have switched to January 2013, while still standing at the footsteps of Congress. The scene repeats itself as the oath of office is being taken. Dr. King realizes that Obama's hair is now sprinkled with white. He pauses and then it hits him.

"Re-elected?" the Reverend blurts out. "How could that have happened?"

"Well, Reverend, he is a symbol of your success. A more than worthy successor to what you started. Remarkably Sir, he has been elected both times by almost half of the country's 72% white majority, and by a large percentage of Asians, African-Americans and Hispanics. The whites were the clinchers, they elected him both times, sir."

They are now in Cairo, Egypt. President Obama is speaking.

"Let's listen to his speech, Reverend."

"For centuries, black people in America suffered the lash of the whip as slaves and the humiliation of segregation. However, it was not violence that won full and equal rights. It was peaceful and determined insistence upon ideals… a tradition that has stretched from the days of the country's founding to the civil rights movement, a tradition based on the simple idea that we all have a stake in one another, and that what binds us together is greater than what drives us apart. That if enough people believe in the truth of the proposition and act on it, then, we might not solve every problem, but we can get something meaningful done."

Dr. King is overwhelmed and yet relieved as he stares into the horizon. His face projects a sense of intense satisfaction, realization and pride.

"It happened, it really happened," he says in a trance.

"Well, Sir, to a large degree, yes, but there is still a lot of work to do. Let me show you, Reverend."

Then the images of the shootings in Orlando, Ferguson and New York flash by.

"I see," says a circumspect Reverend, then he asks, "How did the President react?"

"Let's go there," says the time traveler.

"Violence is a dead end. We will extend you a hand if you unclench your fist," President Obama states.

"We still have a long way to go," declares Reverend King.

"That is true, Reverend, but your dream is not just that any longer, it is now a reality."

The rehearsal has now morphed into reality for the young playwright.

The audience applause does not stop. Each time it fades a bit, its pace and intensity is quickly revived by the enthusiasm of the majority. Now everyone is standing. The public wants more than the three actors bowing their heads. Now, young Billy McCoy steps out from between the closed curtains and the applause becomes an ovation. As he bows his head, there is not a shadow of a doubt in his mind, the President is right, work hard and all the doors are open for you in America... But, he will soon find out that it does not work exactly like that for all.

Another outstanding and gifted Island resident has just burst onto the national scene – the question is whether his family and he are, for a change, regular people or as is common on Paradise Island, just one more facade with plenty of skeletons in the closet.

Island resident, famous criminal attorney Oleg Krull's jury fixer, Emmanuel Oquendo, has committed a catastrophic mistake by bribing his future brother-in-law, Albert Harrington - a juror on a Krull trial. The cost of this mistake will soon become evident.

CHAPTER 30
THE KRULLS (The Trial Begins)

A lbert Harrington is interviewed by the defense, the prosecution and even the Judge. He finds some of the questions intrusive and even offensive, but keeps his composure and answers every inquiry truthfully. The defense attorney's team is particularly aggressive and seems uncomfortable with him. The prosecution, on the other hand, becomes less intrusive as the interview unfolds. It appears to Harrington that there is a bitter fight unfolding between the defense and prosecution about him being selected as a juror. In the end, the Judge decides in favor of the prosecution and appoints Harrington to be an official juror. The Judge even goes as far as to specifically deny a last minute motion put forth by the defense to remove Harrington from the jury.

The lead prosecutor, Dean Hoffman, is obfuscated by the whole skirmish. He talks loudly to his team while on a break. "The jury consultant for the defense must have seen something in regard to this juror that she did not like. As soon as I sensed their problem with juror number four, I knew we had to have him at all costs. What is wrong with Krull? He certainly didn't give up easily. Even at the last moment he tried to get his way!"

"And he could as well have had it, Dean. He may just have had it…" opines assistant prosecutor, Loretta Smith, thinking aloud.

On the other side of the room, Oleg Krull is not missing a bit of it as he reads their lips. Krull is also reading the prosecutor's and his team's body language, including hand gestures and eye movements, and he is a master at it. Oleg Krull thinks to himself, 'I will have the last laugh in this trial, we are now set to win.' Krull is delighted and secure in his knowledge that by the judge sequestering the jury, he is assured victory.

Later that night, official juror Harrington and his fiancée have their farewell. "How long is it going to take, Al?" says Melinda Oquendo, Albert Harrington's fiancée.

"Don't know, Melly, don't know." He is dying inside as his sense of civic duty made him lose sight of his priorities. He knows that any chance to earn the big payoff is now gone for good, as he will be out of circulation.

His mind is still consumed in losing the big money when he is sworn in the next day. The trial begins. Both prosecution and the defense are making their opening statements, but he is barely listening. Albert Harrington does not want to be wasting his time in a courtroom. He should be waiting to be contacted by the man with the red tie and handkerchief…

"… and I respectfully ask the members of the jury to find Justin Dixon innocent." Harrington suddenly comes to and his eyes are about to jump out of his head as he looks at and listens to Oleg Krull.

'A man wearing a red tie and red handkerchief…If you do what he wants, you will be handsomely rewarded.' Oleg Krull's red handkerchief and red tie have been dancing in front of him for the last fifteen minutes before it hits him like a ton of bricks…first comes cold fear, which spreads quickly until it seizes him completely and renders him in a state of panic. All he can think of is to bolt and run away from the courtroom. 'Run, get out of here!' In quick succession, he sees himself being handcuffed and led to prison to serve a very long sentence for jury tampering; then, his fiancée breaking up with him! 'No, I am going to do the right thing and stand up and tell the truth!' He then sees the same scene played out, only this time, they sentence him for conspiracy and his brother-in-law goes to jail with him. 'No, I am going to pretend to be sick, so I am excused.' Finally, he is honest with himself and the only thing he can think of is…the money! 'You corrupt, greedy rat! Just a piece of garbage, that's what you are,' he tells himself. 'I want to kill Oquendo right now!' But he can't, as he is, as the rest of the jury, sequestered until a decision is made. Harrington slowly calms down and starts to feel and taste his upcoming new-found wealth.

Greed clouds all traces of good judgment and common sense from Island resident criminal attorney, Oleg Krull, and corrupt juror, Albert Harrington - neither of them senses the serious trouble they are in.

Island resident, oil tycoon, Mario Angel Restrepo's first wife, is not only his neighbor, but also his best friend. Margarita Lujan-Restrepo is currently one of the four old crows. The couple's story began in Bogota decades ago.

CHAPTER 31
THE LUJAN-RESTREPOS
(Margarita and Mario)

Margarita Lujan and Mario Angel Restrepo met in high school. She was a freshman and he was a senior at Bogota's La Salle Catholic High School. She was the drum majorette of the school band and he was the student with the worst academic and disciplinary record in the school's history. As a matter of fact, nobody knew how he had not been expelled from the school long ago. However, that was easily understood once you looked underneath the surface. His mom was the head of the accounting and collection department of this prestigious high school.

The San Juan Bautista De La Salle School was unique in many ways. It was not only the single boy's and girl's Catholic school in Colombia, but was also run by French Priests, called "Hermanos." The school was prominently positioned at the foothills of a natural park overlooking the city of Bogota. The campus was enormous, with three separate soccer fields, four tennis courts, four volleyball courts, four basketball courts, an Olympic pool, gymnasium, and a full track and field facility. In addition to the outstanding athletic facilities, the campus contained language labs, TV and radio stations, a marine research center, a history and math institute, etc. It all made up for an exceptional educational experience with a uniquely involved student population of hard workers that were very proud of their school.

Margarita had a crush on Mario for as long as she could remember. He was all she ever wanted. He was wild, rebellious, feisty, and vociferous. Half the girls in the school were after him. Margarita was totally convinced she would get what she wanted. She didn't really like his attention-grabbing ways, as she called them, but she saw underneath the surface a good and driven teen that she wanted all for herself. She worked hard at getting him. Both she and Mario were involved in school and community activities, such as school fairs, rollerblade parties, inter-school Olympics, school dances, and community service drives to collect money for the poor. At all the events, Margarita made sure she was physically close to and able to hang around Mario. He never paid much attention to her, but always treated her a little better than the other girls and never got irritated or bothered by her. 'He respects me,' she constantly told herself.

Margarita continued to excel in everything she did. She worked hard at school and hard at out-of-school activities. Finally, there was a magic moment between them that happened unexpectedly during a near tragedy. La Salle was playing Loyola in soccer. It was a classic high school rivalry and the oldest sports rivalry in Bogota. Mario, a La Salle striker, moved quickly forward as a corner kick floated in the air in front of him. He had great momentum as he lunged toward the descending soccer ball. He loaded his head to the side to get ready to execute one of his trademark scoring head shots. He then struck the ball with his head and the angle of contact seemed to be ideal. However, he was violently shaken from contact by a Loyola player crashing into him. At the same time, there was a subtle push that sent Mario headfirst toward the goal post. Mario was precariously close to the metal post, he could not react in time and his forehead crashed violently into the white steel bar. He fell backwards and his bleeding forehead caused a collective gasp of shock from the viewing audience. Margarita was up and running even before he had landed and was by his side holding him within seconds. Using the knowledge from her first-aid training, she ripped off part of her shirt and pressed it hard against his forehead to contain the bleeding. She then started to talk to him to see if he was awake and all right. He suddenly opened his eyes and she was caught by surprise.

"Mario, do you recognize me?"

He slowly acknowledged her by closing his eyes in an affirmative way and gave her a faint smile. "Margarita!" he said, before he passed out again.

Later, the X-rays showed a fracture to the left part of his skull. The attending physician hinted that Margarita's actions may have saved his life. Margarita visited Mario during the four weeks that he was in the hospital. Those were happy days for her, as she had him all to herself. And Mario's attitude towards her noticeably changed. She was no longer the little girl that was always hanging around him, but a young woman he really enjoyed and loved to be with. But, when he was discharged, Margarita was in for a big surprise, as the consummation of their relationship was not going to take place for another ten years. The morning after his discharge from the hospital, Mario quit school and, as she learned later, went to chase oil in the Colombian jungle. But, he never forgot her. She never forgot him either, and waited and waited for the love of her life.

A DECADE LATER

Margarita and Mario did find each other again when one good day, a decade later, he showed up on a Sunday at the doorstep of her parents' home. Now in his late-twenties, Mario was a grown-up man and a very wealthy one indeed, with extensive holdings in the nascent Colombian oil industry. Margarita, in turn, had also matured into a refined and very well educated lady with a degree in clinical psychology. Within a year, they were married in one of the most spectacular ceremonies ever celebrated in the Capital. She was the perfect complement for him as she polished and honed him into a true gentleman that fit the mold of the wealth he possessed. The couple lived the high life and travelled the world incessantly, as his business continued to grow.

Another Decade Later

Ten years after the wedding, their idyllic life came to an abrupt and tragic end. Mario was kidnapped and it took a year of negotiations and an enormous amount of money to free him from the jungle cage where he was held. The man that came back was never the same again. He became taciturn, isolated and secretive. The couple were finally blessed with a beautiful baby girl, but that did not prevent the eventual divorce. However, their bond was never broken as they remained close friends and lived next to each other on Paradise Island. Margarita Lujan never remarried and is now one of the old crow matrons in the card room of the Island Social Club. Mario Angel Restrepo, after several years alone, married the hot little blonde bombshell from Texas.

The Restrepos' only child is the famous model and actress Veronica Lujan-Restrepo, a stunning Latina that is a curse and a blessing for her parents.

CHAPTER 32
THE LUJAN-RESTREPOS
(Veronica)

I t was 2:00 p.m. and everything was messed up. She knows there would be trouble once Tracy finds out about it. Now, her chances of going out Saturday night to Gina's party are zero, nada, as in forget about it. How could she have been so stupid? No, not stupid. Under the circumstances, how about the biggest airhead in the whole wide world. Yes, that's it, mindless, self-absorbed, empty-headed moron.

"Isabela, where are you? I need to see your lying, manipulative, magnificent face right now!"

'Time to get reamed out,' thinks Isabela. Shoeless, but wearing knee-high socks, she walks down the stairs, head down and fearful. Tracy is pacing back and forth as Isabela tiptoes into her office. Her reaction is sudden and violent as she approaches her stepdaughter. For a fraction of a second, it appears as if she is going to either hit or at least slap her, but her raised right hand instead gets a hold of Isabela's jaw. Before Isabela can pull away, Tracy lifts her face and they look at each other eye to eye.

Without releasing the firm grip, Tracy screams at the top of her lungs, "Are you out of your fucking mind? Mind? What mind? You don't have half a brain. There is no rhyme or reason to your senseless actions. All you, excuse me, the only thing you care about, is you, only you. With you it's all about instant gratification, the thrill."

Every time Isabela tries to look away, Tracy's death grip on her stepdaughter's jaw becomes tighter. Flames of angry fire appear in Tracy's eyes. But, wait a second, there is a flicker of weakness and amusement in her eyes. Isabela sees it and responds with a smirk and half smile. Tracy suddenly realizes that her eyes have given her away, the gig is up and both stepmother and stepdaughter explode in screams of unstoppable laughter.

"How on earth did you come up with this?"

"I don't know, I just did."

"Why don't you just start from the beginning? I want to know everything before I ground you until further notice, which means forever." There it was, she was going to miss Gina's party.

"It all started when I was watching a movie on Netflix. The idea seemed stupid at first…"

CUT! Take 32, scene #5. It's a rap. Both actresses relax and smile as they walk off the set.

Veronica Lujan-Restrepo is a stunning Latina and the hottest TV actress in America. At 5'10", she is strikingly tall with long wavy blonde hair. She has green camel eyes, and eyebrows like a cat. The shape of her body makes her look like the younger sister of Sofia Vergara. She is 21-years old, looks 18, and that is exactly the age of the character she plays on her popular weekly sitcom: Totalmente Demais. Veronica's mother is Margarita Lujan-Restrepo, the owner of the home at #4 Paradise Island. The Restrepo's have two homes on Paradise Island. Her father, Mario Restrepo, built a house on Lot #5 when he married the empty-headed bimbo from Texas, who is now her stepmother. Her parents had Veronica in their mid-forties. So, she was raised by parents who behaved more like grandparents. If her parents only knew of Veronica's current lifestyle, both of the Restrepos would need all those years of experience and more...

Island resident and wife beater, Alessandro Baglioni, finally meets his match in his latest escapade.

CHAPTER 33
THE BAGLIONIS AND THE LUJAN-RESTREPOS
(Veronica)

The roar of the twin jet engines of the 92-foot Italian speedboat deafens all sound coming out of the master cabin. At 45 knots per hour, the arrow-shaped boat speeds through the calm seas in the Gulf Stream, heading away from the south Florida coast and towards Cat Cay, in the Bahamas. It is reckless and almost suicidal to activate the autopilot and leave the cockpit, but to Alessandro Baglioni this is part of the thrill. It is the type of tightrope dancing that drives him crazy. He left the controls of the boat unmanned fifteen minutes ago and whatever little common sense he has left is screaming at him to go back and man the boat. But, dirty and depraved sex in the master bedroom is far more alluring or tempting if life itself is on the line.

SIX HOURS EARLIER

The cargo container boat heading north to New York City, ten miles off the Florida coast, is right in the middle of a massive storm. The hull of the boat keeps on crashing against the gigantic waves and every blow is felt by the crew as the thumps of the squalls are hammered off the metal structure. Every few minutes, the boat tilts backward at a seemingly impossible angle as it rides the waves up and down. At times, the boat literally falls forward into a void when it clears the crest and then splashes head first into the waves. This goes on for hours. Finally, the weather system clears. Then, as the crew reviews the damage, they realize they are missing a 40-feet container filled with HDTV's made in Korea.

A Month Earlier

His web name is "Al" and he prowls the Web looking for what he likes. It all begins one evening, when he is browsing an S&M website and chat room he has just heard about, called 'Plepanes.' He is pleasantly surprised, after he requests their services, to learn that one of their representatives is coming to visit and interview him before they accept him as a client. His S&M room should be all his visitor needs to see to welcome him as a client. Alessandro is further delighted that his visitor is one of the co-founders. This gives additional credibility to the escort service.

"What does 'Plepanes' stand for?" asks Alessandro.

"It is pretty obvious, I bet you can figure it out by yourself."

Alessandro does not like the answer, but he likes their claim about the five thousand members. He wants in!

"How is it that an owner has to visit an applicant?"

The young co-founder of Plepanes is observing Alessandro, but says nothing.

'Did I screw up? This guy looks awfully young. What is he? Indian, Pakistani, Sri Lankan? Well, whatever. I don't care. I just want in.'

"Dominatrix?" his interviewer asks.

Alessandro is caught off guard! "Yes," he answers feeling awkward, "how do you know?"

"You like to pay to be dominated. You like to dominate in everything else."

Alessandro now looks at his interviewer with amusement and acceptance and a half smile forms on his face.

"I interview all VIP's like you in person, so we can provide you with the best and fastest service possible."

"C'mon man, what you really want to know is if I can pay!"

"Of course, Sir."

"So who is the most expensive dominatrix you have?"

"I have just the right person for you, money aside!"

"Do you have pictures?"

"No pictures at 'Plepanes.' If you don't like her, just walk away. Until you meet, she won't know who you are and you won't know her either."

"Walk away? I don't go to anybody's place. She has to come to me."

"Excuse me sir… You mean here, at your house?"

"No, of course not, at my boat."

"The one docked outside?"

"Yes, but it will be anchored in Biscayne Bay, 500 hundred yards off the Miami Beach Marina.

"How does she get to you?"

"At the Miami Beach Marina I'll arrange a jet ski rental an hour earlier and she will ride the jet ski to my boat."

Alessandro hands a picture of 'Big Al', as the boat is called, to the interviewer.

The interviewer shakes his head in consent, stands up, and shakes 'Big Al's hand before leaving.

The Encounter (Today, 11:30 A.M.)

Alessandro waits inside the cabin and is unable to relax or distract himself. When he plays these games, he is defenseless. He is not in charge. He is at the mercy of his master. He hears the noise of the jet ski approaching, then, a little docking bump. He hears the steps, 'Man those are high heels. How did she manage?' Then, the legs show up, and sure enough, they are hooked to a pair of beautifully open and red high heels. As each leg takes a step down the steep cabin entrance ladder, all he sees is muscle strength and perfection. Her legs are still wet. Then, as she descends the stairs further, the sinuous and impossible line of her butt emerges. His heart stops. He cannot swallow. Her butt is huge! And her waist is outlandishly narrow. Then she stops, as if she knows he is watching.

"Hello, anybody home?"

'She's got to be Hispanic. She's got to be!'

"Hello!"

She starts moving again and comes down one more step.

'My God, those have to be at least 43 triple-cup jugs.' "C'mon down." She steps one more step down. Now he can see her hair and shoulders and finally her face.

"Al?" She raises the palm of her hand to cover her mouth in shock.

'It is her!'

Then, he does not see it coming, but the lash hits his legs. It is a gentle frontal whip done with lightning speed with just a flip of her wrist.

"Shut up, dirty old man!"

CHAPTER 34
THE LUJAN-RESTREPOS
(Veronica)

Veronica Lujan-Restrepo uses her mother's last name ahead of her father's for artistic reasons, as it rhymes better. But she is just as close to her mom as she is to her dad. Her mom and dad live next to each other, as the family occupies Paradise Island numbers 4 and 5. She literally grew up between the two houses. With two older parents, she was raised with very few rules or restraints. This made her very independent and sexually active from a very early age. She moved out of her parents' homes and off the island at the age of 18. Veronica first worked as a model when she was 16 years old. Soon after beginning her career, she started to grace the covers of the most fashionable magazines in the world and was quickly hired to represent two French cosmetic firms and an Italian fashion brand. After her second year on the runway, Veronica had made more than two million dollars and dropped out of the University of Miami Business School.

Her modeling career soon blossomed into an acting career. During a four-year period, Veronica made six movies, two of them box office hits. But her biggest success has been on a Netflix sitcom called "*Totalmente Demais*" viewed weekly by more than twenty million people.

Her first sexual experience was with her cross-country trainer. She was obsessed with him from the first time she saw him and found a way to seduce him. One afternoon, when they were running along a fifteen-mile-trail she kept intentionally falling behind the team so that the coach would come back to check on her. The third time he came back to check on her, she had fallen so far behind, that they were a good fifteen minutes behind the pack.

"Restrepo, where are you?" yelled an irritated Steven Luzco. Then, from within the marsh, he heard a noise and as he turned, he caught a glimpse of her. "Are you all right?" In the dark marsh area, he could only see her silhouette. He walked towards her. He could now see her moving her finger gesturing him to come to her. Then, as he got closer, he could see that she was totally naked.

"What are you doing?"

"I want you to make love to me, Coach."

As he was contemplating the situation, she stepped forward in all of her naked glory.

Luczo completely lost it and was overcome by an overwhelming desire for the best body he had ever seen. But, as he thrust inside of her, after a bit of pain and hesitation, the fourteen-year-old who had just lost her virginity, took total control. As she started to cum uncontrollably, she began to dictate each sexual act and position. When he started to laugh with pleasure, she slapped him. A few minutes later, she came again and dug her nails so hard into his back that he started to bleed. The pain and pleasure got to him and he came himself as well. Right there on top of a beach towel in the middle of the Everglades, surrounded by all kinds of nature's hazards, Veronica began her sexual journey into the world of sado-masochism.

GROWN-UP VERONICA

She never had boyfriends, just lovers. She had experiences with girls, plenty of them. She had all sorts of men of all types, races, sizes and finally ended up with multiple sex partners. But in the end, she realized that her biggest pleasure came by inflicting pain on men as a dominatrix.

That's when she decided to join an escort service, where the relationships and encounters were non-personal and there was no chance of a relationship other than that of a paid worker. The strict vetting by the agency made her feel safe and she kept a roster of ten men that were her regulars. When she got tired of any of them, she just replaced them. Veronica needed at least two customers every day, so she had to perfect her routine in what she did with each one of them, so no matter what, she was done in thirty to forty-five minutes. She had also come to realize her secret life was going to be discovered. But she did not care and was even thinking about quitting her acting career if the fall-out was too much, as nothing, absolutely nothing, was more important to Veronica than her sexual life.

That is why at first she was concerned while being taught and directed how to handle the jet ski, when she realized that her rendezvous point with her new client was a boat that was well known on Paradise Island and belonged to Mr. Baglioni. It concerned her that Mr. Baglioni might blow her cover. However, her feminist side took over and she became intensely aroused with the notion of beating the crap out of a woman abuser as she humiliated him sexually.

CHAPTER 35
THE BAGLIONIS
AND THE LUJAN-RESTREPOS

Alessandro Baglioni is lost in a sea of lust after being lashed non-stop for an hour by Veronica Lujan-Restrepo. During a short break, he navigates his speedboat away from the Florida coast, then after accelerating to 45 knots, he turns the radar on and sets the autopilot in the direction of the Bimini Islands in the Bahamas. He is bleeding ever so slightly from some of the whipping wounds swelling across his body. No one has taken him this far before, and until now he would not have allowed it. His inner demons are raging today. The masochist side of him craves the pain and the total lack of control, yet it still does not feel enough, even as extreme as it has been. Veronica has broken the wall between Baglioni's two worlds. His one world of masochist activities is impersonal with unknowns. His second world of sadist escapades is, on the other hand, very intimate and personal, to the point that he keeps trophies from each one of his victims. That is what his sadist side wants to do, he wants to hurt her and he wants to do it so badly that he starts to prance like a raging bull. Baglioni returns to the main cabin completely out of control, but when he descends the stairs, he does not see her!

"Straight to the bedroom, Al, I know you want more pain – and you are gonna get it." He grins and walks straight forward. She is trapped, and she doesn't know it! The sadist is now in charge and knows exactly what he is going to do to her in his chamber of horrors. Veronica Lujan-Restrepo is still reeling after the beating she gave to her much-despised neighbor. The pleasure is so intense that she feels overwhelmingly aroused, but the young dominatrix has been very deliberate in her planning and she is also quite experienced. She knows that Baglioni can be dangerous and can turn violent at any time. He walks slowly through the corridor and picks up the voice-activated remote control for his chamber of horrors. He opens the door and sees Lujan-Restrepo looking at him while kneeling on the bed in all her splendor, dressed with black leather belts covering her body, but otherwise totally naked. Her massive boobs, impossibly narrow hips and enormous Latin butt are in full view. He reacts instantaneously, but she is faster. As he is about to voice command his remote control, he is hit with two Tasers on his chest and arms and, as he stumbles toward the bed, Veronica starts another pair of Tasers, one on each leg. He is surprised and in shock, which quickly turns to rage. He tries to move towards her, but when he reaches the bed, he starts to shake violently and collapses face first. As Baglioni slowly regains consciousness, he realizes that he can't move his hands or legs. He is spread eagle, as his hands and feet have been handcuffed to chains secured to the walls of the room. Before he can physically react, Veronica jumps on top of him with her legs spread and bent in a kneeling position. His excitement is instantaneous and her response is as well. First, she leans forward, then she aggressively penetrates herself, literally crucifying herself, with his rock hard cock. Then her wild instincts take over and she squeezes him with her well-trained muscles.

"Oh, my God," he screams completely overwhelmed by her amazing body being nailed to him. Then, she slaps him hard in response to his expressions of pleasure. She tightens her grip on him and her feeling of holding power over him is overwhelming and anger is overcome by lust.

But, as she glances at him, she sees that he did not like being slapped. A masochist does not react like this. That's when she hears the command "straps!" Baglioni's command starts a shower of red infrared light as his remote control blinks. Then, a zapping sound follows as five feet from the floor wide bands shoot across the bed and hit open locks on the opposite side. "Tighten," and in a fraction of a second the bands initiate a downward horizontal movement and quickly tighten against Veronica's middle and lower back. This compresses her against his chest and plunges her even deeper into him. Tightly strapped together in a mixture of extreme pleasure and pain is when Baglioni finally hears the radar emergency signal that has apparently been sounding for some time. Then, before he even has time to react, the speeding boat brushes against a semi-sunken steel container. The impact occurs on the boat's starboard side and throws the speeding boat onto its port side and causes a gaping hole in the bow. Being tightly strapped to each other is one of the reasons that the pair do not get killed by the impact. Baglioni's last command is "unstrap!" This frees Veronica and saves her life and the handcuff keys she held in her clenched fist saves his.

"That boat hit something," says a cargo vessel captain who from a distance witnesses the violent crash and the flip of the boat. He immediately calls in the emergency on his radio, but as he is providing the coordinates he exclaims, "Jeesus, the thing just exploded into a fireball!"

The U. S. Coast Guard helicopter is at the site within record time. Fortunately, for Baglioni and Veronica, a patrolling Coast Guard boat was less than 5 miles away from the crash and gave the location to the helicopter. As it hovers over the flaming debris with video camera rolling, the last thing they expect to see are survivors. It comes as a great surprise when they see two sets of arms flagging them from the calm waters and a good 500 yards from the debris. "That's the only way those two survived, they jumped before the explosion." Then, as the helicopter hovers, the scene turns bizarre for the crew and the nationwide audience.

"These two are totally naked! The man is injured. He is just floating on his back with her help. He seems to be in great pain." "Are there more survivors?" Officer Miller asks over the megaphone. The woman shakes her head and gestures that it is only the two of them. The cameras are ordered to go close up on their faces to avoid nudity. Then as they are lifted, covered in thermal blankets, the scene turns even more bizarre.

"The male victim has a severe injury to his genital area and other injuries that appear to have been caused by lashings, instead of blunt force trauma from the crash."

"The female survivor is uninjured."

"What were these two doing when they crashed?" asks the Coast Guard officers to each other. It is a rhetorical question, as they all have a good idea what the answer is.

Baglioni's command a fraction of a second before the crash set the unstrapping mechanism in motion that completely released Veronica. But this had devastating consequences for Baglioni. When the strap's pressure eased up, she was no longer completely pinned to him. Then, as the G-forces from the crash occurred, there was a slight separation between the two bodies. The quick separation was intense enough to create a massive amount of torque on Baglioni's member and, in a fraction of a second, it snapped and fractured. "The patient seems to have only one severe injury," stated the U. S. Coast Guard medical officer over the helicopter radio.

Silence ensued.

"Copied, go on."

More silence. Then, finally, an embarrassed but chuckling Marine responds in a whisper, "massive fracture of the penis" and his response is heard over their headphones by each of the crew members as they look at the wild twosome. "These two have a lot of explaining to do about what the hell they were doing and why the boat controls were unmanned," states Captain Miller.

In the meantime, Johnny Baglioni watches in disbelief as the whole story unfolds on TV. He gasps in anguish when a renowned doctor comes onto the screen and explains the severity of a penis fracture. This diagnosis is followed by a panel discussion speculating about what kind of S&M activities the twosome were engaged in.

Just a few houses down the block, the scene is not much different. Mario Angel Restrepo and Margarita Lujan-Restrepo sit in front of the TV holding hands as they cry uncontrollably.

"Did you know she was into S&M?" Mr. Restrepo asks.

"No, my love, only that she has always been a very active woman for her age!"

"By active, you mean active sexually?"

An embarrassed Margarita concedes by nodding her head. A very long silence ensues as more embarrassing news of the event are shown. "He is going to pay for this. Nobody messes with my little girl. Nobody. Not even Alessandro Baglioni."

Waiting for a false move from Island resident, lobbyist, Bart Holstein, and the former president are a persistent team of FBI agents.

CHAPTER 36
THE HOLSTEINS

"We are only going to have one shot at this guy," says FBI agent Jim Nash.

"But Jim, we have nothing on him, zilch, zero, nada," replies agent Leon Martinez.

"We have got to be patient," insists Nash.

Leon Martinez is sick and tired of the endless off-duty hours spent in vain and away from his family. "Nothing is going to happen until the ex-president shows up in town. We've trailed Holstein's pimp day and night as he goes about his business. Since the last meeting at Holstein's Paradise Island mansion, there has been no action by either side."

"I say we show up unexpectedly and have a chat with the pimp, I think we should pressure him and offer him a deal," he mumbles without thinking.

"Are you nuts, Leon? Confront him without having him by the balls first? And you expect the dirty weasel to just simply betray Holstein and the ex-president from whom he obviously makes a ton of money? The ex-president obviously has friends everywhere and if we charge forward without this locked up in advance, this whole case will fall apart and we will be eliminated."

"You are right, without verifiable proof, we have to wait."

"And that is what we will do."

Island resident, corrupt lobbyist, Bart Holtein's misdeeds by no means ends by being a pimp for the former president – he also makes his money circumventing the law and exploiting minorities.

CHAPTER 37
THE HOLSTEINS
Southern Illuminated Faith Congregation
Baptist Church Miami, Florida

 We should receive the first financial report and payment this week," says Loretta Brown.

"I'm still uncomfortable with that individual," says Michelle Green.

"How can you say that? He has been a blessing from heaven. How often have you seen a businessman this giving?"

"That's precisely my point, girl. I've never seen it and I'm probably not seeing it now either. There is something definitely wrong with the guy and this week I'll be proven right."

"Really? Something good is finally happening here and you get all pessimistic and sarcastic. Are your trying to attract negativity, woman? What's wrong with you?"

"I ain't saying another word, Loretta. Let us pray that it does happen, otherwise our church is in serious financial trouble."

BART HOLSTEIN

"I have 40% of all the concessions of the Miami International Airport's new American Airlines terminal," says the lobbyist, Bart Holstein.

"How is that possible? I'm sure it's not even legal!"

"Well, I did it."

The lobbyist knows how to manipulate the system, pull the strings of elected city officials and then hide his influence pedaling from any legal ramification. He has no expertise in financial matters, he has hardly ever actually held a real job, but he has a direct ownership or an "economic interest" in most newsstands, cafeterias, fast food restaurants and souvenir shops at the Miami International Airport.

His ownership and control of the airport concessions is contrary to the public interest statutes that seek to give an economic opportunity to minorities in the concessions at that airport. This has taken place in plain sight and nobody seems to care much about it, until a group of resilient members of a church caught wind of the scheme through a church member's attention to detail and her elephant memory.

That morning, she was running late. Anita Kennedy is doing accounting entries on QuickBooks and going over the cash receipts and checks received in the past two weeks. Normally, she is only a few days behind with the books of the church. But, her PhD presentation thesis is absorbing all her time. She enters the check deposit like any other and continues, until her mind wanders off causing her to abruptly stop. She starts to concentrate again and re-reads the name of the issuer. Her eyes widen, she searches the files for the bank record and finds a copy of the check, front and back. She then makes a photocopy of the check and leaves the office.

Antonio Williams, Esq. has been a trial attorney all his life. His specialty is to defend minority businesses that have federal statutory rights of ownership participation in business dealing with the government. He investigates violations of federal statutes or circumvention of minority constitutional rights. Anita Kennedy's aunt and mother are clients of Attorney Williams. They have hired Williams to bring a lawsuit against the lobbyist and it has dragged on through the court system for more than two years.

"Mr. Williams, please explain to me again what this lobbyist did to my aunt and mom?"

"In regard to airport concessions, Federal law requires that minorities have participation in an applicant's roster of shareholders, meaning, African-Americans, Hispanics, Asians, Native Americans or any other minority group," replied Williams.

"So what did he do? He included my aunt and mom. How and why them?"

"After receiving a 40% ownership interest in the concession, the lobbyist got them to transfer 80% of their economic interest back to a company controlled by him. They did this in the form of an economic interest, in other words, unofficially. They officially own 40% of the concession, but they transfer 80% of the economic interest back to the lobbyist as a finder's fee for getting them the economic participation in the concession."

"And nobody knows about this?"

"Everybody knows, but they pretend they don't."

"Are you telling me that the Miami City officials are corrupt?"

"No, some are on the take and others simply owe too many political favors or do it for party loyalty."

"So the minority business people do not actually participate as mandated by Federal law in regard to the airport shops?"

"Right! At least not in the way intended by law."

"Why are we having so much trouble in court?"

"Good question. On one side, lack of evidence and very hard to prove. Many courts won't touch the lobbyist. That's called political clout."

"What if you had good concrete evidence?"

Attorney William's interest is keen, but skeptical. He stares intently at Anita Kennedy. She then responds by saying, "I have the evidence, let me show it to you."

The nation's largest home builder, Island resident, Leon Albert's neglect for his children, especially his eldest Eli, may land him and his son in jail. However, in the American justice system, it is often all about who you know.

CHAPTER 38
THE KRULLS AND THE ALBERTS

"Oleg, this is Leon, I've got a problem," states Leon Albert reaching out to his neighbor, criminal attorney, Oleg Krull.

"Okay, what is it?"

"My son borrowed some guns from my house and one of them is now part of a murder investigation. I have him on the line."

"Hello, Mr. Krull, this is Eli."

"Eli, what kind of gun is it?"

"An AK-47, Sir."

"Holy shit...not good son, not good! How do you know it is part of a murder investigation?"

"A couple of detectives visited me last night and want to talk to me again this afternoon at 4 p.m. at the Miami Beach police station."

"Okay, come to my office with your dad at 3:00, so you can tell me everything. Then, we'll all go together to the police station. Albert, you need to go because you are the owner of the gun."

THE NEXT DAY

The Agusta helicopter lifts up smoothly from the Watson Island helipad. Once in the air, it heads east and flies over the McArthur

Causeway, crosses the Florida coastline and heads out into the Gulf Stream. Inside the air-conditioned cabin, the four passengers sit wearing noise controlling headphones. The state-of-the-art Agusta is the Rolls Royce of helicopters. The flight plan is to take them to a private island in the Bahamas, 90 miles off the coast of Florida. The three college students are giggling and excited.

The 4th passenger and owner of the magnificent flying machine, Leon Albert, is not that excited, as the visit to the Miami Beach police station did not go well at all. A murder was committed with his gun and the ramifications could affect his son. Oleg Krull did seem to be effective with his arguments, but overall, Albert is still concerned. So, the moment the group left the police station, he decided to get away for the weekend and go to his private island. Three small islands suddenly come into view. As they approach the bigger of the islands, on the helipad on top of a small hill, Albert's personal assistant waits with a couple of electric carts.

'What does my deranged boss have in mind for these three girls? They certainly are not going to go back to Miami the same as they came. If they knew what awaits them, I bet they would not have come at all,' thinks Albert's assistant.

Then the beautiful helicopter lowers its wheels and lands softly. "Welcome to Hawks Cay," Albert's assistant states. "Sir, all meals are frozen. Microwave ready. Everything is in place and stacked up." Once she hands the keys to him, she boards the Agusta and as the helicopter lifts up and heads to Miami, Leon Albert and the three teenagers are left all alone on his private island…at least for the time being!

Island resident Lars Johannsen is hopelessly in love. For months he has travelled the world following his tennis star lover. He knows that now is the time to reveal the truth.

CHAPTER 39
THE JOHANNSENS

They start shortly before 6:00 a.m. at Vienna's Ringstrasse. As usual, right from the beginning, everything around them becomes alive, as Lars Johannsen narrates as they jog. He knows the story behind each of the palaces on the classy street.

"Imagine, Gabrielle, how much wealth was generated into this city a century ago and how much hard work and talent was behind it. None of these palaces belonged to the Royal family. They were all owned by business people. This one, for example, belonged to Ludwig Wittgenstein and that one over there, belonged to the Ephrussi family."

Now, as they run through the cobbles of Reisen-Platz, in-between the magnificent Hofburg Palace and the modern Looshaus, Gabrielle, who is in town for a tournament she has played on multiple occasions, feels differently. It seems like everything around her has meaning. At first, she thinks it is because she is no longer alone and is in love, but she realizes that it is much deeper than that. It is his world she is infatuated with. After 45 minutes, they sit down to have breakfast.

"What is it with this city, Lars? It feels magical to me," she asks rhetorically. He is lost in his own world, and does not answer. He just looks at her with sparkling eyes filled with light and full of life…

"Oh, my God, what are you doing to me? This cake is to die for," she says suddenly. Then, as she sips the hot drink, her face seems about to climax. "This coffee is heavenly."

"These Sachertorte cakes are considered the best in Vienna and that, my dear, is a Wiener mélange of foamy steamy milk, mixed into strong and bitter coffee."

"What is it with you?" she says dazzled.

"What?" a bemused Lars Johannsen replies.

"Simple things?"

"What do you mean?"

"A city of kings with palaces, monuments, squares and parks so beautiful that you can hardly breathe, then there was our brunch with what did you call it? Oh, yes, hard cheese accompanied by a bottle of wine sitting on a bench in Michaelerplatz."

"And, the crispy on the outside, flaky on the inside croissant with real butter, marmalade and a large real orange juice in Le Provence."

"We watched the grand operas in Rome, heard Chopin in Warsaw, Beethoven in Berlin and Mozart yesterday at the extraordinary Vienna State Opera. I even loved the hours I spent with you at libraries, bookstores, or looking at works of art. Nine months of this is an entire life in full force."

"Gaby, would you change your life as a tennis pro for all of it?"

"Are you kidding me? I'd been going to all these locations for seven years, but living a miserable lonely life. You opened my eyes with all of your zest for life. You made me realize how much is out there to see if we want to. None of it is even luxurious or expensive.

Just a pair of shoes and jeans and then we have another glorious day alive," she says as she places her arms around him.

"You know what, Lars? You make me immensely happy. I feel safe and fulfilled as long as you are around and like you say, more and more the words such as bored, alone, sad or afraid are becoming totally foreign to me," she says smiling with her heart on her sleeve.

"Gabrielle, I am just following you around the circuit and, thankfully, we have been able to enjoy and share the places together."

"How do you know so much? There are so many things you love so much. I want to be around you all the time, my love," says an effusive Gabrielle. "My sweet and darling language professor," she adds in her blissful ignorance about his real self.

"Ausgleich," he says absentmindedly.

"What?"

"That's what this region of the Austro-Hungarian Empire was called. The Hungarian region was called Magyar and Vienna was the capital. But, the empire was really a broken ..."

"Please, stop, you are deflecting me."

Lars Johannsen crosses his arms and shuts down. She lets him be and does not say a word. Minutes go by and right there in a Viennese Café, under Gabrielle's patient and loving eyes, after six months of a whirlwind of fury, passion and non-stop romance and gifts, he realizes that he has nothing to fear anymore. He finally opens up.

"Ever since I lost my wife I did not want or, as I realize now, never found anyone I wanted to commit to."

"There have been many broken hearts in my life, Gabrielle." She continues not to react. Her instincts are to just let him talk, and so she does, but her eyes betray her.

"But truth be told, I never felt this way. I am not only infatuated and smitten by you, I feel open and relaxed. I want to be with you all the time and never get tired of having you around. Sometimes I just want to hang around and watch you play or go about your routines. Other times I like to listen to your sounds and words. Gabrielle, being with you is a privilege that I will always be grateful for," he says squeezing her hand tightly, and staring mesmerized at who he realizes has become his other half.

"Lars, you've shown me that one does not need much in life except the desire, knowledge or will to learn and love. Also, you've put into perspective the relative value of money. I was spoiled living this opulent 5-star closeted life that was all artificial. A teacher's salary will suffice." She smiles sarcastically.

"But it does not hurt, Gabrielle, that you've made a few million with your racquet, right?" he asks doubling down on Gabrielle's sarcasm.

"No, it doesn't, but honestly what have we needed it for?" she asks with pleasure. "Nothing!" she continues.

Lars knows that the time has come. It is time for her to learn the truth about him. The next day as they land at JFK for her upcoming competition at the US Open, after clearing customs, they are greeted by a limo driver. That surprises her.

"I did not order this," she says.

"Gabrielle, I did," he says to a puzzled face. The limo does not drive out of the airport, but to a private aviation terminal. Gabrielle is confused and a bit lost, but keeps her mouth shut and just goes with the flow. A captain awaits them and greets them.

"Mr. Johannsen, how are you?"

"Mrs. Lareau, how are you?"

They all walk onto the tarmac. She is really upset and asks in a whisper, "Johannsen? What the F is going on?" He does not answer as they board a brand new Agusta Helicopter and within a few minutes they are on their way to Manhattan. However, neither of them speaks and for a moment it seems as if there is a wall between them. As they approach the city, the helicopter circles a tower on the east side of Central Park. Then it proceeds to land on its rooftop.

As they touch down, Gabrielle can see the building is 60-70 stories high. Gabrielle looks around and sees on the rooftop landing pad: 'Johannsen Enterprises.' Her heart stops! When they hop out of the helicopter and walk towards the exit, Lars takes her hand and says, "Gabrielle, it means the world to me that you have fallen in love with me for who I am and not for what I have. Welcome to my town." They then walk one floor down and enter his duplex penthouse that occupies the entire two floors of the building.

"This decadence is a shock! What, am I supposed to be happy?"

"You are already happy! You've been happy with me without any of this and that won't change."

"I need time to think about this. I don't even know if I want to be here. Let me look around and I'll see you in a little bit."

After an hour goes by, Lars goes to look for Gabrielle, but she is long gone. She has left a note, "Sorry, my love I did not sign up for this. Give me some space to think about how I feel. Please don't chase me. I won't like it."

Two days later, he has not heard from her and it is driving him crazy. He drops by Flushing Meadows and sees her practice from a distance. She spends the whole day training. Then, as the sun is setting, she stops and heads to the shower to clean up.

'He looked so sad. Did he seriously think that I would not see him up in the stands?' she thinks distractedly while walking out of the tennis complex with her tennis gear on one shoulder.

"Care for a ride?" She freezes as she hears the voice. Then as she turns around, there he is standing with two bikes and a cloud of balloons on top of him. Dropping everything, she runs and jumps all over him, hugging and kissing him as if there is no tomorrow.

"Why did it take you so long to come and fetch your girl?" she asks and emphatically tells him, "I am in and all yours."

"Nothing makes me happier than hearing you say it," states Lars with a sigh of relief and bubbling with happiness.

Is the philanderer in Lars Johannsen gone for good? Or is Gabrielle another passing fling? Only time will tell.

The Island's young crowd is still not certain about what really happened to Hillary Zathlyn – and how the three vanished Island resident thugs were involved.

CHAPTER 40
THE PESINS

"Explain it to me please, Megan," states Kevin Pesin.

"The three amigos are gone from the Island and the rumor is that they were the ones that molested Hillary. They were whisked away to keep them from the investigators."

"Megan, you are still not telling me anything I don't know already. Say it! Don't dance around it! They raped Hillary. I know it is embarrassing and she is our friend, say it loud and clear, please," says an angry Kevin.

"What do you mean everyone knows?" states Megan.

"Well, it certainly doesn't look like it. They pretend they don't know. In the meantime, it smells like a cover-up. I haven't heard about any police involvement so far. I don't like it Megan," complains Kevin.

"Not everything is what it seems, Kev."

"OK, Meg, level with me, what am I missing?"

"Hillary's dad found out the truth and did something about it, but nobody knows what. All that is known is that the three families were scared enough to send the boys away in a hurry."

"What did Hillary's dad do to them, Meg? Tell me," asks the now smiling Kevin.

"I swear to you I don't know, nobody knows."

The two childhood friends' video call over Apple's video chat Face Time has been going on for about an hour. They are now chuckling, as neither of them likes the three Paradise Island bullies. A text message from Johnny Baglioni flashes on the screen.

"Hey, Yo, what's up?"

"Chillin with Meg, call us over Face Time."

With Johnny on the video call, they all go back to the same subject, but not before talking about Johnny's family being in the headlines.

"What's going on, Johnny?" asks Kevin.

"A bit of trouble at the house between the old folks, but it is getting back to normal."

"Your mom all right?" asks Megan Greenhouse.

"Yeah, those two love each other in a very weird way, but they can't live without each other."

"Enough about me. Meg, tell me all about the three imbeciles," jokes Johnny.

"Do I look like an oracle, clairvoyant, mind reader to you guys. I know about as much as you, Johnny, which is very little."

"That's true, she knows very little…but I know at least something," says Johnny.

"Like what?"

"Hillary's dad did something to them and their parents ran scared and sent them away."

"I wonder what it was?" asks Kevin. And the question resonates with the other two, as they all sense they've got to know more!

"I'll ask the four old crows the next time I see them playing cards at the club. I'll bet you anything that they know," states Megan with curiosity eating her up.

PARADISE ISLAND SOCIAL CLUB (THE NEXT DAY)

The old crows have been sitting and waiting for Margarita Lujan-Restrepo for more than an hour. They have tried to reach her by text and cell phone, to no avail.

"The poor thing is in hiding, she must be devastated," says Sara Pesin.

"Embarrassed and ashamed is what she is," remarks Nicole Albert.

"A bit of both ladies, but we need to find out if she is all right!" chimes in Elizabeth Bell.

Megan Greenhouse walks from the pool area to the clubhouse and knocks softly on the French doors.

"Come in, come in."

Megan is intimidated by the group lounging in front of her. 'Their tongues are dangerous,' she says to herself.

"What brings you here, dear?"

"Johnny, Kevin and myself have been trying to figure out what happened to the three island boys that were sent away?"

The three old crows look at each other, but nobody utters a word.

"Is it a state secret?" asks Megan.

"We've only heard rumors," states Elizabeth Bell.

"Unconfirmed rumors," adds an obviously upset Nicole Albert.

"And what are those rumors?" insists Megan.

Stone silence ensues. Megan decides not to press her luck and prepares to leave.

"Dr. Zathlyn did something to them."

"Shut up, Elizabeth!" shouts Nicole Albert.

With her eyes wide open, Megan continues to stare at Elizabeth Bell, who seems to want to let it out.

"Megan, there is no point in hiding the truth as it is in plain sight and sooner or later it is going to come out," continues Elizabeth Bell ignoring Nicole Albert's outburst.

"The rumor is that Dr. Zathlyn castrated them," blurts out Elizabeth.

Megan covers her mouth with both hands. Her eyes are filled with surprise and fear. Minutes pass with no one saying another word. Megan finally runs out to share the news. The old crows close up shop. But, before they do, they all commit to reaching out to Margarita Lujan-Restrepo to ensure she is all right and persuade her to attend their next card game, so they all can share the latest gossip.

The old crows want Margarita Lujan-Restrepo's presence so that she can give them the latest gossip on the high seas rescue of Margarita's daughter, Veronica, from the clutches of wife beater Alessandro Baglioni.

Island resident, old crow member, Sarah Pesin's granddaughter is one of the most sought after models in the world. Her current photoshoot has taken her to China where she'll meet the man that will steal her heart while at the same time putting her life and freedom at stake.

CHAPTER 41
THE PESINS (ARLENE)
Shanghai, China

Beijing is to Washington as Shanghai is to New York,' she keeps repeating to herself as she strolls through the People's Square and on to Nanjing Road. Just two days in the city and she completely feels that she is in the middle of a Chinese version of the Big Apple. At five foot ten, she stands out in the oriental crowd. Her open coat reveals a long sweater and jeans with the knees cut out. Her shoulder-length black wavy hair follows her runway bouncy steps. Her emerald green eyes shine even in the distance. But, the crowd at the bustling and busy promenade hardly notices. The faces in the crowd, even though predominantly Chinese, are diverse, with people from all over the world. Arlene Alexandra Pesin is on top of the world, jet setting from fashion show to fashion show, cover page to cover page. Regardless of where she is at, she loves to go out and walk for miles. Her goal this morning is simply to wander around, eat local food and then come back to her rented penthouse. As she approaches the Bund waterfront area in central Shanghai, she decides to go into old town to eat noodle soup. Then, as she enters the Bund, she is suddenly shoved forward by someone in the crowd and stumbles and falls hard. As she gets up and regains her balance, an apologetic voice states, "excuse me, I did not see you."

As she is about to turn her head toward the voice, she sees a hand going for her purse that is still laying on the ground. She grabs her purse, yanks it hard and pulls it tight to her chest with both arms. That is when she sees the stiletto blade suddenly coming at her.

"Let go of your purse. Place it back on the ground," a voice states in heavy accented English.

She holds her purse tighter and hears heavy steps around her. Suddenly, her attacker is hit in the face by a military kick. The attacker gets hit again with a karate blow and lands on the ground on his back. Her attacker is knocked out cold and now lies on the ground with a knife lying next to him. The good Samaritan who took the attacker out quickly runs away, but Arlene gets a glimpse of his face. The attacker is a very young, handsome and athletic Oriental boy. She starts to quickly walk away. Suddenly, as she is moving away from the scene, a loud bang occurs. She feels the impact on her back as she is propelled into the air. She lands face down on the pavement, losing consciousness. The few feet that she had just walked from the attempted robbery into the open space of the riverfront end up saving her life.

Two Weeks Later

Arlene wakes up and at first, she can't see a thing. Then, slowly a light appears and finally, she is able to see blurry images and human beings standing in front of her observing and talking to her. The thing is she can't hear them. 'Where am I?' she questions in her mind. Scanning the room, she realizes she is in a hospital and the silver-haired handsome Chinese man is a doctor and the three ladies are nurses. She can sense the nervousness and excitement in the body language of the medical staff in her room. The doctor points a small light at her eyes and asks her to follow it as it moves around. She tries to read his lips as he talks to her, but is unable to understand a word. The doctor then shows her a tablet with a written note: I figured you could not talk or hear, right? She nods by blinking. I'm Dr. Lin. Sound comes to her suddenly as she hears him faintly at first then in full. He then conducts a number of tests to evaluate her motor functions. Once he is satisfied that her motor skills are okay, he concludes she is physically able to discuss the tragedy.

"Mrs. Pesin, what brought you here was a terrorist attack. You were extremely lucky, as 14 people were killed a few steps behind you."

She gasps in disbelief as tears start running down her face.

"Now, Mrs. Pesin, we have been waiting for you to wake up. The police need your help to identify the perpetrators. It is my understanding that you ran into one of them."

Dr. Lin leaves the room for a few minutes and then returns with a couple of detectives.

"Mrs. Pesin, how are you feeling?" asked the shorter of the two.

She makes a waving gesture with her head that translates to so-so.

Both detectives make a quick conclusion she is not a suspect. Her body language and the fear and sadness in her eyes tell them she is an innocent victim.

"Mrs. Pesin, several witnesses have stated that you were knocked down by an individual that you crashed into."

"Yes, I was being robbed," she mouths in anger realizing and surprised that she has now spoken as well.

"We know about that, too. We got your would-be robber that same day. What about the good Samaritan that saved you, were you able to see his face?"

If she understands him correctly, he seems to be asking about the attempted robbery. She drifts back in time to the moment of the robbery. She makes some jerky motions as she remembers.

"Mrs. Pesin, are you all right?"

Arlene nods her head yes.

"Do you remember the face?"

She mouths the word yes.

The answer apparently stuns the detectives and turns the whole investigation upside down.

Yes, a face that will cast a spell of love and danger on the young Island resident.

On the island of Cuba, a talented couple dreams about coming to America.

CHAPTER 42
THE ROJAS-LUGOS

" Life under a Communist system does not offer you many options, so people have to be creative. You take the very little you have, and then, you find as many ways as possible to turn it into what you need," states Juan Carlos Rojas.

"I don't know, Juan, it seems to me so much simpler. Money is unimportant because there is scarcely any to begin with. So all we do on this Island is drink, smoke, have lots of sex, study pointlessly and endlessly and work a little, very, very little, if any at all," replies Ana Julia Lugo.

Juan and Ana have known each other their entire lives, but have only been living together for six months. They are street performers during the weekends and during the week, they are members of a salsa band that plays at government-sponsored events, like award ceremonies, Communist party celebrations, post-military parade festivities, etc. It is 8:00 a.m. on a Sunday and the colonial-style narrow streets of "La Habana Vieja" are still empty. The rows of 'Spanish Colonial architecture' houses look decrepit, with broken roofs and walls swamped with humidity. Yet, from a healthy distance, the city's shining past can be easily imagined. Juan plays five different instruments. Ana is one of the best dancers in the country, but her most unappreciated talent is her voice. They work the tourist crowd because they get tips in hard currency. Their dream is to save enough to pay the smuggling fee to get into America. Both are 20 years old and they dream of a new life in America. Juan's plan has not deviated since he celebrated his twelfth birthday. That day, wearing a red Communist bandana and his school uniform, he had seen, while singing the revolutionary anthem, his teacher being dragged out of the classroom by the community watchdogs who handed him over to the government security forces. As far as Juan could tell, all the teacher did was to voice a complaint about the lack of food. He never saw his teacher again. Thereafter, he vowed to escape from Cuba. Ever since, he made it his mission to devise a plan and implement it.

Ana, on the other hand, had never wanted to leave the island. Recently, however, a powerful government official working directly for President Castro fell madly in love with her and started chasing, calling, inviting and proposing. When rejected outright, the Communist started intimidating and stalking her. He vowed to get her one way or the other. Shortly after, Juan was assaulted on the street by thugs that verbally issued a warning that if he did not stop seeing Ana, they would inflict permanent damage the next time they saw him. That scared Ana to her core and she is now desperate to join Juan and leave the island.

Their opportunity comes in the most unexpected fashion. On a Sunday morning, a small bus is unloading a group of far eastern tourists onto the main square. Juan and Ana unpack their bags and set up the mic and keyboard directly on the well-worn tourist path. Ana starts to dance, but, as always, she needs a partner, as salsa is not a singles' dance. The tourists approach and she picks a professor-type man to be her dance partner. She starts leading him, but he stumbles while trying to keep up with her pace. She can't understand what he says to her, so she simply smiles. The entire group of tourists are clapping and laughing at their friend. Her hips move at a fantastic pace. Her long and tight white dress, commonly used by flamenco dancers, is from Andalusia, Spain. Her long black hair is loose and adds to her sensual movements. She turns her back to the audience and her voice pierces the air with awesome power. Her Caribbean rhythm is now driven by the enhanced fury of the salsa beat. Juan and Ana work in perfect sync and after a 15-minute performance, they receive $75.00 in tips. Then as the group of tourists head into the heart of Old Havana, the bespectacled Chinese man that danced with Ana, stays behind.

"You are a very talented pair."

"Thank you," responds a puzzled Juan in broken English, while Ana bows her head in gratitude although understanding little to nothing.

"Your sound and energy are captivating."

This time they simply smile back.

"I'm Jerry Chen and I am a music producer. You have a unique style and sound that could be marketable. I would like to film you, if that is OK?"

Juan and Ana talk and argue for what seems an eternity. Mr. Chen stands by watching the fiery pair getting in each other's faces with loud, incomprehensible Spanish.

"Juan, don't you get it? He wants to steal our act and music. Chinese copy everything. You are stupid. That's your problem. You are always dreaming, but the reality is that we are stuck in this hell hole."

"Ana, Ana, calm down! What is he going to steal? There are street artists everywhere. Most of them don't make enough money to eat. To me we are as good as many, many others. But, we are lucky that he sees something special in us. Las oportunidades las pintan calvas, Ana! (don't judge a book by its cover)

She is looking at Juan like she wants to kill him, but in reality, as always, he has calmed her down, and her fears are dissipating. His calm and steady spirit always lifts her out of her well-grounded paranoia that in a Communist society, anyone and everyone can turn into an enemy in a fraction of a second.

Juan approaches Mr. Chen with glassy eyes and a broad smile. "It's all right, Sir."

And so begins the story of one of the most successful careers in Caribbean Latin music - an unlikely encounter with a music producer working out of Los Angeles and Singapore with a talented couple sparks greatness. She is the star with the rhythm, energy, moves, stage presence and extraordinary voice. He is the savvy brain with flawless judgment. But, their path to stardom is to take a topsy-turvy road through life before they reach the shores of the United States and, eventually, Paradise Island.

Another future Island resident continues to get closer and closer to realizing her dream through hard work, sheer talent and a huge and loyal client base. But she is going to run into unexpected bumps on the road, closer to home, that she would have never imagined.

CHAPTER 43
THE JOHANNSENS
(Elizabeth Rawlings and Jasper Johannsen)

The ride has been quite bumpy since they entered the Rocky Mountain range and hit clear air turbulence. The Lear-60 is flying at 42,000 feet with head winds of 120 mph. Elizabeth Rawlings is still sound asleep as the jet starts its descent into the Steamboat Airport. It is only when the wheels touch down that she begins to wake up. As she stretches and opens her eyes, she is offered a plate of fruit and a mint tea. By the time they park the airplane, she is ready. Her hair is in place, her makeup is on and her business suit is properly straightened. Then, as she walks down the aisle of the airplane, her longtime assistant hands her the waist-length vest and Elizabeth slides right into it. She is then handed her stiletto high heels and she proceeds down the short ladder with her shoes in hand. This is called by the media, "the Rawlings' grand entrance," as she always uses this technique of putting her impossible high heels on only when she steps onto the tarmac.

Elizabeth Rawlings is a motivational speaker. Her company, Rawlings' Media, grosses in excess of $20 million a year directly from her speeches, books, videos and online productions. The Rawlings'

Institute for Balanced Wellness' week-long retreats have a waiting list and her fledgling social media, the Rawlings' Portal, has over seven million subscribers.

Elizabeth Rawlings was born in Dayton, Ohio, 37 years ago. She has four siblings and grew up in a devout Presbyterian home with a stay-at-home mother and a father who worked in a factory. She was an outstanding student, which got her a scholarship to Wesley College in Boston and subsequently, a scholarship to MIT, where she got an MBA and PhD in computer science. Her career started at Goldman Sachs on Wall Street, where she was an investment banker for six years. During that stint, she found her true calling and launched her present career.

Her career has been a great success, but her personal life has been another story…and today, she will again find out that as much as she succeeds in business, her private life continues to unravel. She will shortly learn that the son of her longtime friend, Lars Johannsen, has unknowingly done something that will cause her great distress.

Island resident, world famous criminal attorney Oleg Krull, always gets his way with juries and the current trial seems to be another business as usual win about to happen. However, he has yet to learn that dangerous undercurrents are building up underneath his world.

CHAPTER 44
THE KRULLS
(The Trial Ends)

The jury foreman decides to take a preliminary vote before the deliberations begin. After all, they've been sequestered for 6 weeks, away from their families, friends, jobs, hobbies and food. He could go on and on and on. Everyone is irritated and tired. They all want to go home. 'So, why not,' he asks himself, 'why not?'

After all, it was as close to a slam dunk for the prosecution as it gets. So, if he could get a unanimous vote or close to it, then the deliberations could be a short affair and they could all be out of here today. 'Could we?' He rhetorically reassures himself. A vote is taken, 9-1 guilty. 'This is an excellent beginning,' the foreman tells himself enthusiastically. So the deliberations begin in earnest, but things do not turn out as expected. Midnight arrives and they are stuck and seem to be going backwards. The third vote has just been taken, 7-3 guilty. It's all due to juror Harrington. He keeps on raising reasonable doubt on every major point the prosecution raised in their closing argument. "How can you condemn a free man if there are reasonable doubts in every aspect of the case?" is Harrington's continuous argument. At first, the foreman is upset and despises the stubbornness of juror

Harrington. He internally labels him as soft, weak on crime, willing to let a guilty man walk free. He is holding everyone hostage to get his way, but as the hours go by, he starts to listen more and more to his arguments and slowly a solid level of respect starts to build.

So he dives right into the process, 'All right, let's debate every issue on our own and get to the bottom of the case and we will persuade everyone to do the right thing.' That was three days ago and now, with the last vote 5 guilty – 5 not guilty, he is facing the stern stare of the Federal Judge and has to explain that they are deadlocked and need more time. He also reassures the Judge that everyone on the jury has behaved in an exemplary manner and everyone is totally involved in the deliberations. The Judge consents and also agrees to respond to all the questions and provide the trial transcripts requested by the jury.

After the jury retires again to deliberate, the prosecution is panicked. Mr. Krull, on the other hand, is very optimistic, as he knows that the cat is almost in the bag and everything is going according to plan.

Twenty-four hours later, at 9:00 a.m., Harrington gives one more impassioned speech; "I will never condemn another human being, as I would never wish to be condemned myself if there is even the slightest shadow of a doubt, and here we have at least a dozen. I hope everyone will follow me and vote not guilty. My vote is not for innocence, as of that I am not certain, no, my vote is that under the law he is not guilty." And that breaks the camel's back as everyone nods and soon after, the 12-0 not guilty vote confirms it.

"How does the jury find the defendant?"

"Not guilty!"

So, it goes for all counts. Oleg Krull bear hugs his scoundrel client.

"You S.O.B., you just got a bust out of jail free card!"

"Not free, Krull, that's why I pay you the big bucks."

Krull looks at the jury and all he sees are faces that just want to go home. 'Yep, that's why they pay me the big bucks,' he thinks with a faint chuckle and smile.

In the meantime, the prosecution team and a couple of FBI agents are not missing one bit of the body language of the jury members or the defense team. 'What the hell happened here?' thinks the prosecutor. As if reading his mind, an FBI agent tells him "everything checks out sir, we don't see anything improper here."

But the end of this trial marks the end of Krull's seemingly unstoppable ascension in his legal career and the beginning of a nightmare, all caused by his long-time jury busting protocol being breached by Oquendo and the revenge on Oquendo by his future brother-in-law.

Island resident, neurosurgeon Richard Greenhouse's oldest daughter, Sarah, is engaged to childhood neighbor, Steve Mizrahi, heir to the largest cruise ship line in the world. Dr. Greenhouse's middle daughter, Lindsey, is a precocious free spirit artist and a source of pride and concern to her parents.

CHAPTER 45
THE GREENHOUSE FAMILY
(Lindsey)

Lindsey Greenhouse is an activist. Her motto is to be against anything and everything. You name it, she is against it. The only time she is not feisty and contentious is when it is about the Greenhouse not-for-profit clinic in Port-au-Prince, Haiti. Ever since she was a child, her father has taken her on 10-day stints, to help him man the clinic overflow of patients that flock to it every time Dr. Greenhouse is in residence. It is her father's altruistic and giving nature that fuels her activist lifestyle. Her father's famous question is, "for your life to have any meaning you have to ask yourself the following question: what have you done today for others in need without truly expecting anything in return?" Over the years he has asked her that same question again and again and he often follows it up with, "and it is not about writing checks to appease your conscience and get a tax break, it is about what you have done or are going to do and what effort or sweat you have made to help others, or are you going to be another one of those ungrateful, egotistical miserable human beings who live every day just for themselves?"

That is how she and her siblings have been raised, giving to others in the form of real work and effort. And these values are part of them as they have been ingrained in them. But, what is really special about the eighteen-year old is that, Lynn, as she is affectionately known to all, has a large following. She provides her followers with the things that they like or crave, and then she lures them into causes she advocates. It is a give and take deal and it works. As of late, her live podcast on the Meerkat and Periscope apps have attracted more than 12 million viewers.

"We are live at the entrance of Club "Blue" on Ocean Drive, Miami Beach, Florida. Sources tell us that Brad Pitt and an unknown companion are in the club. We are staying put until he comes out and perhaps we can extract a few words from him," states Lynn. On this Friday night, Lynn has live video feeds from trendy locations where celebrities are supposed to be. The public loves the suspense and the wait. So, the broadcast goes on and on and, to keep it more interesting, Lynn endlessly adds trivial information about the personal lives of the celebrities. But, it is all choreographed and scripted with the agents and managers of the famous personalities. And, thanks to her massive audiences, her stunts have become part of the celebrities' PR campaigns to simply bring awareness to themselves or to promote a film, a record or a tour. Thus, a huge market has been created from the elaborate "Lynn's Hunt." She is paid handsomely by her "preys" to be, figuratively speaking, "hunted". Hence, she always knows where the celebrities are going to be as they go about their normal routines. She just waits while building up the supposed uncertainty with her audience. For example, getting celebrities while jogging or cycling is one of her audience's favorites. Lynn approaches the celebrities and runs or jogs alongside them. She then interviews them on the spot and according to the comfort level of the conversations, the dialogue goes on and on. It is just a simple marketing ploy in disguise.

"I am here on assignment. I am told he is coming out in a few minutes, stay tuned, don't leave. A live encounter with Brad Pitt is just moments away."

Her breakthrough technique to multiply the suspense has her two other assistants broadcasting live from different locations throughout the city. Lynn then does the narration and the live video feed from wherever she happens to be.

"There he is!! Let me approach him to see if he will give us an interview." Lynn is being filmed as she makes her way through the crowd.

"Brad." He does not pay attention, but she insists.

"Brad, it's Lynn." He then turns around and flashes a big smile.

"Are you following me and hunting me down?"

"Well, you have millions of fans that are waiting to hear from you."

Throughout the web "the buzz" of the encounter goes viral within seconds.

Lynn gets an instant notification on her watch and immediately closes both eyes as she is speaking to Brad. He understands her signal and realizes that the encounter has gone live and is being viewed by millions of people.

"Lynn, I love what you do, care to join us in my limo, then we can find a spot to have a nice chat?"

"Fantastic! I know a place, we can walk along the beach on the boardwalk."

"That's great!"

That night Lynn completes three interviews and her compensation for all of the interviews is $50,000. She first posts the videos on her website and on YouTube. She then posts excerpts on Instagram,

Facebook and Snapchat. For these postings, she earns another $25,000. Not bad for a night's work for an eighteen-year-old.

The next day she has three live video feeds from the back alleys of three of the most famous restaurants in Miami. Standing with her are a couple of food and environmental experts to help her build up the argument on a social cause. Her goal is to show with live images the vast amounts of food thrown away by each of the restaurants every day. She will then contrast that with the many people in the city that are hungry. The experts and she will then quantify the number of homeless people in the City of Miami and Miami Beach living below the poverty level.

She and the experts carry on a live conversation, "The City of Miami has one of the lowest numbers of homeless people of any city in America."

"Why?" asks Lynn.

"Its two homeless centers, Camillus House and Chapman Partnership, do a phenomenal job in bringing people off the street and introducing them back into society."

"What about the hungry?"

"That's a more complex problem. There is hunger around the Miami area like there is across America. It is not widespread, but it is here. People and the media just simply don't like to talk about it."

"Why?"

"It is an uncomfortable and embarrassing problem, especially hungry children."

"So, why don't we, as a society, do more about it?"

"For a host of reasons, including lack of awareness, red tape and regulations."

At that moment, the back delivery door of one of the trendy restaurants opens up and three employees proceed to dump cartload after cartload of food into the garbage dumpsters. Everything is filmed in detail. Several of the customers in the restaurant get the live video feed as they are having dinner and come around back to scope out the situation. Then, one of the owners of the restaurant takes notice and asks one of the diners if there is "breaking news." The diner says that it is a live video feed on the internet. Both the diner and the owner look at the video feed, "fancy Miami restaurants dumping food that could otherwise be donated to the hungry."

The owner watches in horror as he recognizes the back alley of his own place. But, he has to maintain the charade.

"How do they know all that?"

"Lynn Greenhouse, who is broadcasting the video feed, has experts with her."

"Who is she?"

"Lynn Greenhouse of The Lynn's Hunt Show, an internet sensation."

"Does she have an audience?"

"More than twelve million nationwide."

The owner's heart sinks and he just wants to disappear.

At the end of her broadcast, Lindsey reveals the name of the restaurant to her massive audience. All this is watched by the restaurant owner, and Lynn Greenhouse becomes his newly sworn enemy.

MR. AND MRS. GREENHOUSE – LINDSEY'S PARENTS

The Greenhouse home is perhaps the most modest home on Paradise Island. This is the only place in South Florida where Leonore Greenhouse wanted to live, so this is where Dr. Richard Greenhouse bought their home. She is ambitious. He is not. She loves the limelight and the Miami social life. He hates it with a passion. She cares a great deal about how much money they have. He couldn't care less. She is strict, organized and a neat freak. He is the total opposite. She uses harsh words and is quick to criticize. He hardly speaks. Therefore, to see them in public is a study in contrast. Her blonde short hair is neatly combed. Her intense and stern blue eyes frame a small beautiful face. She is always perfectly dressed and has the proper attire for each occasion. He always has an unbuttoned shirt and half of it always hanging out of his pants. He has a noticeable potbelly and his hair is uncombed and grey. He has a hunchback developed from countless hours of doing what he loves. He wears half-rimmed glasses on the tip of his nose that make him look like a humble mad scientist. When he talks to you he always seems distracted with his eyes darting from right to left and then left to right. He is seemingly absentminded all the time.

The Greenhouses live well above their means. Even though he is a renowned neurosurgeon, one of the best in the country, he is a terrible businessman. The life and passion of Dr. Greenhouse can be clearly understood through his family history. Some of the roots of his family lie in post-World War II Russia, in the magnificent City of St. Petersburg, and some in the cornfields of a small town in Iowa.

Island resident/corrupt lobbyist, Bart Holstein, and the cruise line owner's, the Mizrahi family are linked, they just don't know it yet. The connection goes back several decades to the Middle East. Their original last names were not even the same. The Holstein's original last name was Alalu and the Mizrahi's original last name was Mazon.

CHAPTER 46
THE HOLSTEINS AND THE MIZRAHIS
(Part I)

Eladio Alalu was a lady's man. He was also a Sephardic Jew born in the Spanish Sahara, but grown and raised in the streets of Beirut, Lebanon. Alvi Mazon, his business partner, was a very shy man when it came to women. Alvi was also a Sephardic Jew, but born and raised in Istanbul, Turkey. Each man learned to survive on his own, as both of their home countries were predominately Arab and Muslim. Alalu and Mazon would eventually drift apart. One would end up in Cuba and the other in America via Israel. Decades later, their descendants would wind up living next to each other as neighbors on Paradise Island.

Alalu and Mazon were also smugglers and the best in town. After World War II, Beirut lifestyle, culture, art, entertainment and its beach resorts earned it the title of 'the Paris and the Riviera of the Middle East.' They specialized in the finest of everything the world had to offer. Whether it was Cuban cigars, the finest whiskeys, wines and spirits, the finest designer shoes, scarfs and handbags or the finest chocolates, sweets, orchids, roses, strawberries, cheeses, hams, you name it, Alalu and Mazon would get the items through customs, tax free, to be sold to their customers.

It had been the big and physically round, Rocky Shapiro, who had initiated the boys into the smuggling trade. With diamond rings on too many fingers and thick gold bracelets and neck chains, Rocky was flamboyant and charismatic and he reigned as the Beirut smugglers' czar. He reigned until he dropped dead of a stroke in a side street coffee shop while smoking a hooka. But, before he died, he introduced to his imminent successors, Alalu and Mazon, the two ladies that would become their life journey companions and the mothers of their children.

One of the girls, Andrea Holstein, although only 17 years old, was ready for marriage. She had been groomed and educated since childhood that her mission in life was to marry whoever her parents chose for a husband and to procreate as many children as her husband wanted. At 5'8", she was a tall woman for a Jew. She wore her curly black hair flowing down the back of her neck. Her piercing green eyes were her most distinctive feature. They were big, wide and seemed happy most of the time. She was razor thin, but with firm and round breasts and an upright derriere. She spoke Arabic, Spanish, English, Ladino and Hebrew. Andrea had a secret wild side. She was a pretty accomplished amateur singer and performed, without her parents' knowledge, in night clubs in the city center. Her stage name was Isabel Souki and her popularity kept rising. Andrea also loved raw uninhibited sex. Active since she was 15 years old, Andrea had sex almost every day.

Eladio Alalu spotted Andrea singing at an early afternoon gig at a club. He promised himself he would return the next day, but that wasn't necessary, as that night he was in for the surprise of his life when his boss and mentor, Rocky Shapiro, introduced him to the Holstein family as a possible suitor for their oldest daughter.

When he saw her coming down the stairs to greet Rocky and himself, he was smitten in an instant, followed by being amused and intrigued. Her eyes obviously recognized him. 'How could she have? There was a big audience at the club.' At first her eyes denoted fear, but that quickly dissipated when he made an imperceptible, except to the two of them, reassuring move. He requested that her parents let him talk to her alone. This was unusual in a first meet situation, but they happily agreed. Eladio and Andrea walked out and into the privacy of the family room.

"Oh, my God, I'm a nervous wreck," said Andrea.

"Relax, you are safe with me." Eladio then took a step forward and hugged her. But, no sooner had he hugged her when she kissed him hard. He was instantly aroused and she noticed. He felt her hand rubbing his pants. She quickly unzipped his pants and pressed her body tightly against his, then suddenly took a little hop backwards and sat on a small armoire. She grabbed his arms to pull him towards her. Her legs then encircled his torso and pulled him even closer. With a little hop back she penetrated herself with all of him by a gravity thrust. They both gasped with intense pleasure. She was now suspended in air by his penetration with her arms around his shoulders. He then slammed her against the nearest wall and once he had her pinned down, he started thrusting in and out with increased intensity until both climaxed.

"You weren't wearing anything underneath your skirt."

"Yep."

"So you intended to fuck the suitor?"

"Only if I liked him enough."

Just as they had their clothes back in place, her father peeked into the room.

"How's everything?"

"Wonderful, Dad," she replied.

Her father showed a bit of surprise. "That's new, Andrea," he said with a smile. He left the room and started delivering the good news around the house.

"What was that all about?"

"Dad introduced 12 other guys to me and I rejected them all."

"No sex test!"

"Yes, with a couple, but disappointing!"

"Not afraid of being caught?"

"No, they always come back 15 to 20 minutes later to check."

"Didn't we take longer?"

"Nope, we only took 7 minutes."

"Only?"

"Yeah, but it was some of the most intense sex I've ever had."

"So, tell me about your singing career or is it a secret?"

"Yes, it is, but it's what I love to do. After classes and before curfew is the only time I have to do it."

"I think you are great. You have a wonderful voice. I particularly love the way you sing 'la maladie d'amour'.

"Thanks!"

"What's this habit of you not wearing panties?"

"What about it?" she replies defiantly.

"Is that all the time?"

"That's none of your business," she replies angrily.

He looks at her for quite a while without saying a word. He breaks the silence with, "I want to marry you!"

She jumped into his arms, clinging to his neck and says, "I want to marry you as well."

Then, they softly kissed for what seemed an eternity.

"I promise I'll wear panties from now on, but only if you make love to me every day."

"Your wishes are orders to me. I will happily comply. I grew up with all these stories about how hot Jewish girls are. Today, I have experienced this for myself."

As Eladio Alalu left, Andrea Holstein felt satisfied for the first time since she lost her virginity.

CHAPTER 47
The Holsteins
and The Mizrahis (Part II)

Three months after he asked Andrea's father for his blessing to marry his daughter, Eladio and Andrea were married by Rabbi Israel Shamal, a fellow smuggler himself, but only of precious metals and jewels. But Andrea's ways did not change, neither her habit of not wearing panties nor her unstoppable promiscuity and insatiable libido, all of which will eventually bring great tragedy to her life.

Before his death, Rocky Shapiro was also the matchmaker for Eladio's smuggler companion, Alvi Mazon. For years, Rocky had hired and used the Mizrahi family's cargo boats to smuggle contraband goods.

Leon Mizrahi was a burly man with thick curly white hair. His skin was cracked and wrinkled by his excessive exposure to the sun. His deep blue eyes were plagued with cataracts. He had swollen ankles from bad blood circulation. He suffered from hypertension and dizzy spells. At 65, Leon did not have long to live and he knew it. But, as the owner and operator of a fleet of small cargo boats, operating mainly between Europe and Lebanon, he was trapped in a 120-hour work week. A widower, Leon had raised 5 daughters and 4 of them were already married. But, so far, none of his sons-in-law had proven adept enough to take over the business. That's why when Rocky Shapiro brought over Alvi Mazon to meet his unmarried daughter, Leon was hopeful for a match. Leon knew of Alvi's skills, work ethics and tenacity as he was a long-time customer. Finally, a worthy successor. The problem, though, was that his 18-year-old daughter, Eleanor Mizrahi, did not seem to be interested in Alvi at all. For over 2 years, she had been involved in an intimate and secret relationship with a much older man. She loved him deeply, but the relationship was doomed. He was not only much older, but was a Muslim and was married. She lived each day counting the hours until their next encounter. Eleanor Mizrahi was hopelessly in love with Mohamed Masarih, father of 8 and husband of 3. He was her lover, friend and mentor. When they were together, she felt that she was the center of his universe. So it came as no surprise that when her father announced the visit of Rocky Shapiro with a potential suitor, willing to ask for her hand, she showed no interest and pretended to ignore her father.

When Alvi first saw her, he was moonstruck. Eleanor had long curly hair, hazelnut eyes, strong jaw and a Hellenic nose. But it was her poise that got to his core. She was serene, calm and confident beyond her years and when she stared at him, he melted inside. Even though it was not a friendly stare, it did not matter to him. It was what and how he felt that mattered to him. Even against her will, they were left alone to get acquainted with each other.

'What is this brute thug thinking? That I am one of the prostitutes he hangs around with on his trips. A piece of property to be bought. You've been looking at my tits and ass for 5 minutes,' thought Eleanor, as she suddenly stood up and ran to the bathroom. After 10 minutes or so, Alvi went to check on her.

She tried to pull herself together. She was so disgusted with her father for trying to set her up with a marriage she did not want. But, she was even angrier with herself. From the moment Alvi Mazon had laid his eyes on her, she was smitten against her will. His physical presence alone made her shiver, as she had never been that close to someone that strong and handsome. She could not control herself, she had literally lost it and was devouring him with her eyes, when he caught her.

"Eleanor, are you okay?" asked Alvi through the door. "I don't bite."

"Go away, you embarrass me."

"No, no, no! You were the one who made me feel like a roasted turkey waiting to be eaten."

An uncomfortable silence ensued and continued to linger on until...

"Hello, knock, knock!"

Then, suddenly the bathroom door opened slightly without any sound. It took a few seconds for Alvi to get it. But, when he entered there was nothing that could have stopped him and she was ready, willing and able. Their wedding took place 6 months later, and Eleanor's pregnancy only increased and further provoked the sworn vow of revenge by a very angry abandoned Arab.

Two of the most prominent families on Paradise Island originated from the two smugglers operating out of Beirut, Lebanon.

Storm clouds are forming in the horizon for Island resident and corrupt lobbyist, Bart Holstein. The upcoming visit by the former president seems to be the moment when both of them may fall...

CHAPTER 48
BART HOLSTEIN
(Unofficial FBI Investigation)

"" We have learned that three weeks from now the former President will be in town for several fundraisers."

"Ramp up the surveillance on the pimp, then."

"What about the minor?"

"We know they had a minor that night at the Holstein mansion on Paradise Island, but we learned about it after the fact, so we don't know who she is as of today."

"We'll get him this time around."

"Not that easy, surveillance video from that evening does not show any females entering the mansion."

"We are assuming they came by boat."

"This time we'll have video cameras pointed at the dock."

"All right then, lets discuss the Holstein/airport case."

"OK, I have the file right here." He pulled out the file entitled; 'FBI investigation on MIA International Airport violations against minority participants.'

"Mrs. Kennedy's revelations have created a cascade of similar complaints against lobbyist Holstein."

"Up until now, 11 different minority individuals have stated and provided written proof of the side agreements wherein Mr. Holstein was granted up to 80% of their benefits. So, instead of being an owner, he makes them grant him an economic interest in the airport concessions," states the FBI lead investigator.

"Fine, keep me updated."

As his team leaves, special agent Neil Green receives a phone call from one of his supervisors.

"Neil, step down from the Holstein investigation. That's an order!"

"Understood, who will replace me? And what about my team working in the field on this one?"

"No one will replace you. Recall your agents. This matter is dead."

"But there is a mountain of evidence against this guy…"

"Neil, do as you are told, now!"

"Yes, Sir!"

Ten minutes later, Special FBI agent Green has his team back in the office and informs them about the order he got. Then, as the dejected team leaves, each of his three agents receives a folded note. When they read it afterwards it states: "Continue the probe off-the-record. We'll nail this bastard irrespective of his powerful friends protecting him. We'll meet at our homes to update each other. Let's get it done."

This time around not even Bart Holstein's powerful connections are able to stop the investigation.

Island resident, old crow club member, Elizabeth Bell, and her husband are the descendants of two World War II ace pilots. His was an American air squadron commander and hers was a member of the German Luftwaffe.

CHAPTER 49
THE BELLS
(Part I)

J ohn Michael Bell was born to fly. Since childhood, he had read it all, from the Wright Brothers to the Red Baron, Amelia Earhart and Charles Lindbergh. He had grown up on books dealing with aerodynamics and airplane engines. By the start of World War II, even though Bell was barely out of his teens, he had more than six years of experience flying gliders. He enlisted in the Army Air Corps the same week the U.S. entered the war. By the end of the war, he had made it all the way to the rank of Squadron Commander. He was the leader of a couple dozen air fortresses that carpet bombed Germany on a daily basis. He had seen it all!! Death, destruction, narrow escapes, heroism, broken hearts and finally, victory.

Each mission was hell. There was anti-aircraft gunfire coming in at multiple angles that shook the plane to its core. The German Luftwaffe planes were lurking and firing constantly during each mission. He had lost seven crew members to mid-air gunfire, but he had not even been personally grazed by a bullet. Even though emotionally and physically drained from this last mission, he managed to land safely back at the base in Southern England with just a couple of engines left out of four. The fuselage and turrets were riddled with bullets. Even though he had commanded more than 50 missions over Germany, Commander Bell had never been shot down.

Finally, the Allied victory was announced. He celebrated at the base with thousands of other soldiers, officers and airmen. He believed that he was going home to Kansas. That's why when the base commander announced that there was one more mission to run, he felt terrified. Commander Bell felt compelled to break the ice and step forward and ask, "I thought it was over?"

"It is, this is a peace mission. There are no more active troops or air defenses in Germany. The Nazis have surrendered. The orders are to fly your entire squadron to the city of Linz, Austria, where you will pick up 200 French prisoners of war that have been liberated by the allied Russian forces. You are to fly them to the Le Bourget airport in Paris for a hero's welcome. Your planes are already being prepped and refueled. Your ETD is within the hour.

It was Sunday. There wasn't a cloud in the sky. The crystal blue sky contrasted beautifully with the green landscapes beneath the deafening noise of the four engines. The power and intensity of the plane and its engines was a faint distraction to the eerie silence and calmness of the skies. 'Is this what peace feels like?' thought Commander Bell.

As they entered Austria at low altitude and flew over the Danube River, Bell saw life going back to normal and groups of people by the riverside having picnics, swimming and cavorting in small sailing and rowing boats. He thought that this proved that the war had really ended. But, there was one more mission to complete. Shortly thereafter, they landed in the small industrial town of Linz, not far from Vienna. 'Finally down,' thought Bell.

The U.S. Army local liaison introduced the parties, "General Asimov, this is Commander Bell, U.S. Air Force."

"Commander, you have 200 Frenchmen in a general state of malnutrition, but otherwise without any life threatening conditions. Fourteen of them are wounded. One of the wounded is a General who is on a stretcher," said the Russian General through a translator.

"Thank you, General. We will take good care of them and leave immediately. It is my understanding that there are airmen among the French contingent. I would like you to pick one of them to serve as my co-pilot on the trip back."

"I am sure they would be honored, Sir."

"I will also fly the General on my plane."

Commander Bell was sitting in place ready to start the engines when a French airman entered the cabin and quickly sat next to him. As Bell turned to introduce himself, he was rendered speechless. He looked into the eyes of his copilot and was immediately struck by her beauty and sexuality. She was stunning, but obviously rough and tough. She had dark black hair and intense blue eyes. She looked and smelled like she had just come out of the jungle.

"Commander Bell, I am Captain Catherine Claudel."

"Nice to meet you. Your English is flawless."

"Since I was a child, I have studied at the International School at its various locations throughout the world."

"How come?"

"My parents are diplomats."

He was so excited. The attraction was so intense that it was hard to even keep a steady conversation or tone of voice.

"Commander Bell, General Morreau has been brought on board."

He stood up to let Captain Claudel out of the cabin and he followed. The General was laying on a canvas stretcher and seemed to be under heavy sedation. The brief conversation with him yielded the assurance that the General was aware that he was going home.

"His French seemed a bit different, where is he from Captain?" asked Bell.

"He is from Strasbourg, in Alsace, a small region sandwiched between Germany and France."

"Oh, I see."

Then, as they flew back home, Commander Bell communicated with his staff to inquire which side of the aircraft the General was lying in. He then ordered the formation to hold course as he banked left leaving the squadron. Minutes later, as they flew over Strasbourg's city center and the main square highlighted by the cathedral, Bell lowered the right wing of the plane so the General could see his home city. Then, Bell made a sweeping arch so the General could take a long look at the whole city. He then sped ahead and rejoined the squadron. Two hours later they made a soft landing and returned the 200 French Nationals home to a hero's welcome. Later on, Commander Bell's great gesture to the General and the safe return of the French nationals earned him the French Foreign Legion Medal of Honor. But the greatest gift of all was the love story between Colonel Bell and Captain Claudel. After three years of romance jockeyed between the U.S. and France, they married and raised three kids. Throughout the post war, the couple and their kids shuttled back and forth between the two countries. As both integrated into each other's cultures, they were never able to live in just one of the countries. To no one's great surprise, the eldest Bell son succeeded beyond the family's wildest expectations by amassing a fortune through a startup company that became a Fortune 500 enterprise. Bell's son became a billionaire and predictably eventually resided on one of the most expensive pieces of residential property in the country, Paradise Island.

CHAPTER 50
THE BELLS (PART II)
(Ernesto Otto Heindrich)

An endless sea of green surrounded him. He had been flying for nearly two hours in a southeasterly direction. 'How magnificent and unspoiled our planet is,' thought the pilot who was totally absorbed by the views. Then he saw the tepui and knew he was about to arrive. Even after so many flights, these tabletop mesas with jungles at the top never ceased to amaze him.

THE TEPUI

The piper Aztec banked right and came straight at the tepui making a pass just above the tree tops. The Yanomami Indians knew what to do and had their machetes in hand as they ran into the small treeless bush. Twenty of them started to frantically clear the way for their visitor. Ten minutes later, they had cut all the knee-high vegetation to less than ankle height. Then, they started waiving.

Ernesto Otto Heindrich loved to fly into the heart of the Amazon and bring food, medicine and books to the Yanomami Indians. He approached the improvised runway with Teutonic precision.

He stuck the landing on the makeshift runway for the 90th time. He braked hard as the plane bounced on the uneven terrain. He had been making this trip from his home base of Caracas for over 25 years.

"Don Ernesto, bienvenido a casa," (welcome home) said the Chief of the tribe.

"El placer es todo mio, jefe," (the pleasure is mine) replied the delighted aviator.

At 6'3", the 45-year old Venezuelan aviator was also a German national by virtue of his parents' lineage. As he was still sitting in the cockpit and in this serene surroundings, he reminisced about how he had discovered flying.

25 Years Earlier

Originally from the Maracaibo oil field region of Venezuela, Ernesto Otto grew up in an oil camp, as both his parents worked in the oil fields. His mom was an accountant and his dad was a manager of two dozen oil rigs. In spite of the war raging in Europe, his parents started planning his German high school studies when he was just 10 years old. In typical Teutonic fashion, this occurred two years before he was scheduled to finish his elementary school. So, in July of 1940, at the tender age of 12, Ernesto Otto Heindrich boarded a cruise ship at the port of La Guaira and headed straight to Hamburg, Germany. He stayed with his two aunts and started high school that September. His adaptation and assimilation had been difficult for him. Ernesto Otto may have looked German on the outside, but he was Latin on the inside. He became a loner and isolated from the German children his age. He would go on long walks along the Elbe River imagining that he was on Lake Maracaibo where he was born and raised. On one of these long lonely walks he found his calling. He heard a swish of air and instinctively looked up but saw nothing. As he continued to walk along the banks of the river, the landscape cleared into an open green field. This time he heard it coming. A faint sound cutting through the wind. Then, it hovered right over him and he bent down and covered his head. It had huge thin wings and an impossible narrow white body with little aerodynamic sound. As he looked in the distance, the soundless flying object suddenly plunged down. Ernesto gasped, 'it is going to crash!' However, the flying object banked and immediately made a leveling maneuver at ground level for a smooth landing. Young Ernesto walked briskly on to the glider field and right away felt right at home. From that day on, he would come back and observe, take notes and eventually start to mingle with the pilots and crew. In time, he became the mascot of the Hamburg Gliders Club. This new pursuit was far more interesting than school. For starters, several of the pilots were World War I aces and several of them had flown next to the German legend, "The Red Baron."

A couple of years later, when he was 14 years old, Ernesto flew his first glider solo. He had already logged hundreds of hours as a co-pilot. On his solo flight, he circled Hamburg for what seemed an eternity. He was able to catch a nice set of summer hot air jet streams that kept him in the air for 40 more minutes than he had planned. So it came as no surprise, when at the age of 16, Ernesto Otto Heindrich was recruited into Hitler's failing military. The young ace joined the German Luftwaffe in what was already a lost war for Deutschland. He should have known, but he didn't, that Hitler's war was in decline when young teenagers were brought to replenish the Luftwaffe because there were not enough grown men for service. There were heavy losses occurring in all flanks of delirious Hitler's doomed invasion of Russia. Young Heindrich started flying combat missions as a co-pilot. Six months later, he became a full-fledged pilot. However, his first solo flight was his last, as all future operations were halted after this one mission. There were simply no more supplies, not enough fuel, no spare parts, no food and no ammunition. The German Reich was collapsing and the young 16-year old was right in the middle of it, as he was stationed at an airbase deep into Polish territory. Two days after all flights were halted, young Ernesto Otto saw a macabre procession of what remained of the German army as they marched back home through the outskirts of the base in a mixture of retreat and stampede. They were wounded, hungry and in panic mode from the brutality of the Russian armed forces. Once the macabre march went through, the airmen remained stuck without orders, without planes, without hope and just waiting for the worst. It did not take long.

Two days passed and then an entire division of Russian military rolled into town. Young Ernesto Otto was made a prisoner of war and incarcerated at a Russian concentration camp in Poland near the German border. What an irony and role reversal that Russia, one of the victors of World War II, would have concentration camps like their vanquished foe, Germany. However, the Russian camps were not like Auschwitz, Buchenwald and Dachau in that the Russian camps did respect human life and did not gas its prisoners.

Further irony was apparent when one American airman was flying home to Kansas as a Venezuelan-born young German ace was becoming a prisoner of war. Two life paths, both initiated by the love of flying and both having started at an early age piloting gliders; two life paths that would intersect later in life in another era and another place.

Along the way, their two young children will fall in love and eventually become Paradise Island residents.

Future Island resident, Elizabeth Rawlings, is about to experience the shock of her life.

CHAPTER 51
THE JOHANNSENS
(Elizabeth Rawlings & Jasper Johannsen)

Today, Elizabeth Rawlings is fulfilling a lifelong dream and buying herself a hotel on South Beach's Ocean Drive. It is a blue pastel, 5-story, historical landmark. The closing is set for 2:00 p.m. In the morning, she has business to attend to and at noon she'll have lunch with her old friend, Lars Johannsen at his mansion, Paradise Island #7. It is a special occasion, as he wants to introduce her to his fiancée, the young American tennis phenomenon, Gabrielle Lareau. Knowing Lars for so long, she knows he is seeking her seal of approval, and he gets it.

"Wonderful girl, my friend, I am happy for you."

"Your opinion is so important to me Elizabeth, thank you."

"Word of advice though, work on Jasper. He does not seem happy at all with your choice. I love your boy dearly and had a chat with him, but this is a father and son matter."

"All right, copied loud and clear."

At 2:00 p.m. the great moment has arrived and she is surrounded by attorneys eager to conclude the unusual real estate closing.

"Mrs. Rawlings, I've been practicing for over 25 years and must confess, this is my first…"

"Not for me, this is the second property that I have bought in this way."

"All right then, let's get the trading averages of Bitcoin and Ethereum for the last seven days. Let's sign all the documents and put them in escrow and once the confirmation is received that the cyber currency is in the name of my client, the document escrow will end."

Elizabeth Rawlings is deliberately converting her holdings in cyber currency into hard assets after having realized a gain of nearly 20 times on her initial investment. Her offer to pay in Bitcoin and Ethereum was at first rejected, but subsequently accepted by the seller.

"All documents are signed. Mrs. Rawlings, proceed to transfer the agreed amount of coins into the seller's accounts at coin desk."

Elizabeth quickly accesses her encrypted computer and searches for her digital wallets. She panics when she can't find them, then after 3 searches she screams out, "Can't close now, my digital wallets have disappeared!"

Future Island resident, Elizabeth Rawlings, will soon learn that what happened to her hits closer to home than she would have ever imagined.

In the great state of California, a pair of future Island residents are about to meet and begin a relationship that will be filled with passion, love, and secrets.

CHAPTER 52
THE CRAWFORDS

At 5'8", Susan Garland is a sea of contradictions. On one side, she is a voracious reader and at 20-years old, she is on her tenth year of piano lessons and her third year of concert performances. She is mid-way through a degree in Computer Sciences at Cal Tech and in contention to be class valedictorian. She is the captain of the Cal Tech swim team and a NCAA champion. On the other side, she is sexually insatiable. She has four different lovers and on certain days she may have sex with more than one of them. Greg, at 21, is an All American running back, her school mate sex toy and available at any time and close by. Dennis, at 47, is a married teacher in the engineering school and available three days a week, only in the afternoon after class before he goes home. But, he compensates as he is the best and most experienced lover she has ever had. Then, there is Judy, at 25, a dancer and stripper at the Gold Club, the best and most exclusive club in town. For Susan, Judy is a different world of self-discovery and a tenderness she misses from men. They met at a grocery store. Judy relentlessly pursued Susan for a couple of months until she consented. This led to a new world of sexual experimentation. Then, there is Lebron, at 25, a Harvard graduate and a junior attorney at a prestigious law firm. He is full of testosterone and raw energy. Lebron gives her a roughness she has learned to crave, but it is his size and hardness that has become the main reason for her secret preference for black men.

Sue's parents, Sara and Todd Garland, have been happily married for 25 years. Her mom is a West Point graduate and served in the Army for 30 years, retiring with a rank of Colonel. She now works for a think tank that focuses on the defense of conservative values, which is an unusual job for Sara, and puzzling in that she is radicalized. Her dad was a major league player for the Los Angeles Dodgers and played for them for 18 years. He is now a coach for their AAA team. Both her parents travel all year round. Upon closer examination, it is easy to conclude that Susan's sexual appetites have a genetic root. Her parents have an "open marriage" and when they are on the road both freely engage in casual sex with anyone they want to. Her parents have some tacit rules, like not getting into personal relationships and not sharing any aspects of their private lives with any of their other sexual partners.

How does Susan know all of this? Her mom has told her everything since she was 15. Every time mom comes home from a trip, she dumps everything on her daughter. Her mom believes that a women's sexual life is one of her treasures. So, since an early age, she has taught Susan every technique and every way there is to enjoy and give pleasure while having sex. The routine is always the same. She first tells Susan who she slept with on her trip and then describes the quality of each encounter. Her mom also tells her what she learned if anything, what new things she experimented with and which of her partners satisfied her the most. Her mom recognizes that Susan is promiscuous, but cautions her that she shouldn't go to bed with someone she doesn't know at least a little bit. Most of mom's lovers have been from the military, but there have been plenty of civilians too. Because of her high libido, she prefers younger men and she likes them physically and intellectually fit. She prefers straight men, as in nothing kinky.

Susan is also totally open with her mom as well. Mom knows everything about her daughter's sexual life and is totally supportive. Mom believes that her daughter has found what makes her happy and that she enjoys sex as much as her.

Douglas Crawford is about to drop out of Cal Tech with only six months left to graduate. Part of him hesitates, but he doubts he can hold on any longer since he has a double life as an engineering student and an accidental entrepreneur. He is making a fortune from his startup business.

At 6'4", "Doug" is the top freestyler on the Cal Tech swimming team. As he steps out of the locker room on to the pool deck, short on time, he takes a couple of quick steps while mulling his predicament over. He is staring down at the deck as he moves quickly forward, lost in his thoughts. Then it happens. At the very last fraction of a second, a distracted female swimmer crashes into his mass of muscles. The wind is knocked out of her and she starts to stumble. His long arms reach out to her, he catches her and pulls her to him. She winds up in his arms tightly pressed against his chest. She feels dizzy and looks pale. She is groggy, but awake. He tenderly strokes her hair, "Are you all right?" She opens her eyes and nods in slow motion looking straight at him with eyes expressing intense desire. They are skin against skin and their faces are inches away from each other. Their accidental meeting has gone straight into flesh and desire. He feels a little embarrassed because he is getting sexually aroused. She stands back a bit in realization of his predicament.

He goes from embarrassed to shy, but as she tries to untangle herself, his arousal intensifies. When they realize their dilemma, he also tries to untangle. He sees a way out of it and leads the way. He literally lifts her up a little and still pressed against each other, they jump sideways into the pool. Their laughter can be heard throughout the pool area as they hit the water.

"You are the captain of the swim team, right? I am Susan, nice to meet you," and she kisses him right on the lips, a wet and effusive kiss. He reciprocates by letting his tongue caress hers at first and then by a slow and tender exploration under the water.

They slowly surface. "I am Douglas Crawford, where have you been all my life, Susan?" he asks with a look of out of control lust.

"I was just asking myself the same thing," she replies in sensual words as she presses harder against him.

They both look around and see that the pool deck is empty. His hand then reaches under water and soon she is panting and moaning. While staring at him with wild lust and fury, she strokes him with a tight grip and he groans with absolute pleasure. He leads her by the hand out of the pool and into the locker room. He pins her and lifts her against a locker and brings her into his arms. At that time and in that place, the insatiable Crawfords are born as both climax in loud thunderous unison. From then on, the wild pair become inseparable and cannot get enough of each other, day or night, both indoors and outdoors, at his place and her place.

Two weeks later Susan Garland's mom is worried sick. Susan confessed the previous night that she is hopelessly in love.

In the meantime, Douglas Crawford's monetary fortunes are about to skyrocket and will take him and Susan, in a very short time, to the select and small club of U.S. billionaires and a brand new residence on Paradise Island.

At a slow pace but always marching forward, future Island residents, the talented Cuban musicians, inch closer and closer to realizing their dream.

CHAPTER 53
THE ROJAS-LUGOS

I t's been six months since the letter arrived, but for Ana Lugo it seems like years. 'Juan is a dreamer, it is never going to happen. All we've got is $9,000 saved, we are stuck in hell.'

"325," Juan states proudly.

"325 what?" she snaps back.

"$325, not bad for three hours of work when most people do not make that in a year over here."

"Juan, we have to get out of this hell hole."

"Ana, you are obsessed!"

"No, what I am is in constant fear that I'll have to marry that Castro buddie that is obsessed with me. You are not safe either and you know it!"

"The letter was explicit. He would arrange exit visas through the government. He also asked us to be 'patient,' Ana, and the most important thing is that we both will have a job and a career as musicians the moment we arrive in America."

'He always has this calming effect on me,' reflects Ana, as she relaxes once more with the soothing effect of his words of encouragement. Then, the sudden braking makes her jolt. Tires are burning rubber as three brand new Audis stop right in front of them – in the middle of the square.

"Manos arriba!" They are government security forces, the most dangerous of them all.

Both Juan and Ana are quickly handcuffed and loaded into separate cars. Ana is furious and has to be restrained inside the patrol car by two female officers.

"Why are you taking me? I've done nothing wrong. Where are you taking me?"

A sympathetic police woman states "Señorita, you are in a lot of trouble."

"Why?"

"You are being accused of espionage and treason." At first, Ana does not react…

"Ja-ja-ja" is all that can be heard at the high speed they are travelling through the streets of La Habana. But, inside, singer Ana Lugo is scared to death.

Island resident and old crow club member, Sarah Pesin, is raising her two grandkids, Arlene and Kevin, by herself. She is a descendant of a World War II survivor – a doctor and heroic healer that first made his mark on the streets of war ravaged Budapest, Hungary.

CHAPTER 54
THE PESINS

A young Leon Boros was hungry and had not taken a bath in several days. The streets of Budapest, at the end of World War II, were filled with tragedy and sickness. Everyone was simply trying to survive. Food, shelter and medicines were the only things most people could think of. Being a recent graduate, Boros was now an ENT doctor. He spent most of his time tending to others, not himself. Since the war had ended, he had lost 30 lbs. This weight loss was a product of 18-hour workdays and chronic malnutrition.

He worked all over the towns of Buda and Pest, crossing the bridge several times a day. He had not seen his fiancée, Marika Korda, for more than two weeks. Marika was a physicist specializing in ballistics. The Russian Army had her secluded at her lab for no apparent reason.

"Dr. Boros, my wife and I are very grateful to you for saving our son. What we realize now is that what started as an ear infection could have killed him if not for you. Thank you," said the well-dressed stranger.

The flustered doctor quickly glanced at the visitor again. Something was odd and made him uncomfortable, but he could not place it.

"We came to see you at the shelter right off the main square by the city center. We could not get a doctor at any of the hospitals. And we were repeatedly told about you and where to find you and we did, making the line at the shelter like everyone else. You saved our son!"

"I'm glad to hear it," replied an impatient Dr. Boros, in perfect accent-free English.

"Well, before I go, let me introduce myself. I am Bill Landrieux, attaché for the U. S. Embassy."

"Nice to meet you, sir, have a nice day."

"If you are interested, the Embassy is desperately trying to hire a couple of doctors. I will recommend you myself." Landrieux realized that he had Dr. Boros's full attention, even though he was still tending to a patient. "Is this something you would be interested in, Doctor?"

"Yes, how do I apply?"

An hour later, Dr. Boros, with Landrieux's recommendation applied to become a physician at the U.S. Embassy. A week later, he was hired. He would work at the Embassy for two years. During one of his wife's furloughs, they both flew to the U.S. and decided they wanted to stay there for good, so they did. Mrs. Boros was quickly hired by MIT. She taught there for more than 30 years. During her teaching tenure, she also worked stints at the Pentagon and for NASA. Dr. Boros built a great reputation in the United States as an ENT doctor. His private practice became one of the best in Boston. But, neither his wife, nor he and their two kids ever found out that the Boros family was allowed to stay in the United

States because Mrs. Boros's services and expertise in regard to the U.S. Ballistic Missile Defense Program. Unknowingly and flawlessly, she performed for decades. In the future, their daughter, Sarah Boros was going to become a TV personality. Sarah married Saul Pesin, a successful movie producer and lived on Paradise Island for nearly two decades until their only son, Joseph, and his wife, Deborah, perished in an aircraft crash in the Rocky Mountains. Sarah Pesin was then left alone to raise her two grandchildren, Arlene, the fashion model and Kevin, one of the Island's teenagers.

Sarah Pesin has plenty on her plate as her granddaughter, Arlene, has just had a brush with death in Shanghai after a street explosion.

Island resident, renown artisan jeweler, German Lope-Bello, is out of his league trying to climb the famous Matterhorn Mountain in Switzerland. He has also made a huge mistake by carrying such a large amount of cryptocurrency with him.

CHAPTER 55
THE LOPE-BELLOS
Hörnli Hut

The Hörnli Hut is a mountain refuge located at the foot of the north-eastern ridge of the Matterhorn. It is situated at 3,260 meters above sea level, a few kilometers southwest of the town of Zermatt in the Canton of Valais in Switzerland. It was built by the Swiss Alpine Club in 1880. The hut is available only to experienced hikers. From the cable car station of Schwarzsee, a marked trail leads to the ridge and then to the hut. The hut is used as base camp for climbing the Matterhorn on the normal route.

German Lope-Bello slept soundly, but at present, even though he is happy to be well rested, he hasn't yet reached the precipice of the Matterhorn. Part of the trek up consists of going through deep tiny paths carved in the rock. It felt so narrow that even on a windless day, he senses that the slightest breeze would sweep him up and carry him away. He thinks to himself, 'why did I get myself into this predicament?' The argument for this latest adventure had been that the Matterhorn climb was not a technical climb, but a tough hike. Well, how wrong he had been. The moment he saw the mountain and its verticality, he questioned how anyone would want to, let alone have the ability, to climb to the top.

However, German wasn't a fool. The day before, just after arrival, he hopped onto the massive cable car system that ran up the mountain. In total, he had ridden three cable cars up to the Klein Matterhorn and at the 12,000-feet summit, he was able to stand right at the side of the Matterhorn peak. At close range, the mountain looked very impressive with its artistically symmetrical form. But, from an amateur climber's perspective, it was very daunting and intimidating. As he walked through the Klein Matterhorn summery water snow, he saw signs to his left that warned that skiing down in that direction was Cervinia, Italy, and that passports were required. He then looked to his right and tried to distinguish the climbing paths that ran up the Matterhorn. About one-third of the way up, he saw his home away from home, the Hörnli Hut, where the climbers attempted to sleep before the final ascent to the summit. He then looked down and saw the idyllic Swiss village of Zermatt and the steep mountains that surround it. The rock walls are so close to the backs of the chalets or hotels that the perimeter of this tiny village literally lies against the mountain. The town's obelisk is the famous Matterhorn. It is a mountain that can resemble an elongated and a bit tilted horn, depending on what angle one is looking at the mountain.

Upon arrival, German had experienced a wonderful welcome. They had parked 20 kilometers down the valley, as was required, and then had taken a train into the Harry Potter magical train station of Zermatt. Just after arrival, he had taken his three cable car scouting trip up the Matterhorn, and then in the late afternoon, along with a mandatory certified Zermatt guide/climber, he had trekked up to the Hörnli Hut to rest for the next morning's traverse to the summit. The trek had to start before sunrise in order to allow for the maximum amount of sunlight, in case of bad weather or other unforeseen events.

The ascent to the Matterhorn peak started well, but progressively, German Lope-Bello started to feel worse and worse. His head starts to spin. At first he is short of breath, not surprising at 12,000 feet. He then starts to see stars flashing around him. He grips the rope handle. The guide feels it and turns, and to his horror sees German faint and fall pulling him with him.

As Oleg Krull celebrates another trial going his way, inexorably, his jury fixing scheme is unraveling.

CHAPTER 56
THE KRULLS
(After The Trial)

A lbert Harrington is a basket case of mixed emotions after having persuaded the jury to go along with a non-guilty verdict. He feels liberated from a heavy burden, but he is also angry at Oquendo for getting him involved in such a sordid scheme. Then, there is the money that he can't stop dreaming about and all the things he will do and buy. This will change the lives of his fiancée and him. But he also has a sweet and sour feeling. After a lot of debate within himself back and forth, he has found peace. He believes he has done the right thing exonerating the accused. In the meantime, his driving is bordering on reckless as he turns the corner approaching his future brother-in-law's neighborhood. His wheels start to slide, but he corrects with a slight countermove of the wheel. 'Gee, that was close,' he thinks, while trying to get a grip on himself.

The two FBI agents are bored to death. Oquendo's lifestyle and routines do not yield anything of value for their investigation. His phone calls, emails and acquaintances are all consistent with a normal life. His procurement business based in the Caribbean is not only legit, but a very good idea. They know it is about time to wrap this one up, but it is hard to let go after so much time invested. At that moment, while parked across from Oquendo's house, in the otherwise quiet waterfront neighborhood, they hear the sound of an out-of-control car. Then, they see the car careening in their direction at high speed. The driver slams on the brakes in front of Oquendo's house. The unknown driver who steps out is an acquaintance the agents have seen at that address before. But, as soon as he steps out of the car, he slams the car door and the house door opens. Oquendo walks out with a big broad smile to greet him. The body language of the visitor is different as he walks straight up to Oquendo. As he gets closer, they can see Oquendo's smile disappearing. The man approaching Oquendo is yelling at the top of his lungs. Then, as he charges forward, he pushes Oquendo with both arms.

"Uh, what's going on here?" the FBI agent asks.

"Not sure, but we are in for a nice show."

"Who the hell do you think you are?"

"But Al…"

"Shut up, you bastard. How can you put the life of your sister at risk in this way?"

"Let's go inside, Albert," Oquendo pleads as he tries to put his arm around Harrington to walk him inside. But Harrington pushes his arm aside and continues to argue. Oquendo starts walking inside and even though still arguing, Harrington follows him in, albeit reluctantly. They sit right at the kitchen counter. Oquendo knows that he has to get the situation under control and end it quickly.

He instinctively blurts out, "Albert, if you don't want the money that's fine with me. Please accept my apologies. No harm, no foul. I'll return it like nothing happened."

"The only reason I voted not guilty is because I believe he is not guilty."

Oquendo relaxes. 'He has stopped insulting me,' he knows he has him.

"I understand, Albert. You feel you did the right thing and that's what matters. You performed your civic duty and now you are done. Now go home to your family and my sister, they are all waiting for you."

Oquendo stands up to lead him outside, but Harrington does not move.

"Does your sister know?"

"Not a word."

A silence ensues and Oquendo decides to press his luck further.

"Albert, you are going to have to excuse me, but I have to fly out very early tomorrow morning," he says walking to the door to show his future brother-in-law the way out. Harrington still does not move.

"What happens next?" asks Harrington.

"What do you mean?"

"What do we do next?"

"We return the money and forget the whole thing."

"C'mon you are not going to return anything."

"I wish I could, but those people are too powerful."

"I want the money, Oquendo."

'Now you are finally making sense,' thinks Oquendo tasting once more the convincing effect of power and money to break all moral and ethical boundaries. Oquendo does not speak and decides to listen. Harrington explains all of his mixed emotions, including how he feels in his inner conscience.

"And?" asks Oquendo, when Harrington is finished.

"I deserve the money because I did what you asked me to."

"But, Albert, I don't want any hard feelings between you and I."

"There aren't and there won't be any. I just needed to vent, after all I was thrown into a situation that I wasn't prepared for."

"If I give you this money, I don't want any conflicts, Albert. Right now, I feel a lot of tension and anger in you and it worries me."

Albert Harrington smiles and walks towards Oquendo extending his hand. Oquendo extends his and as they shake, Harrington pulls him close and embraces him.

"Thank you, brother. Thank you," he whispers in his ear.

The two FBI agents are sitting outside waiting for dishes to fly and windows to break and even for shots to be fired. Instead they see the visitor walk outside, turn the engine on and drive straight into the home's garage, which opens as he approaches and immediately closes as he drives inside.

"So, what is going on in there?" one special agent asks the other.

"I don't know, but I sure don't like the smell of it."

On a whim, they break protocol and decide to follow the visitor as he pulls out of the garage and drives away.

"Something is in that car and we've got to find out what it is."

"Well, whatever it is, they certainly don't want anyone to see it."

Harrington's "high" quickly evaporates as he drives thinking of Oquendo's words, 'Don't deposit the money, except for a couple thousand bucks here and there. Don't spend it either on big ticket items. Don't buy a new car, new home or wear expensive clothes or jewelry. Pay all of your bills with money orders you can purchase with cash at any grocery store. Purchase cryptocurrencies like bitcoin and ether, and keep the money deposited with solid exchanges. Buy yourself properties abroad, like in Mexico or Central America, and make sure they can generate a rental income for you. Put the properties in the name of offshore corporations with bearer shares. Do not tell! Repeat, do not tell my sister anything, or anyone else for that matter.'

He had no idea it was so complicated. All that cash was his, but it all suddenly felt like gunpowder about to go off with any wrong move.

Harrington arrives home. As he drives through the security gate, parks and takes the elevator, he is in a state of anxiety and confusion. Upstairs, a surprise welcome home party awaits him.

"We need to see your video recordings for the last 30 minutes, sir," states the FBI special agent to the security guard at the entrance to Oquendo's gated community.

The world is falling apart for Island resident, wife beater, now sexually incapacitated, Alessandro Baglioni. His son Johnny couldn't be more different from his father and now, after learning the truth, he needs to decide what to do with him and whether to turn him in or not.

CHAPTER 57
THE BAGLIONIS
(JOHNNY)

Johnny Baglioni has been inside his parents' secret room for hours, but the anger he feels inside has only increased as he has watched video after video and looked at photo album after photo album of his mom being beaten and sexually abused by his father. 'He is a sick dude! He is not in his right mind.' Johnny feels powerless against the man that tortures his mother every day. As his mom always says, "We rely financially on him, Johnny. He holds all the cards. Everything is in his name and I love him the way he is."

He starts throwing things around the room. Then his rage grows until it overwhelms him and he goes on a rampage breaking and smashing everything he sees. Finally, he sits on the floor panting, but he cannot shake off the image of his father doing more of the sick stuff with the girl next door. Veronica Lujan-Restrepo has always been like an older sister to him. And now she is also a victim of his father's twisted ways. Johnny couldn't care less about his father's penis fracture. Hopefully, his father will be sexually incapacitated on a permanent basis.

'So what is it? He likes to punish those that love him and be punished by those that don't. Sick, sick, sick.' Johnny is lost and without a compass. For what appears to be an endless amount of time, he remains motionless, wedged in the corner of the debris cluttered floor. Finally, the pain in his right hand brings him back. He is bleeding from a deep cut on his right thumb. Then, as he is about to stand up, he sees it! And he only sees it because he is right next to it at ground level. He presses down on the loose piece of wood and it pops open exposing a small and rectangular metal door with a lock. 'This is not a safe. It's got to be part of what goes on in this room. It must be the roughest stuff!' he reasons as he makes up his mind and walks to the mansion's utility room to find tools. Minutes later, he cuts the lock and opens the lock-box. And that moment is when his world really comes crashing down!

Former Island resident, Sylvester Antonelli, dreams about coming back to the outside world in Paradise Island. His unlikely return path starts vis' a vis an event that took place five years ago with the sudden death of a prominent tech industry entrepreneur, Leroy Vincent Fiorentina.

CHAPTER 58
THE ANTONELLIS (PART I)
Five Years Earlier

As the early morning sun rose, intense light spread through the snowcapped mountains. Darkness gave way to gray skies, followed by light blue and finally, they became crystal clear and sparkled with yellows. The day had become an intense, pristine and overwhelming sea of white. It was a majestic surrounding that accompanied the helicopter as it glided deep through the high Canadian mountains. Suddenly, a desolate small valley came into view. Fresh powder and steep terrain awaited the sleepy passengers. The mountain was ready to be carved and glided through. As they approached the small landing spot, the mountain guide brought everyone to full attention and started imparting instructions and safety tips.

Once on the ground, the passengers huddled and cuddled while filming and snapping pictures of the moment. Soon thereafter, they started to ski down the hill. The snow was deep, crisp and untouched. The skiers were all knee deep in it, with the snow showering their face masks, as they carved elongated semi-circles while skiing downhill.

He first saw the movement out of the corner of his eye. Then, as he turned, he saw a massive chunk of snow become unhinged.

A massive vertical snow wall had come loose from the mountain. Then came the roar of the avalanche racing towards them. It happened so fast! It had all been so sudden. And, it had caught all off guard with overwhelming force. There was no way out.

In an instant, they had vanished in the monster wave of snow. They had been buried alive.

He was barely conscious. The safety balloon had deployed upon impact and had created the desired space to survive under an avalanche of snow. But, he could not breathe! The safety mechanism had exploded against his chest and he was now hopelessly pinned down by a wall of hard snow and ice. All he could hear was the beep of his emergency beacon sending out his position. Deprived of sufficient oxygen, his thinking was reduced to nothing else than trying to breathe. Leroy Vincent Fiorentina's life was rapidly coming to an end. Neither his avalanche safety equipment, nor his money or power could help him at that moment. The helicopter that had dropped the skiers moments earlier at the top of the mountain was now hovering over the resting place of the avalanche. None of the six skiers could be seen from above the crumbled and rugged snow surface. Was the visionary tech investor and industry oracle gone? His wife Angelina anxiously scanned and searched through the white expanse.

"Are you getting the beacon signal?" she asked.

The helicopter pilot responded, "Nope, nothing yet. They may be under tons of snow and the signal cannot go through."

"Can't you touch down? We could walk through the area and maybe hear or see something," insisted Angelina.

"The whole area is too unstable. We need to wait for search and rescue. They have already sent out a rescue plane, it should be here within minutes."

The former Island resident had plenty of time to chart his return path in the place he is at...jail!

Present Day

Sylvester Antonelli is sitting in a corner watching cable TV on a large flat HD screen. He is listening through a wireless FM headset. On this day, the financial news is boring. There are no major crises or big news events. The stock market has been hovering the whole morning not far from its opening level. Sylvester Antonelli is about to get up and leave when a company name flashes on the screen and catches his attention. CTH (Cloud Tech Holdings, Inc.) reported earnings yesterday, after the market closed, well below analysts' estimates. The stock is off 8%. The company has now lost 95% of its market value in the last five years, since the death of its founder, Leroy Vincent Fiorentina. Tensions are high at the company and rumors are flying about its latest CEO, Alexander Crandoli's imminent departure. The company is a shadow of its former self. 'Boy, so promising,' thinks Sylvester. Every time he hears news about the company or hears its founder's name, something is triggered in Sylvester's memory bank, but he is unable to quite place it. As he walks through the rec room toward the computer room, his mind is still distracted with the nagging thought of what attracts him to CTH or its deceased founder.

As Sylvester walks through the crowded room, he doesn't see the book cart. He feels a sharp pain in his spine as his knee crashes into the book cart's middle shelf. He cries in pain. 'I must have damaged a nerve!' And while contorted in pain with his head down, something catches his attention. It is a glimpse of something, a set of colors…a form. It is a kind of flashback captured through the corner of his right eye. Then, as he limps away, his mind goes blank. Whatever it was, he lost it under a sea of physical discomfort. He tries to stretch out his back, but can't. He sits down trying to relax and breathe deeply. Suddenly he freezes, stands up and limps straight back to the cart. There it is! From a stack in the middle of the cart, he pulls out the magazine with a yellow and red cover. He pages through it. If only he could remember…he stops and stares at the article's headline. Suddenly, everything comes back in a rush. He sits down quickly and pours through all of the information, taking notes. It is all in there, an eight-page article in a magazine that is five years old! Of all the places in the world, this is the last one he could think of to discover and find a treasure trove of information like this. And yet, where else could you find dated magazines lying around, for years, perhaps nowhere else but in a Federal Prison Camp!

Sylvester reads the article quickly. It describes in detail an expansion strategy that Leroy Vincent Fiorentina's company had been planning for over two years. The strategy centered on a series of investments in small startup companies in the fields of search engines, social media and web marketing. The company was awash with cash and Fiorentina, as the founder/owner, wanted to put some of it to work in startup companies that sought to challenge those that controlled 80% of the computer products and services market. It was time to diversify. He did not want his company to have all of its eggs in one basket. The target companies were eager for cash and his plan was that he would allocate about 2% of CTH's cash to these types of investments.

Sylvester stops reading and starts to reflect on the article; 'It is surprising that 2% of the cash to be spent on acquisitions was publicly disclosed in advance. Perhaps this was to reassure the stockholders that the amount to be invested in the startups was only a small percent of the cash the company had. What a difference five years can make.' Since the article was written, Fiorentina's company has gone downhill. The price of shares in Fiorentina's company are pennies on the dollar. The company is also running out of cash. Without Fiorentina's leadership and vision, the company had tanked. What happened? It is obvious and brutally logical. Shortly after the article was published and more than five years ago, Fiorentina had died in a ski accident. Was that the downfall of CTH? Without its founder and leader, the company could not function and yet, there seemed to be more. He had to dig deeper under the surface.

He ordered CTH's financial records. Several weeks pass. He finally receives the printout of Fiorentina's company, including the quarterly and annual reports filed with the Securities and Exchange Commission. He canvasses each of them, all 24 with an average of 25 pages each. They include not only the company's financial statements, business performance, competitive landscape and management data, but also material on transactions or events that the public and shareholders must be made aware of. The story of CTH's decline is all there in black and white. But, the decline is more like a sea of red. Sylvester goes through the material over and over. It appears to him that the company and its management dropped the ball again and again. The company missed the innovations brought in by mobile computing through tablets, smart phones and watches. They also missed the massive development of software applications (apps) for mobile computers; the demise of the keyboard and mouse replaced first by touch and hand gestures then by voice and video; and finally missed the emergence of the Cloud and artificial intelligence imbedded into software applications and smart phones. The once unassailable market dominance of the company had evaporated in five years.

Although it was Fiorentina's vision, it appears that no investments had been made in the lucrative startup computer industry before he died in the avalanche. The public filings in front of him confirmed that. In a small footnote in the financials, he finds a mention of the names of two dozen legal entities that were created as "special purpose vehicles (SPVs)." The purpose of these SPVs was to use them as shelters for each startup company investment that Fiorentina had planned on making before he died. The names of the SPVs, that were now "empty shells", were all listed on a separate appendix. Each of the SPV names was hard to forget, because each of the Delaware-based entities was a flower followed by an extreme attribute... Wild Flower Investments, Blood Rose Capital, Pricey Orchid Equity, etc.

'But there was more to this,' thought Sylvester. Something kept nagging at him about what otherwise was a story of a brilliant entrepreneur that died prematurely and the subsequent and painful demise of his company that he built into a market giant. Sylvester could not let it go...

Then it happens! It is sudden and unexpected. He is sitting on his bunkbed with his legs crossed and is reading and clipping articles from newspapers and magazines when it suddenly dawns on him. This is what he has been hoping for. He has to go and check it out. He lowers himself from his upper bunk with two quick well-practiced acrobatic moves using the bunk and his locker as support. He then pulls out his folder of SEC reports he has developed with regard to Fiorentina's company. He pages through the equity section and goes through the latest stockholder list. He then prepares a detailed letter and puts it in the mail the next morning.

A few weeks later, he gets everything he asked for. He has the annual SEC reports of the top 20 search engine companies in the world. He starts going through their capitalization tables, specifically reviewing the list of shareholders. This is a long shot and he has low expectations about getting anywhere. He goes through every filing, but does not find any shareholder connection between Fiorentina's company and any of the search engine companies. And yet, he still has a feeling that he is missing something. 'The investments have been made…and are about to be completed,' he recalls Fiorentina's statement in the article. What is he missing? He then slowly retraces his steps until he goes through the public filings of the Silicon Valley's darling, the search engine, Zest.

He has been staring at the name for more than an hour, just thinking, just thinking. 'Could it be? LVF!' LVF is the name of the largest shareholder of Zest. Zest in turn, is the most powerful search engine company in the world. Those are Leroy Vincent Fiorentina's initials! Is this one of the special purpose vehicles (SPVs) that were created by Fiorentina to make the investments? If so, why isn't this listed in Fiorentina's company, Cloud Tech Holdings' (CTH) previous SEC filings?'

In his research, Sylvester has obtained every available interview given by Fiorentina. In total, three interviews took place in the month before he died. Pouring through the interviews, he realizes the extent of Fiorentina's commitment to invest and diversify in a series of small startups. The last interview was the most revealing, as he literally predicted what eventually happened to his company. Fiorentina stated in the interview that if his company did not diversify and invest in the new upcoming trends in the computer industry, it would not flourish and would probably fail. Sylvester re-reads the last interview and focuses on one statement:

"Investments we have made and those we are about to complete in this quarter, will be critical for our diversification strategy forward for the next three to five years." Sylvester thinks to himself, 'Have made ... about to complete within this quarter ... it reads as if some investments were in fact made! How could this be? The public filings do not reflect it.'

It is 7:00 a.m. Sylvester has just pulled an all-nighter. The three initials are still staring at him, LVF, LVF!. Could it be possible? He has to proceed with surgical precision and remain objective. It is not a question about what to do, but how? The same night, he posts a letter to his attorney with a detailed list of questions. He wants to know when LVF was created, who its principals are and its shareholders, as well. Does it have a website? Who runs it? Is it an operational company or just a set of papers lying in a drawer in a file cabinet or safe? Additionally, he asks for all of the audited financial statements of Fiorentina's main company CTH.

Now he has to wait patiently one more time. A couple weeks later, he sits late into the night frustrated. LVF's paper trail has taken him nowhere. The company is active, but virtually everything else draws a blank. Then, he canvases its SEC quarterly and annual filings, but can find no evidence of LVF being a subsidiary of Fiorentina's CTH. Hours of going through records, page after page, and he is still at the same spot he was at weeks before. LVF is the largest shareholder of Zest, the largest search engine in the world, by virtue of being one of its earliest investors. Coincidentally, timing wise, LVF invested in Zest at the time that Fiorentina and his company CTH announced to the world that Fiorentina's company was going to diversify by making strategic investments in startups. The plan was that the startups would become future leaders in their fields. But, in spite of the fact that the initials of LVF caught his attention as being the same as CTH's deceased founder, Leroy Vincent Fiorentina, there is no evidence that Fiorentina's company CTH has ownership interest in that company. Hence, it does not have any hidden jewels in its portfolio, or so it appears. It is merely a failing enterprise, run amuck after the death of its founder.

It is now 4:00 a.m. The night is flying by, but Sylvester is utterly oblivious to his surroundings. Sitting in a yoga position, his night light on, the prison camp dorm is a snoring concert hall. He thinks and thinks about the initials LVF. The same question that he had weeks before came back when he saw the letters LVF (the company name and largest shareholder of search engine giant Zest.) These initials, LVF for Leroy Vincent Fiorentina, keep ringing an alarm bell because on Fiorentina's Cloud Tech Holdings (CTH), there is a subsidiary in the public filings called Long View Forward, LLC. It is not the same name, but the same initials. Could it be? He thinks and thinks and mulls this over and over. The answer finally comes to him in a flash! AKA! That's what it is, A/K/A, also known as.

The next morning he posts a letter to his attorney asking the following question to the CTH Investor Relations Department: "A footnote in your annual report for the year 2011 lists a subsidiary called Long View Forward, LLC, then, it is not listed again. Is that subsidiary active? Does that subsidiary have an AKA of LVF?"

The head of investor relations for CTH, Albert Dunn, routinely signs all the authorizations for replies to shareholders, and that is what he does to the recently received request to answer the question: "Is your subsidiary Long View Forward still active?" Dunn answers yes and states that Long View Forward is also known as LVF. He does not think twice about his reply. Unknowingly, he has just triggered into motion what eventually would be one of the largest windfalls ever to occur on Wall Street. Sylvester's under-the-radar approach of research and gum-shoe work is going to hook him up to a financial rocket, the likes of which have never been seen before.

The information shakes Sylvester to his core. Fiorentina's failing company CTH's total market value is down to only $15 million, but its ghost subsidiary, LVF owns 30% of the outstanding shares of Zest, the largest search engine in the world. LVF must have bought the Zest shares before Zest became a giant. The current market value of Zest is $200 billion. So, LVF's shares are worth at least $60 billion. But CTH, a public company on the brink, has not reported this investment. Sylvester's mind is racing: 'What about all the other SPV's Fiorentina had ordered CTH to create before his death? Are there other successful investments that are also not reported?'

Sylvester decides to check Zest's annual shareholders' meeting minutes and requests them by mail through his attorney. The following week he gets a reply. And this leaves no doubt in his mind. LVF is the largest Zest shareholder, but this information is nowhere to be found in CTH's own shareholders' annual meeting minutes. In fact, LVF has never participated or voted at any of Zest's stockholder meetings. Either CTH isn't aware of what it has or it is hiding it! Slowly, but surely, Sylvester makes the decision of his life.

Former Island resident, Sylvester Antonelli, has just bought his return ticket to Paradise Island, he just doesn't know it yet.

Island resident, world renowned architect, Lars Johannsen, has finally come full circle since the death of his wife – to a place where he is ready to commit wholeheartedly to someone and start a family.

CHAPTER 59
THE JOHANNSENS
(Lars and Gabrielle)

“ I gather this is a change in routine for you?”

“Do you mean in a bedroom with a perfect stranger? Yes! Definitely so.”

He smiles at her candor and continues, “I mean living out of a suitcase?”

“Yep, it’s lonely out here, even at the tennis court you feel isolated.”

“How so?”

“When you are hurt, sick or obviously, when you lose a tennis match, you don’t care about being on tour or the money, you just want to be home or with your friends and family.”

“What about being with someone you love?”

She inhales deeply while staring at him. “Yeah, we all want to be…wait a minute…I am not looking for…” she chokes on her own words. “I don’t want to, I can’t afford to…” Her eyes are like lasers directed at him.

“Having a struggle with your mind trying to control your fears?”

She trembles slightly and he gently kisses her lips.

"All that matters is what you feel."

"What about what we feel?"

"What about what you feel?" she says forcefully right in his face.

"I am hopelessly infatuated with you," he whispers to her as he stares back at her with joy in his eyes.

'What am I feeling?' she mumbles to herself.

He leans back and takes a deep breath and tries to ease up the knot of happiness he feels throughout his body. At this moment, he just wants to be with her... "Blissful," she blurts out. There is a long silence while the two just continue to look at each other.

Finally, he says, "I am in bliss, a wonderful bliss as well!"

They are inseparable. Lars follows her around the tennis circuit. Gabrielle follows him to Paradise Island when not on tour. She can't understand why he has stopped teaching, but in fact, it's simply that he has stopped prowling. Tonight they are dining in style in the Johannsen's backyard with the lights of downtown Miami providing a postcard-perfect backdrop. Lars is in awe as he watches Gabrielle gaze at the lights. She is talking, but he is not listening. Just his being there with her makes him feel so alive.

"Lars, are you listening?"

He looks at her and shrugs, while mimicking a childish expression of being caught, "infraganti."

"What are you talking about?"

"Nothing, what were you saying?"

"I was talking about the new French tennis player Sabrina Leconte, she is from Lyon and is currently ranked 6th in the world."

"Okay, what about her?"

"She broke off her engagement."

"Why?"

"Her fiancé wanted to have children!"

"Understandably so, her tennis career is short, she can't have children now," he says.

"Right," says Gabrielle affirmatively, but unconvinced and without enthusiasm.

Gabrielle is caught up in the dilemma and paradox of modern professional women, when to start a family. She's now listening intently.

"But if she wants to have children, now there is a solution for that. The two of them could do in-vitro fertilization and pay for a surrogate mother to have the kid. It will be 100% their child and they are able to be parents and start a family right away without the mother losing any time in regard to her career."

"What if the surrogate mother changes her mind and decides to keep the child?" Gabrielle is now talking out of self-interest.

"That's possible, but the monetary incentive for being the surrogate almost always prevails. Also, if you do it in the right place, like California, the laws make it very difficult, almost impossible, for the surrogate to change her mind."

"Lars, how come you know so much about this?" Gabrielle is catching on to what is coming.

"Because I want to start a family with you." She is trembling and rendered speechless. He then drops to one knee and takes her hand into both of his... "Gabrielle Lareau, will you be my wife?" She is stunned at first and leans back on her chair. Then an awkward silence ensues while she looks at him with her eyes wide open in total surprise, having been caught completely off guard. Then it comes out as a blunt "yesss!" She jumps up and literally piles on top of him, hugging and pulling him close to her. She kisses him all over his face.

"So you want to have a child right away?" she asks with a smile on her face and just inches away from him.

"I was thinking about having five right away."

"What?"

"We will have all the help we need. We can get started right away and have them all at the same time, as opposed to staggered."

She shakes her head in disbelief.

Jasper is eavesdropping on his father and new girlfriend from the balcony of the house. He is in disbelief and thinks to himself, 'c'mon Dad, she is 31 years younger than you.'

Once again, Lars Johannsen has bypassed and totally ignored his son on such an important decision.

Future Island residents, talented Cuban musicians, Ana and Juan Rojas-Lugos are at last on the move and with everything on the line, their dream is either closer and within their reach or it is about to be dealt a death blow.

CHAPTER 60
ROJAS-LUGOS
(The Escape)

The raft has been drifting in the Caribbean Sea for three days and they have hardly gotten any closer to the U.S. coast. The seven occupants have only one goal in mind, to reach land before the Coast Guard gets a hold of them. Once ashore, they will be safe and asylum is automatic. If captured at sea, their future will be uncertain and, in all likelihood, they will be deported back to Cuba. The newlywed Rojas-Lugos fled Cuba the moment they had both been released. They could not wait any longer as both of them were at risk. They joined the first raft they got wind of and within two days they were on the sea, with essentially all of their money tucked in their belts. But, every second at sea they regretted the decision they had made.

As bad as it was, this was nothing compared to what was ahead of them. The weather system comes out of nowhere. First, ominous dark grey clouds form as the sun is setting. Then, the winds pick up and, finally, the waves start to grow in size. As the moonless night falls, the seven dreamers find themselves helpless against the fury of the sea as they teeter violently against the swells. They are now facing a life or death situation. The raft has taken on so much water that some of the seven are overtaken by panic. "Hold her down or she will fall out," screams the group leader. Then, as two young men pull back a young woman by the arms, a massive wave hits the raft and almost tips it over. The threesome is caught off guard and, without warning, are thrown onto the others. But the guttural sounds of pain and agony from bodies slamming into each other are muffled by the roar of nature. Then, as if by the hand of God, the pile on becomes their shield against the onslaught. They are so tightly pressed against each other that they can hear and feel each other breathing. They all react by holding each other even tighter. The ones at the bottom are flattened against the bottom of the boat. The seven sailors weather the storm for hours until calm returns just at the break of dawn. Slowly they untangle themselves and peek out. The would-be captain states, "The water has turned emerald green in front of us, we must be close to land." Suddenly, the shrill sound of the horn makes everyone jump.

"U.S. Coast Guard," can be heard through the sound of a megaphone.

"Nooo! Sh…! Dam..it!"

The Coast Guard vessel moves in quickly. It is now within 500 yards of the raft.

Juan glimpses safety and he zeros in. His survival instincts take over and he jumps into the water.

"There is a sand bar here!"

"Woman what are you waiting for? Jump now!" he yells at his wife. Following her natural instincts, she is about to argue and fight, but the forceful command overtakes her and the fury in his eyes literally makes her jump into the sea. The Coast Guard commands them to stop as it lowers a tender.

Juan sees the sandy bottom rising fast underneath him and within seconds he is able to stand in waist-deep water. Ana is just behind him, swimming frantically and ignoring the Coast Guard orders. They are no more than 30 yards away from the Coast Guard tender. The tender attempts to capture Ana, but in a last desperate effort, Juan reaches out and yanks his wife to safety. As both stand up, a Hispanic Coast Guard officer tells them in Spanish "Qué están esperando? Caminen a la orilla." (What are you waiting for? Walk to the shore.) Once out of the water, the couple hug each other in a bittersweet embrace. They have finally made it. They are now free. But, as they look around at their new-found home, they can see that their five fellow travelers have been captured and plucked out of the water.

A bit of luck, but no doubt about it, it is luck they have made happen. The Rojas-Lugo's relentless and continuous advancement to success and riches is alive and well.

The castrated Island trio are about to find a solution to their sexual predicaments including their inability to have girlfriends, in a way they least expected.

CHAPTER 61
THE KRULLS AND THE MATTHEWS
SAUSALITO BAY, CALIFORNIA

Two of the three boys, Thor Krull and Louis Matthews, III, are at the rehab center and have finally agreed to enter therapy and counselling.

Today at 11:00 a.m., the first session has just begun with routine questioning of the two boys. The psychiatrist doing the evaluation, Dr. James Reed, quickly becomes deeply concerned and steps out of the room for a while to do a bit of research in regard to this highly unusual situation.

"Can anyone help us? Or are we just a lost cause?" says Thor.

"Wackos, that's what we are," answers Louis.

"I don't know what to do. I am so horny. I want to have sex but I can't. It's driving me crazy," says a lamenting Thor.

"Me too! I am ready to explode," adds Louis.

"OK boys, let's take this step by step," states Dr. Reed as he walks back in.

"The fact is that you two feel and act like men, who like women, but you are trapped in bodies that have vaginas. Am I right so far?"

The two teens do not answer out of shame and embarrassment, but at the same time they do not dispute the doctor's assertions.

"Sir, is this ...?" asks Thor as he is interrupted mid-sentence by Dr. Reed.

"Everything we talk about in here is confidential."

"Here is what your profile is. You are both transgender and your shot at happiness and a stable relationship will be to find your opposite equivalent."

Both teens are dumbfounded.

"What do you mean doctor?"

"If you agree, I'll act as a matchmaker and we will search for transgender females of your age that have male organs."

It takes a few seconds to register, but when it does Thor bolts and starts screaming "Are you telling me that I'll find happiness in a weirdo woman who penetrates me with a dick? Are you out of your f..ing mind?"

"Well, Mr. Krull you have no choice but to start accepting the truth. Otherwise, you can become a monk, make a chastity vow and live in a monastery. Or, you can go and pound sand every day for the rest of your life. Or, you can accept your reality and try to find happiness." A long silence follows.

"Are those female looking guys?"

"They can be really good looking women in every respect, manners, features and body, except for their male organs."

Thirty minutes later, the uncooperative teens leave Dr. Reed without a hint of enthusiasm for his proposition. But, as they drive along the Golden Gate Bridge on their way back to Oakland, they are both somewhat relieved, because at least, the overwhelming feeling of uncertainty is finally off their backs.

"Dr. Reed, when can you start" asks Thor as he calls from his cell phone the moment he steps into his dorm room.

"I have already started working on it. I will contact you when I have something." The line goes dead.

"How did he know?" asks Louis to his fellow victim.

"As he said, 'He knows we don't have a choice.' "Besides, what he suggested is genius."

"I wonder if there are any transgenders here on campus?"

"No worries dude, tomorrow we'll start canvassing the whole student body."

The final reality check dawns on Island residents, oil transportation magnet, Louis Matthews, II, corrupt lobbyist, Bart Holstein and criminal attorney ace, Oleg Krull. They are about to find out that there isn't any chance to go after Steven Zathlyn.

CHAPTER 62
The Holstein, Mathews and Krull Families

"Oleg, have you heard anything from General Pinkus?" asked a half-drunk Bart Holstein.

"Nothing, Zilch, Zero."

"Shouldn't we call or pay him a visit?"

"Absolutely not. Let him do his job. He has always been very effective for me, but he marches to the beat of his own drum."

"I am getting restless, Oleg, we paid him a good buck for it."

"All right, if by month's end we haven't heard from him, we'll contact him."

The three parents are hungry for blood and are not letting it go. In the meantime, General Pinkus waits for their approach with a big shocker that should put an end to everything. Of course, he is ready to provide them with a full refund of their monies.

In the meantime, the children of the three frustrated highfalutin parents are about to get started with their new lives.

It has taken a few weeks for Louis Matthews, III to come around. He first erased the email from his therapist upon reading it, then he retrieved it back from the trash bin on his tablet and... then nothing. He just let it sit and fade into oblivion or so he intended at first. That is, until around midnight when he woke up from a bad dream and half asleep went straight to his tablet and opened the unsettling email again. 'Hell with it,' he thought and clicked the attachment.

The JPEG opens and shows the picture of a gorgeous young woman with long curly blond hair, big, deep hazelnut eyes and perfect lips. Then he opens a second picture. She is in a bikini. She has a stunning body and beautiful suntanned skin. Then, in an instant, reality hits him with a vengeance.

'How can she be a man? I don't get it.' He reads her profile.

Name: Caroline "Carol" McNerney
Age: 19
Sex: Transgender
Studies: Stanford (currently), majoring in applied mathematics.
Sports: All American golfer for Stanford
Status: Single

He is impressed with what he sees, but for a while he can't get himself to act.

Finally, Louis texts Carol and introduces himself. A couple of days go by without a response. At 2:00 a.m., he is lying awake filled with anxiety when he hears the buzz of an incoming text message.

"Louis, are you awake?"

"Yes." A full minute goes by.

"???" he texts.

The screen remains blank, and he senses that it is better not to push back.

One, two, three, four, five, ten, fifteen minutes go by and, as he is falling asleep, the buzz awakens him.

"Are you still there?" she texts.

"Yes, but falling asleep."

Another full minute goes by.

"This is very difficult for me," she adds.

'For me as we…' impulsively he erases it before sending it.

"I understand how you feel," he finally texts.

The gap this time is shorter. Thirty seconds or so.

"When did you find out you were a transgender?" she asks.

"I didn't."

"What do you mean?"

"I was born a man, feel and act like one, but lost my penis by a surgical procedure," he replies.

"I read on your file that you have a vagina."

"Once my organ was gone, they reconstructed my genital area into a vagina," he states, not feeling ashamed for the first time since the incident.

Again, silence ensues, but this time he takes the initiative.

"What about you?" he asks.

"I was born a woman, but with male genitals. Everything about me is absolutely feminine and straight. That's the way I feel."

"But you have never had the surgery? Why?" he presses.

"That part of me is totally suppressed. I've thought more about it recently and I guess eventually I'll do it."

"Do you go out? Do you date anyone?"

"I go out, but no I don't date anyone and never have had a boyfriend. I guess that being a transgender has made me kind of a dating hermit because I am afraid of being rejected by men and really don't know how others will look at me when we are intimate."

"Well, in the pictures you look spectacular and very beautiful to me."

Silence.

"Thank you."

"What about your friends and classmates, do they know?"

"Oh yeah, everyone knows, but I am lucky as, at least at Stanford, I have never been mistreated and my privacy has been respected. I guess everything about my everyday life, friends and academic life is 100% normal. It is only on the intimate side where I am left alone and thought of as a freak. So, I am simply not dating – period!"

"I don't think I would have contacted you in a moment like this, in the middle of the night when I feel vulnerable, except there is something about you!" she adds.

"I guess, Carol, all we have to do is find out if we like each other."

"Yeah," she replies hesitantly.

"When can I see you?" he asks anxiously.

Silence again. He refrains from texting and forces himself to wait while literally biting his nails.

"What about now?" she texts.

Now the silence comes from him. Then, although in panic and with part of him rejecting it, he lets what he learned in therapy take over.

"Your orders are my command, text me your address and I will be on my way."

Island resident, Louis Matthews III, is on his way to meet a beautiful girl for the first time since the "incident" where his manhood wings were clipped – the only problem is that she is biologically speaking, a man.

The Island teen's curiousity about what really happened to Hillary Zathlyn has been raging.

CHAPTER 63
PARADISE ISLAND SOCIAL CLUB, POOL AREA

After several weeks, Hillary Zathlyn is finally back. Since it is a Sunday, she wastes no time and goes to join her friends at the Paradise Island pool. As she walks in, everyone is surprised. Kevin Pesin, Megan Greenhouse and Johnny Baglioni are sitting poolside.

"When did you get back, girlfriend?" asks Megan.

"Last night."

After she walks in, she sits down into one of the pool side chairs. Her childhood friends stand up and huddle around her, each one kissing and hugging her as if trying a bit too hard to welcome her and also a bit too close for comfort, considering the emotional state she is in.

"Guys, calm down. I'm here. I'll be here tomorrow and the next day and so on. I am back and I am fine!" She waves them off.

They are all excited to have her back, but they are also full of questions built up inside of them. What happened to her? Why was she away for so long? What happened and where are the three island bullies? What did her dad do to scare them away?

Hillary looks at her friends and they seem like strangers to her now. She feels so detached.

"Hm, hm, hm." Johnny Baglioni clears his throat trying to draw her attention.

No one is talking and there is an eerie silence among them.

"Guys, no one has died. I am here and in one piece. Also, I did plenty of sightseeing in Europe."

Everyone stays quiet, they are waiting for the good stuff, but Hillary clams up.

"Hillary, let's start from the beginning. What really happened to you on that day?" asks Johnny Baglioni, trying to break the ice.

"I can't talk about that, sorry!"

Everyone looks at each other with disappointment.

"I gather you can't talk either about the three bullies that your dad and the big mean looking investigator asked me about that day. You know that, right?"

Hillary remains silent.

She is fighting tears and wants to leave, but her dad is out of town so she needs their company.

"Guys, I am not ready to talk about anything yet," she says sheepishly.

"Leave her alone," says Megan Greenhouse.

"Why don't we switch subjects?" asks Kevin Pesin.

"So, Johnny, what was the deal with your dad the other day?" asks Kevin Pesin.

Livid, Johnny Baglioni stands and leaves. As he walks out, he hits and punches everything near him.

"That's quite a temper," states Kevin.

"Well it's worse than that. Why would he press you so hard when he has much more serious problems to deal with at home?"

"What kind of problems?" asks Hillary.

"Well girl, you've missed a lot of stuff about the Baglionis."

She is shocked after being told of the events. The whole thing creates a strong desire to reach out to Johnny and stand with him as a friend and, who knows, maybe more. Ever since he held her in his arms after the rape, she has been fantasizing about this moment. All she can think of is to make sure he is all right.

'Johnny, call me back,' Hillary texts.

Five minutes go by before her phone buzzes.

"Hi."

"Hi."

"Where are you?"

"Why?"

"I have to see you."

"You have to see me?"

"No, I want to see you, Johnny Baglioni."

"Where are you?"

"At my cabaña at the Island's club."

"On my way. I will see you in a couple of minutes."

The natural attraction that existed from the beginning between Hillary Zathlyn and Johnny Baglioni has never gone away – besides he was the first one by her side after the rape.

Young Jasper Johannsen is about to go in quick succession from outlaw hacker, to thief, to villain, to hero and savior of his father's old friend and future Island resident Elizabeth Rawlings.

CHAPTER 64
THE JOHANNSENS
(Elizabeth Rawlings and Jasper Johannsen)

The head of the security detail protecting Elizabeth Rawlings has just witnessed his boss break down in tears. Rawlings and her long-time friend, Lars Johannsen, are having a pointed discussion. Her words are loud and clear on how her digital wallets have simply disappeared. The two friends are sitting together at the poolside of Johannsen's Paradise Island mansion.

Rawlings' head of security is equally angry, but not for what happened to his employer, of that he could not care less, since he is the one who stole the bitcoins and the ether cryptocurrency from her. He is upset about the digital wallets evaporating from the computer he parked them in. Now, without his retirement package, he again faces years of continuous work as a slave to the bitch, as he calls her.

Earlier in the day, he saw the face of the man who assaulted the woman whose computer he'd just hacked. Ever since, Jasper Johannsen has not left his room. He is scared to his core. He is in a state of panic. He is paralyzed and unable to get out of bed. His phone has been buzzing for a while, but he has ignored it. He looks at his cell phone, 'son, are you home right now?' He hesitates for a moment, but he knows he better answer his dad.

"Yeah, why?"

"An old friend of mine has some computer related problems. They are serious. Can you come down? Perhaps you can help her."

"Right now? I don't feel like it dad. Maybe later."

"Jasper, get up and come down right now. That's an order!"

A very unhappy and scared Jasper Johansen shows up at the pool minutes later.

"Jasper, do you remember Mrs. Rawlings?"

Jasper's face changes immediately from a smirk on his face to a broad and shiny smile when he recognizes her. He spontaneously approaches her and warmly hugs and kisses her.

"Of course dad. She always gave me the best gifts and she was the one who took me out when you were busy. Thanks to her, I went to candy shops and ice cream parlors. How could I not remember her?"

"Your dad was raising you as a single parent so I happily gave him a hand," states Elizabeth sensing the veiled criticism of her dear friend, Lars. Young Johannsen and Elizabeth Rawlings look at each other in smiling complicity. Jasper relaxes a little.

"Mrs. Rawlings, what's up?" asks Jasper. "My dad told me you are having computer problems. Perhaps I can help you."

Jasper then spots the lead security guard and immediately tenses. That is the face that sent him to bed in a panic. Rawlings notices it right away and responds swiftly by ordering her security detail to leave the pool area.

"Guys, we need privacy. Leave us alone."

"Mrs. Rawlings, dad, let's take a ride on the water-ski boat. I am not comfortable talking cyber with anyone near or in the vicinity that can listen in." The two old friends are a bit surprised, but go along with it. They all walk to the house dock and within minutes lower the boat into the water and hop in.

In the meantime, the head of security is enraged when the listening device that he usually leaves behind is giving him no voice sounds. When he peeks at the pool area, he sees the threesome leaving the estate on a small powerboat.

Safely out a mile away, Jasper feels comfortable and eager to help someone that has always cared about him. Even though he is not sure what the nature of the problem is, one way or another he is pretty certain he will be able to help her.

"Alright Mrs. Rawlings, what happened?"

"My bitcoin and ether – digital wallets were stolen! As a consequence, earlier today an important real estate transaction I intended to make here in Miami Beach could not close."

Jasper becomes white as a ghost. His atypical reaction is not lost on the other two on the boat.

"Son, are you all right?" Johannsen senior asks approaching him and placing the palm of his hand on his cyber-thief son's shoulder.

Rawlings on the other hand gets a sinking feeling that she cannot shake off and her intuition screams at her: consciousness of guilt. An uneasy silence follows. Jasper cannot look the other two in the eye and intensely bites his lower lip.

"He did it!" he babbles.

"Who did what?"

"Your lead bodyguard stole your wallets."

"How do you know?"

"Because I stole them from him."

"Jasper, you better explain yourself. I have no patience right now for any of your bullsh…," states his dad.

Jasper looks intensely at both of them.

"Dad, I'm a hacker and you know it. A few days ago, I was prowling the net. It was rather easy to break into a computer that turned out to belong to a woman called Teske. When I break in, it's my usual practice to turn the invaded computer's video camera on. I do this regardless if it's a smart phone, a tablet, a desktop or in this case, a laptop. This is my way to be certain that no one is around the device I'm busting into. On that particular night, I was in for the shock of my life as I found two digital wallets on the hacked laptop with a total amount in the eight figures between the two cryptocurrencies. I am sure they were yours, Mrs. Rawlings, even before we verify the amounts and ID numbers.

"Why Jasper? How can you be sure before we check the IDs," asks Rawlings, while starting to breathe a little easier as she instinctively senses light at the end of the tunnel.

"Here's how I know. As I was downloading the digital wallets, a bleeding and badly beaten woman came running and stumbling her way into the room. She then hid under the bed. Not long after that, a man came into the room and dragged her out from under the bed and out of the room. Before he left, he turned the lights off. So, I was left in total darkness. Because the hacked computer video camera had low resolution lenses, I didn't have a real good look at either the woman or the man involved in the altercation. As I was about to disconnect, a flashlight was pointed at the camera blinding me out for a second. Then when I peeked, I saw the face of the man that had done the beating looking straight at me through the camera lens. It scared the hell out of me, so I turned the connection off. I presumed that in the darkness, as he was leaving, he must have caught a red light or something in the corner of his eye that indicated the camera was on. As I later cleaned all of the data out of the hacked computer, I saw no one had come back in. I concluded that I had nothing to fear, as in all likelihood the user and the abuser were both computer neophytes.

In horror, Elizabeth Rawlings blurts out… "Teske… the person you saw is my lead bodyguard and the woman was his girlfriend, who he regularly beats up."

"Yeah. The abuse victim. At first, I thought she was dead, but then I accidentally ran into her the next day when, out of morbid curiosity, I checked her ID information. I located her place of work, which turned out to be a Google office on Alton Road, Miami Beach. To my great surprise, she looked like nothing had happened to her physically and she didn't look at all like she had lost millions the night before. I figured that in all likelihood, she didn't know that she had been robbed or she didn't know about the currency sitting in her computer, as she didn't look like someone who was well healed.

"What to do now?" Rawlings asks.

"Call your attorney and ask him to bring the attorney for the seller back for the closing. Perhaps you can still catch them if they are still around. Where were you going to close?"

"Lincoln Road, Miami Beach."

"Perfect, because we do not have to return home. We can navigate you within a couple of blocks of Lincoln Road."

"Jasper, do you have access to the wallets?"

He smiles, "of course, always wherever I am."

"What an advantage guys like you have in today's world."

"Only if they put it to good use. Young man, you and I will have a very serious talk once this is over," warns his dad.

Rawlings reaches her attorney who in turn asks the others to drive back. 'Money moves mountains' she realizes as all agree.

The parties are eager to go back. 'Everyone wants their share of what amounts to a big real estate closing,' she reflects as she gets to do a redo.

Two hours later as the sun is setting, they navigate back to Paradise Island and when they dock, Rawlings' security details are there waiting. Rawlings intentionally left her smartphone at a poolside table, so they have no idea that the threesome spent the majority of their time away at an attorney's office closing the largest real estate transaction ever paid for with cryptocurrencies, bitcoin and ether.

"Not a word about what happened," states Johannsen senior.

Another run of the mill day on Paradise Island – unfettered talent and mischief, unwavering loyalty and discretion, reckless danger and adrenalin junkies. And after everything is said and done, moving on quickly to the next "rush."

Island resident, the old crow club member, Sarah Pesin's granddaughter Arlene, is getting tangled in a dangerous web of international terrorism as she has become mesmerized by a mysterious and magnetic young oriental American student.

CHAPTER 65
THE PESINS

Arlene Pesin has been sitting for at least an hour viewing picture after picture and they all look the same to her. She can hardly differentiate one from the other, Koreans from Japanese, let alone Chinese. She is getting tired of hearing the same questions over and over. How can she know what Chinese look like from different regions of the vast country? "Mrs. Pesin, we are trying to differentiate the key features of the face of the suspect in order to do a portrait. This individual may be a very dangerous terrorist. Please help us."

"To me they all look the same. A little while ago, I thought that I had figured out Koreans and Japanese as one group versus Chinese as another, but now you have just shown me a bunch of pictures of Chinese from the northeastern region and they all look Korean and Japanese. I am totally confused."

The Chinese police team huddles and their body language, especially their hand gestures, denote equal frustration. After a few minutes, they seem to reach an agreement and quickly disappear into the vast office space of the Shanghai police department headquarters. Within ten minutes, they are back.

"Mrs. Pesin, instead of drawing a picture of the subject, we are going to show you headshots of possible suspects. Let us know if you recognize the subject."

"OK, but I am tired, so it has to be quick. I am losing my ability to concentrate."

A large computer screen is rolled in and placed in front of her. Then, one by one, blown up images of mostly male suspects are shown to her. Surprisingly, she can distinguish one face from another thanks in part to the grueling previous session of her interview, where she learned something about the features of the different kinds of oriental men. Nevertheless, as the number of faces mounts, they start to turn blurry and soon the session turns monotonous again. The agents sense they are losing her again, so they speed up the scrolling. Each time she sees a resemblance, she stops the scrolling and looks at the image for a second time, but deep inside she is not expecting to find him in this gallery, or perhaps she does not want to find him… then to her horror, she sees him! Thankfully, her face and eyes are looking straight at the screen, so no one around her sees her reaction. Her first reaction is fear and the adrenaline rush keeps her scrolling. By the time the full impact of the sighting hits her, a couple of images have gone by.

"You seem tired, Mrs. Pesin."

"Yes, I am."

"We'll let you go then. Perhaps, you can stop again tomorrow so we can finish the interview and look at a few more pictures."

"Sounds fine to me."

Fifteen minutes later, Arlene Pesin walks once again through the streets of downtown Shanghai and feels a sense of déjà vu. She does not like it, as she can't help thinking about the last time she was walking the same city streets and she almost got robbed and killed. Nevertheless, she does feel healthy and clear-headed for the first time in weeks. Her modeling calendar and other professional engagements are all upside down, but she doesn't mind as her agent has already given her the heads up that everything is being rebooked. 'Like nothing has happened,' she reflects, while acknowledging the reality that something did freaking happen and scared the hell out of her. Then, as she walks, she keeps bumping into people trying to lure or convince pedestrians to enter their stores or dine at their restaurants. 'Gee, they are so aggressive and want the business so badly that they try almost anything,' she reflects as a young kid is offering an all-you-can-eat lunch for the equivalent of $3. The kid suddenly approaches her and whispers, "look at the restaurant display window on your left." She is surprised and tenses, but nevertheless turns her head and then sees a small electronic sign on the restaurant window that reads 'Thank You' followed by 'Thank you for what you did this morning.' She freaks out, then suddenly the message is gone. The lone policeman following her would later state, 'she seemed tempted to enter into a restaurant, but changed her mind. Besides that, she had limited physical contact. We have reviewed the video footage of her walk in great detail and can confirm that she had no contact with anyone except a beggar kid who tried to sell her something.'

Arlene walked as fast as she could back to her suite. She was rattled and scared.

'How the hell does he know what happened at the police station? I've got to get out of town right away. Right away, as in right now!'

She enters into her rented penthouse in a hurry and starts packing. Within 15 minutes she is ready to check out, when a text flashes on her smart phone.

"Mrs. Pesin, I hope you get a good night's rest. We will see you tomorrow at 10:00 a.m. unless you have a scheduling conflict that is work related. In that case, let us know as soon as possible, so that we can mutually agree on another time that is more convenient to you, but it must be tomorrow as well."

She sits down and realizes that the street experience has made her panicky and she totally forgot about the Shanghai police. She can't leave, at least not yet. She is stuck in Shanghai for the night and she intends to bunker down.

"10:00 a.m. would be fine, sir," she texts back.

"Have a pleasant evening, Mrs. Pesin."

"Thank you."

She goes to bed and drifts into a heavy sleep. When she wakes up she has no idea what time it is, except that it is dark outside. She stretches and feels hungry so she decides to get something to eat. She gets out of bed in a daze and as she turns to head to the kitchen, she lets out a muffled scream as she sees a figure sitting in the chair across the room.

"Mrs. Pesin, I did not want to wake you up, so I let you sleep." He turns on the lamp next to him and she immediately recognizes him.

"You!?!"

"Yep, it's me again."

The man sitting across from her is very young. The same age or a bit older than her. He is also extremely handsome and fit. She is attracted to him. The feeling is very intense and in a way, she cannot control it. Just like the first encounter when she saw his face in a flash, she feels very comfortable around him.

"The police are after you. They think you're a terrorist and that you planted the bomb on Nanjing Road," she says.

He stays silent, but staring intensely at her with a tiny smile in the corner of his face.

"You also know my name. You are obviously following me. You know what happened inside the police station. Now you have slipped uninvited into my room and then, to top it off, you laugh when I tell you that the police are after you, who are you?" she says trying to be angry.

"Do you believe what they are saying?"

She looks at him and is not paying any attention to the question, as she is mesmerized by him.

"Do you?" he insists softly and sexy.

"I don't know. How can I know? On first impressions, no. You are dangerously too handsome for me to think straight."

His smile is replaced with shyness and an expression of discomfort, even embarrassment.

'He is not accustomed to being anatomically praised,' she realizes as if intuitively detecting a weakness in him.

"Do they know who I am?" he suddenly asks with cold scary eyes.

"Are you kidding me? You know what I said over there and you don't know that? What is it? Do you like to play rhetorical games with people?"

"Mrs. Pesin, you haven't answered any of my two questions."

"Tell me who you are first."

"I am Lewis Wang, 24 years old, born in Santa Barbara, California. I am a computer science major from CalTech and have a Master's degree from Stanford University. At present, I am finishing my doctorate degree in applied mathematics. I came to China through an exchange program for three months, which is about to end. Born in Beijing, my father is a heart surgeon in L.A. Born in

Savanna, Georgia, my mom is a pediatrician, also in L.A. They met in med school."

She feels like a heavy weight has been lifted off her chest. However, as much as she wants to, her inquisitive mind does not let go. There are still things she cannot understand.

"How did you get in here?"

"I also live in this building, it just took a bribe." Her head is spinning.

"So when you ran into me that day, it wasn't a coincidence?"

"No, it wasn't. Ever since I first saw you downstairs in the lobby, I've been obsessing over you. That day I was following you, I was looking for an opportunity to introduce myself."

"What about the restaurant display window?"

"That was a long shot. I assumed you were coming back here on foot, which seems to be your preference."

"How do you know what happened at the police station?"

"I can't tell you that."

"Why?"

He stays quiet and does not respond.

"They don't know who you are, but they have your picture. Why would they have your picture?"

Again, he stays silent and she gets a chilling sensation that there is something dark and sinister about him. What she does not realize is that she is falling into a web of danger that will turn her life upside down.

Lewis Wang knows exactly why his picture was shown to Arlene Pesin. They have him as a person of interest in the investigation. But, for the moment, he is still free to move around town and even leave the country if he wants. How does he know this? Because the second highest ranking officer in the Shanghai police department is part of his team. It is time for him to fold his tent and fly back to the U.S.

Later that night, Arlene finds herself thinking about Lewis and after an uneventful second visit to the police, she is also ready to leave China. Once out of the country, Lewis stays in contact via text and as the days and weeks go by, the two form a bond.

"When are you coming back?" he asks knowing that a world-class model lives the life of a gypsy.

"Maybe never," she teases him.

"Well, after never ends and you feel like coming back, I want to see you."

"Well, my dear Lewis, that will be possible only after you answer some questions for me."

"Not through this channel, Arlene!"

"However you wish, but those questions come first."

"Then, we definitely have to meet because that has to be in person."

"So you'll have your way with me, Lewis? Is that how you operate with girls? Because if that is the way it is, it will not work with me."

"I'll see you when I see you, then," texts Lewis before signing off.

"Bye, stranger," replies Arlene as she leaves the conversation as well.

Unknowingly, the young globetrotting model is playing with fire as she falls for her rescuer hook, line and sinker.

Future Island residents, the hardworking and immensely talented Cuban musicians continue their inexorable march towards the American dream of stardom and success.

CHAPTER 66
THE ROJAS-LUGOS

The Rojas-Lugos have been living in a small condo in Hialeah for the last six months. The largely Cuban community has been a blessing for them as they have helped them with a smooth transition and assimilation into the American way of life. They straightened out their immigration status and legalization process by filing for green cards under the Cuban Adjustment Act. Then, they started their journey in pursuit of the American Dream. Everything is a discovery for the young couple. They open their first bank account and start using a debit card to withdraw cash or simply pay for things. Ana cries the first time she visits a supermarket. Juan also cries when he steps into the largest music store in town. Ana has to drag him out after several hours. He still cannot believe that there are so many brands of his favorite musical instruments. For a while, both become TV addicts and it takes a couple of months for them to learn how to record and play back whatever they want to watch. TV is what gets them going with the language and, amazingly, Ana progresses a lot faster than Juan, picking up the language at lightning speed. It takes a while for them to get a computer and it takes even longer for them to start to use it as both not only are PC illiterate, but they are also afraid of the device in a paranoid sense because somehow it reminds them of the Island's regime. Their fear is totally irrational, but they both act as if somehow, someone is going to spy on them, or worse, have some form of control over them. But when they finally become PC literate, it becomes an immediate replacement to their TV habits. They sit together for hours in front of the screen and learn how to navigate it. Then comes the purchase of a tablet, which makes it far easier to master and soon they are doing everything electronically, like paying bills, watching movies, listening to the radio or their music library and, in Juan's case, even playing musical instruments. Ana and Juan never learn to use the keyboard or mouse as they skip right into hand gestures and voice to command their tablet and soon after, their smart phones. They also are a bit crazy, shopping and spending more than they can afford, but that is understandable after years and years of repression with no ability to purchase anything and virtually nothing to buy.

Ana and Juan find work relatively quickly with a local salsa band and within weeks of their arrival they are doing gigs several times a week. On their six-month anniversary of arrival, Juan announces that they have enough money saved, plus what is left of their original savings that they brought along from Cuba, to move to a much nicer condominium. They chose one in Miami Beach, four blocks from the ocean. Juan also asks Ana if she agrees with putting $5,000 down on a small piece of land in Miami. She says, yes! He is actually going against the stream, as prices are depressed in that part of Miami. Juan still has to get the rest of the money, but soon learns that there is a banking system out there that is eager to lend. Juan's knack for real estate would develop over the years and he would gain a real estate investor's mind that would eventually earn the Rojas-Lugos enormous wealth, along with a beautiful home on Paradise Island. However, there are still vast oceans of uncertainty and hardship to navigate in their steep climb to success.

"Juan, your act is good. Really good, but we need a rhythm. A unique sound that will distinguish you from everyone else," states their Chinese-American producer on their first meeting since their arrival in the U.S.

"OK, we will work on it," replies Juan, while Ana smiles and both nod their heads. 'They have come a long way since those frantic times in Cuba, where she behaved like a caged wild animal,' reflects the producer, remembering their first encounter.

After their foray into real estate, this proves to be the second pivotal moment in the Rojas-Lugos' lives, as the request from their producer is the trigger and the catalyst for Juan to start composing, writing and producing music. In due order, Juan and Ana's musical accomplishments will become pure and simple, the stuff of genius.

In no time at all, the Rojas-Lugos go from victims of a communist totalitarian system to being postcards for capitalism entrepreneurship.

Island resident, largest home builder in the country, Leon Albert, is a very sick and deviant individual as his young guests will soon find out.

CHAPTER 67
THE ALBERTS' BAHAMAS PRIVATE ISLAND

As the afternoon sets in, the ocean breezes slowly bring the temperature down, and this makes the idyllic setting simply perfect. The postcard emerald-green waters and sandy beaches surrounding Leon Albert's private island in the Bahamas adds wonder to the perfection. The three teenage visitors waste little time in jumping into the pristine and translucent water. The three beautiful girls splash and play, enjoying themselves with the carefree attitude of youth.

"Why don't you girls swim out to the platform?" asks Albert from the edge of the beach. The girls look at him and turn their head to the floating deck a couple of hundred yards out from the shore. One of them shrugs her shoulders.

"Why not?" she replies and starts to swim. Then, the other two follow.

Shortly thereafter, they are all at the side of the platform and climb up the side ladder. Immediately, they start going down the water slide, which even though short, propels them into the water, flying first forward 7-8 feet in the air before dropping a good 6 feet into the water. The girls are soon having a blast. But, underneath the surface something is happening. A net in the shape of a ring fence around the platform is deployed from the bottom of the sea all the way to the surface. Nothing under the water can swim through it. Then, as the girls go up and down the ladder, the blood laced mesh starts to have its desired effect. Leon Albert watches from a short distance with his eyes zeroed in on his preys. The first girl to spot the shark fin is the tall blonde cheerleader and she screams from the top of her lungs. "Shaaark!"

The girls scramble up onto the platform. Soon there are half dozen sharks around. The sharks are on the other side of the fence, but they don't know this. Soon there is a shark frenzy biting at the steel fence. The three girls are in total panic and their screams get louder and more frantic. One of them finally remembers that Albert is close by and turns towards him, but the beach is empty.

"Help, somebody help!" But their cries for help are lost in the winds of the deserted island. Leon Albert, in the meantime, sits in his specially-built cabin. With his binoculars and video camera, he records every second of the terror he is causing his three guests. Leon Albert is a very sick individual that thrives and gets excited sexually only when he inflicts fear, panic and terror on his victims. He derives maximum pleasure when they fear for their lives and are helpless. When he sees one of the girls falling into the water, he knows the show is over. He runs to the beach, as the two girls are pulling the third one back onto the platform. The fence is now down and the blood source is gone. The sharks quickly retreat.

"What's going on, girls?"

"Sharks!" they yell back.

Leon Albert then unties a dingy that is ready for the occasion and within a couple of minutes he is at the platform rescuing them.

"Didn't you see us?"

"No, I am very sorry. I went inside the house for a minute."

"Why did you let us swim in shark infested waters?"

"Girls, that platform has been there for years. After 25 years coming over here, I have never seen a single shark on this beach." He lies, as he has done this countless times before with other victims.

That night as they sit on the open air living room floor of the main house, the three girls slowly at first, but then in earnest, start to relax and joke about the incident. On Sunday evening when they all go back together on his helicopter, the incident is just an anecdote to remember. But, to Albert, it is one more win on his insatiable quest for victims to inflict sheer horror upon.

But Leon Albert's games of fear and terror will soon come back to haunt him in the most unexpected of ways.

Island resident, world-famous neurosurgeon, Richard Greenhouse's vocation is grounded in deeply rooted childhood experiences and traumas.

CHAPTER 68
THE GREENHOUSES

The world-famous neurosurgeon, Richard Greenhouse, grew up as a farmer, like most everyone else in the Town of Triumph, Idaho. It has a population of 500. The whole town is like an extended family that lives together. Rich, as he's called ever since he can remember, is an optimist. Everything about Rich is upbeat, cheerful and funny. Seemingly, he wakes up happy, goes to sleep happy and greets everyone happy. Around town, whether at the community fairs or the religious services, everyone refers to him as the happiest boy on earth.

"What is it with this boy?"

"He must have been bitten by some kind of bug."

"I guess he has, but I have never heard of a happiness bug. Have you?"

"You think I'm kidding, but I'm not. How else do you explain, in the face of so much tragedy, that he's always cheerful and always has a big smile on his face?"

Today Rich is running late. He overslept and has to rush just to make it on time to school. His chores in the cornfields and the containers of freshly squeezed milk have been left unattended. Worst of all, he had no time to tell either of his parents about it.

Richard Greenhouse, Sr., Rich's father, gets up from his chair and as he walks out he states, "Well woman, now you can add irresponsibility to happiness."

"Honey, when are you going to stop being so negative. You're as cranky and grumpy as your son is sunny and joyful."

"Now I have to go and do 'Sunny's job. This is the way it's going to be from now on, right?"

"Richard, Sr., get over it. Oh, my lord, you can be a miserable and nasty old man when you want to be," yells Maryanne Greenhouse at her husband.

He turns his back on her with a poignant smirk on his face. Nothing has been the same for the Greenhouses ever since the oldest and vivacious daughter, Megan, was stricken with the polio virus when she was 8 years old. The disease had been terrible. It left her unable to walk or breathe on her own. Then, about a year ago, she died during the night, suffocated by the fluids from a cold. Megan was Rich's best friend, as well as his older sister, and her sickness had been the reason for his first interest in medicine and why he would later in life name his youngest daughter after her. He wanted to cure polio so little children like his sister could be saved. However, a dramatic and demanding incident in his personal life is about to happen and, through tragedy, Rich is going to make something extraordinary out of the most trying of circumstances.

Denzel Steele is also running late, but in his case, this is no rare occurrence, but a habit. His backpack over his right shoulder is moving from one side to the other as he runs down the sidewalk. His balance is precarious as he breathes even harder to pick up speed. After peaking at his watch he realizes he only has two minutes left to make it to his classroom.

If he doesn't make it, he is going to be suspended from school. "No more chances," the principal has stated. As he is preoccupied with the prospect, he thinks about his mom and how he has let her down on more than one occasion. He sprints forward even faster along the storefronts.

'Ain't gonna happen,' he thinks, as he glances right and left and sees an empty street. He is about to cross. He never sees Rich coming from the left side of Main Street. All he sees is the extended feet of the other runner as if perfectly placed to trip him. He gets hit cleanly, is propelled into the air and lands face first on Main Street. Denzel's broken neck, subsequent paralysis and a strong sense of guilt will be the other determining factors that will drive Rich to become a doctor. His goal becomes to cure paralysis and, in honor of the Steeles, he eventually spends part of his life offering his skills and knowledge to the people of Haiti.

Future Island resident, world class Italian shoe designer Laureen Krall, conceives of an idea that will bring her to Paradise, but her private life preferences will put her whole life course at risk.

CHAPTER 69
LAUREEN KRALL
(Part I)

5 3-year old Laureen Krall is a Wharton Business School graduate and an expert and icon in the Italian women's shoe industry. Earning $3-$5 million per year including bonuses, she has been in the industry for 30 years and knows it inside and out. She knows the best leather tanners, the best shoe designers and the best shoemakers in Italy. For the last fifteen years, she has been working for the same shoe brand. For the last five years, her employer has been, thanks to her, acquiring smaller shoemakers from around the northern Italian region. She has developed into an operational executive that organizes and sets up systems that integrate and commercialize small artisan shops that produce some of the best shoes in the world. Since she was hired, revenues at her company have increased from $100 million to $1.7 billion per year.

'A lifetime dedicated to a brand,' reflects Laureen, as she stretches in her bed at 35,000 feet. It is a dark, moonless night. Her double decker Emirates airline airbus cubicle gives her almost complete privacy. Her giant touch screen offers her hundreds of on-demand movies and TV shows. She has a huge music library to choose from and access to email and the internet. The "à la carte" menu is close to gourmet. On this plane, she can get a massage, take a hot shower, sit down at the bar to have a drink or perhaps just finish her current read, Andrew Carnegie's bio by David Nasaw. But, Laureen does not care about any of it, she is sick and tired of this lifestyle, except for the sex, of which she never gets enough. Just the thought of it makes her wet and horny and she wants it and wants it now. She checks her watch. It's time. She presses a button on her armrest and opens the cubicle's sliding doors. She now has a full view of the front section of the plane's cabin. She quickly goes commando and waits. As planned, her "boy toy" comes into view shortly after walking up from the economy section. He seems only half-awake when he stumbles his way into one of the front bathrooms. As agreed, the "busy signal" red light flashes on the wall panel. She then stands up and walks around the cabin. Then, exactly two minutes later, she is standing in front of the same bathroom door and on the dot the door lock is released and she quickly steps in. So begins the most exciting part of the flight for her. Being 30 years younger, her stud easily pins Laureen's back against the door while he parts her legs and quickly lifts them all the way up to his waist. He then lets her drop on him and thrusts harder and harder, deeper and deeper, for the next 15 minutes until he literally nails her. She convulses and pants in pleasure. Part of the thrill is doing it right there next to everyone on the flight.

"You are so wet today," he whispers.

"Sweetie, you don't talk, you just fuck," she snaps back. "Capisce!"

Then, as she explodes and contorts by squeezing and choking him in a sexual clash, he is barely able to contain himself. But, he knows better not to have an orgasm, as she only wants it her way.

Sure enough, once she relaxes, he lifts her legs up a bit so she becomes "unplugged" and then lowers her down so she can stand up. She quickly swaps places and he is now standing against the wall. Then, she kneels and grabs his boy toy with both hands and starts stroking it up and down while tightly squeezing it. She then swallows it like a big piece of candy and starts to suck it up and down with him not moving as previously instructed. She also plays with his sack as she continues the assault on her favorite instrument. She knows when his defenses are about to crumble and grabs it with both hands and points it at her face. He loses it. She sprays herself in sheer delight. Then, as she sits down on top of the toilet, he kneels down and she opens her legs wide for him to feast on her. Then, minutes later, as he is drawing circles around her clitoris with his tongue, she explodes again, this time louder, also trembling and shaking in pleasure. He then lifts her up and slides his hands underneath her blouse and rips her bra.

Aroused again she then eagerly takes her "send away" package, the tools to continue to pleasure herself while at her seat.

Ten seconds later she walks out of the bathroom and it immediately goes back to "busy" as he stays in. She walks gingerly on pins and needles back to her cubicle. Two crew members are watching through the corner of their eyes. Smiling, one tells the other, "I told you that around midnight she was going to have him for a late night snack. Always on this flight and always with the same man."

"How do you know all this?"

"Because he does me before and after the flight."

"But aren't they a couple?"

"No, he works for her and literally hates what he does."

"You know a lot about these two."

"He has to take Viagra before doing her in order to be excited enough by the time they meet in the bathroom."

"What a twisted world, she can have anything she wants except somebody to love that loves her back."

"She is not the loving type. She is all business, but let me tell you what happens now. The bathroom is just the beginning."

"I only see that she is back in her cubicle with the lights off."

"Well, let me tell you how and what she likes after her bra has been ripped. It's always the same. Just before she comes out of the bathroom, Laureen starts to tremble as her breasts are suddenly liberated. His hands slide under her blouse once more and she prepares. Then pain comes like a jolt, then intense pleasure as the clamps bite and pinch both her nipples. She then feels his hand moving down her back and gently applying a lubricant. Once again, pain is followed by an even more intense pleasure as an enormous butt plug slides in. Then his right hand moves even more deftly and he quickly inserts three Ben Wa balls linked by a string in her vagina."

"Now, I understand why she walked back so gingerly."

Five minutes later, Laureen is lying in bed and uncontrollably having one orgasm after another as she pleasures herself. She goes at it for another hour before she realizes what time it is. She abruptly stands up and heads through the dark corridor straight into the bathroom again.

"I told you she would head back there after an hour," says the crew member smiling.

"OK, partner, how do you know all of this?"

"How do I know? I told you he does me before and after," she says smiling with a mischievous look as the bathroom door sign on the wall monitor goes to busy.

"In a minute or so when she is ready, it is going to go back to open."

"And?"

"And now, I'm going in to do her," she says marching straight into the restroom.

As she walks in, Laureen is completely naked, which means that she can do with her whatever she pleases

Three hours later as they are landing, the two crew members are seated next to each other.

"Are you going to tell me what happened during those 45 minutes?"

"Eventually," the other replies nonchalantly.

NEW YORK (Laureen Krall's home office) (Part ii)

The idea comes to her by accident. A sleek Apple computer arrives via FedEx. Excitedly, Laureen opens the box and unpacks her new tool of trade. Then as she is about to throw the shipping box into the trash, something catches her attention. She starts to analyze the shipping labels on the box and right away her advanced expertise in logistics and supply chain kicks in. A few minutes later, she logs into her Apple account and goes straight into the "track your shipment" option.

'There it is,' she thinks.

'Point of origin, Shanghai,' her head is spinning.

'This mammoth company has just shipped my tiny order directly from their factory in China to my home. No inventory. Basically, my computer has been made/built to order.' This becomes the trigger for a business idea that will launch her as an independent entrepreneur. She then spends the next several weeks developing and researching her concept. She immediately quits her job and, as she expected, her non-compete contract clause (prepared and executed in Italy) does not include internet sales. This provides her with "carte blanche" to immediately start executing her plan.

NORTHERN ITALY (Near the City of Torino)

"I'm working for myself now, Vittorio," states Laureen.

"I see. So, you want to buy the leather from me?" states the tannery owner Vittorio Tomba, in broken English.

"Yes, I do, Vittorio. There is no better leather in the world than in Italy."

"That is very true, mia signora," he states.

Then, seemingly an endless silence ensues as they both stare intensely at each other. She knows full well that it is almost impossible to gain access to the finest Italian tanneries.

"Well, my doors are open to you. You're a long-time friend and I trust you. Whatever you need," announces Vittorio.

She gets emotional and hugs him. This successful event gives her the self-confidence she needs and she now goes after the Italian tanners who produce the finest leather in the world.

MILANO (Café de La Fontana)

"$1 million per year plus a bonus of 1% of sales working exclusively for me," proposes Laureen. Laura Cacciopo is enjoying her double espresso. She smiles at her friend.

"I don't need the money. I know you have the means to make me the offer. All you need to do is ask and even though I don't know what your strategy is, I'll be in. I know the money will come in bunches because you know this industry as well as many of the owners of the biggest brands. You're asking me to give up my independence as a freelancer?"

"Yes, I am and I know that you are the best freelance designer of women fashion shoes in this country, perhaps in the world," replies Laureen praising her old friend.

"It is only because of you that I accept. I hope you realize that!" states the exceptional 29-year old.

"Well, I understand there is trepidation but, trust me, we are going to disrupt this industry."

"I'll follow you anywhere, Laureen. Let's do it. My customers can always be regained as they need people like me on their never ending quest for newer/cutting-edge designs."

Laureen knows that Laura's customers are among the top Italian brands in women's fashion shoes and that makes her respect her decision even more.

"Laura, I want you to hook up with your favorite designers and come up with 10-20 new designs to choose from. Besides market rates for time spent on the designs, I'll pay every freelance designer behind it, $100,000 for each of the selected designs. This is in addition to the portfolio design that you have proposed."

"As always, provoking competition. I like it. Hopefully, you'll pick only mine, right?" asks an excited Laura.

"That's the idea, mia cara, that's the idea."

TORINO (MASTER SHOEMAKER GIUSEPPE VERDI)

"How would it feel to be on your own, Giuseppe?"

"Ahh, after 40 years in the industry, I would feel liberated."

"But you still want to stick it to them, right?"

Giuseppe shoots back at Laureen with a look of steely resolve.

"You have no idea how much."

"What if I were to propose for you to join me on a brand new venture. I'll guarantee to pay you the same income you have now plus 1% of the total sales. Furthermore, You'll be able to stick it to them!"

She's hardly finished when Giuseppe walks towards her and effusively embraces her, perhaps a bit too tight, then Laureen finds herself being lifted off the floor.

SHENZHEN, China
(30 DAYS LATER) (OFFICES OF LTN EXPRESS)

"Mrs. Krall, you asked us to prepare a report on how Apple exports products via courier to their customers around the world directly from their factories in China?"

"Right," answers Laureen Krall.

"The courier companies and Apple have agreements with Chinese and U.S. Customs for their products and they use pre-agreed bar codes that are scanned upon exit from China. When the products reach the U.S., they are scanned again. Taxes are levied automatically when the products are scanned. For random inspection purposes, products can also be identified by box dimension, weight and even box color, all of which are pre-approved and pre-registered for each product," states the LTN representative.

"I want to do the same, but for women's fashion shoes. Is it possible?"

"Yes."

"How long will it take to set this up?"

"Six to nine months on the customs side, from the moment we receive the sample products in their shipping boxes and four to six weeks on the IS systems (software) side, from the moment we are hooked up with your IS team or contractor. The process could be shorter, as the product is not electronics, but just apparel. Additionally, being luxury goods may also keep you away from quotas or special tariffs on garments."

"All right, we will have 10 to 20 models of shoes and their shipping packages ready for you within the next 180 days."

"We will research the matter further and reconfirm everything we've just told you about copying the Apple process. We will ship shoes from factory to consumer, instead of iPhones."

HONG KONG ISLAND

"What is your recommendation, Giuseppe?"

"You asked me to locate leather shoe manufacturers in mainland China that had the quality control and quality assurance standards to punctually manufacture and deliver products of the kind we are seeking. I started with a roster of possible candidates that exceed several dozen. However, upon closer look, I narrowed the number of companies to 20. I have spent the last four weeks visiting them, their resellers and even interviewing consumers."

"And?"

"I recommend three factories that are far superior to the others and have the financial strength to handle high volume. Choosing the three will give us the opportunity to spread the 20 models among them."

"Concerns?"

"You know that we will be copied!" states Giuseppe.

"Yes, quid pro quo, that's the price you pay in China."

"However, they don't have the leather."

"Yes, exactly. We march ahead, take advantage of their manufacturing prowess and the lower costs of manufacturing in China. Then, when they start copying us, we enter the market with our products that are of a far better quality," states Laureen.

"Boss, what's the next step?"

"If they accept our terms, we will sign manufacturing agreements with the three you recommend. Essentially, we will pay them a manufacturing/assembly fee per shoe, plus handling and transportation costs. After the contracts are signed, you will train them and when ready, we'll start shipping the leather from Italy to begin trial runs. You'll be present at all times. You must be here essentially all of the time for the first few months of operations, followed by frequent visits to ensure the quality of production."

"What about the rest of the shoe parts?"

"Everything can be sourced locally; the quality is up to standard and the price is much lower."

"All right then, I'll instruct the attorneys to contact you tomorrow. You can then begin contract negotiations with the three manufacturers."

SHENZHEN, CHINA (ONE WEEK LATER)
Offices of Dansyst, Inc. a software developer
of web based logistics and supply chain solutions

"Gentlemen, I've brought with me today the folks from LTN Express. They are a Dutch-based logistics provider with local offices here in Shenzhen," states Mrs. Krall. After introductions are made, she opens the meeting.

"LTN is working the customs and logistics angles. However, I need to hook them up with your company so you can work in tandem. Dansyst, Inc.'s job is as follows: You will set up a website, that after each U.S. customer places an order and pays for it, will transmit the order to our three Chinese contract manufacturers. The original order will be received first at our company's computer terminal in the U.S. The orders will then be transferred into your computer system. You will print the shipping instructions for the order and you will ensure that all of the orders will be shipped by these factories only to LTN Express in Shenzhen. At the same time, you will send the consumer's shipping information for the orders to LTN Express and only to them. A computer terminal will be installed at LTN for this purpose. Today's meeting is to ensure that you guys work hand in hand." Everyone nods in agreement.

"What's your business model, Mrs. Krall?"

"To sell Italian fashion shoes for women directly from the factory to the U.S. consumer at 1/3 of their regular price. We will sell them at $250 each, versus a market price of $750. We will offer 2-3 days delivery directly from the factory with the convenience of shopping through the web." Laureen can see that everyone is totally tuned-in and on the same page.

"The second reason I am here today is to inquire about the progress of the front end of the website. You know that I want to exhibit the shoes through gorgeous and stunning images. I also want 3D, so the clients can rotate the shoe on their tablets or smart-phones just by moving the mouse or with hand gestures." They all walk over to Dansyst's lab and spend the next hour watching a demo of web page screen shots showing stunningly vivid high-resolution 3D images.

"When will you be ready?"

"Website in six weeks. The logistics and ordering back end will be ready in 4-6 months."

"Make it quicker," she says even though the time schedule is perfectly fine.

NEW YORK (Laureen Krall) (Part III)

By using her deep knowledge of the Italian women's fashion shoe industry, as well as the world of logistics, supply chain management and web marketing, Laureen has been able to create a model of a global corporation for the future. Just a year in business and her company is already selling its products in over 30 countries. It sells north of 10,000 Italian design women's shoes every day at $250 each, for a gross of $2.5 million per day. She has done this by offering only 20 different models at 1/3 the regular market price. She sells only through her website, which showcases gorgeous images of shoes in 3D images that can be rotated to show every possible view of the shoe. Also, each customer's feet are digitally recorded for perfect fitting shoes. Customers receive their orders via courier in three to five days, directly from the factory. Perhaps the most amazing aspect of her company is that it operates at a run rate of $800 million in sales per year with no inventory of finished products. The shoes are built to order. She is paid in advance for her sales before she builds her products. She has done all of this with only 25 direct employees, which include an Italian master shoe designer and a world-class Italian shoemaker. She has no corporate offices, as all her employees are spread around the world and work out of their homes on company-owned computer terminals. She has no need for warehouses, plants, or equipment of any kind. Her company is organized under the laws of Hong Kong and all of her sales and profits worldwide are booked through it. Her mainland China branch makes all of the leather shoes, pays a manufacturing fee for the shoes to be built, pays the logistics provider to handle the finished products all the way to the consumer, and keeps books of all the export sales to and from China. This is the future. No infrastructure or financial burdens of inventory of finished products or accounts receivable. Laureen estimates that the cost of production and transportation is $70, and overhead does not exceed $5 per shoe, which means that she is netting up to 70% on her sales of more than $500 million a year.

"Mrs. Krall, congratulations," states the realtor to the stars, Regina Keys. Laureen Krall snaps to attention and comes back to reality. 'Where am I?' Then she remembers. "Congratulations, you are a brand new homeowner on Paradise Island. She stands up and shakes hands feeling a great sense of accomplishment.

But Ms. Krall's celebration is to be short lived as her tacky sexual practices will soon come back to threaten what she has worked so hard to build.

Island resident, surgeon to the stars, Steven Zathlyn's private life is not only kinky but his ways of deriving pleasure border on exploitation and promiscuity.

CHAPTER 70
THE ZATHLYNS
(The Bay Area Mandarin Hotel) (Part I)

Steven Zathlyn's hotel suite is a fitting reward as a final destination after a hectic day. In town for a conference and a couple of lectures, he has spent the whole day shuttling back and forth from the city's downtown convention center and the Stanford University campus. The room is in impeccable condition. It has a soft smell of flowers in the living room. The entire space smells like a forest in spring. The temperature is perfect. The carpeting is super cushioned and thick. The lighting is on dimmers. His favorite tune is playing in the background. He likes the feeling that everything is brand new. This is the time of the day for him to relax before what is going to be a 24-hour drill with stopovers in three states.

He turns his iPad on, but deliberately stays away from reading any email messages, news and especially the web. However, he does activate his iTunes favorite playlist and plugging in his waterproof wireless headphones, he jumps in the shower activating the powerful jet streams of hot water. He lets the water pressure massage his neck. He starts to think ahead and how unique and special the night is going to be as he intends to push boundaries and seek plain, straight and raw pleasure. Still dripping as he dries himself off, he looks at the illuminated bay area bridges through the wrap-around floor to ceiling windows of his suite's living room. The adrenaline rush of playing the great doctor and healer is starting to fade away, being replaced by rapidly building testosterone levels.

He types in the website's name, then after logging in, a home screen box promptly asks, "What are you looking for?" He quickly replies narrowing the search to a simple request. "20-25 years old, the most expensive companion money can buy." He then scrolls by sweeping left on the pad screen and one by one headshots roll by. Not satisfied, he then becomes more specific and narrows the search even further.

"Show me the top three only."

"Same age bracket?"

"Yes."

He quickly scrolls through the three images and is quite satisfied.

An hour later, Dr. Zathlyn, the surgeon to the stars, meets the three stunningly beautiful women in the lobby of a 20-story glass tower in downtown San Francisco. The three women have never met before and not even the $5,000 rate each is charging, makes any of them feel comfortable with this arrangement. It is only Dr. Zathlyn's calm and reassuring demeanor when he arrives, that prevents them from leaving. He kisses each one on both cheeks while gently pressing his hands on the top of their hips. 'Not an iota of fat on any of them,' he tells himself.

"Ladies, follow me, please. Let's have some drinks." They ride the elevator to the 20th floor and are greeted by a butler.

"Dr. Zathlyn, good evening."

They all walk into a glass structure with a magnificent bar where every liquor, wine and spirit is on display through the glass shelves that run wall to wall up to the 12-feet ceiling. They all sit down and after a few drinks, the ladies become relaxed and chatty. One lady is married with one child and works this job to support their lifestyle. However, Zathlyn suspects that there is more to that story. 'She likes it,' he guesses. The second lady is a college graduate working on her master's degree. She says she needs the money to pay for her tuition, but Zathlyn believes that that is not the whole story. The third one, is a track and field athlete. She is on the Stanford University track and field team. She is at least honest and says she does it because she loves sex.

"Ladies, which one of you has had sex with another woman?" They all look at each other and he can see that there is some common ground between the track and field star and the married woman.

"I never have," states the MBA student.

"What about group sex?"

This time nobody comes forward, but the sexual tension and anticipation are palatable. Zathlyn does not sense any descent or rejection.

'This bunch is ready to experiment,' he tells himself.

"Have any of you had sex with multiple partners?"

"What do you mean?" asks the athlete, not sure of what he is asking.

Obviously, two of them do not know what he is talking about, but the married woman does and she whispers an explanation to the others. An uneasy silence ensures, but again, nobody pushes back. An hour goes by and several drinks later the foursome is now totally relaxed, except for the sexual tension and libido, which are running wild.

"All right, let's move to more comfortable accommodations," he commands.

They stand up and walk together to the back of the bar where two sliding glass doors open. They step into a large living room in semi darkness. The room is filled with all kinds of sofas, framed by floor to ceiling glass windows that face the city. As the four adjust their eyes, they can see people all around them sitting or lying on the furniture. Some of them are chatting and laughing, but the vast majority are having sex. Girl with girl, girl with man, girl and girl with man, etc. Many of them are naked, but several are dressed. It does not take long for both women and men to start to approach the foursome. Before Dr. Zathlyn can intercede, a hostess approaches at a quick pace. "Dr. Zathlyn, please follow me." He follows and gestures for his three companions to do the same. They walk around the room until they enter a separate living room and, once inside, the hostess closes the door and leaves.

"Ladies, get yourselves comfortable, as we are going to have the time of our lives."

Veronica Lujan-Restrepo's turn to come back into the public eye has arrived, but even drowning in work by spending grueling hours filming her smash hit soap opera is not enough to protect her from all the attention.

CHAPTER 71
VERONICA LUJAN-RESTREPO

The set of the # 1 Spanish TV soap opera in the nation is filled with a lot more people than usual. There is a buzz in the air as the star of the show, Veronica Lujan-Restrepo, is making her first appearance since "the incident" with her neighbor.

In the final scene of the current season, Veronica's character tries to come back to her husband after she deserted him.

"I can't do only one side of the equation."

"What do you mean, I don't get what you are trying to say," she questions, with fear in her voice.

"I mean doing only for richer, but not for poorer, doing in health, but not in sickness and doing when in good, but not when in worst."

The tune in the background takes over. Alejandro Sanz's "Amiga Mía" fills the air with a magic melody.

"What did you expect me to do? I had no choice," she replies with a hollow voice.

He smiles, but says nothing. She then does what she always does when feeling guilty, she goes in for the attack.

"How can you be smiling at this moment?" she starts.

"It is not a smile of joy, but of sadness," he quietly replies.

"Something is wrong with you, no one smiles when they are sad," she counters in sheer ignorance.

"Even though knowing you so well makes your words so predictable, looking at the state you are in and what you've become saddens me deeply."

"You did this to me!"

"Blame and guilt do not work anymore."

She doubles down, when blaming and guilt does not work, she insults the other party in such a way that they fight back in anger.

"Nothing matters to you. That's one of your biggest problems, you have no empathy for others."

Again, the silence is replaced by the music and this time the trumpets of Sanz's "A la Primera Persona" take over.

Still no reaction from him. He listens and smiles. This infuriates her even more.

"And you are such a narcissist. Look at you so full of yourself. That's another problem you have, you think you are something you are not. You really think that you are better than the rest, but I've got news for you, you aren't." She ups the ante totally obfuscated by his lack of reaction and also feeling fear creep all over her as she gets a sense that she has no longer control over him whatsoever and she may have lost him for good. He just continues to stare at her with a benevolent smile. Sanz's "Corazon Partio" plays now and puts things into perspective. She then abruptly stands.

"You know what? I am going to leave. You are a coward. You have no balls. And you are sooo afraid of your mother, mamma's boy..." She is yelling at the top of her lungs, seemingly on the verge of getting physical. But panting and unhinged, she remains standing and does not leave. Not being able to provoke a fight completely rattles and exasperates her. Normally, the situation should have evolved into a shouting match by now. Without a confrontation, she is simply not in control.

Sanz's "Eres Mía" plays in the background. It evokes profound love. Misty love.

"Look at you, even at this moment you are lying. Lying to yourself. And that's your biggest problem, you lie about everything. You are sick and need help. It is a sickness and you can't control it." She is now crying inconsolably.

"I love you too," he says in response.

She knows that this is the moment when he delicately caresses her face and her hair, then a kiss followed by passionate love and that's how they'll make up.

Mecano's "Tu" takes over their silence and impregnates the air. The music gets to both of them as they look intensely at each other. But, nothing happens and fear spreads like wild fire through her. Sanz's "La Fuerza del Corazon" now irrupts through the stillness.

"But it does not work anymore. Nope. Blame and guilt do not work anymore. The magic spell is broken." He says dropping the gauntlet.

"You don't call. I never hear from you. I have been waiting for you. I still love you. I've always loved you." She now pleads, absent any histrionics.

"I simply can't reach out to you anymore as when it really mattered, you didn't answer my calls. That will never happen again. But you are always free to reach out and I will always be there for you." His reply evidences that he has reflected on what he is talking about.

Sanz's "Ellos son así" fits right into the moment, softening the building tension.

"And I can't see you either, unless you specifically request it. You always leave in moments when you know you could get away with it. That won't happen again," he says, adding to his previous thoughts.

"But, if there is love, why not try?" she asks.

"There is the love of a fantastic and magical life together and there is true love that we were able to find and that will never go away, and even though a breakup happened, you did not lose the father of your children."

"I have simply run out of words about us and you, I have nothing else to say." And these are his final parting words.

Cut. Scene No. 7. That's a wrap.

Everyone celebrates, kisses and hugs. The season is over and with the ratings through the roof, the show continues to be a mega hit. But soon everyone notices that Veronica is nowhere to be found. She left as soon as the scene ended.

Veronica Lujan-Restrepo is lost with the music in her dressing room at full blast.

Mecano's "Dali" fits right in with the piano and violin, as a prelude to the great artist's lyrics about his life and genius. That's the way she feels, as a misunderstood character, an eccentric, talented, extra-terrestrial. Why are her preferences so out of tune with society's norms? Don't we all have the choice to live however we want as long as we don't break the law. She feels judged. In a way, she feels like she is walking the plank about to be thrown to the sharks by a society that seems to be condemning her because of the media fascination with her.

The Pretenders' Chrissie Hynde's voice on "Sense of Purpose" takes over the room. Veronica thinks to herself, 'the power in her voice is like the power behind a strong modern woman.' Then, the lyrics hit her … What was she thinking? Her sexual drive and desire to hurt had taken control of her and she had literally lost her mind and almost got herself killed.

Then her entire room is inundated by the powerful notes of Mecano's "Aire." Yes, that's what she needs. Air. Air to drown the feeling of being judged and suffocated by public opinion.

She knows that Baglioni lost control of himself as well. And it went way beyond leaving the boat unmanned, that room was a trap and something made him snap.

Sinead O'Connor's version of Bernard Taupin "Rocket Man" pierces through the air and O'Connor's deep voice makes Veronica shiver.

Now that her secret is out, she feels like she is careening out of control. It is public news. She has not faced her parents yet, but she knows they are in pain and deeply embarrassed.

Laura Pausini's "Amare Veramente" slips through unnoticed at first. Then, as its magic spreads steadily throughout the room and the notes go higher and higher, Veronica's mind shuts down and floats as if in space.

Then, the Gypsy Kings' "Un Amor" comes across as music filled with pain. Through its beauty she can feel love and romance as the tune touches every string in her heart.

'Why can't I just love someone and live a normal life? Open my heart, be vulnerable, let myself be loved.'

Amaia Montero's "Quiero Ser" starts with a bang and quickly takes over the room and further elevates and heightens her spirit. She now feels like she is in a slow dance that never ends.

'Yes, that's what I'll do. Fall in love…find that someone.'

Her phone rings breaking the spell. It's her dad.

'OK, time to face reality. I have to find out if I still have a family and a career. I have to spend time with my parents, letting them vent while still being loving and respectful, but most important of all, I have to keep my dad under control and out of his vengeful ways.'

Veronica Lujan-Restrepo and her parents meet up...

CHAPTER 72
THE BAGLIONIS
AND THE LUJAN-RESTREPOS

M ario Angel Restrepo has not spoken to his young wife for weeks, but that has not stopped him from keeping a close eye on her. Whenever she leaves home, the tracking device in her car keeps tabs on her and when he is busy, a security firm has been engaged for the same task. So far, nothing seems out of the ordinary, except her solicitous and lately anxious requests to talk to him. All to no avail, as he is determined to keep her on ice for a little while longer. Besides, he's got a feeling that old habits die hard and somehow, somewhere, she is going to find a way to screw someone younger, fitter and stronger than him. That, he will not tolerate. He hopes and prays for it not to happen, because this time she will feel his rage, as well as her lover.

At present, what consumes Restrepo is another fire. He has Alessandro Baglioni in his sights. Another type of father would have perhaps chuckled when learning about the devastating injury Baglioni suffered, but for Restrepo that is not enough. For him that is nothing compared to what he has in mind for his daughter's corruptor. The only thing that has kept him from starting to plan the assault on and ultimate demise of Alessandro Baglioni is the fact that he has yet to see Veronica since the well-publicized boat orgy and crash. He needs to hug, kiss and assure her that he will take care of things. She has promised to drop by today, but she did not specify what time, so he canceled all his activities for the day and is simply waiting at the house for her to arrive.

"Sr. Restrepo, your daughter is just entering her mom's house," says the long-time housekeeper, Dora.

Restrepo heads right out and walks next door to his ex-wife's home. When he walks in, he finds mother and daughter fused together tightly hugging each other.

"Hija, hija, what are you doing with your life? This is not what we've taught you! This is not what God wants from you!" states her visibly shaken mom.

Restrepo walks over, hugs his daughter and states, "that bastard is going to pay!"

"Dad, I was not there against my will."

"But he could have gotten you killed!"

"Leaving the boat unmanned was reckless, but that happened in the heat of the moment," Veronica replies.

"So, what were you doing? Beating the guy up?" asks her father.

"Sort of," she replies in a whisper.

"And he asked you to do that?"

"Yes, and even though I hesitated at first, I went ahead nevertheless, as that is a man that needed a beating."

"Hija, and that is what you like? To hurt men?" asks her mom, Margarita.

"Yes and no. I play games with people that derive pleasure from pain. But, it usually is not dangerous. In this case, though, once I made up my mind, I did want to hurt him and badly as everyone

342

on the island knows that he abuses his wife," states a slightly embarrassed Veronica Lujan-Restrepo.

"Veronica, what is it with you and hurting men? Have I ever done anything to you to cause such anger?" asks Mario Angel Restrepo, entering the conversation.

Veronica does not know whether to laugh or keep a straight face. How can she explain her private life to her parents without causing them more pain and embarrassment? She thinks long and hard and decides a course of action.

"I do not like hurting men. Not one bit. But, I like to experience sex while inflicting pain. It has to be intense like that, otherwise I am not satisfied. Dad, you have been and are still the best father any daughter could ask for."

"Hija, perhaps you can go to therapy to cure your problem." Margarita interjects.

"Oh, Margarita, shut up! Your daughter is not sick and does not need therapy. She has sexual preferences that are different than yours or mine. That is all."

Veronica feels relief and acceptance from her father. She walks towards him and embraces the old man like a little girl and then starts kissing him on each cheek.

"I love you dad, and always will."

Later on after they finish dinner, Veronica wants to make sure that her dad has abandoned any thoughts of revenge against Alessandro Baglioni.

"Dad, I want your promise that you won't do anything to our neighbor. Believe me, he is facing a very uncertain future as it relates to his most important, at least for him, organ."

"It's a promise Veronica," states Mario Restrepo. Mario believes what he is saying. However, he is unaware that Baglioni is planning his own revenge.

Island residents John Bell, Jr. and old crow club member Elizabeth Bell, are the children of a pair of World War II ace pilots. He is the son of John Bell, an American squadron commander and war hero. She is the daughter of Ernesto Otto Heidrich. They are both heirs to the mammoth pharmaceutical company their parents started decades ago

CHAPTER 73
THE BELLS AND THE HEINDRICHS
(Part I)

The black Rolls-Royce Phantom is moving at 90 mph, but on the magnificent back leather seats it feels as if the car is hardly moving.

70-year-old John Bell Jr. has just finished his customary round of golf at his club in West Palm Beach and is now heading south on I-95 to his home on Paradise Island. He has a luncheon meeting with a prospective new executive director for his company. If the candidate is suitable, all he has to do is sell the candidate why a move to Miami is a great thing. He intends to do this hopefully with the help of his wife, Elizabeth Bell. She is one of the old crows of Paradise Island. She has been calling him incessantly, but he has yet to answer the phone. He'll be home exactly at the agreed time, so what is there to talk about!

"Sir, I have your wife on the phone," says his long-time chauffeur, Jean-Philippe.

"Yes, Elizabeth, what is it?"

"My dad has just passed away. Since I could not reach you in the meantime, I've informed your father."

'For his 98-year-old father John Michael Bell, Sr., the news must have been pretty hard. After all, Ernesto Otto Heindrich was his lifelong best friend.' He quickly snaps back to reality and realizes that his wife is still on the phone.

"Sorry darling, I am on my way home, I'll be there shortly. I am so sorry." But the line is already dead. She is upset and she has the right to be. John Bell, Jr. starts remembering the time his father first met Heindrich.

Houston, Texas (1955)

"Dad, this is my new friend, Elizabeth," says 8-year-old John, Jr.

"Hi, Elizabeth," says American hero and flying ace, John Michael Bell, Sr.

"Sorry, but she does not speak English very well."

"Where is she from?"

"From what I gather, South America."

"But she looks European."

"I don't know anything about that, dad, all I know is we get along well together. She is a lot of fun. Also, I think from her body language she is trying to explain, that her dad has something to do with aviation. That is why I brought her to meet you. Her dad will come soon."

"Very interesting, let me know when he arrives. In the meantime, go and have fun and don't forget to let me know when he shows up even if I am busy."

"Hi there," says the tall young man with a thunderous voice.

John, Sr. is in a deep sleep as he lies on the grass next to a picnic basket. This is his only time in the week to completely disconnect, a Sunday, when he takes his kid John, Jr. to the park. John, Jr. comes running and starts shaking his dad awake.

"Dad, dad, wake up, Elizabeth's dad is here!"

John, Sr. makes a half turn on the ground and then opens his eyes as he looks up.

"Yes?"

"I'm Ernesto Otto Heindrich, Elizabeth's dad."

"Oh, I'm sorry," replies Bell as he quickly stands up and shakes hands.

"The kids get along quite well," says Heindrich.

"Did you just get here?" asks Bell.

"No, I have been on that pavilion over there, far enough away to have peace and quiet, but close enough to keep an eye on my daughter."

"So, where are you guys from?"

"Venezuela."

"But you look like…"

"Yes, we do, my parents are from Hamburg, Germany."

"So, tell me what brings you here?"

"I'm a test pilot for the Venezuelan Air Force."

"My first stop is here in Fort Worth to take some training courses, then onwards to the Mojave Desert in California to do a series of test runs on fighter planes bought by our government from Lockheed."

"What about you?"

"Well, I guess the world is small sometimes. I was also a test pilot, but the U.S. Air Force recently transferred me to NASA, the U.S. space agency."

"Mr. Bell, perhaps you can help me. Where can I fly gliders around here?"

John Sr. suddenly gets hit by a torrent of emotions. He looks at his new acquaintance with total joy.

"Mr. Heindrich, today is your lucky day."

"You know about gliding?" asks Heindrich.

Both Ace pilots spend the next hours dumping their extraordinary lives on each other. One a hero of the victorious allied forces, the other an accidental recruit and then a prisoner of war, sharing not only their passion for flying, but also their passion for gliding. Even though Bell is a bit older, they are both veterans of the same war.

Bell and Heindrich set out to fly together and they did so with a vengeance. They glided, flew antique and acrobatic planes and a solid friendship emerged.

Not only were Bell and Heindrich great at aviation, they were great at making money. They started a company together that had its roots in events that happened in Hamburg, Germany, just as the war was ending, right after Heindrich had been liberated from a prisoner of war camp …

THE BELLS AND THE HEINDRICHS (Part II)
The Ruins Of Hamburg, Germany (August 1945)

"Young man, we as family don't have much left, but we don't want to send you back to South America with nothing but two years as a prisoner of war at a Russian concentration camp," said Uncle Kurt to young Ernesto Otto Heindrich.

Heindrich and a friend had just completed a walk from Frankfurt Oder, Poland, all the way to Hamburg, Germany, and part of the trek they did barefoot. Ernesto Otto had arrived looking like a walking skeleton. Both of them had been released from the camp because their captors did not believe they were going to survive their lung infections. But both did. They started deep into Polish territory, now occupied by Russian forces, and had first walked shirtless and shoeless for several days. People in a small village at the Poland-Germany border gave them clothes and food. Their trip was from town to town, from hand out to hand out. Heindrich had arrived at his uncle's home with a single idea in mind - to get back to his home country of Venezuela. Realizing that he needed traveling documents, he hitched his way across the devastated and hungry Germany to Bern, Switzerland. Once his nationality was confirmed at the Venezuelan embassy in Bern, he had a passport issued. Back in Hamburg, he had made plans to travel back home in ten days' time on a cargo vessel via Oslo, Norway. A life changing event was about to take place, as he was thanking all of his relatives for the two years they had hosted him before he was recruited into the German Air Force, the Luftwaffe.

"Ernesto, these are matters that at your young age of 18 perhaps don't matter much," continued his Uncle Kurt. "I'll explain them to you, as they may shape your future someday. I am a patent attorney and before the war, I ran the largest law office in Germany dealing with intellectual property." Young Heindrich looks at his uncle with a puzzled face not really knowing what he was talking about.

"Since the 19th century, my country has been at the forefront of many scientific developments. In the area of chemistry, we have led the world in recent decades. Chemistry, young man, is the backbone of the development of modern medicines. Thus, many of the formulas for thousands of modern medicines were developed here. Unfortunately, the war destroyed most of the industrial apparatus of Germany and with it most of the labs and enterprises dedicated to the production of medicines. The good news is that most of those patents and formulas are in my possession and I have secured either exclusive rights, licensing or outright ownership of a significant amount of my country's intellectual property in the area of medi-caments. So this is my gift to you, my boy. I am transferring to you all of the rights, licenses and patents for your eventual commercial exploitation. Always remember this, once you have the maturity and are ready, your starting point, the market you want to start your efforts in is North America. Do not look anywhere else. Additionally, I am also assigning to you the exclusive representation and distribution rights that I have secured from current or former clients. I control 50 of the largest German manufacturers of industrial machinery. This should be a good springboard to get you started in South America. Anyone in need of German machinery in South America or the Caribbean will have to go through you."

Young Heindrich understood what his uncle had given to him and he realized the wisdom and the value of what Uncle Kurt had said to him. Ernesto Otto Heindrich was to remain his uncle's benefactor for the rest of his life and he was going to give his uncle the gift of immense joy and pride in his nephew's future accomplishments.

Ernesto Otto Heindrich finally arrived back in Venezuela a couple of days after his 19th birthday. He had left 7 very long years ago. It seemed to him that he had lived several lives in one. He established a company within a month and dedicated himself to promoting German industrial machinery and equipment, first in Venezuela and soon thereafter throughout Central America, South America and the Caribbean. For each sale, he would process the order, secure payment in favor of the manufacturer in Germany, then arrange shipment, installation, training and maintenance. As the equipment and machinery were big ticket items, young Heindrich was already, in his early twenties, making hundreds of thousands of dollars. Also, each year, as the region developed and grew, his income also grew. By 25, Heindrich was already a millionaire. However, Heindrich's passion in life continued to be flying. Even after he married and had his daughter Elizabeth, Heindrich spent all of his free time flying away from work and family. He started to fly into the Amazon jungles to bring food and medicines to the Indians. He loved to help and to explore. In that effort, he also became a reserve in the Venezuelan Air Force as a test pilot.

THE COMPANY

Two months into their friendship, Heindrich mentioned to Bell Sr. that he had secured exclusive rights, through a family-owned law firm in Hamburg, Germany, to a large portfolio of German licenses and patents for pharmaceutical products. The German companies, factories and labs involved in the manufacturing of the products were in disarray because of the war. This caught airman Bell's full attention and he took it upon himself to check and vet thoroughly their value and commercial application in the United States. It did not take long for Bell to realize that his young ace mate had in his possession a treasure trove of unique drug formulas that could be the basis for a major business. So it came as no surprise that the company they founded together, equipped with the best German manufacturing equipment available and then ran with the same precision they piloted planes, had made both of their families among the wealthiest in the country. The fortuitous encounter in a park in Houston, Texas, was the beginning of a long friendship and partnership. Then, when their kids, John Bell, Jr. and Elizabeth Heindrich married, the ace pilots went from close friends to becoming family.

But a patent and intellectual property rights problem is about to explode and threaten the company the two ace pilots founded.

Island resident, corrupt lobbyist Bart Holstein's parents met in "the Paris of the Middle East." That is what Beirut, Lebanon was called then. Everyone in the family knew that the stormy relationship between Eladio Alalu and Andrea Holstein had started in the most unlikely of fashions, but no one would have ever predicted how it was going to end.

CHAPTER 74
THE HOLSTEINS
La Habana, Cuba (1950's)

From the beginning of their romance in Beirut, Lebanon, through their marriage, Eladio Alalu and Andrea Holstein's relationship was doomed. She was simply too hot to handle. Andrea liked men too much and literally could not keep her panties on, as she seldom wore them. Sex was always a flick away for her. Their marriage was the laughing stock of the large Sephardic Jewish community in Havana. On the other hand, Eladio Alalu's fortune in everything else had a Midas touch. Ever since his arrival on the island, Eladio had prospered into one of the wealthiest merchants in the capital.

First, he used his knowledge about gourmet products and delicacies from his old smuggling days in Beirut to import into Cuba fashionable and hard to get products from Europe, especially from Italy and France. His trading company exploded in sales as he not only opened stores, but also distributed to his competitors on the island. Eventually, he secured exclusive rights and a monopoly on the island for all the products he carried. Eladio also started acquiring real estate with all his burgeoning income. He bought small buildings, large colonial houses and empty lots all around Havana. He then renovated the properties and put them up for rent. He kept some of the space for his own stores. In the larger spaces, he opened hotels. Within five years of his arrival in Cuba, Eladio Alalu was a multimillionaire. He frequently flew to Miami for business or as a connection point for trips to New York, the west coast, Europe or Asia. He finally realized that it was perhaps in his best interests to move to America and shuttle back and forth to the Island. So, he started planning the move. In 1957, based on his eye for good land, he purchased three one-acre parcels for $10,000 each on the semi-empty Paradise Island in Miami Beach. He immediately started to build his new family home on one of the parcels. His plan about the move and new home was kept a secret from his wife and family. His plan was to surprise them on a future visit to Miami Beach. He also started to move cash from his Cuban businesses to Miami.

As his fortune grew, Eladio's old pirate's physique changed, but unfortunately in the wrong direction. He had arrived in Cuba at a lean and buff 180 lbs., an ideal weight for his 6'7" frame. Seven years later, Eladio's weight was just short of 300 lbs. He became prematurely obese through the thousands and thousands of hours of zero physical activity, except work, and eating the rich and fatty local Cuban food.

Eladio Alalu adored his wife. For him, she could do nothing wrong. Whatever she wanted, he provided. However rude, loud or insulting she was with him, he always responded lovingly and gave her anything she was demanding. There was nothing more important in Eladio's world than his family. So, on one of the sporadic occasions when they had sex, they had conceived and were blessed with a boy they named Bart, the future lobbyist and best friend of a U.S. president.

Life seemed idyllic and perfect in Eladio's mind and heart. The problem, though, was that seemingly he was the only one on the entire island that did not know that his wife was screwing any pair of pants that crossed her path. Andrea Holstein was insatiable. She was deep into an almost sick fascination for the male anatomy. She liked them young, strong and with perfect bodies. She liked them from any ethnic group and she even took them in pairs at the same time. What Andrea Holstein did not like one bit was her husband. She actually despised him. At home, her rejection levels reached intolerance and she could not even bear to hear his voice or be in his presence. He was an obstacle to her living the way she liked and she hated depending on him for money. For Andrea Holstein, like with all men, she grew sick and tired of Eladio. After seven years of marriage, he had transformed himself into a walking meatball that had driven her from fondness for him as a likable friend, to loathing him. Eventually, their dissonance was to evolve into a discord with an unimaginable crash!

It all began when Andrea deliberately avoided sex with Eladio after she got pregnant. Then, she kept him in the dark about the pregnancy. This was compounded by her continuing her old ways, since her teens in Lebanon, when she sang in night clubs, dressed in skimpy clothes and performed in front of rowdy patrons, many of whom she later took to bed.

"She looks and dances like a Middle Easterner," says the visiting Syrian who has experience in selling Persian rugs.

"She has been the hottest little thing in town for the last few years," adds the host.

"How old is she?"

"She is in her mid-twenties," answers his local customer and an Iranian rug importer.

"I love her body, it's tight and strong. I also like her boobs, not too big, not too small, but round and firm and I can see she has really big nipples. I also like the way she moves and her energy. I still believe she is from the Middle East," the Syrian responds to his client and friend.

"She indeed is."

Now the Syrian is really interested.

"How do you know she is a Middle Easterner?"

"Because she is the wife of a friend."

"Is your friend a pimp?"

"No, she is not a prostitute, she is a nymphomaniac."

"And him?"

"A very good man who is completely oblivious to her promiscuity. Hence, only a decorative figure that provides her with a very nice life during the daytime."

"A cornuto! A cornuto!" the Syrian voices aloud.

"What?"

"An Italian expression which is a pejorative for someone that his or her spouse puts or places horns on."

The Syrian is gone. He is hooked and on fire. Sure enough, a couple of hours later in her dressing room, he has her, or at least that's the way he sees it, when perhaps it's the other way around, she has him. But for him, it's an "out of this world" experience. No one has pumped and squeezed him that hard and intensely ever before in his life and although he is done in a couple of minutes, he is obsessed. She, on the other hand, is not all that pleased. 'First and last, a softie with two minutes of fuel in the tank and a very large ego,' she thinks. She has forgotten the way men behave in the Middle East. The rug trader has already made up his mind and he not only wants her, but he wants her all for himself so she can join his modern harem consisting of four wives and six concubines.

"Leave your husband, come with me to Damascus. I'll give you anything you want," he pleads with veiled authority.

"How do you know I am married?" she asks, on guard and quite angry.

"A little bird told me, but don't worry, no one has to know. We leave today and in a few days you send him a letter."

"Get out!"

"One hundred thousand dollars in cash."

"What?"

"One hundred and fifty thousand dollars in cash before you leave."

She is flustered and about to explode. She does not care about money beyond what she already has. All she cares about is sex and singing. She detonates, jumps at him, and with her face inches from his, yells at him from the top of her lungs. "Get out or I will call security!"

"I know you like me very much. I know you enjoyed squeezing me out. Let me be your man. I'll satisfy your every need. I'll give you everything you ever dreamed of."

She now wants to hurt him and decides to be simply just her, blunt and brutal.

"Actually, I did not like it very much."

"You did not like what?"

"The sex and your penis is too soft and not big enough for me. C'mon man you were done in less than two minutes," she says, humiliating him.

"For me it was a one-time thing only. I am just being very honest with you," she continues with a sardonic smile and smirk on her face.

"Too quick and soft for you then! So for a whore like you what does it take to impress you?" he states with fire and venom in his eyes. He takes a step forward and tries to grab her by the neck, but being well trained in defensive maneuvers she stops him cold with a kick to his nuts, followed by an intercom call to security to rush to her dressing room.

"You'll hear from me again, dirty bitch," he screams, as two security guards forcefully drag him out of the room and then throw him out of the club. She does not pay much attention as she's had her share of similar situations with obsessed sex partners who she has ditched. In every instance, she forgets the whole thing after a few days. But none of her jilted lovers had come from that part of the world where men reign supreme and where wounded pride always has only one remedy, one where women never win.

A couple of days later, she walks back home at her usual time of 10:00 p.m. She knows that within an hour her husband will be back, so after checking on her son Bart, who was already put to bed by his nanny a couple hours earlier, she heads to the kitchen to fix dinner for Eladio before he arrives.

"Andrea, I am already here."

She is surprised to see him sitting in the living room reading the newspaper.

"You're home early," she says flustered and already irritated.

"And you're late. Quite late. Where were you?" Eladio asks. Her nerves explode.

Up to that very night, Eladio always thought that every day she was home early enough to care for Bart and put him to bed.

"I was out with friends," she replies boiling inside. Her tone is nasty, seeking to stop him from asking anything further.

"No, you weren't," he says standing up.

"What do you care? You are always busy and never available to give me any attention," she says going on the attack, trying to play the blame game. But at the same time she starts to panic.

'What does he know?' Soon enough she finds out.

"I saw you, Andrea. I was there the whole time."

A long silence follows until she blurts sheepishly. "You've always known that that's what I love to do."

"That I know."

'OK, he knows I sing, so what?'

"And I will still continue to do it. Nothing will stop me," she states trying to regain her normal role of dominatrix of their relationship.

"What is it that you are not going to stop? The singing or the fucking?"

"You bastard! Don't insult me like that!" She jumps over him trying to slap and kick him, but his smuggler street-fighting ways take over and in a second he is bear hugging her from the back and without a single blow he completely neutralizes her. She is impressed by his strength and manhood. Andrea Holstein is aroused and hot as a volcano. His power awakens her insatiable appetite.

"I want you," she says in a seductive voice filled with desire.

As angry as Eladio is, he is also filled with sexual tension. Without a word, he lets go of his grip a little bit and she turns around still trapped by it. Facing him she commands, "Tear my clothes off. Tear them off now."

His anger then turns into sexual energy and he tears her clothes in four brusque movements. She then throws herself on him.

"Do you like me?"

Before he answers, she kneels down and opens his fly and starts to suck him in rapid and intense movements. He moans in pleasure and ecstasy. She then lays down on the living room rug and facing him opens her legs and starts touching herself while slowly moving her hips in wide circles.

"Come," she asks in between panting sounds. "Come."

He is about to undress when she stops him.

"Come now, dressed as you are, come."

He obeys and drops to his knees and swiftly thrusts inside her. No sooner has he done this when she turns him around and sits on top of him penetrating herself through sinuous movements that quickly become faster and faster and faster as she tightens her muscles.

"This is a crab claw," she tells him while she squeezes him into sheer delight.

Then, as a dormant volcano becomes alive, both husband and wife climax at the same time with an intensity that relieves all of the tension that floated above them just a few minutes ago. But, Eladio, feeling powerful and sexy, takes off his shirt exposing all his rolls of fat, cellulitis and the thick hair on his chest. Although, Andrea is in a rush as she has just climaxed like she has not in a long time, when she catches a glimpse of her husband's physique, she becomes nauseated. Her anger then rises again and she explodes yelling and screaming.

"You're a fat, good for nothing husband, except for your money. What did you expect? Look at you. I can't stand the sight of you. I had to look for real dicks and real men out in the world. And yes, I've had hundreds of them since we got married. You hear me? Hundreds of them. Every day and every night. Since the beginning of our marriage, I have had them of every color and size there is in the universe." She vents more out of fear of herself than anger at him, as the coitus she just had is the best she's had in years.

However, she is too depraved and damaged to allow herself to depend on anyone emotionally. Thus, her instincts are to push back as hard as she can.

With deep sadness in his eyes, Eladio starts to stand as he looks at her fiery eyes filled with contempt and total rejection. Eladio Alalu's veins on his neck start to explode. His eyes are bloodshot, throbbing and bulging out of his eye sockets. He slaps her so suddenly that she has no time to react. The blow is so hard that it snaps her head to the side and her lip starts to bleed. She tries to swing back at him, but before she does, he slaps her again, this time harder.

"I swear to you, disgusting ball of fat, that I am going to have you killed, so you better kill me first."

This time he lands his fist with full force on her upper cheek and catapults her up into the air. She flies for a second and then lands hard on the floor, head first.

"I love to fuck, don't you get it? It is not that you didn't give it to me good this time. We just had a great time, but when will we do it again? …in two to three days? That's nothing, Eladio. I need that two or three times a day. You see, you don't give me enough. You never will. You are pathetic and impotent. I hate you. You hear? I can't stand you …" she stops as she suddenly sees a gun pointed at her, but she does not care anymore about anything.

'I am going to let him have it before I go,' she screams in her mind.

"Bart is not yours. He is Alvi's son. Yes, your partner and best friend from the old days has been fucking me each time he has visited the Island. I wanted Bart to be his, so for two months I had sex with no one except him."

Eladio Alalu looks like he has been shot. He starts shaking and trembling and then hits the floor hard with a heavy thump.

A shot is involuntarily fired upon impact and an entire glass cabinet in the dining room is shattered by the bullet. She slowly stands up, only to meet the intense, wide eyed stare of her dead husband lying on the floor.

After the fact, the coroner determines that he suffered a massive heart attack.

Soon thereafter, Andrea Holstein leaves Havana for good. She takes with her a significant fortune, after liquidating all of the family assets in Cuba. She adds this to the fortune already in place in Miami. She barely beats the fall of the dictator Fulgencio Batista and the ascension to power of the communist Fidel Castro. Andrea Holstein, in her late twenties, moves into her brand new mansion on Paradise Island, Miami Beach.

Her ways never changed. She never married again and she never went by the last name of her dead husband. She was Andrea Holstein, rich matriarch of Paradise Island. She continued to have sex with as many men as she could. Over the years though, the age of her partners went precipitously down, as the number of her cosmetic and plastic surgeries went up. Bart grew up in this environment, where a promiscuous, distant and uninterested mom always thought about herself first and always got what she wanted. He made it to Harvard, partly because of her generous contributions to his future alma mater. In her sixties, Andrea Holstein developed Alzheimer's disease. Bart took over the Paradise Island mansion, got married, started a family and became a powerful and successful lobbyist. However, the traumas of his upbringing and the dark secrets of his mom that she hid from him since birth, eventually all caught up with him.

And that is how Island resident and corrupt lobbyist Bart Alalu became Bart Holstein. But in reality, he should have been named Bart Mazon as Alvi Mazon was his real father. Bart did not have the foggiest idea about any of this – but eventually when he finds out, it will come to haunt him.

Island resident, owner and CEO of the largest cruise line in the world, Ariel Mizrahi's parents did not tell him the truth either about the events that led to his birth or his mother's greatest love.

CHAPTER 75
THE MIZRAHIS

Alvi Mazon and his wife stayed in Lebanon after their marriage. Her father had retired and Alvi took over the fleet of cargo ships. He streamlined the operations and doubled the volume of business within a year. The ships were at first repaired, then retrofitted and finally replaced one by one by much faster and more fuel-efficient vessels. He also expanded the fleet with larger boats to accommodate all types of cargo. He opened additional routes and the Mizrahi fleet soon covered all of North Africa, from the Spanish Sahara all the way to Egypt; the Middle East to the Mediterranean; and Israel all the way to Turkey.

In addition to his business prowess, by all accounts Alvi's marriage was a success. They seemed to love each other. Yet, after several years as a couple, there were still no kids. However, behind the scenes, the Mazon-Mizrahi union had friction that derived from Alvi's philandering when he traveled out of town. As soon as his wife learned about his activities through crew members loyal to her father, she went back to her married Arab lover. For a couple of years, the marriage seemed to function with each having a double life. They both seemed content and happy when together. However, both found a need to be in the arms of others.

Five years into their marriage, Alvi made a business decision that would be the catalyst for the Mizrahi family fortune to become one of the largest in the world. Alvi decided to start a passenger transport business to shuttle people back and forth between Europe, Africa and the Middle East. He introduced brand new and comfortable vessels. This was his first spectacular success. His second success, the acquiring of luxury transatlantic boats with luxury cabins, massive dining rooms, entertainment halls, pool decks, etc., was the big winner. The first route he opened was a cruise of the Balearic Islands in Spain. Then, he opened a route to the Adriatic Sea vis-à-vis the Northeastern coast of Italy and across the Croatian Coast. Then he added the Greek Islands and the Turkish Coast, including Crete. The cruise ship fleet grew steadily as not only Europeans, but people from all over the world, discovered the pleasures of cruising the Mediterranean Sea and the beautiful ports of call in high comfort and style through the Mizrahi cruise line.

Alvi and Leonor decided to try their Mizrahi cruise experience for themselves and booked passage to the Greek Islands, honeymoon-style in the presidential suite. The honeymoon ended for Leonor when she found out that her husband cheated on her on the cruise. He was intimate with one of the female officers on the ship, who apparently was a long-time lover of her husband, and hooked up with him when he was on board any of the Mizrahi family ships where she was a crew member. When loyalists to her father informed her about the officer's presence on the cruise, she thought that Alvi, out of respect for her, would refrain from any extramarital activities. The first couple of days, she remained hopeful as they hardly left the cabin and had sex non-stop day and night. But the hurtful news came on the third day, when Alvi was absent for about an hour. He was supposed to be attending a briefing with the ship's captain, which turned out to be a 10-minute conversation, followed by 50 minutes in the cabin of the female officer. Leanor's informers confirmed to her that the brazen duo had wild and loud sex for nearly an hour. Leanor said nothing to her husband and managed to enjoy him for the rest of the journey, hardly allowing him to leave their cabin.

However, although she passionately loved him, she decided that it was time to solve the problem once and for all. So, in the following weeks, she expressed her desire to take another cruise. Eventually, Alvi relented and agreed to take her on a cruise going to the Adriatic Sea, including the Italian and Croatian Coasts. As she expected, this boat had not one but two of her husband's flames on board. What he did not know, though, was that she had her own Arab lover on board, as well. So, this time, during the cruise, when her husband went about his ways, she did the same in a separate cabin she had reserved. Then, as her screams of pleasure could be heard from outside, the crew members rejoiced and celebrated as the daughter of the only boss they recognized got even with her philandering husband.

"Are you sure?" asked her infatuated Arab lover.

"Well … Ah… OK."

Later that evening, as Alvi walked back to his cabin through the upper deck of the cruise ship, he whistled in joy about his polygamy. 'I am too smart to be caught,' he thought. 'Besides, no single woman can satisfy me.' In hindsight, it was being so out there and so full of himself that did him in. He did not see the blow coming and the impact on the back of his head knocked him out on the spot. He came to a while later, first just seeing a blurry image in front of him, then slowly things came into focus, but he did not recognize who was standing in front of him.

"Someone hit me?" he asks, holding his damaged head.

"I did."

Alvi tries to move and attack the stranger, but he fails miserably as his legs cannot sustain him.

"I have been looking forward to doing this for a long time," says the Arab.

"Who are you?" Alvi asks.

"Your wife's lover before and after you were married."

Alvi is overcome with rage, but still cannot move.

"Hey, you don't like your wife doing to you what you do to her?"

"But, I am the ..."

"Don't give me any male privilege babble. I have to hand it to her. She left me and did not want anything to do with me until her sources within your fleet told her what you did when you were away. It was only then that she took me back. From then on, our relationship has been even better, as we are now both married and she is playing at the same level as I am."

"But, she never told me."

"That's where she is far brighter than you and me. That's right, she never told you anything. Instead of getting mad, she simply started to do the same as you and concealed it in the same way you did, but she has an edge on you."

"What...why?"

"Because, wisely, she did not see you in her long-term plans."

"But we love each other very much."

"Even if it hurts, I have to admit to that, but even feeling like that, she is absolutely clear about you not lasting as her husband."

"I'll change and make amends."

"No, you won't."

"How dare you? You don't know me."

"Oh, yes I do because I know your type. You will never change, as nothing will prevent you from putting your dick into any hole that crosses your path."

"Well, I am a man, what do you expect me to do when one woman is not enough for me?"

"Obviously, you were not enough to satisfy Leanor, so she has me in addition to you."

"You SOB, I am going to kill you."

Alvi tries to get up, but can't as his legs do not respond.

"Mr. Mazon, she does not want you back after tonight."

"In your dreams, I only have to talk to her and we'll patch things up."

"Perhaps I did not make myself clear. She does not want you back on planet Earth after tonight."

"What?"

Those are the last words ever uttered by Alvin Mazon. The Arab hit him unexpectedly on the head again and knocked Alvi out cold for the second time that night. Then, with the help of two crewmen lying in wait, Alvi was thrown overboard never to be heard from again.

The search for Alvi Mazon was called off on the third day and it was ruled an accidental death by falling overboard.

For Leanor Mizrahi, Alvi's absence was a hard hit pill to swallow. She loved him dearly and was accustomed to spending a great deal of her life with him, so the void was bigger than she ever anticipated.

Her rage and burning desire to get even had turned into an obsession, and the decision to get rid of him had been impulsive. Now, she regretted it with all her heart.

It didn't take long for her family to find a suitor, but this time much closer to home. Six months after the "disappearance" of her husband, she married her first cousin, Aaron Mizrahi. She was not in love with him and even though they had a son together, Ariel, their union was never real. After her husband's murder, she lived a very sad and lonely life, except for her encounters with her long-time Arab lover.

In the meantime, the Mizrahi cruise ship line continued to grow and expand. It was time for her son, Ariel, to take over the business so she could retire. Their cruise ship line had become the largest of its kind in the world.

Then, for reasons of convenience, Ariel decided to move their world headquarters from the Middle East to Miami, Florida. Leanor and Aaron stayed behind in the Middle East and moved to Tel-Aviv, Israel. Ariel, on the other hand, chose a location for his company right in the Miami city center. He subsequently built his home along with his wife Deborah (Debbie) and raised their only child, Steve Mizrahi, on Paradise Island, Miami Beach, Florida. When Steve Mizrahi grew up, he became engaged to Sarah Greenhouse.

Ariel Mizrahi's father and his neighbor on Paradise Island, Bart Holstein's father, turn out to be the same person. And, that is how Ariel Mazon became Ariel Mizrahi – his father Alvi Mazon crossed a line that cost him his life.

CHAPTER 76
THE ZATHLYNS (SAN FRANCISCO)
(Part II)

“ Ladies, tonight is going to be all about you. I'll simply be an observer until the very end.”

“And then?” asks the university student.

“Then we'll see, but now it is only about you. Make yourself comfortable and enjoy.”

Steve Zathlyn has planned every detail like he always does. Drinks flow, laughs begin in earnest, everyone opens up. Then, the three women start to share some of their most memorable encounters as escorts including scary moments which they all have experienced.

“So, what are you going to do with us?” asks the married woman.

“I already gave you a hint, you'll explore things that you have never experienced before.”

“But I don't want to do anything I don't like,” states the student.

“And you won't, because you are all free to stop at any time.”

“Well, if there is any S&M, I am out now,” states the married woman.

"There isn't any whatsoever," assures Dr. Zathlyn.

These last words have a calming effect on everyone and the vibe becomes relaxed, but sexual tension is building up. What none of the women know is that their drinks are laced with Viagra so their libido has been rapidly rising to the point that they are not able to control their sexual desires.

Suddenly, a group of gorgeous women enter the room through a back door. They split up in groups of three and sit around each of the three women. Dr. Zathlyn takes center stage to enjoy the show. The three women that sit around the university student/athlete start touching her hair and arms, then her legs. It all happens simultaneously and even though she seems surprised at first, she does not push back. The three ladies then start caressing her boobs and one of them initiates a passionate kiss with her mouth wide open. The student lets herself go. Her previous experience with a woman happened once and she liked it, but it was only one on one, and not three on one! A hand goes underneath her skirt and softly starts caressing her most intimate parts. Suddenly, she realizes where she is, looks around and is shocked to see that the same thing is happening to the two other girls. Her clothes are now being taken off of her very delicately. She is undressed slowly until she is totally naked. Then, as one woman kisses her, another one plays with and then gently sucks her boobs and the thigh parts of her legs while kneeling in front of her. Then, the third woman starts licking and kissing her vagina. She has a sudden violent orgasm where she pants and trembles in ecstasy. They gently bring her back by caressing her hair and face. The three ladies sit on the floor in front of her and one of them opens her legs again and starts inserting a warm vibrator. Then they all take turns pressing it against her G-spot until she cums again. This time it is an eternity of panting with moans of pleasure. She passes out from the Viagra laced cocktails. When she wakes up, she is in the same room lying naked on one of the sofas covered with a blanket. When she moves, she realizes that her two other escort companions are lying next to her, naked as well.

"How do you all feel?" asks Dr. Zathlyn.

The three women slowly wake up enough to respond.

"It was nice," the athlete replies.

"Nice? It seemed more than nice to me," responds Dr. Zathlyn. Nothing could be heard for a while.

"C'mon girls."

"It was really great, but I guess we are all a bit embarrassed." The other two nod their heads in agreement.

"That's natural. It was a first for all of you. Now let me ask you a question. Did you discover something new about yourselves tonight?" Again, no response.

"I will let you mull it over. But, you have to ask yourselves, are you straight, gay or bisexual?" The question has the desired effect as they are all aroused again. He gets honest spontaneous answers from them. Two declare themselves as bisexual and one straight, but open to making love with women occasionally.

"OK, girls, what about putting into practice with each other what you have just learned." Dr. Zathlyn pulls the big blanket from them and now they see each other naked. It does not take long and the three engage in uninhibited and freewheeling sex as a group. In an hour, Zathlyn is left with the impression that the three have now become bisexual. But they are in for another surprise. This time a group of six men come in (two for each woman).

"Ladies, these gentlemen are porno film stars. They will introduce you to the world of double penetration. I caution you that once you experience it, you will never be totally satisfied ever again with just one man. The threesomes then engage in foreplay. The women are made to suck both men separately. Then, the men pleasure each lady with their hands and mouths. Then as each lady sucks one, the other penetrates her vaginally. Then soon after, the second man penetrates her as well from behind. An hour later, the three women lie exhausted on the sofas, but all sporting faces of absolute satisfaction.

"So, what are you going to do to me now, depraved ladies?" asks Dr. Zathlyn finally arriving to the end he wants.

Hillary Zathlyn's father's lifestyle is a vulnerable item that his adversaries could take advantage of, only if they knew about it.

Paradise Island residents are endlessly capricious and seek immediate gratification – otherwise, for many of them, there is no pleasure in life.

CHAPTER 77
THE MIZRAHIS (ARIEL)

 How do you want to pay for the car?"

Ariel Mizrahi simply pulls out his wallet and hands the salesman his black American Express card. The salesman knows better than to lose his composure in front of a very rich man, so he walks a way still maintaining an expressionless façade. Inside his head, the salesman is thinking, 'Gee, how cool is it to pay for a $135,000 brand new Aston Martin with your credit card? He just got here 15 minutes ago and out of impulse he is getting a better car than his neighbor.' Juan Ortiz, the star salesman of the Coral Gables dealership walks into the credit department and explodes, "I've just sold a $135K Aston Martin in 15 minutes and here is the payment." The credit manager takes the credit card and immediately recognizes the name and realizes that not only is it a kosher transaction, but he better hurry up and not make a member of the wealthiest family in Florida wait.

"But, there is only one caveat," states the salesman.

"What is it, Juan?" asks an irritated credit manager who is accustomed to, but never in acceptance of Ortiz's twists and turns when selling a vehicle.

"He wants to drive out in the car in 15 minutes, otherwise he is gone."

The credit manager calls the insurance broker himself while his staff completes the computer templates and then prints the invoices, insurance, waivers, temporary tag and delivery documents. He calls out for the car to be driven to the entrance for immediate delivery.

"But sir, we need time to at least clean it up."

"You've got exactly five minutes to accomplish whatever you can do in that time period and don't waste any more of my time or yours, just get it done." Amazingly, less than 15 minutes later Mizrahi drives away in his brand new metallic grey Aston Martin.

Ariel gives Juan Ortiz his card. But, on a closer look, he realizes that the number on the card is the switchboard of the Mizrahi cruise lines main office in Miami Beach. As Juan is daydreaming about taking a cruise, he gets a call. "Is this Juan Ortiz at the Aston Martin dealership in Coral Gables?" the caller asks.

"Yes," replies Juan.

"I noticed that my neighbor just arrived on Paradise Island with a new Aston Martin V8 Vantage. Do you have a more expensive model in stock?"

"Yes," replies Juan.

"I will be in..." replies Ariel Mizrahi's neighbor on Paradise Island. Afterwards, Juan thinks to himself 'I guess those are the prerogatives and tribulations of a billionaire. That's what I want and will be someday.

But the Island residents are also extremely jealous of one another and competitive on everything, especially material things. And the reasons for jealousy are the silliest and most banal of all (namely vanity and ego) about who has the latest, newest and the best.

Former and future Island resident Sylvester Antonelli is about to strike gold.

CHAPTER 78
THE ANTONELLIS (PART II)
SYLVESTER'S MONEY SUPPLY

Sylvester started writing from the first day he arrived at the Federal Prison Camp and he has written five to seven pages per day since then. His first action thriller ended up being a seven book series written over two years. But, strangely enough, that ended up being the easy part. First, the handwritten pages had to be transcribed to typewritten pages and that took a long time. After that, he would mail them out to where they would be scanned and converted into Word files, printed and sent back to him for grammar, syntax and typos. He would then make corrections and mail back for conversion into a Word file. This rotation went on forever. Finally, three years after starting the process, the first book was ready. The cover was chosen. The book was registered with the Library of Congress. And finally, it was published on-line through Amazon, Apple and Google iBooks. The book was published under a pseudonym. Social media campaigns were initiated through Facebook, Twitter, Instagram and Snapchat. He released the book by chapters every two weeks, with the first five chapters free. The book broke out quickly and became a top seller within a week. Sylvester then negotiated a seven-book deal with the second largest publisher in the country. He also sold the movie rights for a percentage of the box office. All in all, he had grossed enough money to pay his restitution to the government and was left with enough money to bring his family back to solvency, put his kids through college and he had some chump change to spare. Sylvester was waiting for a court reply to his request for a sentence reduction. He felt this was fair, as he had paid back everything he owed as a result of the ramifications of his own business's failure years earlier. Now, it was time to begin his entrepreneurship and buy as many shares as possible of CTH - shares that seemingly nobody wanted.

It is 9:00 a.m. and the instructions that were received by mail by his lawyer are clear and precise, as well as the timeline that is to be followed. Sylvester's attorney, John Hill, Jr., has a mission to fulfill, so he places the call: "I want to purchase a block of shares of the company, CTH, that at present is a penny stock trading at 3 cents. Can you find out if any shares of this stock can be bought?"

The stock trader on the phone looks up the information on his computer screen. The stock has virtually no recent trading history. Who would want to buy this worthless stock? But, that is not for him to judge.

"This is an over-the-counter stock, let me find out for you." He starts to call around and finds out that some large institutional shareholders are still holding the stock since its heyday as a high-flying company. They quickly offer to sell large blocks of shares, just to get it off their books.

"Sir, I can get you as many shares as you want and some of the holders are willing to sell at a discount so they can unload what they've got. How many shares or better yet, what is the dollar amount you want to spend?" reports back the stock trader.

Sylvester Antonelli's attorney, Hill Jr., ignores the question and simply continues to follow instructions: "I want you to buy all of the available shares owned by institutional shareholders. You will deal with each institutional holder separately during the course of the day. Before we start, you need to be specific with me about the quantity of shares these companies hold."

"400 million shares, at 3 cents each, that's $12 million."

"Take all you can, but only in large batches and today. Each time you have a block of shares, confirm the price and number of shares with me for approval. I'll expect a significant discount of the market price in order to buy those parties out of their stock position."

The stockbroker checks Sylvester's account and it holds $13 million in unencumbered funds. Showtime! At 9:30 a.m. when the market opens, he begins to buy and does not stop until 4:00 p.m. By then, 250 million shares have been bought in large blocks for an average price of 2 cents, for a total investment of $5 million. He has generated $600K in commissions for his firm and his client now owns 33% of the available stock of CTH. Additionally, some of the largest institutional investors in the company have finally been able to unload an undesirable stock that has cost them significant grief and losses. Everyone is a winner, the stockbroker reflects, and his client is a total moron or he knows something no one else does and is, in fact, the smartest kid in the room. Somehow, he has an inkling that the truth is closer to the latter.

SYLVESTER'S NEWFOUND GAIN

Nat Manning, the stockbroker, is surprised. This is an unusual request. The client wants physical possession of the shares. Normally, shares remain in possession of custodians. In fact, most physical shares/titles never move physically from the storage areas kept by the highly regulated custodians. What changes is the names of the owners of the shares, but, the owners rarely ask for physical possession because, when shares stay with the custodian, the shares can be sold in an instant and the change of ownership can be made by a book entry. If a shareholder of a publicly-traded company were to keep the shares in his or her possession, the shares could not be readily sold. For Sylvester, considering his situation, a custodian is not sufficient. If there was going to be a rapid rise in the price of the shares he had just bought, speculators could come in and bet against the price increase. This process is called shorting. Speculators would come into the market and bet big against the stock rise. However, for this to happen, there would have to be sufficient shares available in the market that could be traded. This is called the float.

'Without a float, the speculators will stay away,' concludes Sylvester.

"Are you sure about this? When your client presents the physical shares to us, he is not going to be able to sell for weeks because the shares would have to be authenticated first," the broker states to Sylvester's attorney, J. Hill, Jr.

"I understand, but that is the way he wants it," replied the attorney.

CEO CRANDALL'S NEWFOUND LOSS

CTH's CEO, Alexander Crandall, isn't planning to stick around for much longer as the company is on the verge of insolvency and the shareholders are asking for his head. The company's sales are dismal, there is an ongoing rapid contraction of its customer base with corresponding shareholder losses. But he does not care. He couldn't care less. Four years of careful planning are about to produce immense wealth for both him and his partner. It was four years ago that CTH's CFO, Ramesh Sidhu, quietly left the company, while Alexander Crandall stayed behind to guard the payout. They are in it together. Four special purpose companies (SPVs) were set up five years ago to engage in strategic investments for CTH that had been planned by the late Leroy Vincent Fiorentina. Fiorentina's plan to diversify the company was about to be unwound and closed at the value of the money deposited for investment in each company, plus interest, meaning there would be no loss on the books of CTH. These investment funds, totaling $12 million between the four companies, would add to CTH's liquidity position.

It has been a long process for Crandall and Sidhu to generate the exact amount needed to be reimbursed to CTH. At times, it seemed impossible, as CTH's bad performance kept diminishing Crandall's bonuses and stock options at CTH. But, 30 days ago, they finally reached their goal and funds were ready for transfer. What they are doing is illegal, since they are trying to cheat CTH's shareholders out of tens of billions of dollars of value. The reality is that the four CTH subsidiaries invested in four startups and the startups are all now public companies with a market value of several hundred billion dollars. The search engine Zest, where CTH's special purpose vehicles (SPVs) invested $5 million, has become the biggest payoff.

The sudden death of Fiorentina, five years ago, left these investments in limbo. Weeks after Fiorentina's untimely death, CFO, Ramesh Sidhu, requested a private meeting with Crandall.

"Alexander, we have these four subsidiaries that made investments in four startup companies under their a/k/a (also known as). For example, the search engine and special purpose vehicle Long View Forward, invested under the name LVF. But, in our books the name LVF does not exist."

"Where are you headed with this, Ramesh?"

"Do you want me to spell it out for you, Alexander? LVF was a name Fiorentina made up out of his initials, he never registered it and it does not exist in our records. Officially, we did not make that investment."

"This is a very delicate situation, Ramesh. What exactly are you proposing?"

"To keep things the way they are, unreported, in other words, let sleeping dogs lie."

"And?"

"If any of the investments pays off, then, quietly unwind the investment vehicles and reimburse the original investment amounts plus interest to the company.

"And all of this works because, one, we never registered LVF as an 'a/k/a', and two, we know something no one else does. Yes!"

"Brilliant, but very dangerous, Ramesh."

So, it has been five years now. The two crooks, Crandall and Sidhu, set up four offshore companies, all of them with the same three letter names and with registration dates prior to the investments made by Fiorentina and CTH. The offshore companies will hide the crooks' loot. Alexander Crandall reflects alone in his office, 'the Fiorentina investments have skyrocketed and CTH has never reported or acknowledged them. Our delay in not finalizing the transaction as planned has been caused by our inability to put together the money to reimburse CTH. But, now we are ready, money in hand, to wire the money to CTH.'

Then, his heart stops and he loses it as he reads the routine memo over and over. The memo was prepared in response to Sylvester's inquiry and has just reached Crandall's desk.

"Please drop by my office on your way out," says Crandall to the CTH's investor's relations manager.

"Come in," Crandall replies 5 minutes later, when he hears the soft knock at the door.

"Have a seat, please."

Crandall hands the memo to the preparer. "What is this?"

"A shareholder requested information on whether Long View Forward is also known as LVF."

"Why would anyone ask that?"

"It beats me, came out of left field," the investor relations manager replies.

"I have never heard those three letters being used as a company name in regard to our business dealings," says Crandall, hoping and praying.

"But I did, Mr. Crandall, I did."

"When, where?" says Crandall with a knot in his throat, unable to breathe deeply and trying to camouflage his concern.

"It is mentioned as a name because these letters are the initials of our founder, Leroy Vincent Florentina."

A long silence ensues.

"But it was never registered, right?" asks Crandall.

"We didn't register it."

Only then is Crandall able to take a deep breath and exhale with a deep sigh of relief.

"But, Mr. Crandall, then I made a mistake when we replied to the stockholders."

"You did what!?"

"What we normally do, always reply within 24 hours as per our instructions."

"And?" asked Crandall apprehensively.

"I told the stockholder making the request that the answer was yes, that Long View Forward, our fully owned subsidiary, is also known as LVF."

A couple of minutes later, the investor relations manager walks out of the CEO's office. His boss, Crandall, just stood there staring at him, his eyes not moving and being non-responsive to any words or questions. So, he stood up and said good-bye and left him to his own devices.

THE NEXT DAY

Sylvester's plan for the coming out party is simple. The stockbroker confirmed to Sylvester's attorney that he has received the actual physical shares of stock from the custodian. So, he is going to tell the truth. First, he instructs his attorney to call CTH and ask, "Sir, recently you confirmed to me that a subsidiary of yours, Long View Forward, is also known as LVF."

"Actually, I'm glad that you called. Can you hold a minute? I want to conference in a colleague of mine."

"That's fine, but hurry, I don't have much time."

Crandall was paged and he agreed right away to join the call.

"Okay, here we are. CTH's CEO, Mr. Crandall is on the line."

"Nice to talk to you."

"Nice to talk to you as well."

"May I ask who you are?" asks Crandall.

"Sorry Mr. Crandall, my fault, John Hill, Jr., Attorney for a large shareholder of yours."

"Okay, thanks, Mr. Hill. Are you a long term shareholder?"

"No. My client has just become your largest shareholder. He owns 33% of the outstanding stock of your company and will be forthwith filing notice with you and the SEC today."

The investor relations manager jumps into the conversation. "Welcome on board, Sir. So, you obviously see opportunity in our company."

"Mr. Hill, we may have made a mistake when we confirmed to you that Long View Forward was also known as LVF," states Crandall tentatively.

"No, you didn't. I believe that you have a serious mistake in your books ever since the unfortunate death of Mr. Fiorentina. A number of investments made just prior to his death by specialty created subsidiaries seem to have remained unrecorded. This seems to be a mistake!"

"And the mistake would be what?" asks Crandall already in panic mode.

"For example, LVF invested $5 million in the search engine Zest, that in the meantime went public and is currently worth a couple hundred billion. Zest's records show that the special purpose investment vehicle created by CTH, Long View Forward, AKA LVF, has never been part of any of Zest's shareholders meeting and does not have any Board representation for such a large shareholder. And, on the CTH side, the company has never reported the investment. It is like it does not exist. But, it does and needs to be disclosed right away."

"But, how do you know it is our investment?" asks Crandall sheepishly, as the reality of the mess he has gotten himself into is already sinking in.

"Because it was done and announced by you guys shortly after your diversification investment strategy was put into place. And the announcement was shortly before Fiorentina's death. So, somehow it must have slipped through the cracks."

"Mr. Crandall, any comments?"

Silence

"Mr. Crandall?"

More silence.

'Oh, my God' he realizes, 'he is not on the line.'

"Mr. Hill, can we get back to you while we sort this out?" asks the investor relations manager.

"Absolutely. Please get back to me at your convenience. In the meantime, get ready because I am going public and will report this to the SEC immediately. The public cannot be kept in the dark a minute longer. Good bye."

The investor relations manager immediately recalls the previous day's meeting with Crandall. His behavior, his reaction and then today, when he simply left the call. Does he know? Is he involved in it? He stands up and heads to the in-house legal department. He has to check, verify and act quickly for his own and CTH's sake.

After a 30-minute wait, Sylvester is on the phone with his attorney. Hill reports to him the results of the conversation and then they go over the upcoming public filing and disclosure with the Securities and Exchange Commission. They discuss the memorandum outlining CTH's lack of due diligence about its investment through LVF, in the search engine giant Zest. Sylvester's input is that the public filing and memorandum should include the background of the transaction, the timing, CTH's announcement at the time, and "the mistake" about the name.

Sylvester signs off on the public filing and memorandum and agrees to follow up with his attorney in 30 minutes to verify the filing. Within minutes, Sylvester's memorandum and disclosures are filed. Thereafter, there is a call between his attorney, John Hill, Jr., and two journalists from the Wall Street Journal. Following Sylvester's instructions, this is not an interview or fact-finding exercise, but rather a "dump." The journalists record it all and as soon as they hang up, they go and do their fact checking in regard to the search engine giant and CTH's public filings. Then, they engage in a feisty and testy debate with their editor in order to get a sign-off to publish.

The enormous wheels of the SEC bureaucracy get moving slowly at first, but then get up to full speed as it is soon deemed an emergency. After a frantic series of meetings take place, a recommendation by the Agency's Director causes a perfect storm, as CTH's own press release comes out disclosing the problem alongside an SEC press release of its own, disclosing the shareholder's inquiry about the company's actions and ordering the halting of trading of its shares. Then, the SEC sends agents to CTH's headquarters. A few minutes later, almost in synchronization with the SEC events, The Wall Street Journal breaks the news just after trading has been halted.

Alexander Crandall's blood pressure is out of control. The Highway Patrol had clocked him at 105 mph. They are deciding whether to arrest him or just issue a speeding ticket.

The 10 boxes he kept in storage with all the documentation, bank records and investments of the SPV's are there in the trunk of his car.

"Sir, this is your lucky day, I'm going to give you the maximum ticket I can and send you on your way," says the officer.

The rest is history. When trading resumes the next day, the shares explode. Crandall is fired and a criminal investigation is initiated against him and the co-conspirator, Ramesh Sidhu, CTH'S former chief financial officer, by both the SEC and the U.S. Attorney's office. Massive class-action lawsuits are filed by former shareholders alleging that they missed out on the financial gains of the company. Notwithstanding the litigation, CTH's market value explodes, making Sylvester's stake in the company worth north of $3 billion, and this is just for starters.

One thing is certain, Island residents, current and former, all possess not only relentless drives and oversized ambitions but also extraordinary talents. So, behind their illegal, decadent and materialistic lives lie outstanding skills, abilities and knowledge – all of it worthy and existentially valuable if they used it in the right way, which by and large they never do.

Island resident, wife beather and pervert, Alessandro Baglioni, is about to meet his match.

CHAPTER 79
THE BAGLIONIS
(Part I)

Alessandro feels excited, maybe even happy, as the majestic doors of his Paradise Island mansion open up and he presses his remote key and hops out of his Rolls-Royce Black Phantom. He has spent the last six weeks convalescing at the hospital, as his recovery was slow and plagued with setbacks. In the end, he was discharged with a questionable diagnosis about his ability to ever again have natural erections. He knows that money can buy almost anything. So, in a day or two he plans to be on his plane to Zurich, Switzerland, where he will be fitted with tubes through his penis and a tiny pump on his stomach. He will be able to have endless hard-ons simply by pressing the pump multiple times.

Now he has to face his family. He hasn't seen or heard from them since the short visit his wife, Ornella, paid to him the day after the accident. 'They'll get over it,' he thinks without even an iota of embarrassment or guilt. He opens the door and walks into an eerie silence. The normal sounds, smells and noises that are familiar to him are all absent. He walks around and after just a few steps, he notices the dust and traces of unfamiliar scents. He goes through the whole house. The house is empty of both furniture and people. Frantically, he calls Ornella's phone. "This phone has been disconnected." As he walks to his studio, he calls Johnny and hears "this number is no longer in service." He is now getting really angry. 'What the hell is going on?' Then, as he enters his home office, anger is quickly replaced by panic and fear. The whole place is trashed, nothing is left. But all of that is irrelevant as his sights are zeroed in on the hole in the floor. His treasure hideout has been found. He takes a couple of quick steps and sees in horror that his secret compartment is empty! The scream that follows is primal and atavistic. All of a sudden his phone rings.

"Alessandro, I gather you've made it back home safe and sound," says Ornella, in a matter of fact way.

He struggles to compose himself as an uneasy panic follows. 'You've got to be nice to her. Besides, she just called this place home.'

"Yes, I am back, but not in one piece. I have got to go to Zurich for one more tweak," he says struggling to be Jekyll instead of Hyde.

"I know, Dr. Reed told me," she says.

"Oh, you kept in contact with him," he asks.

"Why shouldn't I, we were all worried about you," she says.

"I am fine, Ornella," he says, already a bit exasperated.

"All right then, take care," she says, parting ways.

"Wait a minute, where are you guys?"

"Alessandro, the children and I are all fine. We also brought the staff with us."

"I said, where are you, Ornella?"

"Far away from Miami and you."

"I'm coming to get you all and bring you back home. Your pick. Nice or painful? Your choice. No matter where you are, I'll find you and it will only take a few hours."

"Well, it won't be that easy, as I have your passports and we did not fly on the family plane. We did not fly out of any Florida airport. I know you'll find us, but you may want to think twice about it."

"You don't talk to me this way, Ornella! You'll pay for this!"

"If you want to ever see us again; if you value your freedom; I suggest you contact our attorneys as soon as possible," she says just before hanging up her satellite phone.

Alessandro slams his phone to the floor with such violence that it breaks into countless pieces that fly all over the place. The moment he is done, he regrets it. Now, he is also without a phone. "Who does she think she is threatening me this way?" he yells aloud while panting with uncontrolled rage. But, Alessandro Baglioni's survival instincts remain intact. Within minutes, he is on his way out of the house and driving off the island heading straight to his attorney's office. He zooms past the two Restrepo-Lujan homes and his revenge plans on Veronica all flash through his perverted mind. 'One thing at a time, Alessandro. One thing at a time.' His obfuscated mind prioritizes his collection of bad deeds yet to be done.

Law Offices of Larkin, Donaldson and Benton

Alessandro Baglioni looks like he is about to have a stroke, followed by a heart attack. The veins around his neck are seemingly about to explode. His face is flushed red. He has just thrown all of his attorneys out of the conference room. 'Miserable rats. 25 years working for me and they sell themselves to the best offer.

All lawyers are rats. Low, stinky, putrefactive rats,' he vents, completely out of control. The envelope keeps on staring at him. He wants to shred it to pieces. 'Who does she think she is,' he repeats to himself once again in total frustration. Alessandro is about to lose it. He is not in control. He is being forced to act against his will. His release valve is a giant glass ashtray that goes flying in an angry and violent backhand throw. It crashes into a massive video screen and for a moment it seems like a real explosion with glass fragments being propelled all over the place. The law partners are watching the video screen images of the conference room in horror.

"I am calling security."

"Leave him alone. What you are witnessing is a wild animal in a cage. If he felt in control, he would have fired us on the spot. He knows he has no choice."

Finally, Alessandro opens the letter and starts to read. "Alessandro, the attorneys have, per my instructions, drafted the necessary documentation for you to transfer 50% of the family assets into my name. Additionally, you and I, in turn, are each contributing 25% of our divided assets to trust funds for our kids that will be funded today when you sign the documents. You will find that I have already executed all of them. Your latest escapade made me realize that the interests of this family must be safeguarded against your worsening acts of irresponsible recklessness. Yours, Ornella."

His rational side finally takes over. 'She has evidence of crimes that would send me to jail for the rest of my life. I've got no choice. Besides, isn't she right? She isn't asking for more than she is entitled to. I can get it all back,' reasons Alessandro. With a tiny, almost imperceptible smile on his face, he walks to the intercom.

"Guys, you can come back in. Let's get all of the papers signed."

"I told you he had no choice."

Minutes later, the three law partners walk in with a mountain of documents. A short while later, Alessandro Baglioni starts to sign. But his movements are all mechanical and uninterested. He is not paying any attention to what he is signing. He is already somewhere else and far away. He is already planning how he is going to kill his wife. 'That little bitch is going to find out what happens when anybody defies me.'

"Mr. Baglioni, your wife and son have deposited with us a locked box with sealed instructions that we are to execute only in case anything were to happen to either of them."

Baglioni's blood is boiling and he is about to explode once again!

"Here is an envelope from your son." With disdain and a pronounced smirk on his face, he opens it. It contains his passports and a letter.

"Dad, if you ever touch my mother again, I will go to the police."

A long silence ensues and Baglioni does not move or blink. He just stares straight ahead at nothing. He then stands up and leaves without saying a word. As all psychopaths do, he now shifts his focus on the trip to Switzerland that will hopefully bring back his manhood, everything else does not matter at all, for the time being.

First things first for Alessandro Baglioni. He has to get his manhood back before he can even think about anything else. His sole focus is on the procedure he will undergo in Switzerland.

CHAPTER 80
THE BAGLIONIS (PART II)
(Zurich, Switzerland)

"Herr Baglioni, just press your belly right where you feel the implant. Then press again and keep on doing it until you have a full erection. When you want it over, just press continuously. Don't let go until the erection is over."

"So what am I doing? Just pumping air?"

"That is correct, Herr Baglioni."

"Well, I've got to try this before I leave this town."

"Now that, mein herr, is your prerogative."

"Can you recommend a good service to me?"

"Of course, Herr Baglioni, here is the number."

BAGLIONI'S HOTEL SUITE (LATER THE SAME DAY – 8:45 P.M.)
The woman that walks in is stunning. She must be 6'1" with long thick blond hair, green eyes and wearing a tight business dress accentuating her body. 'Well, that's what money can buy you,' he thinks.

"Come here. There is a service I want you to render before we go out and have dinner." She is surprised and reacts with a gesture demanding respect.

"I am supposed to get to know you first. That's our policy. Then I decide if I like you."

"Well, decide now, otherwise you can leave."

Baglioni approaches her and simply stands close waiting for her to sense his wild lust. She waits for him to sit, but he doesn't.

'I guess $5,000 is worth it to please this bastard. Besides, he is not bad looking,' she thinks to herself kneeling down.

Baglioni begins to pump and within seconds feels as hard as a rock. He then runs his fingers through her hair as her mouth swallows his newly found member. He tightens his grip over her head and now starts driving her head in rapid movements up and down. Then in a rush, Baglioni suddenly explodes in ecstasy and screams, "hallelujah, I am back, baby, I am back." He looks at the call girl who now seems to be mesmerized by and lost in Baglioni's world of sex.

"Let's go have dinner and gather some strength. Wait until you see what I have planned for you later," he says.

"Did you just come as well?" he asks noticing her almost imperceptible spasms.

"Yes, and that is also a very good sign of things to come later on tonight," she replies with a wink.

The next morning, Birgette Schmidt decides to leave the escort service for good and quits. She is hot and cold about the previous night. She took such a beating on her behind that she can't sit. Her nipples are swollen and they hurt after being tightly clamped throughout the night. She was supposed to tell him to stop when he handcuffed her, but she said nothing. Then, she thought about leaving after he whipped her the first time, but she didn't. She liked the whole thing. And at present, she does not like herself for that very reason! Part of her simply wants to go to him in America and be totally his and let him do whatever he pleases forever. The other side of her just wants to continue her studies in the Politeknique Institute of Zurich. She is now a tortured soul. Did she quit the escort service for her or him? He didn't ask her to. He actually hardly spoke to her except to give commands. Did she like that so much? 'What should I do? Who should I be?'

Baglioni's G-650 Gulfstream Private Jet

Any thought of the escort woman quickly vanishes. He knows he totally depraved and damaged the woman, and that gives him pleasure. 'Maybe she'll even show up in America!' He soon drifts away into a deep sleep while he heads over the Atlantic to Paradise Island.

Baglioni's Mansion

The moment he pulls in, he knows they are back. Is he feeling excited? Happy? Him? Maybe. All his social behavior control mechanisms are at work. He has to be at his best. 'Relax. Smile. Be empathetic. Be humble for once. Your family is back. Apologize.' He walks in the house, tip toeing but to no avail. The whole family is standing in the living room. Sheepishly, he says, "Hi, guys."

"Have a seat, dad. We brought some fold-up chairs."

His impulses jump and he feels rage. His son commandeering him! Everyone is dead serious. They are looking at him with stern faces. He walks to one of the plastic chairs next to his son. Lava starts to flow as he sits. Everyone remains silent, still staring at him straight in the eye. Time goes by until he finally gets it. 'OK, I will give it to them,' he calculates.

"Sorry. I am really sorry."

His kids' and wife's faces relax a bit, but not Johnny's, not him.

"One chance," Johnny declares.

Silence again and lava is about to explode.

"Dad, that's what you've got. One more chance with us."

"Who do . . . .," he starts, but he stops as Ornella and Johnny stand up followed by the rest of the kids. He then sees the suitcases.

"All right, son, what is it?"

Nobody sits, only him, and he remains so.

"Dad no more hanky panky with mom or anyone or we are gone in a flash."

Everyone goes silent again. Baglioni is in a corner and against his worst instincts, he lets himself be driven by his son.

"All right," he whispers.

"I did not … we did not hear you dad," Johnny replies.

"All right!"

"That's not enough," states Ornella.

'Wait until you and I are alone' his eyes are on fire, but he keeps under control. Ornella turns and heads for the door and everyone follows.

"Johnny, please bring the luggage out."

On his way out, Johnny turns and stares back at his father.

"You have to go to therapy," Johnny demands.

"All right."

"I can't hear you again."

"I said all right, I'll go!"

"Mom and I will attend also."

He again starts to burn inside, but this time it does not last.

'Let the pile on continue,' remembering the street beating he had taken as a teenager.

"OK. I agree that you and mom shall join me."

"You'll treat us with respect at all times. No bullying. For the foreseeable future, you are in the dog house in this family."

"I'll do my best."

'That's what happens when you give your family half your money,' he thinks.

"That's not nearly good enough."

"All right, I'll do it."

"And the dog house hyperbole is correct. You'll be sleeping in the guest house annex until further notice. Mom does not want you near her until she sees a real change."

Baglioni now feels defeated. His son has been relentless. What is he supposed to feel? Proud? Well, he feels something like that for his son. Respect, that's what he feels, man to man respect.

"Dad?"

"What? Ah, yes, I'll sleep in the guest house until your mom sees a change in me."

"Real change, dad."

"Real change, son."

The word son comes out of him unintentionally and at first it shocks everyone. But as it settles in, it breaks the ice and for the first time the word 'son' begins to endear Alessandro Baglioni to his family. He notices it at once. His psychopathic mind finally finds satisfaction. He is going to play them.

"Dad, this is the first time ever you've called me son and you did it out of your heart and it touched me, but I'll know when it is phony. You won't sweet talk your way out of this," states Johnny, while being dead on about his dad's thought process.

'Tough cookie this one. Like father, like son,' he reasons while his narcissistic personality provokes a phony self-congratulation.

A faint smile crosses Alessandro's and Johnny's faces. Alessandro stands up and walks towards his son. Johnny tenses, but

Alessandro appears to just want to hug him. Johnny senses the gesture and puts up his hand to block him. But, Alessandro moves forward quickly and bear hugs his son anyway. Johnny is stiff and uncomfortable until he and the whole family hear the paterfamilias crying like a baby. No one has ever seen such a display from the tough macho man. Slowly at first, but then in earnest the whole family approaches. It all ends in a pile on hug of love for their 'enfant terrible'.

But, after everything is said and done, it still does not earn him the ticket to the lady of the house's bedroom!

Who would have thought that it was going to be the son that would say to Alessandro Baglioni – Enough is Enough!!

Island resident, powerful criminal attorney, Oleg Krull's life and reputation are hanging by a threat. He just does not know it yet.

CHAPTER 81
THE KRULLS
(Part I)

"Sir, after several weeks of surveillance we've found no evidence of Emmanuel Oquendo being involved in drug smuggling or money laundering. We still have a few holes in that we don't have a record of all his entries into the United States. He obviously comes back incognito and that can't be a good sign," states the FBI agent to his boss.

"Right! We will leave that for others to look into or perhaps he will fall on his own sword. OK, that's it then. It's a wrap," orders senior officer Martinez.

"Well, not exactly, sir. As to what we were investigating, yes. But, we ran into a situation involving Oquendo and we want to run it by you."

"All right, go ahead," says Martinez.

"Earlier today, as we were parked near Oquendo's home, doing surveillance, a speeding car almost crashed into us. The vehicle slammed on its brakes in front of the suspect's home and the driver then jumped out of his car and appeared to be out of control. He proceeded to have a very heated argument with Oquendo right there on the front lawn. Oquendo tried to bring him inside, but he was having none of it. For a moment we thought they were going to get physical right there, but Oquendo finally persuaded the man to go inside. That's when things got really weird. The mad driver suddenly walked out of the house, drove his car inside the garage and closed the garage door. A short while later, he backed out of the garage and drove away. On a hunch, we guessed that he may have picked up something at Oquendo's house that they did not want anyone to see."

"He may have dropped something off for Oquendo as well," interrupts Martinez.

"Right, we acted on a hunch and did not consider that scenario. That could have been a serious error in judgment, but as you will see later, we were probably right. It is highly unlikely that the daredevil driver dropped off something at Oquendo's."

"Alright go on, then," says Martinez.

"We followed the car to the Beach House condominiums where the driver parked in the tenant garage. When we approached, the car was empty with the trunk slightly ajar, but it was also empty.

"Are you sure the trunk was ajar?" asks Martinez.

"Yes, sir, and if need be, the garage cameras will show it."

"Let me warn you, I am growing uncomfortable by the second, but go on," warns Martinez.

"We went to security and asked to see the security video recordings of the last 10 minutes. We saw video of the driver, but he was empty-handed. Then, as we were about to leave, we see Oquendo get on one of the elevators. We were both surprised. The security guard noticed our reaction and volunteered the following: "The owner of the car you are concerned about is Mr. Harrington and he lives in Building B, Unit 207. There is a surprise welcome home party organized for Harrington at his condominium."

"Where are you heading with this?" the exasperated Martinez lets out in anger.

"Sir, as we were about to leave, the security guard blurted out that Harrington was coming back home after several weeks sequestered on jury duty." Captain Martinez' eyes widen ever so slightly and the two special agents now have his undivided attention.

"Additionally, sir, just before this meeting, we were having lunch in the Bureau's cafeteria and overheard a couple of agents, male and female, and an attorney talking about a case they had just lost. A case, that according to them, was a slam dunk. However, the jury came back rather quickly with a not-guilty verdict."

Both of the agents can sense in his stare that Martinez is thinking exactly what they are thinking.

"Sir, we have just verified that Mr. Harrington was one of the jurors in that trial."

"Apparently, after being released from jury duty, Harrington, before going home, went to have a heated argument with his future brother-in-law, Oquendo. Then he drove his car inside his garage – why? Then he went home."

"OK, stay on it," directs Martinez.

The two special agents look at each other, then turn back to face their boss and hear the magic words.

"Go and find out what the hell is going on with these two," orders Martinez.

But in the world of the powerful and the well connected, the alliances are what always moves the needle in the right direction. Alliances are what stop investigations, even indictments, or gets them started.

Island resident, reknowned criminal attorney, Oleg Krull's world is all of the sudden unraveling or isn't it after all?

CHAPTER 82
THE KRULLS
(Part II)

"The bank records show nothing sir. Their phone calls also show nothing. Harrington and Oquendo have not met or spoken again."

"Did you check all of the camera recordings in the condominium complex?"

"We saw him on a recording from the night in question. He was carrying something across the parking lot, but that's about all we got on him."

"What about Oquendo's business in the Caribbean?"

"Sir, we've had total cooperation from both the local government authorities and his banks. Nothing. Zilch. All our forensic accountants found is regular business activities."

"OK, gentlemen, I am going to give you a bit more leeway on this. Otherwise, we will shut it down as well."

KRULL MANSION (1:00 A. M. SAME DAY)
"Krull, we've got a problem" says the deep voice with a tone of urgency.

"Do you want to come over now?" Krull responds.

"I am on my way already, just a couple of minutes from your home."

Krull gets up from bed, puts on a bathrobe, glances at his wife peacefully sleeping and heads down, just in time to see on the kitchen's security camera, the lights of his visitor's vehicle. Then, as he lets him in, it hits him, 'this can't be good.'

"Your jury fixer, Oquendo, is compromised," states the visitor.

"How so?" asks Krull.

"The last juror you picked up, Harrington, happens to be Oquendo's future brother-in-law and he still went ahead and recruited him," the visitor states.

Krull is processing the information and alarm bells start ringing.

"Is his cover blown?" he asks with cold fear in his bones.

"No, at least not yet," the visitor responds.

"How did this come about?"

The visitor narrates everything in detail. He starts with Oquendo and Harrington's fight on the day of the jurors' decision. He then goes into Oquendo's business and bank records as well as the phone taps.

Krull is relieved that the firewalls have held. Now he has to get into preservation mode.

"I'll take care of this immediately," states Krull.

"You better, Krull, for all of our sakes," replies FBI senior officer, Martinez. Then as Martinez drives away, he almost crashes head on into another car on Paradise Island's single lane road. "Isn't that officer Martinez?" they ask each other in disbelief. The two that see Martinez are also FBI agents who are staking out lobbiyst Holstein's home. What startles them the most is the expression on Martinez's face when he recognizes the two.

"Did you see his eyes?"

"Man, they were wide, wide open. Like a beacon."

"Yep, like the last thing he wanted to see was for us to see him here."

"Smells like a rat to me."

"What house was he coming out from?"

"Criminal attorney Krull's home."

Silence follows, as both know the implication of such a visit at that hour.

"He is on Krull's payroll!"

"We've got to report it to internal affairs, otherwise we'll get into serious trouble."

"I hear you."

EMMANUEL OQUENDO'S HOME (1:30 AM)

Oquendo is deep asleep but his computer won't let up. The pre-programmed beep keeps on coming back every few seconds. He feels something far away at first. Then, the sound becomes louder and louder. Suddenly, he opens his eyes and listens attentively to make sure that it is the dreaded sound. In seconds he is on his computer and opens the message. 'Your payroll will be delayed by one day.' He swallows hard, but his training kicks in. He goes to his emergency situations location list. He searches the place assigned for the present month and week. There it is, Bimini.

He checks the hour on the message and realizes that his instructions tell him to be at the location first thing in the morning. He has to move fast, as he must be in Bimini in five hours. Thirty minutes later, Emmanuel Oquendo quietly unties his 36' Intrepid boat from the back of his house's dock, hops in and lets it float for a while into the open bay. Once far enough away from his house and with the lights still off, he turns on the engines and starts to slowly coast in the direction of government cut, the exit point for him to go into the Atlantic Ocean. Thirty minutes later he is in the open sea heading to the Gulf Stream in the direction of Bimini. He is going intentionally slow. His only goal is to make it to his destination before sunrise.

THE ISLAND OF BIMINI

The bulky and tall Bahamian lawyer contemplates the message in disbelief. He asks for authentication and a few seconds later the cryptographic confirmation arrives and as he deciphers it, his attitude changes. He checks the instruction manual and is relieved that he is not being asked to terminate someone. It's been more than 10 years since he left the Interpol front lines. And, he now feels completely out of step for what used to be routine. "Subject has to extract his target from the U.S. by tomorrow. If successful, use either of the following options: target to be enrolled in a one-year course of his preference at any of these institutions (a list follows with names and addresses in Asia and Europe) or target to embark on an around the world journey with a duration of no less than one year. If subject is unable to extract target or target refuses, further instructions will follow tomorrow. Subject will arrive to meet you early this morning. If subject fails to show up, notify us immediately." The Bahamian lawyer who is Krull's agent checks the assigned address for the meeting.

BIMINI MARRIOTT LOBBY (7:30 AM)

Oquendo is rendered speechless as he listens to the instructions from the Bahamian lawyer. He realizes that he, Oquendo, is the subject and Harrington, his brother in law, is the target.

"So what happens to me?"

"This is only a guess, but based on experience, you'll be on ice for a year and during this time you have to focus on whatever it is that interests you."

Later that same day, persuaded by Oquendo, Harrington and his fiancée take a flight to London and then take a train across the channel to Paris. In Paris, they connect to a Geneva-bound bullet train. They finally disembark in Grenoble, Savoie, where they have been enrolled in the local business school. Tuition and board have been paid for by one of Krull's European subsidiaries.

In the meantime, Emmanuel Oquendo decides to take the year-long boat trip and embarks on that journey the day after his sister and Harrington leave the U.S.

FBI HEADQUARTERS, MIAMI

"Sir, Oquendo and Harrington are gone."

"What do you mean?"

"Gone from the U.S. At least Oquendo is, and we think Harrington and his fiancée have traveled to London. Their ultimate destination is unknown. What do we do now?"

"We wait. Put it all on ice until they are back," states Martinez.

Yeah, that's how Island residents avoid being accountable under the law. With only a few exceptions, it is not about what they know or did but about who they know.

Island residents corrupt lobbyist Louis Mathews II, the Venezuelan oil transport magnate and ace criminal attorney Oleg Krull have not been careful about what or when they ask for help. Today, the Island resident parents of the three teen rapists are going to get far more than they bargained for – to basically back off – no questions asked.

CHAPTER 83
THE HOLSTEIN, MATHEWS & KRULL FAMILIES

The three anxious parents have been waiting in the lobby of General Pinkus' security firm (Zapco) for quite some time. It took a week of constant calls to finally get hold of him. Pinkus' response had been terse: "Meet me at my office two days from now, Friday at 2:00 p.m. I have information for you."

"Who does this guy think he is?" states Mathews II.

"We all have things to do," complains an angry Holstein.

That's when the elevator doors open and the massive figure of General Pinkus walks out.

"Gentlemen, my apologies. I was actually being briefed about your matter and it took much longer than expected. Follow me, please."

They go into the conference room. A projector and screen have been set up.

"Have a seat, gentlemen."

"You asked me to look into Dr. Zathlyn. However, we were stopped right in our tracks by this."

The projector shows DNA lab results for three subjects. The three parent faces denote discomfort, as if they want to stop the show.

"Bear with me a little longer, please."

The image now shows four different DNAs in a single test. The next image shows the four DNAs separated and three of them have an attached legend "match".

"Gentlemen, it appears that your three boys raped Dr. Zathlyn's daughter and the tests you have just seen are from your three boys' DNA. The fourth DNA was retrieved from Ms. Zathlyn. There is a conclusive match. I submitted the DNA findings to a second lab and their conclusion is the same. Your three boys did it."

"But this is not what we hired your for," complains Holstein.

"That is precisely why I have your retainer check here. We never cashed it."

"But ..." states Mathews II.

"Gentlemen, I can no longer be involved in this matter. Now it's up to you to do what you have to do. Dr. Zathlyn in the meantime is unequivocal. If you don't back down, he is taking this matter to the authorities."

Pinkus stands up and leaves. The check lies on the table and the three angry parents feel that this may be the end of the road.

Game, set and match never applies to the wars between Island residents. Highly successful individuals accustomed to getting their way are simply too resourceful and driven to be easily defeated much less when three of them are going against one – watch out Dr. Zathlyn.

Another storm is brewing between the Baglionis and the Zathlyns families as the relation between Hillary and Johnny blossoms.

CHAPTER 84
THE BAGLIONIS AND THE ZATHLYNS

Johnny and Hillary have been going out for about a month. In many ways, they are typical dating teenagers. They have a lot of common interests and they spend lots of time together. They both love music and they plan to go to the next Ultra Fest. They argue and fight for silly reasons. They spend lots of time on the phone and texting each other. As they get more and more serious, they both become extremely possessive and jealous of anyone of the opposite sex approaching the other. The area where they have struggled, though, is sex. Johnny's lack of experience and her recent traumatic experience made for several failed attempts. However, today they are both drunk and they go to her cabaña at the island's social club to lay down for a while. Johnny has been teasing Hillary about her new haircut all afternoon.

"Why do you embarrass me in front of everyone? It is hurtful and uncalled for," Hillary complains.

"I thought it was funny," Johnny jokes back.

"Don't do it anymore."

His Italian blood is flowing, but he channels his negative reaction in the right direction.

"Hill, I react that way when you look sexy."

"What are you talking about? You are babbling!" Hillary quickly sees his hungry look. "Sexy in what way?" she teases him.

"I don't know, it is just you, all of you. The way you move, the way you act. It is so sexy."

Hillary bites her lip. "Which way, Johnny Baglioni, show me."

Johnny then tries to imitate her moves and gestures. His mimicking act makes her laugh and she copies every one of his playful movements until she starts just being herself and moving to her inner self. Johnny is mesmerized as her rhythm is so sensual and inviting. He can hardly control himself.

"You are so f...ing beautiful, Hill!" he blurts out.

"So what are you waiting for, then?" she teases him while continuing to move.

"Waiting for what?" asks Johnny under the influence.

"You just said I am so beautiful."

"No, I said f...ing beautiful." Johnny moves toward Hillary. He starts undressing his girl slowly and with patience, but she wants none of it. She is hungry and in a hurry. So, it becomes her undressing him and herself and literally tearing the clothes off. Johnny was going to make love to her with tenderness and care, but she jumps on top of him and forces the issue.

Johnny manages to turn her and sets up a pace, rhythm and cadence of tender love making as opposed to dirty sex. The first time she climaxes is an explosion of pleasure. She trembles and shakes, then smiles with relief as if a big weight has been lifted off her shoulders.

Much later down the road, they both will look back at that moment as the instance when Hillary Zathlyn overcame the trauma of her rape. Johnny and Hillary go on making love throughout the evening and finally fall asleep. When they wake up, their union becomes even closer than before. Dangerously close.

Why some of the Island residents get along and others don't is impossible to discern and neighbor relations in the "paradise place" do not follow any common sense, civic rules or etiquette as practiced in the "real" world. This is certainly the case between the Baglionis and the Zathlyns, who are like oil and water. That is not so with their offsprings and this will inevitably create a major rift on the Island.

Island resident and Colombia oil tycoon Mario Angel Restrepo is still hurting and boiling inside. But that still doesn't take anything away from the fact that he is still passionately attracted to his current wife...

CHAPTER 85
THE RESTREPOS

L ynn Restrepo is all excited. After almost three months, her husband has started to acknowledge her and utter a few monosyllables. Finally, after a prolonged cold stone silence, that had her worried that a breakup was around the corner, dinner will be served for two.

'So that's it, today we'll make up,' she thinks, but not totally convinced about it. Lynn wears a tight and provocative low-cut dress and takes a place at the table 15 minutes earlier than the customary Hispanic dinner hour of 8 p.m. This has never suited her. She is hungry. She waits for her husband, nervous and jittery. At exactly 8 p.m., Mario Angel Restrepo shows up. He is freshly shaved and with pressed clothes. 'He is dressed for the part,' she observes.

"Lynn," he greets from afar.

"Mario," she replies, trying to show affection with her tone.

"Let us pray," Mario states. They both bow their heads. He recites a Catholic prayer.

"Bon Apetit," he says as he starts to eat in earnest.

Halfway through the meal, as he is not talking or even looking at her, she decides to break the ice.

"Mario, are you going to talk to me or what?"

"What is there to talk about?" he snaps.

"Anything, I am your wife, you know."

"Are you?"

She is about to snap but doesn't. She knows this is not the moment or the place.

"Yes, I am."

He finally looks at her with eyes of steel.

"You better start behaving like it then."

"I know you've been upset, I am rea…"

"Stop it Lynn, I don't need your B.S. I don't want to hear any apologies. Just be grateful that you are still here."

All she feels at the moment is loathing and contempt for him.

"The only thing I am interested in is your behavior. And don't make the mistake of ever underestimating me again. If I catch you fooling around again, next time it will not only be your lover."

Lynn shivers inside as cold fear spreads throughout her body. But, she does not show it. She isn't giving him that pleasure.

"Is that understood?" Restrepo demands.

She bats her eyes in agreement.

"All right, now go and undress and wait for me in my room without any clothes on." She is shocked and looks at him in panic and fear.

An hour later, Lynn lies in his bed alone with a smile on her face. She let him do what he wanted and she even climaxed several times. She enjoyed the sex and she knows he liked it even more.

'It is that damn sagging skin that I cannot get over. I like them young and tight,' she muses.

"Not bad for an old fart," Mario Angel Restrepo winks as he leaves the bathroom.

"Not bad, husband, not bad," she replies as she is thinking what could be the best way to get rid of him for good.

'If he will not let me have my way with men, then, he is in my way and I have to knock 'em out of the box,' she diabolically reasons as she smiles and waves him away.

Reckless, dumb and doomed, Lynn Restrepo has still not learned enough from the "jungle law" lesson her trainer, Piero Tomba (R.I.P.) received.

Island resident, surgeon to the stars, Steven Zathlyn's, secret preferences are going to eventually land him in trouble. He just does not see the danger he is facing.

CHAPTER 86
THE ZATHLYNS
(SAN FRANCISCO BAY AREA)

Steven Zathlyn is back in the bay area after a two-month absence. He has conferences both at Berkley and Stanford that will take up all of tomorrow. So, tonight is his night of freedom and pleasure. And, he has been dreaming about his three call girls for weeks. 'Bad girls is how I call them now. I made them into really bad girls,' he naughtily reasons.

An hour later, he waits in the lobby of the 'tower of passion', as he calls it. Then, at the exact agreed upon hour, they show up. At first, he sees them in the distance and his senses start to go into overdrive. Their movements and cadence are super sensual and he visualizes them naked.

'They are arriving together, that's strange.' They look like coordinated fashion models on a runway wearing extremely high heels. As they approach, he sees the three holding hands. The realization hits him that there's more to it than three friends holding hands. So, when they finally stand in front of him, he is perplexed and bewildered.

"How are you, girls?"

"Dr. Zathlyn, we moved in together. We have been a three-some for a month. We are happy to have found each other."

"So what, no men anymore?"

"Oh yeah, lots of them. But only in the way you taught us."

'I really damaged these girls,' thinks Zathlyn.

"So what are we going to do to you tonight, doctor?"

"I guess you are in charge, whatever you want."

"All right, naughty boy, follow us."

That evening became a memorable one indeed as it marked the beginning of Steven Zathlyn's unraveling.

Future Island residents, talented Cuban musicians, Ana and Juan Rojas-Lugo, discover their beat.

CHAPTER 87
THE ROJAS-LUGOS

Happy birthday to you!" The group of 50 or so Cuban expatriates, plus a few other Hispanics and some Americans, are celebrating Juan Rojas-Lugos's b-day with a double surprise. First, the party was kept secret from both Juan and Ana, and second, essentially all of the invitees are musicians by trade. The Rojas-Lugos have progressed admirably in just over a year. Their English is almost perfect. They are proficient users of tablets and cell phones. They have no debt and own three small pieces of land. They have a lot more savings than when they arrived. They live a couple blocks from Miami Beach and perform in one of the best bands in Miami. Between both of them, working day and night, they are netting $12,000 per month.

The night becomes an encounter among friends that not only share their love for music, but for most of them, they share their journey and sacrifices in leaving their home countries and moving to America. Then it begins, like it always does when musicians get together. A couple of Dominicans start playing their instruments. A couple of Venezuelans join in. Soon Ana is humming their tune and the ensemble is off to the races. They start an all-night jam session. Improvisation sparks more improvisation and after a while musicians replace musicians on the stage. Everyone gets to jam. Then, as time goes by, the synchronization gets better and better until the whole group of musicians starts to follow the beat of the leaders. By 4:00 a.m., the energy has not diminished and the ritual continues, where ten to twelve play and one sings, while the rest watch. After a while, Ana's turn comes. She sings a couple of romantic songs to her husband and then asks for some Cuban rhythm. She starts to dance while continuing to sing. Then, magic happens within the permutations of the instruments and sound. One rhythm starts to stick out and the players stay with it. As the rhythm is played again and again, each musician keeps on adjusting and homing in on it until the beat and the rhythm suddenly clicks.

"Right there, that's it, you got it," says the bespectacled Chinese guest. "You got it guys, that's the sound that will take you to the stars and beyond."

And that's how the rocketed rise of Juan and Ana Rojas-Lugo's musical career gets started. It is a combination of their immense talent and the guidance of their faithful and original manager and producer, who spotted them the first time while they were performing on the streets of "La Habana Vieja."

*Renowned Italian shoe entrepreneur, Laureen Krall, literally hooks up
with General Pinkus in order to solve a threatening situation.*

CHAPTER 88
LAUREEN KRALL

“General, I'm a new resident of Paradise Island and a neighbor
of mine, Oleg Krull, recommended that I see you when I went
to him to seek advice,” states a visibly upset Laureen Krall.

“Yes, Mr. Krull contacted me. How can I be of help?” replies
General Pinkus, head of the security firm Zapco International.

“I'm being blackmailed.”

Pinkus pauses in delight. Blackmails are always to his liking
and he has 100% success rate. He explains his perfect track record
to Laureen's delight.

“OK, Mrs. Krall, give me the details of the matter and be can-
did if you would, please.”

“An airline stewardess and a boy toy are threatening to release
videos of me having sex with them on commercial airline flights.”

“Where?”

“In the restrooms.”

“I see. Anything controversial in the type of sex?”

“If you mean is there dirty sex involved, yes, there is. How
could it not be if one of my lovers is a woman?”

"I can see that," he replies as he struggles to not start laughing out loud at the woman sitting across from him and spilling her sexual guts out to him.

"Do you have data on the two culprits?"

"Yes."

"How do they know each other?"

"They told me that they are lovers."

"You didn't know that?"

"I didn't even have a clue that they knew each other."

"Did they set you up?"

"Not exactly. I hired the boy toy from the market, but he definitely set me up with her."

"Are you paying the boy toy for his services?"

"I pay him a monthly salary."

"So, what do they want?"

"They want money. A lot of money."

"How much?"

"A million dollars."

"I gather you came to me for discretion and results."

"Absolutely. This cannot come to light, otherwise, it could hurt my business."

"Which is?

"Italian designer shoes. I have been in the industry forever."

Pinkus likes her, in more ways than one, but business before pleasure. Thus, after signing a contract and getting paid a retainer, the general gets into motion. It takes a couple of days only, as after being subjected to military torture techniques, including waterboarding and electric shock, both blackmailers turn all of the material over and run away.

"Next time you'll lose your body parts permanently," warns Pinkus sternly to both of them.

"Mrs. Krall, problem solved. Do you want us to burn the material or do you want us to bring it to you?"

"Get rid of it, please. Thank you, General."

"You are very welcome, Mrs. Krall."

"Call me Laureen, please.

"I'll do that, call me Robert."

"So what are you waiting for? When are you going to ask me out?" she says teasing him.

"Yes, ma'am. How's tomorrow at 8 o'clock?"

"It will be a pleasure, Robert."

But theirs is not a match made in heaven - to the contrary, it is one made in hell.

New Island residents, Susan and Douglas Crawford, welcomed by the four old crows, are soon involved in an encounter that will alter and potentially shatter their lives.

CHAPTER 89
THE CRAWFORDS

" Douglas Crawford."

"Susan Garland-Crawford."

"Nice to meet you too. You are a lovely couple."

The Island's four old crows welcome the shiny and impossibly young new Paradise Island owners.

"When are you moving in?" asks Margarita Lujan-Restrepo.

"After a few renovations, we will move right in," Douglas replies.

"Well, we are all available for anything you may need. Also, for practical day to day matters you may need, a family doctor, dentist, gynecologist, etc.," says Nicole Albert.

"Thank you so much," Susan says.

"You two are an amazing success story," says Elizabeth Bell.

"Douglas is the genius businessman. I am just tagging along."

"Not true. Behind every great man there is an even greater woman," states Sarah Pesin.

"I couldn't agree more," proudly states Douglas.

"When you get settled, the four of us are going to tell you about the nuances and occurrences on the island, including its funky and peculiar residents," states Nicole Albert.

"We'll also introduce you to the people in your same generation," states Elizabeth Bell.

"That'll be fantastic, Mrs. Bell," states Douglas.

"By the way, Mrs. Bell, are you the same Bells from Heinb Laboratories?"

"Yes."

"So You're the daughter of an American hero? A WWII Ace pilot?" asks Douglas.

"Right. Actually, both my husband and I are. He's the son of a German Ace pilot as well, but how do you know all of this?" replies Elizabeth.

"My father has worked for Heinb all of his life. He actually started as an apprentice when both your husband's father and your father were still running the company," Douglas replies.

"Oh my, You're the son of Jeremy Crawford? Wait until I tell my husband. You know that my father, Ernesto Otto Heinrich just passed away."

"I didn't know, my condolences," says Douglas, paying his respects.

At that moment, lightning strikes when the most voluptuous and stunning woman both Douglas and Susan have ever seen walks in.

"Mom, I'm leaving. See you."

"Veronica wait! Let me introduce you to our new neighbors. A lovely young couple, the Crawfords." The rush is so intense that Douglas does not know himself and has a hard time staying expressionless on the outside. 'Oh my, this is a bombshell of a woman.'

Susan is experiencing the same feelings and sensations, but out of experience, her reaction is more controlled. 'I am going to have this woman,' she thinks blowing through and shattering her newly married restraints. When Veronica Lujan-Restrepo finally locks eye contact with each, she is equally attracted to both and immediately perceives their desire as well. Then as she kisses both on the cheek, she squeezes their hands a bit as they greet. She then predicts the future, 'I am going to have both of them.'

'Wait until you see what I am going to do to you,' is what her eyes tell the young couple as she, intensely albeit briefly, stares one more time at them. Right there begins a storm that will threaten their young marriage and test its endurance after both youngsters are severely damaged by the insatiable Veronica.

Modern technology will enable Island residents, the Holsteins and the Mizrahis, to uncover the truth about their past and their blood lines.

CHAPTER 90
THE HOLSTEINS AND THE MIZRAHIS
(Part I)

B art Holstein has been so busy putting out fires of the criminal kind that he almost forgets about the letter that has been laying on his desk for weeks. It took him almost a year to make up his mind. Then as if by magic, the intense national marketing blitz had persuaded him to do it.

'Perfect! This is exactly what I needed,' he reasons when he reads the advertising in detail. "Find your long lost loved one. Send your DNA in and it'll be compared to millions of others to find your relatives." Bart had ordered the package. Once received, he had sent back the DNA samples as requested. Then, he had forgotten about it until the results came in the mail. He forgot them again, as he was overwhelmed by the two criminal probes being conducted against him. But, today is the day. His long quest to find who his father is or was, might be inside this envelope in front of him. Bart spends the next hour wandering through his life as a child and the wild ways of his mom who seemed insatiable for men. 'How am I to know among the countless lovers she had who had knocked her up?' he thinks. He feels tortured. Finally, he opens the envelope. Actually, rips it open on impulse. He reads it carefully and when he gets to the last page, his eyes widen in shock and disbelief. 'You've got to be kidding me. This must be wrong. There is some kind of mistake here.' He calls the provider. Thirty minutes later he hangs up with the realization that there is no mistake. There can't be a mistake with DNA matches. Bart Holstein reads the final message once more already trying to guess who it could be, but has no clue. Then, he reads it aloud once more. "We have found someone that must be your half sibling as he shares half of his DNA with you, meaning you have a common parent. He lives on Paradise Island. If you consent, we can connect you with each other." 'Stupid computer system cannot discern that we live on the same island in Miami Beach, Florida!' Nevertheless, he answers yes and waits.

Sitting on his computer, Ariel Mizrahi gets a reply to his quest for ancestors. The message is the same as Holstein got. He is immediately on the phone to Israel, with his father and mother on the line, he narrates what has just happened. "Mom, dad, I don't know who this DNA match of mine is, but you have some explaining to do. C'mon spill the beans," states an obfuscated Ariel while both his parents realize that the ghost of Alvi Mazon, the Jewish Lebanese smuggler thrown overboard on the Mediterranean, on orders of Ariel's mom, has come back to haunt them.

The longtime Island residents, Ariel Mizrahi, the cruise line tycoon, and corrupt lobbyist, Bart Holstein, are half-siblings. How is that for a bombshell in any normal environment? However, on Paradise Island, it is just one more daily occurrence.

CHAPTER 91
THE HOLSTEINS AND THE MIZRAHIS
(Part II)

A fter spending the first three nights of their honeymoon on the private island of Mustique, in the Caribbean, Sarah Greenhouse and Steven Mizrahi are asleep in the Gulfstream G-650 bedroom. They do not notice the plane's descent into their next destination, the Galapagos Islands, off the coast of Ecuador in South America. The Mizrahi family yacht is already in position waiting for them.

Once on the ground, the crew wakes up the newlyweds. Minutes later, they scramble their way in shorts, sandals and lobster sunburns to the waiting Augusta helicopter. Thirty minutes later, they land on the mammoth yacht and in five minutes they are back to sleep for the next eight hours. They spend the next four days cruising and sightseeing the flora and fauna. This is only the prelude for Sarah and Steven's main reason for visiting the islands. At 8:00 a.m., everything is ready and with four crew members in tow, the young couple takes a plunge into the waters off the exotic island. A crew member, a former professional diver, leads them into a prolonged descent which finally ends up underneath a massive rock ledge. Then, they wait. From underneath the massive underwater stone, the light filtering through the water looks like white laser beams. Then, they see the first group of sharks swimming calmly above them. The divers have never seen so many bunched together. Then, just like that, they are gone. And then, the party really begins as the divers are treated to a spectacle of colors and a variety of tropical fish. Suddenly, the tropical fish are gone and it is time for the day's main attraction. At first, there is one, then a couple, until there are at least 50 of them. The hammerhead sharks are bunched much tighter together than their relatives earlier on. Sarah keeps a tight grip on Steven's forearm, but the site of the massive and menacing hammerheads makes her arm hold feel as if her nails are about to cut through his thick wetsuit. As he looks at his wife, her eyes seem ready to pop out of her head in fear. He gestures with love for her to calm down. Looking straight at him Sarah gestures amazement to Steven.

The dive is over and they are now watching in the media room of the yacht, both the pictures and the videos of their adventure. Steven's satellite phone starts to ring. He picks it up right away as he knows that the call has to be important, otherwise no one would be bothering him except at the agreed times.

"Mom? We are fine, mother, happy and healthy, what's up?"

"Huh?"

"What's the problem?"

Sarah steps towards her husband with a bit of alarm.

"Wait, let me put you on the speaker. Sarah is here and I want her to be in the conversation with us."

"Dear, how are you?"

"Fine, Mrs. Mizrahi, thanks for asking."

"Well, you let me know if that son of mine does not treat you like a queen. All right?"

"I will, count on it."

"Son, we got some rather disturbing news last night."

"Go ahead, mom, we are listening."

"You dad got an email from a DNA databank where he registered for them to look for long lost relatives."

"And?" asked a bemused Steven while smiling at his wife.

"Well, the message we got states that they located a half sibling of your dad´s."

"What?"

"Yes, that is what I said."

"Maybe it is a prank or a trick to hack you."

"No, son, we already checked it out. It is kosher."

"So, what's next?"

"Wait, wait, there is more."

"OK," replies Steven cautiously.

"The email message also stated that if we want, they can put us in contact with your dad's half-sibling."

"That's to be expected and seems like a sound approach to ask at first."

"That's not the catch son."

"What is it then mom? Spell it out."

"The half-sibling's location is the issue."

"Why?" Steven asks, but the line remains silent.

"What's the mystery, mom?"

"Lives on the island, son."

"What! Is… you mean our island, Paradise Island? You've got to be kidding me. This is a prank. We have to find out who is putting you through this."

"Son, it is not a prank. The company's system just generated the information automatically. They can put us in contact. They will do it, however, only if the two parties agree."

"Who could it be?"

"We have an idea, but your dad is already on his way to Tel Aviv to talk to your grandparents and clarify this before we set any contact up."

"Whoa, mom, this has lots of ramifications. I've got to think about this. Keep us informed, please."

The following day, as the yacht heads west into the South Pacific, the young couple takes a short flight into the Andes Mountains in Peru. They hire a guide and he takes them right into the beginning of the Inca trail.

"We have the daytime hours to cover the equivalent of a marathon distance. Our destination is the ruins of Machu Picchu," he states.

The young couple had been preparing for this trek for almost a year. They have been high altitude training in Telluride, Colorado. The trail turns out easy in steepness, but trying in altitude. It is almost 4 p.m. when they finally see Machu Picchu in the distance. Steven waits until the final moment and with full provenance view in front of him, does his promise. With the help of his satellite phone, he sets up a live video connection through Periscope and sends the link to both his and his wife's family. As he starts playing the host for everyone, text messages start arriving, one after another.

"Here is my lovely wife," he says, with her smiling with the ruins in the background.

"He is killing me, this is not a honeymoon, but an athletic competition," she says, mocking him and showing her biceps.

The next morning, their flight path takes them all along the West Coast of South America. Several hours later, they land in the

City of Puerto Montt, deep in southern Chile. Right after arrival, they board a small cruise ship reserved just for them and head to Argentina through the magical, unspoiled and postcard-perfect traverse of the seven lakes in Patagonia. It is late into the evening and they are both tucked in bed and exhausted when his satellite phone rings again.

"It's mom again, should I put her on speaker phone, honey?" he states to his lovely wife.

"How are my two lovebirds?"

"Mom, we are exhausted and already in bed. What do you want?" says an irritated Steven.

"I pray you guys are making lots of babies …"

"Bye, mom."

"Wait! Your dad is back."

"Let me talk to him, please."

"Son, how are you?"

"Happy dad, but worried. What's going on?"

"Well, son, the news is, how should I call it? Shocking."

"Yes, shocking, but also unavoidable as well."

"I'm listening."

"Turns out that your grandfather is not my dad. I'm the son of my mother's first husband, who no one ever told me existed. He was lost at sea before I was born."

"Who was he dad?"

"His name was Alvi Mazon. He was a smuggler of fine goods when he met grandma. It turns out that he was the genius behind the Mizrahi cruise ship line. He was the one that transformed your great grandpa's ocean cargo company into a Mediterranean cruise line. He was the head of the company when he fell overboard on a cruise with grandma."

"Why hide his existence that way?"

"He was quite a womanizer …"

The line goes dead. Sarah and Steven look at each other with startled faces.

"Well, I guess they will call back and finish the story."

"And we still don't know who the half-sibling is," she says.

At the Bavarian influenced town of Bariloche, located on the final lake of their journey, Nahuel-Huapi, the young couple disembark. After a breathtaking hike over Cerro Cathedral, with magnificent vistas of the Andes, they head back to their Gulfstream G-650 stationed and waiting for them at the Bariloche Airport. Within minutes they are in the air heading west. Now, their destination is the middle of the South Pacific. Hours later, as they are arriving on Easter Island, his dad calls again.

"Hi, again."

"What took you so long to call back dad?"

"Long story, son, but bottom line is I had to reacquaint myself with somebody."

"Who is it, dad?"

"Coming shortly, but let me finish first. Grandma confessed to me something that has been a well-guarded secret in the family."

"OK, dad, enough of this, spell it out."

"Alvi Mazon was the love of her life." Both youngsters are in shock.

"But what about grandpa?"

"Her cousin, a marriage of convenience."

"Like you said, shocking."

"Well, among Alvi Mazon's conquests was the wife of his childhood friend and fellow smuggler."

"This is getting more intense by the minute, dad."

"His name was Eladio Alalu and they grew up on the streets of Lebanon. Under the tutelage of a master smuggler named Rocky Shapiro, they learned all the tricks of the trade. Rocky also introduced them to their future wives. Alalu moved to Havana with his young wife, while Mazon stayed in Beiruit running the ship line for the Mizrahis, your grandma's family business. So the two friends distanced themselves."

Sarah and Steven are not missing one bit of the story.

"Your grandma found out …"

The satellite signal drops again as their flight path gets them deeper into the Pacific Ocean. The young couple enjoys extraordinary weather while visiting Easter Island and its mystical moai statues. The highlight of the stop is a video that shows how the stones were moved by pulling and rocking them back and forth to put them into position to form the statues. All the stone carvings were completed between 1000 and 1500 CE.

That same day, the young couple is off again to Port Douglas, Australia, to dive in the Great Barrier reef. This time Steven calls his dad as they travel through the South Pacific.

"Dad, please finish the story and be quick."

"Alalu amassed a fortune in Cuba in real estate by developing a smuggling operation on the island. The problem though was that his beautiful young wife was too hot to handle and liked to dance and sing in the nightclubs. She started to perform at an early age in Beirut, Lebanon, and continued to do it in the streets of La Habana. She was insatiable with men. Apparently, she came to despise Alalu physically, as he put on an enormous amount of weight. Apparently, Mazon got her pregnant on one of his trips to Havana."

"So Mazon is your dad?"

"Right."

"What happened to Alalu?"

"Died of a heart attack in Havana."

"OK, dad, enough. Who was Alalu's wife and who is her son then?"

"She is Andrea Holstein and her son, Bart, is my half-brother."

"Oh, my god, the lobbyist. She's got Alzheimer's and her son is a crook," states Steven in disgust.

The newlyweds' honeymoon will eventually take them to Fiji, the Seychelles and finally, Botswana, before returning to the States. But, during the remaining three weeks they did not stop talking about their newly acquired family.

Inexorably, dumb and clumsy repeats itself. Have the three rapists jeopardized their wellbeing again?

CHAPTER 92
THE HOLSTEIN, MATHEWS AND KRULL FAMILIES
(Paradise Island Social Club – Sunday at Noon)

T hor Krull, Louis Mathews, III and Andy Holstein are flaunting their three gorgeous girlfriends at the Paradise Island pool.

The Island's old crows are not even pretending to peek, as they all stand watching through the glass doors of the card room. The Island teens by the pool are frozen in their chairs. Their mouths are open as they watch the spectacle.

"That's the problem with unverified rumors," states Elizabeth Bell whose police contacts again take center stage.

"Something is not right. I thought the story was accurate," states Sarah Pesin.

"To the contrary. Everything is right, Sarah," states Margarita Lujan-Restrepo.

"They all seem in one piece to me," confirms Nicole Albert.

Sitting by the pool, the island teenagers are equally startled.

"Guys, this is insane. These three morons got away with it and their parents took them away from here until the waters calmed down," says Megan Greenhouse.

"Well Johnny is full of …everything he said wasn't right," states Kevin Pesin.

"Not exactly, Kevin. Something happened to Hillary. We just don't know yet what it was," replies Megan.

"Come to think of it, she hasn't even said… that they actually did something to her," replies Kevin.

At that moment, the old crows and the teenagers stop talking as Johnny and Hillary approach the pool. The Krull, Mathews and Holstein boys are caught by surprise. From afar and to their backs, Johnny calls them out.

"So we've got here the three cowards in person or should I say the three she's?" The three boys freak out as they face the Baglioni-Zathlyn twosome. Hillary is in a state of terror. She starts shaking and convulsing and in an instant, she passes out.

Minutes later, surrounded by her childhood friends, the four old crows and Johnny, Hillary comes to with a tired look on her face and her eyes open in fear.

"Where are they?"

Johnny turns towards the pool area, but the three bad boys are gone. Shaken, the Holstein, Mathews and Krull boys have left the Island Social Club dragging their girlfriends with them.

"Thor, what was that all about?" asks his girlfriend.

"Our breakup was nasty and her new boyfriend is jealous."

"It seemed like a lot more than that, Thor. Are you being honest?" she presses on while deciding to find out more once they are back in the bay area.

Later that day, when the boys are alone at the Krull mansion, Louis Mathews, III, explodes.

"Thor, I told you this was a very bad idea."

"Well, our families pushed it and our girls as well. Besides, our girls wanted to see where we came from. Louis, you are always doing 'Monday Morning Quarterbacking.'

"Keep your mouth shut, Holstein. I'm the one who got you out of your junky rehab downward spiral."

"Thor, our three girls are very smart. They are going to find out," Andy Holstein states.

"Find out what?" states Krull, Sr. as he walks in to greet the boys.

Has Island resident and corrupt lobbyist Bart Holstein and his pal (the former president) run come to an end? Is this the time when they are finally going to fall?

CHAPTER 93
THE HOLSTEINS
(MIAMI FBI HEADQUARTERS)

FBI special agent Neil Green has a decision to make. If he gives the order, the sting operation will start up and may end up with the arrest of a former president and his close confidant, the lobbyist, Bart Holstein.

"Let me see that video again," he demands. His nerves are about to fry.

Video Title: "Interrogation of Lou, a/k/a the pimp"

"Lou, we got you on conspiracy to money launder. You are going down for 20 plus. Your choice! Are you going to help us or not?" asks the FBI agent to Holstein's pimp.

"Sometimes it is better to be locked up, than having a price on your head for being a snitch."

"As you wish. We are going to arrest you right here and you will be arraigned this afternoon. Think hard, because when we walk out of this room, the deal is off!" The two agents stand up and get ready to leave as the ashen faced low life seems frantic and in panic mode.

"Wait, guys. Wait."

The agents stop on their heels. They did not expect their bluff to work or Lou Manzetti to break that easy.

Special agent Green stops the video.

"You see guys, that is my problem."

"I can't see him caving under stress. It is too easy. We cannot afford to be wrong."

"And we aren't. Sir, the facts are simple and straightforward. We checked the President's schedule and he is going to be in town the days Lou indicated. As you know, the schedule, even for ex-presidents, is confidential. But the point is that Lou says Holstein alerted him to find girls," states the special agent to his boss.

"It is a fact that he is coming into town. So, what matters is the girls Lou has chosen," states his partner.

"Well, we checked them and they are all under 18. We can nail the bastards, sir."

"Wait a minute, what about us knowingly letting a group of underage girls walk into the wolves liar."

"We will bust them right at the moment we get their intent on tape."

"But if anything were to happen to the girls, it will all be on us."

"Your call, sir. We recommend to move forward."

"Are the three going to be wired?"

"Yes, with body cameras as well."

A long pause ensues for what seems like an eternity.

"Our jobs are on the line. Let's do this right."

HOLSTEIN MANSION (PARADISE ISLAND)

The three girls hidden in the back seats of an SUV arrive at the Holstein mansion with their recording devices on.

"Sir, we have live video and sound feeds. The SUV has left the premises and the girls have been dropped off. The teams to execute the arrests are in the vicinity, both on land and sea."

There is high tension among the FBI personnel. Then, the first glitch happens.

"Sir, we've lost the signal. It does not mean the devices are not recording, but only that we are not getting the video and sound feeds."

"We cannot be out of touch with the minors. Do whatever is necessary to restore the connection, otherwise we will have to move in."

"Sir, the three girls are in the house."

"Go in, immediately," orders Green.

Two different contingents of FBI agents move on the house. One agent disables the front entrance door and another one comes into the house from the Biscayne Bay back entrance.

"Mr. President, Mr. Holstein, we need you to verify the identities and ages of your three female companions."

"This is an outrage! How dare you to barge in here like this! There will be hell to pay for this," Holstein replies.

"Let's ensure that neither of you have broken the law, sir, because if you have, we'll arrest you right now."

"Go ahead and do what you have to do before you all have to walk the plank."

As he listens and views his agent's actions through the body cameras, special agent Green gets an eerie feeling and it is soon validated.

"Sir, we've got an issue here."

"What is it?"

"Their three companions are all adults!"

"How …? Show me their faces now."

In disbelief, Green and his colleagues see the faces of three women in their mid-twenties.

"Is there a problem, officer?" asks an obfuscated president.

"No sir. None other than you were about to commit adultery."

"What I do privately is none of your damn business. Get the hell out of here now!"

Then, as the agents leave, the former president has one last word. "You all know or should know that your careers are over. You will not even be able to find a job as a street sweeper."

FBI agent Green goes into preservation mode and broadcasts: "Get the hell out of there. The SUV with Lou and the young girls still in the back of the vehicle just surfaced on the other end of Paradise Island. They were never dropped off."

"Did he double cross us, sir?"

"We'll find out, but my gut tells me that he didn't. He is scared and now the deal is off, so I doubt it. He has too much to lose."

Holstein Mansion (Paradise Island)

"Mr. President, they fell for it. That should keep them at a distance for a quite a while."

"It was brilliant, Bart, but Paradise Island and Miami are too hot to handle, so let's move the party somewhere else."

"Yes, sir. But first let's call our three guests to render a good and honorable service to their country."

"Let's do it!" states the president, as he walks alongside his long-time friend towards the three most gorgeous ladies money can buy. They are an experienced threesome and, after the fact, they will do their utmost to bring down the ex-president as a payback to the depraved acts they were subjected to on that night.

Longtime Island resident, old crow club member, Sarah Pesin's, granddaughter is falling into a dangerous rabbit hole.

CHAPTER 94
THE PESINS

Paradise Island resident, Arlene Pesin, has been doing a photo shoot nonstop in Central Europe for a French luxury brand during the last three weeks. The first shoot was in Prague's Wenceslas Square; then the baroque architecture streets and the Charles Bridge over the Vitava River; then it was Budapest's magnificent structures over the Danube River, and finally, Saint Petersburg, Russia, at the Hermitage Museum.a After the final ten-hour session in the magnificent Russian city, she is tired and anxious to get back home. When she goes to her hotel to pack and enters her suite, her iPad is flashing a text message on her encrypted chat app. "What about meeting me in Budapest tomorrow night?" writes Lewis Wang.

"I was just there, Lewis. I want to go home. I am so tired," replies Arlene in terse language.

"Home is where your heart is," he shoots back.

"How do you know where my heart is, Lewis? You are so full of yourself," she texts with a chuckling emoji attached. "Not full of myself, but smitten by you, and I recognize it."

"Mystery man, you know how much I like you, but I still don't know who you really are underneath your academia cover."

The screen goes quiet for what seems to be an eternity.

"Arly, there is only one way for you to find out."

"And that would be …"

"By checking the goods."

"Yeah, right!"

"Why not?"

"Well, I was planning to visit you at the bay area next week."

"That sounds great, but why not tomorrow?"

"As I said, I don't know, I was just there."

"What does that matter? We won't be staying there anyway."

"Why go there, then?"

"We'll get started from there."

"All right, explain yourself, Louis Wang."

"Arly, we'll be taking the ride of a lifetime if you want."

"Which is, if I may ask?"

"I'll see you tomorrow at 6:00 p.m. at the Budapest Main train station, where we will be boarding the Orient Express to travel to Istanbul."

"But …" the chat app on the other end is gone.

Arlene is anxious, but she slowly lets herself doze off while dreaming about the tempting magic ride.

Orient Express Train, Budapest Main Station (6:00 p.m.)

Lewis has a gut feeling that 'she is not coming.' He is seated in the train's main salon. The train starts to move and anxiety and pain fill Louis.

"This train is straight out of an Agatha Christie movie," a familiar voice states from behind him. He smiles and turns around, but all he sees is a newspaper fully opened. The paper drops and there she is, in all her glory.

"I thought you would have noticed me by now. I have been here all along. In fact, I got here way before you," she mocks him with panache.

Lewis walks over. Their faces get really close and at that moment she kisses him with hunger and passion.

"If you are really into the cloak and dagger game, you are pretty lousy at it, Mr. Wang."

Lewis is embarrassed, but at the same time euphorically happy.

On this, their first real date, they chat to no end under the old Victorian luxury of their cozy surroundings. They wine and dine and finally dance to the romantic classic tunes of Frank Sinatra and Ella Fitzgerald. When it's time to retire, they are both in high spirits.

"Well, my beautiful dame, my cabin is next to yours and if you need anything, just holler. I'll see you whenever you wake up. You need to rest." Wang approaches her to kiss her goodbye, but she wraps her arms around him.

"Lewis, don't behave like a schoolboy. You don't really think I flew all the way to freaking Budapest to behave like a good girl. No, my dear, I came to check out the goods in person per your offer," she says while gently squeezing him right in the middle of his pants.

Istanbul, Turkey (days later)

Among the Persian rugs, arabesque utensils and adorns, the souvenirs and the pushy salesmen of Istanbul's market bazaar, Arlene and Lewis float on a carpet ride of infatuation and desire as they walk the streets of old Constantinople. Later, they walk towards the Szechenyi Chain Bridge that separates Asia and Europe. They wish they could stay a bit longer, but, his invite to visit Vienna and

Salzburg is too tempting to pass up. So, they find themselves back on the Orient Express, this time heading north, back to Europe. But, the moment they disembark in the Austrian capital, the news is all over the newsstands and TV screens; "Terrorists attack Istanbul's market bazaar – 200 dead."

Twice in a row, Arlene Pesin's boyfriend, Lewis Wang, has been present when terror attacks have occurred in two major cities – Shanghai first and then Istambul. And the young model is right in the middle of all of it.

Island resident and the largest homebuilder in the United States, Leon Albert's, luck is about to run out on his reign of terror.

CHAPTER 95
THE ALBERTS
(Liv Night Club, Miami Beach)

Jennifer is half wasted and in a bathroom line with a friend when she blurts it out. "This guy has gazillions. The one who flew us to his private island in the Bahamas the other week."

"Is he single?"

"I think he is divorced."

"You think? If you are going to date him, you better find out."

"Are you crazy? I am not dating that creep. Besides, there were four of us on the island."

"A foursome, then? That is really naughty."

"None of that, I promise, none of that."

"No action, I can't believe it."

"There was plenty of action, believe me."

"Of which kind, then?"

"We were almost eaten by sharks."

"Get out of here. What happened?"

"We were swimming close to shore. Suddenly, we were surrounded by them."

"How did you girls get away?"

"There was a platform that we rushed to in a frenzy. Going up the ladder was terrifying as I thought a shark was going to come and bite my ass!"

"So nothing happened?"

"The whole thing scared the hell out of all of us. I swear to you we were so scared that one or all of us could have drowned just out of the panic we were in."

"Excuse me," states a tall and striking brunette.

"Yes?" replies an intrigued and uncomfortable Jennifer.

"Sandra," she extends her hand.

"Jennifer."

"I need to apologize to you because I overheard your conversation."

"Don't worry it was just silly stuff."

"No it wasn't," states a dead serious Sandra.

"I beg your pardon?" responds Jennifer in discomfort.

"Jennifer, the same thing happened to me and three of my girlfriends weeks earlier," states Sandra.

"This guy sure is sick," states Jennifer in disgust.

"What are we going to do about it Jennifer?" asks Sandra in anger.

On Paradise Island almost everyone deceives the others, and the others them. Bottom line, money changes hands for the strangest of reasons and seldom for the right ones.

CHAPTER 96
THE KRULLS AND THE ALBERTS

"$250,000," states criminal attorney, Oleg Krull.

"For what?" asks Paradise Island neighbor, Leon Albert.

"To make it go away," confirms Oleg Krull.

"You're kidding, right?" asks an incredulous Leon Albert.

"No, I'm not, otherwise your son and maybe yourself are in legal jeopardy of the criminal kind. And believe me, the state prison system is not a place you ever want to be in."

"C'mon Oleg, that is a lot of money."

"Call it the price of freedom. That's how the system works. If you can pay them off, the odds are all stacked in your favor."

"Even in murder cases?"

"Those are on a whole different level. Depending on the case, money can buy you the best chance you would ever have to beat one of those raps."

"It's still a lot of dough, Oleg."

"Not for you or me, Leon."

"So, how do I rationalize this high payout?"

"Peace of mind, my friend. Just piece of mind."

"I am going to kill Eli," says Leon, talking about his eldest son.

"No, Leon what you should do is pay attention to him. What he needs is a real father," states Oleg Krull, while scolding both his long-time neighbor and himself for not being exactly that.

'Thor is now crippled for life thanks in part to me being an absent father,' he mulls over in anger.

"All right, I'll send you a check today. Should I consider the matter closed?"

"Closed forever," confirms Krull as he has indeed put the gun issue to rest, but without spending a penny on it.

'Some favors and relationships are worth their weight in gold,' Oleg reasons. He has now cashed in on another fee without putting much effort into it.

"Am I getting the weapon back?"

"It is already in my office. I'll bring it to you tonight."

Upon hanging up, Leon Albert calls his son right away. "Eli?"

"Yeah, dad?"

"The matter is closed and I'll have the item back tonight." He can hear his son sobbing in relief.

"Thanks, dad. Once more, I am sorry."

"Don't do it again."

"I learned my lesson."

"I love you, son," pleads Leon, not really knowing what promoted it. He can hear his son's gasps for air in surprise.

"Me too, dad. Me too."

As other clouds gather on the horizon, at least the $250,000 is an OK price to pay to get father and son closer together.

Island resident, world-famous architect Lars Johannsen and his fiancée, tennis star Gabrielle Lareau, ride perhaps the most enchanting and magical train in the world – what they don't know is that at their destination, they will run into the mysterious disappearance of one of their Island neighbors, German Lope-Bello.

CHAPTER 97
THE JOHANNSENS (LARS AND GABRIELLE)
GLACIER EXPRESS TRAIN, SWITZERLAND

❝ Gabrielle, this is the most picturesque train in the world."

The fairytale route of the Glacier Express is taking them from Saint Moritz to Zermatt. After a day of doing 35 miles of cross-country skiing on the massive frozen lake of the Swiss town, Lars and Gabrielle are ready for the ride and the rest. They first traverse the mountains of the Italian-Swiss Canton of Ticino and view the precipices and the winter ice. It overwhelms them.

"This landscape is breathtaking," states Lars.

"I thought I'd travelled a lot, but in fact, I haven't. Hotel rooms and tennis courts do not count for much. I have played tennis in London, Paris, Rome and Barcelona, but I do not know them."

"Let's focus on the present, my love."

"I try to do that with all my heart each day I am with you. You know so many places. Do you realize, Lars, that you know by heart the top 50 cities in the world and when you are in those places, you breathe them? You run and cycle their streets. You have your breakfast spots, favorite lunch places and usual dinner spots. In every place you take advantage of the best they have to offer. In London, it is the plays. In Paris, it is Le Vaudeville. In Florence and Milano, it is the fashion. You also enjoy their music and art. It is overwhelming and fascinating. It is hard to keep up with you. Do you realize this?" she says, while trying to make him laugh.

"Lars, sometimes I ask myself why do you need me? Why would you need anyone in your amazing world?" She turns again to face him and the snoring sound finally makes her realize he is deep asleep and has probably not heard a word she has said, but she does not care.

"I love you, my amazing Swede," she says while kissing her sleeping fiancé on the lips.

'I love you too. More than you can imagine. You actually saved me from myself,' he reasons as he is actually fully awake, but acting as if he is sleeping.

Hours later, as they approach Zermatt, Gabrielle is all excited at the sight of the Matterhorn far away in the distance, awaiting them.

LATER IN ZERMATT, SWITZERLAND (JASPER)

"Honey, what did Mrs. Rawlings do with her head of security?" asks Gabrielle.

"She fired him, of course. She didn't press charges for the theft of the bitcoins, but she did persuade his live-in girlfriend to press charges for domestic abuse. He's now facing jail time."

"What about Jasper?"

"He was the hero of the whole matter. I'm proud of him. At the beginning, I was a bit upset, until I processed the whole thing. As part of his reward, I invited him over here. He'll be joining us."

"Super," she says, happy that he was not hard on his son.

Little do they know that while in Zermatt, the father, his son and the tennis player will run into the strange disappearance of their Paradise Island neighbor, German Lope-Bello, while he was climbing the fabled Zermatt Mountain, the Matterhorn. Once more, Jasper's bitcoin expertise will be put to the test.

There is no question that Island residents are great when it comes to not paying taxes and hiding money – an army of accountants and attorneys makes sure of that. This works of course until the bankers that hold their stashed away money, give them away.

CHAPTER 98
THE MATTHEWS FAMILY

The banker from Lugano, Switzerland, has sweaty hands and is a nervous Nellie, as he stands on the Miami International Airport U. S. immigration line. It is always the same thing. He never carries case files, valuables or information about his clients with him, so the fear is irrational and unfounded, but he can't control it. He knows that the reason for his edginess is the awareness that what he does is illegal and, if caught, could be punished with a very long prison term. Klaus Lehman is a private Swiss banker. He has been honed and trained on the strictest traditions of the country's banking systems; discretion and first-class customer service. He visits his U.S. clients three times a year. Along the way, he picks up one or two additional clients per trip. The in-person conversations with his clients are always checked for listening devices. The conversations invariably are about untaxed funds, either deposited in his bank or, hopefully, on the way to his bank. A full 50% of his time is dedicated to explaining and plotting off-shore and off-country deposit methods. Mr. Lehman also performs additional services for his clients, like paying bills abroad. He organizes the purchasing and paying for precious metals, stones, jewelry, real estate, art, designer clothes, rents, condominium fees, travel expenses, jets, limos, boats, etc. If a client needs cash, no matter where they are in the world, a security guard with a briefcase will show up in short order with the money. He is dependable and responsive and his clients know it. The line is impossibly long and his angst is only growing. 'Klaus, they don't even know who you are,' he thinks, but he couldn't be more wrong.

"Sir, face recognition has picked up the Swiss banker about to enter the country."

"Is all the paperwork in order?"

"Yes sir."

"OK, pick him up."

Lehman stands in front of the immigration officer for his routine clearance.

"What's the purpose of your visit to the U.S.?"

"I am "

"Sir, please come with us," states one of the two Homeland Security agents that are standing behind him.

Alarm bells go off inside Lehman's head. His worst fears come to fruition. Three hours later, still sitting in the same windowless room, a couple of FBI agents finally show up. A man and a woman.

"Mr. Lehman, I am Mr. Rossen, a Federal prosecutor."

"And I am FBI special agent, Mr. Brown."

"Mr. Lehman, we want the names and account balances of all of your clients. If you cooperate with us, we'll grant you immunity. If you don't, we'll charge you with crimes that'll send you to prison for a very long time. This is the only time we will make you this offer. Your choice."

Lehman's eyes dart in all directions as he sizes up the two government officials.

"All right, Lehman, what is it going to be?"

"I want the immunity in writing."

"That's not a problem. Keep in mind it'll be good, as long as you are truthful."

"All right, I'll do it."

'So much for Swiss banking discretion,' the prosecutor reasons.

"We will need written bank statements."

"That's easy to get."

"That'll be a condition of the immunity."

"That won't be a problem."

"You'll need an attorney to review your immunity agreement."

"I have one, let me call her."

They hand a phone to Lehman and within an hour, the attorney is sitting across from him.

"Mr. Lehman, as long as you are truthful, they are granting you full immunity. Are you willing to sign?"

"Yes."

"Then sign here, please."

Thirty minutes later, the document is fully executed by the prosecutor's office, as well.

"Mr. Lehman, how much is deposited with you?"

"1.2"

"1.2 what? Don't start playing games with me."

"$1.2 billion."

"Holy Guacamole! How many clients?"

"112"

"Who's your largest client?"

"Louis Mathews II?"

"The oil tycoon from Paradise Island."

"Yes."

"How much is he holding with you?"

"The total, in Swiss banks including ours, is $550 million. We administer all of his funds in Switzerland."

Silence engulfs the room as the government official's expectations have just been blown out of the water.

"I guess Mr. Mathews will be seeing a lot of us in the near future," the prosecutor says.

"I am sure he will," replies the FBI agent, already salivating at the beginning of the chase of a very large prey.

From now on, Island resident and Venezuela oil transport magnate, Louis Mathews II's fate, fortune and wealth are no longer under his control but under the control of the government.

The parents of longtime residents, John and Elizabeth Bell, an old crow club member herself, founded decades ago, one of the largest pharmaceutical companies in the world – Heinb – which stands for Heindrich and Bell. The company was founded with a treasure trove of patents and formulas that originated from Elizabeth's dad, Ernesto Otto Heindrich, who had received them from his uncle.

CHAPTER 99
THE BELLS AND HEINDRICHS

In the beautiful city of Bonn that served as the German capital while Berlin was occupied after World War II, but the riverside sits a nondescript six-story building that dates back over one hundred years. It is one of those old European buildings that is more humid and cold inside than on the street. On its third floor lies the office of 77-year-old Isaac Perlman. As his father did before him, Perlman is an asset hunter. His office is a treasure trove of information perfectly indexed and arranged in countless file cabinets. Over the years, his father and he have uncovered thousands of assets stolen from Jewish families during World War II. Contrary to conventional wisdom, the perpetrators have come from across Europe. When his father started back in 1946, Isaac was barely 6 years old and Germany was in ruins. He quickly found out that the Nazis had not done all the stealing. He learned that as Jews were sent to concentration camps, whether in France, Poland, Austria, Czechoslovakia, Hungary, the Netherlands or Belgium, the locals did as much pilfering as the Nazis. The biggest of illegal acquisitions took place in Switzerland, where thousands upon thousands of art treasures and numbered bank accounts disappeared from the face of the Earth.

The Perlmans' ability to recover art, jewels, memorabilia, family heirlooms, real estate and cash caused their reputation to grow. Their client base grew and grew over the years. Perlman's latest battle had been to uncover a set of long lost bank statements at a shady accountant's office in Basel, Switzerland. The Zurich-based bank that had issued the statements back in 1940 had been denying the existence of the accounts or even that Perlman's client ever had an account with them. To complicate matters, the actual bank did not even exist anymore, as it had been bought by another Zurich-based bank. But fate was going to smile on the descendants of the account holder who had perished at the Buchenwald concentration camp.

The Swiss bank that bought the accounts had sizeable operations in the U.S. So, the U.S. Judge where the claim was filed, ordered them to pay up from their U.S. assets. The family received $89 million, including interest. Perlman, keeping with his father's tradition, immediately contributed 75% of his fee to the Holocaust victim's fund.

Today is an important day for Perlman. Loaded with thousands of scanned documents, he is riding the bullet train to Hamburg, where he'll be taking the deposition of several members of the Heindrich family. He has been working on this particular case for several years. It is an unconventional, but noteworthy case. He is representing a large number of Jewish families of German descent that all have the same claim. The formulas and patents for thousands of medicines were stolen from them by the Heindrich patent office in Hamburg. Back then, they were the largest in Germany. The principals at the time are long deceased. Perlman has engaged in a long legal war to get to this moment.

"Mr. Heindrich, what did your father do with all of the patent certificates and secret formulas?"

"I guess they were lost during the bombing of Hamburg. As you know, nothing was left."

"No records, no ledgers, no paperwork left?"

"Gar nicht. Nothing left."

Perlman is totally frustrated as, after a couple of hours, he has been totally stonewalled. During the break, he paces back and forth in the corridors of the reputable patent office and feels he has reached a dead end. He decides to wrap up the deposition and reassess his strategy going forward. Dejected, he walks back. Because he is distracted, he does not see the document stack on the far corner of the corridor until it is too late, and he literally runs it over knocking three feet of documents and files all over the floor. Embarrassed, he starts gathering and picking them up. Heindrich, the witness and the attorneys hear the commotion and come out. Everyone helps out and quickly everything is back in its place. Perlman is kneeling on the floor when he sees it. It is a stock market plaque, or more like what the Americans call a declaration to memorialize public offerings of stock. It is so far down on the wall of awards and newspaper clippings that it literally can only be read while sitting or kneeling.

Heindrich Bell a/k/a Heinb Inc., 50,000,000 common shares at $12 per share...$600,000,000

'So, that's where my clients' stolen intellectual property ended up - controlled by an American pharmaceutical giant,' he suddenly realizes. He now knows exactly where he has to go next.

The decades old company is now in jeopardy. Now the lives and futures of longtime Island residents, John and Elizabeth Bell are threatened.

EPILOGUE

PARADISE ISLAND, MIAMI BEACH, FLORIDA

Alessandro Baglioni is a caged animal, desperate to get back "total control" of his family. He is also raging to get even with Veronica Lujan-Restrepo.

Veronica, in turn, has "moved on" under the false assumption that Mr. Baglioni and Veronica's father are "under control." Her new objects of desire are The Crawfords, a young new couple that have just moved onto Paradise Island.

Veronica's father, Mario Angel Restrepo, in turn has warned his young wife to cut out her wild ways. However, his wife, Lynn Restrepo, has her own ideas about how to get her husband, once and for all, off her back.

Father and son, Lars and Jasper Johannsen, team up to solve the mystery of the disappearance of their Paradise Island neighbor, German Lope-Bello, while he was climbing the Swiss Alps' Matterhorn.

Lars Johannsen's close friend, Elizabeth Rawlings, is threatened and accosted by her former "head security guard."

The Island's "gossipers," the four old crows, Sarah Pesin, Marguerita Lujan-Restrepo, Nicole Albert and Elizabeth Bell's loose tongues get them into serious trouble.

Steven Zathlyn's depraved secret life is uncovered by his enemies, Oleg Krull, Louis Matthews II, and Bart Holstein. His enemies are the parents of the three teens who he performed sex change operations on after they raped his daughter. The parents take notice and use it to seek revenge.

Private security firm owner, General Robert Pinkus' relationship with new Paradise Island resident, Laureen Krall, flourishes until he realizes that she is playing him.

Oleg Krull's witness tampering activities go public.

Louis Matthews II, runs into serious trouble with the IRS, thanks to his Swiss bank account information going public.

The three teens, Thor Krull, Louis Matthews III, and Andy Holstein's past "sin" is exposed to their "girlfriends."

Ariel Mizrahi and his newly discovered half-brother, Bart Holstein, find out the truth about their father, Lebanese smuggler, Alvi Mazon.

Sylvester Antonelli's newfound wealth puts him a step closer to moving back to Paradise Island.

Leon Albert's S&M play-outs on his private Bahamian island predictably cause a tragedy and, as a consequence, his private life unravels.

Isaac Perlman, the Jewish hunter of Nazi stolen assets, lands in Miami and his target is the mammoth pharmaceutical company owned by one of the families of Paradise Island residents.

Lindsey Greenhouse's relationship with phenom and Paradise Island resident playwright and movie director, Billy McCoy, runs into trouble with the Hollywood establishment and it affects her popular web broadcast, "Lynn's Hunt."

The Cuban immigrants, the Rojas-Lugos, achieve wealth and fame through their revolutionary Latin "beat". However, the price of fame causes them tragedy and pain.

Arlene Pesin is on a tightrope, as her Japanese-American boyfriend, Lewis Wang, is a hot number but she starts to suspect he is an international terrorist.

Billy McCoy is headed for nationwide stardom but first he will run into a series hidden obstacles waiting for him.

Index

Paradise Island. Miami Beach
was printed in
the United States of America
in October 2018